AMAZING GRACE

In the Ritz-Carlton ballroom in San Francisco a glittering, celebrity-studded crowd gathers for a charity dinner dance. The evening is perfect—until, just minutes before midnight, the room begins to sway. Glass shatters. And as the lights go out, people begin to scream . . .

In the earthquake's aftermath, the lives of four strangers will converge . . . Sarah Sloane, the beautiful wife of a financial whiz, watches her perfect world fall to pieces . . . Grammy-winning singer Melanie Free, comes to a turning point in her life. . . Photographer Everett Carson, a former war correspondent, finds new purpose amid the carnage . . . and Sister Maggie Kent, a nun who normally works with the homeless, searches through the rubble—and knows instantly that there is much work to be done . . .

As the city staggers back to life, a chain reaction of extraordinary events will touch each of the survivors . . . and each discovers the unexpected gifts in a tragedy's wake . . and the amazing grace of new beginnings.

AMAZING GRACE

Danielle Steel

WINDSOR

PARAGON

First published 2007
by
Bantam Press
This Large Print edition published 2008
by
BBC Audiobooks Ltd by arrangement with
Transworld Publishers

Hardcover ISBN: 978 1 405 61928 8
Softcover   ISBN: 978 1 405 61929 5

British Library Cataloguing in Publication Data available

Printed and bound in Great Britain by
Antony Rowe Ltd., Chippenham, Wiltshire

To my beloved children,
Beatrix, Trevor, Todd, Nick, Sam,
Victoria, Vanessa, Maxx, and Zara,
all of whom have amazing grace,
all of whom I admire so immensely,
and of whom I am so very, very proud,
and whom I love with all my heart.

with all my love,
Mom / d.s.

In each loss there is a gain.
As in every gain there is a loss.
And with each ending comes a new beginning.
—SHAO LIN

If you become whole,
everything will come to you.
—TAO TE CHING

Chapter 1

Sarah Sloane walked into the ballroom of the Ritz-Carlton in San Francisco and thought it looked fantastic. The tables were set with cream-colored damask cloths, the silver candlesticks, flatware, and crystal gleamed. They had been rented from an outside source, which had donated their use for the evening, and offered fancier options than those provided by the hotel. The plates were rimmed with gold. Silver-wrapped party favors were on the tables at each place. A calligrapher had written up the menus on heavy ecru stock, and they'd been clipped into little silver stands. The placecards with tiny gold angels on them had already been set down according to Sarah's carefully thought-out seating chart. The gold sponsor tables were at the front of the room, three rows of them in fact, with the silver and bronze tables behind them. There was a beautiful program on every seat, along with an auction catalogue and numbered paddle.

Sarah had organized the event with the same meticulous diligence and precision that she did everything, and in the way she had run similar charity events in New York. She had given every detail a personal touch, and it looked more like a wedding than a benefit, as she glanced at the cream-colored roses encircled with gold and silver ribbons on every table. They had been provided by the city's best florist at one-third of the normal cost. Saks was providing a fashion show, Tiffany was sending models to wear their jewelry and wander through the crowd.

1

There was an auction of high-ticket items, which included jewelry, exotic trips, sports packages, celebrity meet-and-greet opportunities, and a black Range Rover parked in front of the hotel with a huge gold bow tied on top. Someone was going to be very happy driving the car home at the end of the evening. And the neonatal unit at the hospital benefiting from the evening was going to be even happier. This was the second Smallest Angels Ball that Sarah had organized and run for them. The first one had netted them more than two million dollars, between seat prices, the auction, and donations. She hoped to make three million tonight.

The high caliber of the entertainment they were providing would help them get to their goal. There was a dance band, which would play on and off during the night. One of the other members of the committee was the daughter of a major Hollywood music mogul. Her father had gotten Melanie Free to perform, which allowed them to charge high prices for both individual seats and particularly the sponsor tables. Melanie had won a Grammy three months earlier, and her single performances like this one usually ran a million five. She was donating her performance. All the Smallest Angels had to pick up were her production costs, which were quite high. The cost of travel, lodgings, food, and the set-up of her roadies and band was estimated to cost them three hundred thousand dollars, which was a bargain, considering who she was and the cataclysmic effect of her performance.

Everyone was so impressed when they got the invitation and saw who was performing. Melanie Free was the hottest musical artist in the country at the moment and dazzling to look at. She was nineteen years old and had had a meteoric rise in the last two years, due to her consistent hits. Her recent Grammy was the icing on the cake, and Sarah was grateful she was still willing to do their benefit for free. Her greatest fear had been that Melanie would cancel at the last minute. With a donated performance, a lot of stars and singers dropped out hours before they were expected to show up. But Melanie's agent had sworn she would be there. It was promising to be an exciting evening, and the press were covering the event in force. The committee had even managed to corral a few stars to fly up from L.A. and attend, and all the local socialites had bought tickets. For the past two years, it had been the most important and productive benefit in San Francisco—and, everyone said, the most fun to attend.

Sarah had started the benefit as a result of her own experience with the neonatal unit, which had saved her daughter, Molly, three years ago, when she was born three months premature. She was Sarah's first baby. During the pregnancy everything seemed fine. Sarah looked and felt fabulous, and at thirty-two, she assumed she wouldn't have any problems, until she went into labor one rainy night, and they couldn't stop it. Molly was born the next day and spent two months in an incubator in the neonatal ICU, with Sarah and her husband, Seth, standing by. Sarah had been at the hospital day and night, and they had saved Molly with no ill effects or resulting damage. She was now a happy, bouncy three-year-old, ready to start preschool in the fall.

Sarah's second baby, Oliver—Ollie—had been

born the previous summer, without any problems. He was a delicious, chubby, gurgling nine-month-old now. Her children were the joy of Sarah's existence and her husband's. She was a full-time mom, and her only other serious activity was putting on this benefit every year. It took a monumental amount of work and organization, which she was good at.

Sarah and Seth had met at Stanford Business School six years before, which had brought them both out from New York. They married as soon as they graduated, and stayed on in San Francisco. Seth had gotten a job in Silicon Valley, and just after Molly's birth he had started his own hedge fund. Sarah had decided not to join the work-force. She got pregnant with Molly on their wedding night, and wanted to stay home with their babies. She had spent five years working on Wall Street in New York as an analyst, before going to business school at Stanford. She wanted to take a few years off now, to enjoy motherhood full-time. Seth had done so well with his hedge fund that there was no reason for her to go back to work.

At thirty-seven, Seth had already made a considerable fortune, and was one of the brightest young stars in the heavens of the financial community, in both San Francisco and New York. They had bought a beautiful large brick house overlooking the bay in Pacific Heights, and filled it with important contemporary art: Calder, Ellsworth Kelly, de Kooning, Jackson Pollock, and a handful of promising unknowns. Sarah and Seth were thoroughly enjoying their life in San Francisco. It had been easy for them to move since Seth had lost his parents years before, and Sarah's had moved to Bermuda, so their family ties to New York were no longer strong. It was obvious to everyone on both coasts that Sarah and Seth were there to stay, and they were a wonderful addition to the business and social scenes of the city. A rival hedge fund had even offered Sarah a job, but she had no desire to do anything except spend her time with Oliver and Molly—and Seth when he was free. He had just bought a plane, a G5, and flew to L.A., Chicago, Boston, and New York often. They had a golden life that only got better year by year. Although she and Seth had both grown up in comfortable circumstances, neither of them had had the extravagant life they had now. It worried Sarah a little from time to time that maybe they were spending too much money, with a fabulous house in Tahoe in addition to their city house, and their own plane. But Seth insisted they were fine. He said that the kind of money he was making was meant to be enjoyed. And there was no question that he did.

Seth drove a Ferrari, and Sarah a Mercedes station wagon that was perfect for her with two kids, although she had an eye on the Range Rover that was going to be auctioned off that night. She had told Seth she thought it was really cute. And most of all, it was for a good cause, one they both really cared about. After all, the neonatal unit had saved Molly's life. In a less high-tech, medically sophisticated hospital, their adorable three-year-old wouldn't be alive today. It meant the world to Sarah to give back by organizing the benefit, which had been her idea. The committee turned an enormous profit over to them after the evening's expenses were paid. Seth had kicked things off for them with a two-hundred-thousand-dollar donation in both their names. Sarah was very proud of him. She always had been and still was. He was the star of her heavens, and even after four years of marriage and two children, they were very much in love. They were even thinking about trying for a third baby. She had been overwhelmed with the benefit for the past three months. They were chartering a yacht in Greece in August, and Sarah thought that would be the perfect time to get pregnant again.

Sarah walked slowly around each table in the ballroom, double-checking the names on the placecards against her list. Part of the success of the Smallest Angels Ball was that it was exquisitely run. It was a first-class event. As she made her way toward the silver tables, after checking the gold, she found two mistakes, and switched the place-cards with a serious expression. She had just finished checking the last of the tables, and was going to check on the party favor bags that six of the committee members were filling to hand out at the end of the evening, when the benefit's assistant chair made her way toward Sarah across the ballroom, with an excited look. She was a beautiful, tall blonde married to the CEO of a major corporation. She was his trophy wife, had been a model in New York, and was twenty-nine years old. She had no children and wasn't planning to have any. She had wanted to be on the committee with Sarah because the benefit was such a big deal and so much fun. She'd had a ball helping Sarah put it together, and the two women got along well. Sarah's hair was as dark as Angela's was blond. Sarah had long, straight, dark brown hair, creamy skin, and huge green eyes. She was a beautiful young woman, even with her hair in a ponytail, no makeup, a sweatshirt, jeans, and flip-flops. It was just after one o'clock, and in six hours both women would be transformed. For now, they were hard at work.

'She's here!' Angela whispered with a broad grin.

'Who?' Sarah asked, resting her clipboard on her hip.

'You know who! Melanie, of course! They just arrived. I took her to her room.' Sarah was relieved to note they had come in on time, on the private plane the committee had chartered to bring her and her entourage from L.A. Her band and roadies had come by commercial jet, and had already been in their hotel rooms for two hours. Melanie, her best friend, her manager, assistant, hairdresser, boyfriend, and mother, had come up in the chartered plane.

'Is she okay?' Sarah asked, looking concerned. They had gotten an advance list of everything she required, including Calistoga bottled water, low-fat yogurt, a dozen kinds of natural foods, and a case of Cristal champagne. The list was twenty-six pages long, referring to all her personal needs, her mother's food preferences, even the beer her boyfriend drank. And then there were another forty pages referring to the band, and all the electrical and sound equipment they'd need on stage. The eight-foot grand piano she required for her performance had been brought in at midnight the night before. She and the band were scheduled to rehearse that afternoon at two. Everyone else had to be cleared out of the ballroom by then, which was why Sarah was finishing her rounds at one.

'She's fine. The boyfriend is a little odd, and her mom scared me to death, but her best friend is cute. And Melanie is really beautiful and very sweet.'

Sarah had had that impression the one time she spoke to her on the phone. The rest of the time, Sarah had dealt with her manager, but she had made a point of calling and thanking Melanie personally for doing their benefit. And now the big day was here. Melanie hadn't canceled in favor of a performance somewhere else, the plane hadn't crashed, they'd all arrived on time. The weather was warmer than usual. It was a sunny afternoon in mid-May. In fact it was hot and muggy, which was rare in San Francisco, and more like a summer day in New York. Sarah knew that it would break soon, but it always created a festive atmosphere in the city when the nights were warm. The only thing she didn't like about it was that someone had told her that days like this one were considered 'earthquake weather' in San Francisco. They'd been teasing her about it, but she didn't like hearing it anyway. Earthquakes were the one thing that had worried her about the city since they'd moved there, but everyone assured her that they rarely happened, and when they did, they were small. In six years of living in the Bay Area, she hadn't felt one yet. So she dismissed what they had said about 'earthquake' weather. She had other things to worry about right now, like their star singer and her entourage.

'Do you think I should go up to see her?' Sarah asked Angela. She didn't want to intrude, nor be

8

rude by neglecting them. 'I was going to meet her here when she comes down for rehearsal at two.'

'You can just stick your head in and say hello.'

Melanie and her group had two large suites, and five other rooms on the club floor, all provided on a complimentary basis by the hotel. They were thrilled to host the event, and gave the benefit committee a total of five free suites for their stars and fifteen rooms and junior suites for their VIPs. The band and roadies were on a lower floor, in lesser rooms that the committee had to pay for out of the benefit budget, which came from their profits for the night.

Sarah nodded, put her clipboard in her handbag, and checked on the women stuffing the party favor bags with expensive goodies from a variety of stores. And a moment later she was in the elevator on the way to the club floor. She and Seth had a room there too, so she used her key for the elevator. Otherwise there was no way to get to that floor. She and Seth had decided it would be easier to dress at the hotel than go home and rush back. Their babysitter had agreed to stay overnight with the kids, which made it a nice night off for Sarah and Seth. She could hardly wait till the next day, when they could lie in bed, order room service, and talk about the event the night before. But for now, she just hoped everything would go okay.

As soon as she got off the elevator, Sarah saw the huge lounge on the club floor. Pastries, sandwiches, and fruit were set out, bottles of wine, and a small bar. There were comfortable chairs, tables, telephones, a vast array of newspapers, a gigantic wide-screen TV, and two women sitting at a desk, to help guests in any way they could, with dinner reservations, questions about the city, directions, manicures, massages, whatever whim a guest could have. Sarah asked them for the directions to Melanie's room, and then continued down the hall. To avoid security hassles, and fans, Melanie was registered under the name Hastings, her mother's maiden name. They did that at every hotel, as did some of the other stars, who rarely registered in their own names.

Sarah gently knocked on the door of the suite number she'd been given by the woman in the lounge. She could hear music inside, and a moment later the door was opened by a short, heavy-set woman in a halter top and jeans. She was carrying a yellow pad, with a pen stuck in her hair, and carrying an evening gown. Sarah guessed correctly that she was Melanie's assistant, whom she had also spoken to on the phone.

'Pam?' Sarah asked, as the other woman smiled and nodded. 'I'm Sarah Sloane. I just came to say hello.'

'Come on in,' she said cheerfully, as Sarah followed her into the living room of the suite, and saw chaos all around her. Half a dozen suitcases were open on the floor, with their contents spilling everywhere. One was full of slinky gowns. Out of the others poured boots, jeans, handbags, tops, blouses, a cashmere blanket, and a teddy bear. It looked as though an entire chorus line of women had dumped their belongings on the floor. And sitting on the floor beside them was a small elfin-looking blond girl. She glanced up at Sarah, and then went back to pawing through one of the bags, obviously searching for something specific. It

10

didn't seem like an easy task to find anything in the heaps of clothes.

Sarah glanced around the room then, feeling out of her element, and then she saw her, Melanie Free, sprawled out on the couch in exercise clothes, her head leaning on her boyfriend's shoulder. He was working hard with the remote, with a glass of champagne in his other hand. He was a handsome boy, and Sarah knew he was an actor who had recently left a successful TV show, due to a drug problem. She vaguely remembered that he was recently out of rehab, and he appeared sober as he smiled at Sarah, despite the champagne bottle sitting next to him on the floor. His name was Jake. Melanie stood up to come and say hello to Sarah. She seemed even younger than she was, with no makeup on. She looked about sixteen with long, straight golden-colored hair. The boyfriend's was jet black and spiked, and before Melanie could say a word to either of them, Melanie's mother appeared from nowhere and shook Sarah's hand, until it nearly ached.

'Hi, I'm Janet. I'm Melanie's mom. We love it here. Thanks for getting everything on our list. My baby loves her familiar treats, you know how that is,' she said with a wide, friendly grin. She was a pretty woman in her mid-forties who might have been beautiful once, but had seen better days. Despite the handsome face, she had gotten wide in the hips. Her 'baby' still hadn't said a word. She hadn't had a chance to in the face of her mother's chatter. Janet Hastings had bright-red dyed hair. The color was aggressive, particularly next to Melanie's pale blond hair and almost chidlike looks.

'Hi,' Melanie said quietly. She didn't seem like a star, just a pretty teenage girl. Sarah shook hands with both of them as Melanie's mother went on talking, two other women walked through the room, and the boyfriend stood up and announced he was going to the gym.

'I don't want to intrude. I'll let you settle in,' Sarah said to Melanie and her mother, and then she gazed directly at Melanie. 'Are you still rehearsing at two?' Melanie nodded and then glanced at her assistant, as her manager spoke up from the doorway.

'The band says they'll be ready to set up at two-fifteen. Melanie can go on at three. We only need an hour, so she can check out the sound in the room.'

'That's fine,' Sarah reassured them, when a hotel maid arrived to take Melanie's costume away to be pressed. It was mostly sequins and net. 'I'll be waiting for you in the ballroom, just to make sure you have everything you need.' She had to be at the hairdresser herself at four, to get her hair and nails done, and then back at the hotel at six, in order to dress and show up in the ballroom at seven, to assess things one last time, make sure everyone was on deck, and greet the guests. 'The piano came last night. And they tuned it this morning.' Melanie smiled and nodded again, and then flopped down in a chair, while her best friend on the floor next to the suitcases gave a victorious shriek. Sarah had heard someone call her Ashley, and she had the same childlike appearance as Melanie.

'Found it! Can I wear it tonight?' The item she held up for Melanie to see was a slinky leopard-

12

print dress. Melanie nodded, and Ashley giggled again when she found the matching platform shoes with what looked like eight-inch heels. She scampered off to try the outfit on, and Melanie smiled shyly at Sarah again.

'Ashley and I went to school together from the time I was five,' Melanie explained. 'She's my best friend. She goes with me everywhere.' She had obviously become part of the entourage, and Sarah couldn't help thinking that it was a strange way to live. There was an almost circuslike feeling to their lifestyle, in hotel rooms and backstage. In a matter of minutes, they had given the elegant suite at the Ritz the feeling of a college dorm. And once Jake had gone to the gym, there were nothing but women in the room. The hairdresser matched a thick fall to Melanie's blond hair. It was perfection.

'Thank you for doing this,' Sarah said, looking into Melanie's eyes with a smile. 'I saw you on the Grammys and you were terrific. Are you going to sing "Don't Leave Me" tonight?'

'Yes, she is,' her mother answered for her, handing her daughter a bottle of the preordered Calistoga water, while standing between Melanie and Sarah, speaking for her as though the beautiful blond superstar didn't exist. Without further conversation, Melanie sat down on the couch, picked up the remote, took a long drink of the water, and turned on MTV. 'We love that song,' Janet said with a broad smile.

'So do I,' Sarah agreed, a little startled by Janet's forcefulness. She appeared to run her daughter's life, and seemed to think she was as much a part of her stardom as Melanie was

13

herself. Melanie didn't appear to object, she was obviously used to it, and a few minutes later, her friend came back into the room, teetering on the leopard heels, in the borrowed dress. It looked a little big on her. She immediately sat down on the couch to join her childhood friend in staring at the TV.

It was impossible to figure out who Melanie was. She seemed to have no personality of her own, and no voice, except to sing. 'I was a showgirl in Las Vegas, you know,' Janet informed Sarah, who attempted to look impressed. It was easy to believe, she looked the type, in spite of lavishly filled jeans, and huge breasts, which Sarah correctly suspected weren't real. Melanie's were impressive too, but she was young enough to pull it off on her slim, sexy, well-toned frame. Janet looked a little over the hill. In fact, she looked like the hill. She was a robust-looking woman, with a loud voice and a personality to match. Sarah was feeling overwhelmed as she struggled for excuses to leave the room, while Melanie and her school chum were mesmerized by the TV.

'I'll meet you downstairs to make sure everything is set for your rehearsal,' Sarah said to Janet, since she appeared to be the full-time proxy for her daughter in real life. Sarah calculated quickly that if she stayed with them for twenty minutes, she'd still have time to get to the hairdresser. Everything else would be done by then, and in fact already was.

'See you there.' Janet beamed at her, as Sarah slipped out of the suite and headed down the hall to her own room.

She sat down for a few minutes, and checked

14

the messages on her cell phone. It had vibrated twice while she was in Melanie's suite, and she hadn't wanted to pick up. One was from the florist, telling her that the four huge urns outside the ballroom would be filled by four o'clock. The other was from the dance band, confirming their start time at eight o'clock. She called home to check on the children then, and the sitter told her they were fine. Parmani was a lovely Nepalese woman who had been with them since Molly was born. Sarah didn't want a live-in, she loved taking care of her babies herself, but Parmani was there in the daytime to help her, and she stayed in the evening when Seth and Sarah went out. She was spending the night, which she seldom did, but she was more than happy to help on a special occasion like this. She knew how important the benefit was to Sarah, and how hard she'd worked on it for months. She wished her good luck before they hung up. Sarah had wanted to say hi to Molly, but she was still having a nap.

By the time Sarah finished, checked some notes on her clipboard, and brushed her hair, which looked a mess, it was time to go back to the ballroom to meet Melanie and her crew for rehearsal. She had already been told that Melanie didn't want anyone in the room when she rehearsed. Thinking about it now, Sarah couldn't help wondering if it was her mother's edict, and not the star's. Melanie didn't look as though she'd care who was around. She seemed oblivious to what went on around her, who came in and out, or what they did. Maybe it was different when she performed, Sarah told herself. But Melanie seemed to have the indifference and passive

15

manner of a docile child—and an absolutely incredible voice. Like everyone who had bought tickets, Sarah couldn't wait to hear her perform that night.

The band was already in the ballroom when Sarah walked in. They were standing around, talking and laughing, while the roadies finished unpacking equipment and setting it up. They were almost through, and the entire group looked like a motley crew. There were eight men in Melanie's band, and Sarah had to remind herself that the pretty blond girl she'd seen watching MTV in the suite upstairs was currently one of the biggest singing stars in the world. There was nothing pretentious or arrogant about her. The only thing that gave it away was the size of her entourage. But she had none of the bad habits or behaviors of most stars. The singer they'd had at the Smallest Angels Ball the year before had had a major tantrum over a problem with the sound system right before she went on, threw a bottle of water at her manager, and threatened to walk out. The problem had been fixed, but Sarah had nearly panicked at the prospect of her canceling at the last minute. Melanie's easy ways were a relief, whatever her mother's demands on her behalf.

Sarah waited ten more minutes while they finished setting up, wondering if Melanie would come down late, but she didn't dare ask. She had discreetly inquired if the band had everything they needed, and when they said they did, she sat down quietly at a table, out of their way, and waited for Melanie to appear. It was ten to four when she walked in, and Sarah knew she would be late for the hairdresser. She was going to have to rush like

16

a maniac afterward to get ready on time. But she had to attend to her duties first, and this was one of them—running interference for their star, being available, and paying court to her, if need be.

Melanie walked in wearing flip-flops, a skimpy T-shirt, and cut-off jeans. Her hair was lumped up on her head in a banana clip, and her best friend was at her side. Her mother marched in first, her assistant and manager brought up the rear, and there were two ominous-looking bodyguards close at hand. The boyfriend, Jake, was nowhere to be seen. He was probably still at the gym. Melanie was the least noticeable member of the group, and nearly disappeared in their midst. Her drummer handed her a Coke, she popped it open, took a swig, hopped up on stage, and squinted as she looked into the room. Compared to the venues where she was used to performing in concert, this was tiny. The ballroom had a warm, intimate feel to it, particularly the way Sarah had it set up, and once the lights were dimmed and the candles lit that night, it would look beautiful. The room was brightly lit now, and after Melanie looked around for a minute, she shouted to one of her roadies, 'Kill the lights!' She was coming alive. Sarah could see it happen as she watched, and cautiously approached the stage to talk to her. Melanie looked down at her with a smile.

'Does everything look okay?' Sarah asked, once again feeling as though she were talking to a kid, and then reminded herself that Melanie was a teenager after all, even if she was a star.

'It looks great. You did a really nice job,' Melanie said sweetly, and Sarah was touched.

'Thank you. Does the band have everything they

need?'

Melanie turned and looked over her shoulder with a confident glance. She was happiest when on stage. This was what she did best. It was a familiar world to her, even though this was a lot nicer than where she usually played. She loved the suite, and so did Jake. 'You got everything you need, guys?' she asked the band. They all nodded, said they did, and started getting their instruments in the right key, as Melanie forgot Sarah and turned to them. She told them what she wanted to play first. They had already agreed on the order of the songs she was going to sing, including her current smash hit.

Sarah realized she was no longer needed then, and started to leave. It was five after four, and she was going to be half an hour late for her hair appointment. She'd be lucky if she could get her nails done. Maybe not. She made it to just outside the ballroom door when one of the committee members stopped her with a catering manager in tow. There was a problem with the hors d'oeuvres. The Olympia oysters weren't in, what they had on hand wasn't fresh enough, and she had to pick something else. A minor decision for once. Sarah was used to bigger ones. She told the committee member to make the choice, just so it wasn't caviar or something that would destroy their budget, and with that she ran into the elevator, rushed across the lobby, and claimed her car from the valet. He had left it parked nearby. The big tip she'd given him early that morning had served her well. She pulled sharply onto California Street, turned left, and headed up Nob Hill. Fifteen minutes later, she was at her hairdresser, and out of breath when she walked in, apologizing for how late she was. It was

18

four-thirty-five, and she had to leave no later than six. She had hoped to be out by five-forty-five at the latest, which was no longer possible. They knew she was chairing her big benefit that night, and whisked her into the chair. They brought her some sparkling mineral water, followed by a cup of tea. The manicurist went to work on her as soon as her hair was washed, and they blew it out carefully.

'So what's Melanie Free really like?' her hairdresser asked her, hoping for some dirt. 'Is Jake with her?'

'He is,' Sarah said discreetly, 'and she seems like a really sweet kid. I'm sure she'll be great tonight.' Sarah closed her eyes, trying desperately to relax. It was going to be a long and hopefully successful night. She could hardly wait for it to begin.

*   *   *

Sarah was getting her hair swept into an elegant French twist, with little rhinestone stars pinned into it, as Everett Carson checked into the hotel. He was six foot four, originally from Montana, and still looked like the cowboy he had been in his youth. He was tall and lanky, his slightly-too-long hair looked uncombed, and he was wearing jeans, a white T-shirt, and what he referred to as his lucky cowboy boots. They were old, battered, comfortable, and made of black lizard. They were his prize possession, and he had every intention of wearing them with the rented tux that the magazine had paid for him to wear that night. He showed his press pass at the desk, and they smiled and said they were expecting him. The Ritz-Carlton was a lot fancier than the places where

Everett usually stayed. He was new to this job and this magazine. He was there to cover the benefit for *Scoop*, a Hollywood gossip magazine. He had spent years covering war zones for the Associated Press, and after leaving them and taking a year off, he had needed a job, so he took this one. On the night of the benefit, he had worked for the magazine for all of three weeks. So far he had covered three rock concerts, a Hollywood wedding, and this was his second benefit. It was definitely not his cup of tea. He was beginning to feel like a waiter, in all the tuxes he'd been wearing. He actually missed the miserable conditions he'd gotten used to and felt comfortable in, during his twenty-nine years with the AP. He had just turned forty-eight, and he tried to be grateful for the small, well-appointed room they escorted him into, where he dropped his battered bag that had been all over the world with him. Maybe if he closed his eyes, he could pretend he was back in Saigon, Pakistan, or New Delhi . . . Afghanistan . . . Lebanon . . . Bosnia, during the war there. He kept asking himself how a guy like him had wound up going to benefits and celebrity weddings. This was cruel and unusual punishment for him.

'Thanks,' he said to the clerk who had shown him to his room. There was a brochure about the neonatal unit on the desk, and a press kit for the Smallest Angels Ball, about which he didn't give a damn. But he would do his job. He was there to take pictures of celebrities and cover Melanie's performance. His editor had said it was a big deal to them, so here he was.

He pulled a bottle of lemonade out of the

20

refrigerator in the mini-bar, opened it, and took a swig. The room had a view of the building across the street and everything in it was so immaculate and incredibly elegant. He longed for the sounds and smells of the rat-holes where he'd slept for thirty years, the stench of the poverty in the back streets of New Delhi, and all the exotic places his career had taken him to for three decades.

'Take it easy, Ev,' he said to himself out loud, switched on CNN, sat down at the foot of the bed, and took a folded piece of paper out of his pocket. He had printed it off the Internet before he left the office in L.A. It must have been his lucky day, he told himself. There was a meeting a block away, in a church on California Street called Old St. Mary's. It was at six, would last an hour, and he could be back at the hotel at seven, when the benefit started. It meant that he'd have to go to the meeting in his tux, so he wouldn't start late. He didn't want anyone complaining about him to his editors. It was too soon for him to start cutting corners. He always had, and had gotten away with it. But he was drinking then. This was a new start, and he didn't want to push the limits of the envelope just yet. He was being a good boy, conscientious, and honest. It felt like going to nursery school again for him. After taking photographs of dying soldiers in trenches, and having shellfire all around him, covering a benefit in San Francisco was pretty goddamn tame, although others would have loved it. He wasn't one of them, unfortunately. This was a hardship post for him.

He sighed as he finished the lemonade, threw the bottle in the wastebasket, peeled off his clothes, and got into the shower.

The water felt good pelting down on him. It had been a hot day in L.A., and it was warm and muggy here. The room had air-conditioning, and he felt better when he got out of the shower, and told himself to stop bitching about his life, as he got dressed again. He decided to make the best of it and helped himself to the chocolates at his bedside and ate a cookie from the minibar. He looked at himself in the mirror as he clipped on his bow tie, and put on the jacket of his rented tux.

'My God, you look like a musician . . . or a gentleman,' he said grinning. 'Nahh . . . a waiter . . . let's not get crazy here.' He was a damn good photographer who had once won a Pulitzer. Several of his shots had made the cover of *Time* magazine. He had a name in the business, and for a time had screwed it all up by drinking, but at least that had changed. He had spent six months in rehab, and another five in an ashram figuring out his life. By now he thought he had. Booze was out of his life forever. There was just no other way. By the time he hit bottom, he had damn near died in a fleabag hotel in Bangkok. The hooker he had hired had saved him, and kept him alive till the paramedics came. One of his fellow journalists had shipped him back to the States. The AP had fired him for having been missing in action for nearly three weeks, and blowing all his deadlines, for about the hundredth time that year. He couldn't keep it together anymore, and he had put himself in rehab against his better judgment, and had only agreed to thirty days. It was only after he got there that he realized how bad things were. It was either dry out or die. So he had stayed six months and

22

chose to dry out instead of dying the next time he went on a binge.

Since then, he had gained weight, looked healthy, and went to AA meetings every day, sometimes as many as three. It wasn't as tough for him now as it had been at first, but he figured if the meetings didn't always help him, his being there would help someone else. He had a sponsor, was one, and had been sober now for just over a year. He had his one-year chip in his pocket, his lucky boots on, and had forgotten to comb his hair. He picked up the room key, and headed out at three minutes after six, with his camera bag slung over his shoulder, and a smile on his face. He was feeling better than he had half an hour before. Life wasn't easy for him every day, but it was a hell of a lot better than it had been a year ago. As someone had once said to him in AA, 'I still have bad days, but I used to have bad years.' Life seemed pretty sweet to him, as he walked out of the hotel, turned right on California Street, and walked a block down the hill to Old St. Mary's Church. He was looking forward to the meeting. He was in the mood for it tonight. He touched his one-year sobriety chip in his pocket, as he often did, to remind himself how far he'd come in the past year.

'Right on . . . ,' he whispered to himself, as he walked into the rectory to look for the group. It was exactly eight minutes after six. And as he always did, he knew he would share at the meeting.

*   *   *

As Everett walked into Old St. Mary's, Sarah jumped out of her car, and rushed into the hotel.

She had forty-five minutes to dress, and five to get downstairs from her room. Her nails were freshly done, although she had messed up two of them reaching into her bag too soon for the tip. But they looked fine, and she liked the way they'd done her hair. Her flip-flops made a flopping sound as she ran across the lobby. The concierge smiled at her as she sped by, and called out, 'Good luck tonight!'

'Thanks.' She waved, used her key in the elevator to get to the club floor, and three minutes later, she was in her room, ran the tub, and took her dress out of the plastic zipper bag it came in. It was sparkling white and silver, and would show off her figure to perfection. She had bought silver high-heel Manolo Blahnik sandals that were going to be murder to walk in, but they looked fabulous with the dress.

She was in and out of the tub in five minutes, sat down to do her makeup, and was clipping on diamond earrings, when Seth walked in at twenty to seven. It was a Thursday night, and he had begged her to do the fund-raiser on the weekend, so he didn't have to get up at the crack of dawn the next morning, but this was the only date that both the hotel and Melanie had given them, so they went with it.

Seth looked as stressed as he always did coming home from the office. He worked hard, and kept a lot of balls in the air. A success like his didn't happen by being relaxed and casual about it. But she noticed that he looked particularly harassed that night. He sat down on the edge of the tub, ran a hand through his hair, and leaned over to kiss his wife.

'You look beat,' she said sympathetically. They

24

were a great team. They had gotten along brilliantly since the day they met in business school. They had a happy marriage, loved their life, and were crazy about their kids. He had provided her with an incredible life in the past few years. She loved everything about their life together, and most of all, she loved everything about him.

'I am beat,' he confessed. 'How's everything lining up for tonight?' he asked her. He loved hearing about the things she did. He was her staunchest supporter and biggest fan. Sometimes he thought her staying home was the waste of a great business mind and her MBA degree, but he was grateful that she was so devoted to their babies, and to him.

'Fantastic!' Sarah grinned as she answered his question about the benefit, and slipped on a nearly invisible wisp of white lace thong underwear that wouldn't show underneath her dress. She had the figure for it, and just watching her do it turned him on. He couldn't resist reaching out and fondling her upper leg. 'Don't start, sweetheart,' she warned him, laughing, 'or I'll be late. You can take your time coming downstairs if you want. If you get there in time for dinner, that'll be fine. Seven-thirty, if you can.' He glanced at his watch and nodded. It was ten to seven. She had five minutes to get dressed.

'I'll be down in half an hour. I've got a couple of calls to make first.' He always did, and tonight was no different. Sarah understood. Running his hedge fund kept him busy night and day. It reminded her of her Wall Street days, when they were doing an IPO. His life was constantly like that now, which was why he was happy and successful, and they had the lifestyle that they did. They lived like fabulously wealthy people twice their age. Sarah was grateful for it, and didn't take it for granted. She turned so he could zip up her dress. It looked terrific on her, and he beamed. 'Wow! You're a knockout, babe!'

'Thank you.' She smiled at him, and they kissed. She put a few things in a tiny silver handbag, slipped on the sexy shoes that went with it, and waved as she left the room. He was already on his cell phone talking to his best friend in New York, making some arrangements for the next day. She didn't bother to listen. She left a small bottle of scotch and a glass of ice beside him, and he was pouring it gratefully into a glass as the door to the suite closed behind her.

She got into the elevator and rode down to the ballroom, three floors below the lobby, and everything was perfection. The urns were filled with creamy white roses. Pretty young women in jewel-colored evening gowns were seated at long tables, waiting to hand people escort cards and check them in. Models were wandering around in long black dresses, wearing fabulous jewelry from Tiffany, and only a handful of people had arrived before she did. Sarah checked that everything was in order, just as a tall man with disheveled sandy gray hair walked in with a camera bag over his arm. He smiled at her as he admired her figure, and told her he was from *Scoop* magazine. She was pleased. The more press coverage they got, the better the turnout next year, and the more appealing they'd be to performers who might donate their performances, and the more money they stood to make. Press was a big deal to them.

'I'm Everett Carson,' he introduced himself, and clipped a press badge onto the pocket of his tuxedo. He looked relaxed and entirely at ease.

'I'm Sarah Sloane, the chair of the benefit. Would you like a drink?' she offered, and he shook his head with a grin. It always struck him now how that was the first thing people said when welcoming someone, right after introducing themselves. 'Would you like a drink?' It came right after 'Hello' sometimes.

'No, thanks, I'm fine. Anyone special you want me to keep my eye on tonight? Local celebrities, the hot social types in the city?' She told him the Gettys would be there, Sean and Robin Wright Penn and Robin Williams, along with a handful of local names he didn't recognize, but she promised to point them out to him as they came in.

She went back to stand near the long tables then, to say hello to people as they got off the elevators, near the check-in tables. And Everett Carson started taking photographs of the models. Two of them were sensational-looking, with high, round artificial breasts and interesting cleavage they had draped diamond necklaces on. The others were too skinny for him. He came back and took a photograph of Sarah, before she got too busy. She was a beautiful young woman, with her dark hair swept up, the little stars sparkling in it, and her huge green eyes that seemed to smile at him.

'Thank you,' she said politely, and he gave her a warm smile in return. She wondered why he hadn't combed his hair, if he'd just forgotten, or maybe that was his look. She noticed the worn black

27

lizard cowboy boots. He looked like a character, and she was sure there was an interesting story to him, though she'd never have a chance to know it. He was just a journalist from *Scoop* magazine who had come up from L.A. for the evening.

'Good luck with your benefit,' he said, and then sauntered away again, just as the elevators disgorged about thirty people all at once. For Sarah, the night of the Smallest Angels Ball had begun.

Chapter 2

The schedule was running late because it took longer for people to get into the ballroom and take their seats at their tables than Sarah had anticipated. The emcee for the evening was a Hollywood star who had had a talk show for years on late-night TV and had just retired, and he was terrific. He urged everyone to take their seats while he introduced the celebrities who had come up from L.A. for the evening, and of course the mayor, and local stars. The evening was going according to plan.

Sarah had promised to keep speeches and acknowledgments to a minimum. After a brief speech by the doctor in charge of the neonatal unit, they ran a short film about the miracles they performed. Sarah then talked about her own personal experience with Molly. And from there, they went right into the auction. The action was hot. A diamond necklace from Tiffany went for a hundred thousand dollars. The celebrity meet-

and-greets went for an astonishing amount of money. An adorable miniature Yorkshire terrier puppy went for ten thousand. And the Range Rover went for a hundred and ten. Seth was the under-bidder and finally lowered his paddle and gave up. Sarah whispered to him that it was all right, she was happy with the car she owned. He smiled at her but looked distracted. She noticed again how stressed he seemed, and assumed he'd had a tough day at the office.

She caught a glimpse of Everett Carson a couple of times during the evening. She had given him the table numbers of the important socialites. *W* was there, *Town and Country, Entertainment Weekly,* and *Entertainment Tonight.* There were TV cameras waiting for Melanie to go on. The evening was turning out to be a huge success. They made over four hundred thousand in the auction, thanks to a very aggressive auctioneer. Two very expensive paintings from a local art gallery had helped, and there had been some great cruises and trips. Added to the price of the seats, the funds raised so far had exceeded expectations, and checks always came in for days afterward, with random donations.

Sarah made the rounds of the tables, thanking people for coming, and saying hello to friends. There were several tables at the back of the room that had been donated to charitable organizations, the local Red Cross chapter, a foundation committed to suicide prevention, and a table that had been filled with priests and nuns, purchased by Catholic Charities, who were affiliated with the hospital that housed the neonatal unit. Sarah saw the priests in their Roman collars, and several women with them in dark, simple navy or black suits. There was only one nun in a habit at the table, a tiny woman who looked like a pixie, with red hair and electric blue eyes. Sarah had recognized her immediately. Her name was Sister Mary Magdalen Kent, and she was the city's version of Mother Teresa. She was well known for her work on the streets with the homeless, and her position against city government for not doing more for them was very controversial. Sarah would have loved to talk to her tonight, but she was too busy with the thousand details she had to keep an eye on to ensure the success of the event. She whisked by the table with a nod and smile to the priests and nuns sitting there, obviously enjoying the evening. They were talking and laughing and drinking wine, and Sarah was pleased to see they were having a good time.

'I didn't think I'd see you here tonight, Maggie,' the priest who ran the city's free dining room for the poor commented, grinning. He knew her well. Sister Mary Magdalen was a lioness in the streets, defending the people she cared for, but a mouse when out socially. He couldn't remember ever seeing her at a benefit before. One of the other nuns, in a trim-looking blue suit, with a gold cross on her lapel and short, well-cut hair, was the head of the nursing school at USF. The other nuns looked almost fashionable and worldly, sitting at the table, enjoying the elegant meal. Sister Mary Magdalen, or Maggie as her friends called her, had appeared uncomfortable for most of the evening, and embarrassed to be there, with her coif slightly askew, as it slipped around on her short bright red hair. She seemed more like an elf dressed up as a nun.

'You almost didn't,' she said in an undertone to Father O'Casey. 'Don't ask me why, but someone gave me a ticket. A social worker I work with. She had to go to a rosary tonight. I told her to give the seat to someone else, but I didn't want to seem ungrateful.' She was apologetic about being there, and thought she should be on the streets. An event like this one was definitely not her style.

'Give yourself a break, Maggie. You work harder than anyone I know,' Father O'Casey said generously. He and Sister Mary Magdalen had known each other for years, and he admired her for her radically benevolent ideas, and hard work in the field. 'I'm surprised to see you in a habit though,' he chuckled to himself, pouring her a glass of wine she didn't touch. Even before she went into the convent at twenty-one, she never drank or smoked.

She laughed in answer to what he'd said about what she wore. 'It's the only dress I have. I work in jeans and sweatshirts every day. I don't need fancy clothes for what I do.' She glanced at the other three nuns at the table, who looked like housewives or college professors more than nuns, except for the small gold crosses on their lapels.

'It does you good to get out.' They started talking about church politics then, a controversial stand the archbishop had taken recently about ordaining priests, and the latest pronouncement from Rome. She was particularly interested in a currently proposed city law being evaluated by the board of supervisors, which would affect the people she worked with on the streets. She thought the law was limited and unfair and would hurt her

31

people. She was very bright, and after a few minutes, two of the other priests and one of the nuns entered the discussion. They were interested in what she had to say, as she knew more about the subject than they.

'Maggie, you're too tough,' Sister Dominica, who headed up the nursing school, said. 'We can't solve everyone's problems all at once.'

'I try to do it one by one,' Sister Mary Magdalen said humbly. The two women had something in common, as Sister Maggie had graduated as a nurse right before entering the convent. She found her skills useful for those she tried to help. And as they continued their heated discussion, the room went dark. The auction was over, dessert had been served, and Melanie was about to go on. The emcee had just announced her, and slowly the room fell into silence, alive with anticipation. 'Who is she?' Sister Mary Magdalen whispered, and the rest of the table smiled.

'The hottest young singer in the world. She just won a Grammy,' Father Joe whispered, and Sister Maggie nodded. The evening was definitely way out of her league. She was tired, and ready for it to be over, as the music started up. Melanie's signature song was being started by the band, and then in an explosion of sound, light, and color, Melanie came on. She drifted onto the stage like an exquisite waif, singing her opening song.

Sister Mary Magdalen watched her, fascinated, as did everyone in the room. They were mesmerized by her beauty, and the stunning power of her voice. There was no sound in the room except hers.

'Wow!' Seth said as he looked at her from a

front-row seat, and patted his wife's hand. She had done a fantastic job. He had been distracted and worried earlier, but now he was loving and attentive to her. 'Holy shit! She's fantastic!' Seth added, as Sarah noticed Everett Carson crouched just below the stage, taking shots of Melanie while she performed. She was breathtakingly beautiful in the nearly invisible costume. The dress she wore was mostly illusion and looked like glitter on her skin. Sarah had gone backstage to see her before she went on. Her mother was running interference for her, and Jake was half smashed, drinking straight gin.

The songs Melanie sang mesmerized the audience. She sat down at the edge of the stage for the last one, reaching out to them, singing to them, ripping their hearts out. Every man in the room was in love with her by then, and every woman wanted to be her. Melanie was a thousand times more beautiful than she had seemed to Sarah when she hung out in her suite. She had a stage presence that was electrifying and a voice that no one would ever forget. She had made the evening for everyone, and Sarah sat back in her chair with a smile of total satisfaction. It had been an absolutely perfect night. The food had been excellent, the room looked gorgeous, the press was there in full force, the auction had made a fortune, and Melanie was the big hit of the night. The event had been a total success, and would sell out even faster the following year as a result, maybe even at higher prices. Sarah knew that she had done her job, and done it well. Seth had said he was proud of her, and she was even proud of herself.

She saw Everett Carson get even closer to

Melanie, as he took more shots. Sarah felt giddy at the thrill of it all, and as she did, she felt the room sway gently. For an instant, she thought she was dizzy. And then, instinctively, she looked up and saw the chandeliers swinging overhead. It made no sense to her, and at the moment she looked up, she heard a low rumble, like a terrifying groan all around them. For a minute, everything seemed to stop, as the lights flickered, and the room swayed. Someone near her stood up and shouted, 'Earthquake!' The music stopped, as tables fell and china clattered, just as the lights went out and people started to scream. The room was in total darkness, the groaning sound grew louder, people were shouting and screaming over it, and the rolling movement of the room turned into a terrifying shudder as it went from side to side. Sarah and Seth were on the floor by then, he had pulled her under their table before it overturned.

'Oh my God,' she said to him, clutching him as he put his arms around her and held her tight. All she could think of were her babies at home with Parmani. She was crying, terrified for them, and desperate to get back to them, if they all lived through what was happening to them now. The undulating of the room and the crashing sounds seemed to go on forever. It was several minutes before it stopped. There were more crashing sounds after that, and people shouting and pushing and shoving as the exit signs came back on. They had gone out, but a generator somewhere in the hotel had gotten them going again. There was a sense of chaos all around them.

'Don't move for a few minutes,' Seth told her from where they lay. She could feel him, but no longer see him in the total darkness. 'You'll get trampled by the crowd.'

'What if the building falls in on us?' She was shaking and still crying.

'If it does, we're fucked,' he said bluntly.

They, and everyone else in the room, were well aware that they were three floors underground. They had no idea how to get out, or by what route. The noise in the room was deafening as people shouted to each other, and then hotel employees with powerful flashlights appeared beneath the exit signs. Someone with a bullhorn was telling them to stay calm and proceed with caution toward the exits and not to panic. There were dim lights in the hall beyond, while the ballroom remained totally dark. It had been the most terrifying experience of Sarah's life. Seth grabbed her arm, and pulled her to her feet, as five hundred and sixty people pushed their way toward the exits. There were sounds of people crying, others groaning in pain, some shouting for help, saying that someone next to them was hurt.

Sister Maggie was already on her feet, moving into the crowd rather than out of the room. 'What are you doing?' Father Joe shouted after her—they could see dimly now in the light from the hall beyond. The enormous urns of roses had fallen over, and the scene in the ballroom was one of total chaos and disorder. Father Joe thought Maggie was confused as she made her way deeper into the room.

'I'll meet you outside!' she shouted, as she disappeared into the crowd, and within minutes was on her knees next to a man who said he thought he'd had a heart attack, but had nitroglycerin in his pocket. She reached in unceremoniously and helped him find it, took out a pill, and put it in his mouth, and then told him not to move. She was sure help would come soon to assist the injured.

She left him with his frightened wife, and moved along a littered path wishing she was wearing her workboots and not the flat pumps she had worn. The ballroom floor was an obstacle course of tables lying on their sides or even upside down, with food, dishes, and broken glass everywhere, and some people lying amid the debris. Sister Maggie made her way systematically toward them, as did several other people who said they were doctors. There had been many of them in the room, but only a few had stayed to help the wounded. A crying woman with an injured arm said she thought she was going into labor. Sister Maggie told her not to even think about it until she got out of the hotel, and the pregnant woman smiled as Maggie helped her stand up and start moving out of the ballroom holding tightly to her husband's arm. Everyone was terrified of an aftershock, which might be even worse than the first quake. There was no doubt in anyone's mind that it had been greater than seven on the Richter scale, maybe even eight, and there were groaning sounds in the room all around them as the earth settled again, which was anything but reassuring.

At the front of the room, Everett Carson had been next to Melanie when the quake hit. As the room tilted crazily, she had slid right off the stage into his arms, and they both fell to the floor. He helped her up when the shaking stopped.

'Are you okay? That was a great performance,

36

by the way,' he said lightly. Once they opened the ballroom doors and light filtered in from the hall he noticed that her costume had torn, and one of her breasts was exposed. He slipped his tuxedo jacket on her to cover her up.

'Thank you,' she said, sounding dazed. 'What happened?'

'About a seven- or eight-point quake, I believe,' Everett said.

'Shit, now what do we do?' Melanie looked scared, but not panicked.

'We do what they're telling us, and we get our asses out of here and try not to get trampled.' He had been through earthquakes, tsunamis, and similar disasters in Southeast Asia over the years. But there was no question, this had been a big one. It had been exactly a hundred years since the last big San Francisco earthquake in 1906.

'I should find my mom,' Melanie said, looking around. There was no sign of her or Jake, and no way to recognize people easily in the room. It was too dark. And so many people were shouting, and there was such pandemonium going on around them that you couldn't hear anyone except the person standing next to you.

'You'd better look for her outside,' Everett warned her, as she started to make her way to where the stage had been. It had collapsed, and all the band's equipment had slid off. The grand piano was teetering at a crazy angle, and fortunately hadn't fallen on anyone. 'Are you okay?' Melanie looked a little stunned.

'Yeah . . . I am . . .' He headed her toward the exits then, and told her he was staying for a few more minutes. He wanted to see if there was anything he could do to help the people in the ballroom.

A few minutes later, he stumbled over a woman helping a man who said he'd had a heart attack. The woman moved away to help someone else, and Everett helped get the man outside. He and a man who said he was a doctor put him on a chair and lifted him up. They had to carry him up three flights of stairs. There were paramedics, ambulances, and fire trucks outside, helping people pouring out of the hotel with minor injuries and reporting on others who were hurt inside. A battalion of firemen rushed in. There was no evidence of fires around them, but electric lines were down, and there were sparks shooting into the air as firemen with bullhorns shouted at them to stay clear, and set up barricades. Everett noticed quickly that the city all around them was dark. And then by instinct more than design, he reached for the camera still slung around his neck, and started taking pictures of the scene, without intruding on the gravely injured. Everyone around him looked dazed. The man who had the heart attack was already on the way to the hospital in an ambulance, along with another man who had a broken leg. There were injured people lying on the street, most of whom had come out of the hotel, and others who hadn't. The stoplights were no longer functioning, and traffic had stopped. A cable car at the corner had jumped the tracks, and at least forty people were injured, as paramedics and firemen ministered to them. One woman was dead and had been covered by a tarp. It was a grisly scene, and Everett didn't even notice till he got outside and saw blood on his shirt that he had a cut on his cheek. He had no idea how it had happened. It appeared to be superficial and he wasn't worried about it. He took a towel when a hotel employee handed it to him and wiped his face. There were dozens of them handing out towels, blankets, and bottles of water for the shocked people all around them. No one could figure out what to do next. They just stood there, staring at each other, and talking about what had happened. There were several thousand people crowded into the street as the hotel was emptied. Half an hour later the fire-men said that the ballroom was clear now. It was then that Everett noticed Sarah Sloane standing near him with her husband. Her dress was torn and covered with wine and the remains of dessert that had been on their table when it tipped over.

'Are you all right?' he asked her. It was the same question everyone was asking each other again and again. She was crying, and her husband looked distressed. So was everyone else. People were crying all around them, in shock, fear, and relief, and worried about their families at home. Sarah had been frantically calling on her cell phone, which didn't work. Seth had tried his too, and looked grim.

'I'm worried about my babies,' she explained. 'They're at home with a babysitter. I don't even know how we'll get there. I guess we'll have to walk.' Someone had said that the garage where all their cars were parked had collapsed, and there were people trapped inside. There was no way to access their cars, and everyone whose car had been in it was now stranded. There were no cabs. San Francisco had become a ghost town in a matter of minutes. It was after midnight, and the quake had hit an hour before. The Ritz-Carlton employees were being wonderful, wandering through the crowd, asking people what they could do to help. There wasn't much anyone could do right now, except the paramedics and firemen trying to triage those who had been hurt.

A few minutes later, the firemen announced that there was an emergency earthquake shelter two blocks away, and gave them directions. They urged people to get off the street and go there. Power lines were down, and there were live wires on the street. They were warned to steer a wide berth around them, and to go to the shelter rather than try to go home. The possibility of an aftershock was still frightening everyone. As the firemen told the crowd what to do, Everett continued taking pictures. This was the kind of work he loved. He wasn't preying on people's miseries, he was discreet, capturing this extraordinary moment in time that he already knew was a historical event.

There was finally a shift in movement in the crowd, as they walked on shaking legs toward the earthquake shelter down the hill. People kept talking to each other about what had happened, what they had thought at first, and where they'd been. One man had been in the shower in his room at the hotel, and said he thought it was some kind of vibrating feature in the tub for the first seconds. He was wearing a terrycloth robe and nothing else, and his feet were bare. One of them was cut, from glass lying in the street, but there was nothing anyone could do. And another woman said she thought she had broken the bed as she slid toward the floor, and then the whole room rock-and-rolled like a carnival game. But this was no game. It was the second-biggest disaster the city had ever known.

Everett took a bottle of water from a bellman handing them out. He opened it, took a long swig, and realized how dry his mouth was. There were clouds of dust coming out of the hotel from structures inside that had broken, and things that had collapsed. No bodies had been brought out. The firemen were covering those who had died with tarps in the lobby as a central location. There were about twenty so far, and there were rumors that people were trapped inside, which made everyone panic. Here and there, people were crying, unable to find the friends or relatives they had been staying with in the hotel, or still hadn't located in the group from the benefit. They were easy to identify from their torn and soiled evening clothes. They looked like survivors of the *Titanic*. It was then that Everett spotted Melanie and her mother. Her mother was crying hysterically. Melanie looked alert and calm, and was still wearing his rented tuxedo jacket.

'Are you okay?' he asked the familiar question, and she smiled and nodded.

'Yeah. My mom is pretty freaked out. She thinks there will be a bigger one in a few minutes. Do you want your jacket back?' She would have been nearly naked if she'd given it back to him, and he shook his head. 'I can put on a blanket.'

'Keep it. It looks good on you. Everyone accounted for in your group?' He knew she'd had a large entourage with her, and he saw only her mother.

'My friend Ashley hurt her ankle, and the paramedics are taking care of her. My boyfriend was pretty drunk, and the guys in my band had to carry him out. He's throwing up somewhere over there.' She gestured vaguely. 'Everyone else is okay.' She looked like a teenager again now that she was off the stage, but he remembered her performance and how remarkable it was. So would everyone else after tonight.

'You should go to the shelter. It's safer there,' Everett said to both of them, and Janet Hastings started pulling on her daughter. She agreed with Everett and wanted to get off the street before the next quake came.

'I think I might stay here for a while,' Melanie said softly, and told her mother to go on without her, which only made her cry harder. Melanie said she wanted to stay and help, which Everett thought was admirable. And then for the first time, he wondered if he wanted a drink, and was pleased to realize that he didn't. This was a first. Even with the excuse of a major earthquake, he had no desire to get drunk. He broke into a broad grin as he thought it, while Janet headed toward the shelter, and Melanie disappeared into the crowd as her mother panicked.

'She'll be okay,' Everett reassured Janet. 'When I see her again, I'll send her to you at the shelter. You go on with the others.' Janet looked uncertain, but the movement of the crowd heading toward the shelter and her own desire to get there swept her away. Everett figured that whether or not he found her, Melanie would be fine. She was young and resourceful, the members of her band were near at hand, and if she wanted to help the injured in the crowd, that didn't seem like such a bad idea to him. There were a lot of people around them who needed assistance of some kind, more than the paramedics could provide.

He was taking pictures again when he came across the small red-headed woman he'd seen help the man with the heart attack and then move on. He saw her assist a child, and turn her over to a fireman to try and help her find her mother. Everett took several photographs of the woman, and then dropped his camera again as she moved away from the little girl.

'Are you a doctor?' he asked with interest. She had seemed very confident in her treatment of the man with the heart attack.

'No, I'm a nurse,' she said simply, her brilliant blue eyes locking into his briefly, and then she smiled. There was something both funny and touching about her. She had the most magnetic eyes he'd ever seen.

'That's a good thing to be tonight.' Many people had gotten hurt, not all of them severely. But there were a multitude of cuts and minor injuries, as well as bigger ones, and several people had gone into shock. He knew he'd seen the woman at the benefit, but there was something incongruous about her plain black dress and flat shoes. Her coif had vanished in the aftermath of the quake, and it never occurred to him what she was, other than a nurse. She had an ageless, timeless face, and it would have been difficult to guess her age. He figured her for late thirties, early forties, and in fact she was forty-two. She stopped to talk to someone as he followed her, and then she paused for a bottle of water herself. They were all feeling the effects of the dust still billowing from the hotel.

'Are you going to the shelter? They probably need help there too,' he commented. He had thrown his bow tie away by then, and there was blood on his shirt from the cut on his cheek. But she shook her head.

'I'm going to head out when I've done all I can here. I figure the people in my neighborhood can use some help too.'

'Where do you live?' he asked with interest, although he didn't know the city well. But there was something about this woman that intrigued him. And maybe there was a story in it somewhere, you never knew. His journalistic instincts came alive just looking at her.

She smiled at his question. 'I live in the Tenderloin, not far from here.' But where she lived was worlds apart from all this. In that neighborhood, a few blocks made a huge difference.

'That's a pretty rough neighborhood, isn't it?' He was increasingly intrigued. He had heard of the Tenderloin, with its drug addicts, prostitutes, and derelicts.

'Yes, it is,' she said honestly. But she was happy there.

'And that's where you live?' He looked startled and confused.

'Yes.' She smiled at him, her red hair and face streaked with dirt, and the electric blue eyes grinning impishly at him. 'I like it there.' He had a sixth sense about a story then, and knew intuitively that she was going to turn out to be one of the heroes of the night. When she went back to the

44

Tenderloin, he wanted to be with her. For sure, there was going to be a story in it for him.

'My name is Everett. Can I come with you?' he asked her simply, as she hesitated for a minute and then nodded.

'It might be dicey getting there, because of all the live wires on the street. And they're not going to rush to help people in that neighborhood. All the rescue teams will be here, or in other parts of the city. Just call me Maggie, by the way.'

It was another hour before they left the scene outside the Ritz. It was nearly three in the morning by then. Most people had either gone to the shelter or decided to go home. He never saw Melanie again, but wasn't worried about her. The ambulances had left with the critically injured, and the firemen seemed to have things in good control. They could hear sirens in the distance, and Everett assumed fires had broken out, and water mains had broken, so they were going to have a tough time fighting the fires. He followed the little woman doggedly as he accompanied her home. They walked up California Street, then down Nob Hill, heading south. They passed Union Square, and eventually turned right and headed west on O'Farrell. They were both shocked to see that almost all the windows in the department stores on Union Square had popped out and broken on the street. And there was a similar scene outside the St. Francis Hotel to the one they had just left at the Ritz. The hotels had been emptied, and people had been directed to shelters. It took them half an hour to reach where she lived.

People were standing around on the street, and looked markedly different here. They were

45

shabbily dressed, some were still high on drugs, others looked scared. Store windows had shattered, drunks were lying in the street, and a cluster of prostitutes were huddling close together. Everett was intrigued to note that almost everyone seemed to know Maggie. She stopped and talked to them, inquiring how everyone was doing, if people had gotten hurt, if help had come, and how the neighborhood was faring. They chatted animatedly with her, and eventually she and Everett sat down in a doorway on a stoop. It was nearly five A.M. by then, and Maggie didn't even look tired.

'Who are you?' he asked, fascinated by her. 'I feel like I'm in some kind of strange movie, with an angel who came to earth, and maybe no one can see you but me.' She laughed at his description of her and reminded him that no one else was having a problem seeing her. She was real, human, and entirely visible, as any of the hookers on the street would have agreed.

'Maybe the answer to your question is a what, not a who,' she said comfortably, wishing she could get out of her habit. It was just a plain, ugly black dress, but she was missing her jeans. From what she could see, her building had been shaken up but not damaged dangerously, and there was nothing to stop her from going in. Firemen and police were not directing people to shelters here.

'What does that mean?' Everett asked, looking puzzled. He was tired. It had been a long night for both of them, but she looked fresh as a rose, and a lot livelier than she had at the benefit.

'I'm a nun,' she said simply. 'These are the people I work with and take care of. I do most of

46

my work on the streets. All of it, in fact. I've lived here for nearly ten years.'

'You're a *nun*?' he asked her with a look of amazement. 'Why didn't you tell me?'

'I don't know.' She shrugged comfortably, perfectly at ease talking to him, particularly here on the street. This was the world she knew best, far better than any ballroom. 'I didn't think about it. Does it make a difference?'

'Hell, yes . . . I mean no,' he corrected himself, and then thought about it further. 'I mean yes . . . of course it makes a difference. That's a really important detail about you. You're a very interesting person, particularly if you live here. Don't you live in a convent, or something?'

'No, mine disbanded years ago. There weren't enough nuns here in my order to justify keeping the convent going. They turned it into a school. The diocese gives all of us an allowance, and we live in apartments. Some of the nuns live in twos or threes, but no one wanted to live here with me.' She grinned at him. 'They wanted to live in better neighborhoods. My work is here. This is my mission.'

'What's your real name?' he asked, totally intrigued now. 'I mean your nun name.'

'Sister Mary Magdalen,' she said gently.

'I'm utterly blown away,' he admitted, pulling a cigarette out of his pocket. It was the first one he'd smoked all night, and she didn't seem to disapprove. She seemed to be totally at ease in the real world, in spite of the fact that she was a nun. She was the first nun he'd talked to in years, and never as freely as this. They felt like combat buddies after what they'd just been through, and in

47

some ways they were. 'Do you like being a nun?' he asked her, and she nodded, thinking about it for a minute, and then she turned to him.

'I love it. Going into the convent was the best thing I ever did. I always knew it was what I wanted to do, ever since I was a kid. Like being a doctor or a lawyer or a ballet dancer. They call it an early vocation. This has always been it for me.'

'Have you ever been sorry you did it?'

'No.' She smiled happily at him. 'Never. It's been the perfect life for me. I went in right after I finished nursing school. I grew up in Chicago, the eldest of seven children. I always knew this would be right for me.'

'Did you ever have a boyfriend?' He was intrigued by what she said.

'One,' she confessed easily, with no embarrassment about it. She hadn't thought about him in years. 'When I was in nursing school.'

'What happened?' He was sure some romantic tragedy had driven her into the convent. He couldn't imagine doing that for any other reason. The concept was totally foreign to him. He had grown up Lutheran, and had never even seen a nun until he left home. The whole idea of it had never made much sense to him. But here was this happy, contented little woman who talked about her life among hookers and drug addicts with such serenity, joy, and peace. It utterly amazed him.

'He died in a car accident in my second year of nursing school. But even if he'd lived, it wouldn't have made a difference. I told him right from the beginning that I wanted to be a nun, although I'm not sure he believed me. I never went out with anyone else after that, because by then I was sure.

I probably would have stopped going out with him too. But we were both young, and it was all very innocent and harmless. By today's standards, for sure.' In other words, Everett understood, she had been a virgin when she entered the convent, and still was. The whole idea seemed unbelievable to him. And a waste of a very pretty woman. She seemed so alive and vibrant to him.

'That's amazing.'

'Not really. It's just what some people do.' She accepted it as normal, although it seemed anything but to him. 'What about you? Married? Divorced? Kids?' She could sense he had a story, and he felt comfortable sharing it with her. She was easy to talk to, and he enjoyed her company. He realized now that the plain black dress was her habit. It explained why she hadn't been in evening clothes like everyone else at the benefit.

'I got a girl pregnant when I was eighteen, married her because her father said I had to or he'd kill me, and we split up the following year. Marriage wasn't for me, not at that age at least. She filed for divorce eventually, and got remarried, I think. I only saw my boy again once after we divorced, when he was about three. I just wasn't ready for fatherhood right then. I felt bad about it when I left, but it was so overwhelming for a kid the age I was then. So I left. I didn't know what else to do. I've spent his whole life and most of mine running around the world covering war zones and catastrophes for the AP ever since. It's been a crazy life, but it suited me. I loved it. And by now, I've grown up, and so has he. He doesn't need me anymore, and his mother was so furious with me, she had our marriage annulled by the church later, so she could remarry. So officially, I never existed,' Everett said quietly as she watched him.

'We always need our parents,' she said softly and they were both quiet for a minute as he thought about what she'd said. 'The AP will be happy with the pictures you took tonight,' she said encouragingly. He didn't tell her about his Pulitzer. He never talked about it.

'I don't work for them anymore,' he said simply. 'I picked up some bad habits on the road. They got out of hand about a year ago, when I damn near died of alcohol poisoning in Bangkok and a hooker saved me. She got me to a hospital, and eventually I came back and dried out. I went into rehab after the AP fired me, and they were justified doing that. I've been sober for a year. It feels pretty good. I just started the job at the magazine I was covering the benefit for. It's not my kind of thing. It's celebrity gossip. I'd rather be getting my ass shot off somewhere uncivilized than in a ballroom like tonight, wearing a tuxedo.'

'So would I,' she said, laughing. 'It's not my thing either.' She explained that she was at a donated table and a friend had given her the ticket, even though she didn't want to attend, and she had gone so as not to waste it. 'I'd much rather be working on the streets with these people than doing anything else. What about your son? Do you ever wonder about him or want to see him? How old is he now?' She was curious about Everett too, and brought up his boy again. She was a great believer in the importance of family in people's lives. And it was rare for her to have a chance to talk to someone like him. And even odder for him to be talking to a nun.

'He'll be thirty in a few weeks. I think about him sometimes, but it's a little late for that. Or a lot late. You don't walk back into someone's life when they're thirty and ask them how they've been. He probably hates my guts for running out on him.'

'Do you hate your guts for it?' she asked succinctly.

'Sometimes. Not often. I thought about it when I was in rehab. But you just don't spring up in someone's life after they're all grown up.'

'Maybe you do,' she said softly. 'Maybe he'd like to hear from you. Do you know where he is?'

'I used to. I could try to find out. I don't think I should. What could I say to him?'

'Maybe there are things he'd want to ask you. It might be a nice thing to do for him, to let him know that your moving on had nothing to do with him.' She was a smart woman, and Everett nodded as he looked at her.

They walked around the neighborhood for a little while after that, and everything seemed to be in surprisingly good order. Some people had gone to shelters. A few had gotten hurt, and been taken to hospitals. The rest seemed to be doing okay, although everybody was talking about the force of the quake. It had been a huge one.

At six-thirty that morning Maggie said she was going to try and get some sleep and then go back out on the street in a few hours to check on her people. Everett said he was probably going to try and get a bus, train, or plane back to L.A. as soon as he could, or rent a car if he could find one. He had taken plenty of pictures. For his own purposes, he wanted to cruise around the city a little and see if there was anything else he wanted to shoot before he went back. He didn't want to miss a story, and he was taking some great material back with him. He was actually tempted to stay a few more days, but he wasn't sure how his editor would react. And for San Francisco and the surrounding areas, there was no phone communication with the outside world at the moment so he couldn't check out his reaction.

'I got some nice shots of you tonight,' Everett told Maggie as he left her on her doorstep. She lived in an ancient-looking building that looked as disreputable as it did old, but it didn't seem to worry her. She said she had lived there for years and was a fixture in the neighborhood. He jotted down her address and told her he'd send prints of the photographs to her. He asked her for her phone number, in case he ever came back to the city. 'If I do, I'll take you to dinner,' he promised. 'I had a nice time talking to you.'

'So did I,' she said, smiling up at him. 'It's going to take a long time to clean up the city. I hope too many people weren't killed tonight.' She looked worried. They had no way of getting news. They were cut off from the world, without electricity or cell phones. It was a strange feeling.

The sun was coming up as he said goodbye to her, and he wondered if he'd ever see her again. It seemed unlikely. It had been an odd and unforgettable night for all of them.

'Goodbye, Maggie,' he said as she let herself into the building. There were bits of broken plaster lying all over the hallway, but she commented with a smile that it hardly looked worse than usual. 'Take care of yourself.'

'You too,' she said as she waved at him and

closed the door. An evil smell had drifted toward them as she opened the door into the hallway, and he couldn't imagine how she could live there. She was truly a saintly woman, he realized as he walked away, and then laughed softly. He had spent the night of the San Francisco earthquake with a nun. He thought she was a hero. He could hardly wait to see the pictures of her. And then oddly, as he walked away from her building, back through the Tenderloin, he found himself thinking about his son, and the way Chad had looked when he was three, and for the first time in the twenty-seven years since he'd last seen him, he missed him. Maybe he would look him up one day, if he ever got back to Montana, and if Chad was still living there. It was something to think about. Some of what Maggie had said had gotten under his skin, and he forced it out of his head again. He didn't want to feel guilty about his son. It was too late for that, and would do neither of them any good. He strode off then in his lucky boots, past the drunks and the hookers on Maggie's street. The sun was coming up, as he walked back into the heart of the city to see what stories of the earthquake he would find there. There were endless opportunities to shoot. And for him, who knew, maybe even another Pulitzer one day. Even after the shocking events of the previous night, he felt better than he had in years. He was back in the saddle as a journalist, and felt more confident and in control of his life than ever before.

Chapter 3

Seth and Sarah started the long walk home from the Ritz-Carlton after the benefit. Her high-heeled sandals were nearly impossible to negotiate, but there was so much broken glass on the streets that she didn't dare take them off to go barefoot. She got blisters with every step she took. There were lines down and sparks spitting from live wires which they carefully avoided. They were finally able to hitch a ride from a passing car for the last dozen blocks or so, from a doctor returning from St. Mary's Hospital. It was three o'clock in the morning, and he had gone to check on his patients after the earth-quake. He told them things at the hospital were relatively under control. The emergency generators were working, and only one very small part of the radiology lab on the main floor had been destroyed. Everything else seemed to be in good order, although patients and staff alike were visibly shaken.

Like everyone else in the city, at the hospital, they had no phone communications, but they were listening on battery-powered radios and TVs for news bulletins, to see which parts of the city had suffered the worst damage.

He also told them the Marina had taken a terrible hit again, as it had in the smaller '89 earthquake. It was built on landfill, and there were fires burning out of control. There were also reports of looting downtown. Both Russian and Nob Hills had survived the 7.9 earthquake relatively well, as had been witnessed by everyone at the Ritz-Carlton. Some of the western areas of the city had suffered severe damage, as had Noe Valley, the Castro, and the Mission. And parts of Pacific Heights had been badly shaken. Firemen were attempting to rescue people trapped in buildings and elevators, and still have enough manpower to fight the fires that had erupted in many parts of the city, which was no mean feat with broken water mains nearly everywhere.

As their benefactor drove Seth and Sarah home, they could hear sirens in the distance. And both of the city's main bridges, the Bay Bridge and the Golden Gate, had been closed since minutes after the earthquake. The Golden Gate had swung wildly, and several people had been injured. Two sections of the upper deck of the Bay Bridge had collapsed onto the deck below it, and several cars were reported crushed with people trapped in them. So far, the highway patrol had not been able to effect a rescue. Reports of people blocked in cars and unable to get out, screaming as they died, had been horrendous. So far, it was impossible to even guess at the death toll. But it was easy to assume there would be many, and thousands injured. The three of them listened to the car radio as they drove carefully through the streets.

Sarah gave the doctor their address, and was quiet on the way home, praying for her children. There was still no way to communicate with the house or the babysitter for reassurance. All telephone lines were down, and cell phones weren't working. The badly shaken city seemed completely cut off from the outside world. All she wanted to know now was that Oliver and Molly were okay. Seth was staring out the window in a daze, and kept trying to use his cell phone, as the doctor drove them the rest of the way. They finally arrived at their large brick house perched on top of the hill on Divisadero and Broadway, overlooking the bay. It appeared to be intact. They thanked the doctor, wished him well, and got out. Sarah ran to the front door as Seth followed behind her, looking exhausted.

Sarah already had the door open when he reached her. She had kicked her impossible shoes off, and was running down the hall. There was no electricity, so the lights were off, and it was unusually dark, with not even streetlights outside. She ran past the living room to go upstairs, and then she saw them, the babysitter asleep on the couch, with the baby dozing in her arms, and Molly snoring softly beside her, and candles lit on the table. The sitter was out cold, but stirred as Sarah approached.

'Hi . . . oh . . . such a big earthquake!' she said, waking up, but whispering so as not to disturb the children. But as Seth walked into the room and the three adults talked, the children began to stir too. Looking around, Sarah could see that all their paintings were wildly askew, two statues had fallen down, and a small antique card table and several chairs had tipped over. The room had a severely disordered look to it, with books spilling all over the floor, and smaller objects strewn around the room. But her babies were fine, which was all that mattered. They were uninjured and alive, and then as her eyes got accustomed to the dim room, she could see that Parmani had a bump on her forehead. She explained that Oliver's bookcase had fallen on her as she ran to get him out of his

56

crib when the quake began. Sarah was grateful it hadn't knocked her unconscious or killed the baby, as books and objects had fallen off the shelves. A baby in the Marina had been killed in the 1989 earthquake that way, when a heavy object had slipped off a shelf and killed the infant in its crib. Sarah was grateful that history hadn't repeated itself with her son.

Oliver stirred as he lay on top of the sitter, picked up his head, and saw his mother, and then Sarah picked him up and held him. Molly was still sound asleep curled up in a little ball beside the babysitter. She looked like a doll, as her parents smiled at her, grateful for their safety.

'Hi, sweetheart, were you having a big sleep?' his mother asked him. The baby looked startled to see them and puckered his face as his bottom lip quivered, and he started to cry. Sarah thought it was the sweetest sound she had ever heard, as sweet as the night he'd been born. She had been terrified for her children all night, ever since the earthquake had begun. All she had wanted to do was run home and take them in her arms. She leaned down and gently touched Molly's leg, as though to reassure herself that she was alive too. 'It must have been so scary for you,' Sarah said sympathetically to Parmani, as Seth walked into the den and picked up the phone. It was still dead. There was no phone service in the entire city. Seth must have checked his cell phone a million times on the way home.

'This is ridiculous,' he snarled, as he walked back into the room. 'You would think they could at least keep our cell phones going. What are we supposed to do? Be cut off from the world for the next week? They better get us going again tomorrow.' Sarah knew, as he did, there was little chance of that.

They had no electricity either, and Parmani had wisely shut off the gas, so the house was chilly, but fortunately the night was warm. On a typical blowy San Francisco night, they would have been cold.

'We'll just have to camp out for a while,' Sarah said serenely. She was happy now, with her baby in her arms, and her daughter within her sight on the couch.

'Maybe I'll drive down to Stanford or San Jose tomorrow,' Seth said vaguely. 'I have to make some calls.'

'The doctor said he heard at the hospital that the roads are closed. I think we're pretty much cut off.'

'That can't be,' Seth said, looking panicked, and then glanced at the luminous dial on his watch. 'Maybe I should head down there now. It's nearly seven A.M. in New York. By the time I get down there, people will be in their offices on the East Coast. I'm completing a transaction today.'

'Can't you take a day off?' Sarah suggested, and Seth ran upstairs without answering her. He was back downstairs in five minutes, wearing jeans and a sweater and running shoes, with a look of intense concentration on his face and his briefcase in his hand.

Both their cars were trapped and perhaps lost forever in the garage downtown. There was no hope of getting either of them out, if they could even be found, and not for a long time anyway, since most of the garage had collapsed. But he turned to Parmani with an expectant look and

58

smiled at her in the soft darkness of the living room. Ollie had gone back to sleep in Sarah's arms, comforted by her familiar warmth and sound.

'Parmani, do you mind if I borrow your car for a couple of hours? I'm going to see if I can head south and make some calls. Maybe my cell phone will even work down there.'

'Of course you can,' the babysitter answered, looking startled. It seemed like a strange request to her, and even more so to Sarah. This was no time to be trying to get to San Jose. It seemed inappropriate to Sarah for him to be obsessed with business now, and leaving them in the city.

'Can't you just relax? Nobody is going to expect to hear from anyone in San Francisco today. This is silly, Seth. What if there's another quake or an aftershock? We'd be here alone, and maybe you couldn't get back.' Or worse, an overpass could collapse and crush him on the road. She didn't want him going anywhere, but he looked determined and intent as he headed for the front door. Parmani said her keys were in it, and the car was in their garage. It was a battered old Honda Accord, but it got her where she wanted to go. Sarah wouldn't let her drive the children in it, and she wasn't enthusiastic about Seth traveling with it either. The car had over a hundred thousand miles, had no current safety features, and was at least a dozen years old.

'Don't worry, ladies.' He smiled at them. 'I'll be back.' He ran out the door. It worried Sarah to have him venturing out, with no streetlights to drive by, no stoplights to control traffic, and maybe fallen obstacles on the road. But she could tell that

59

nothing would stop him. He had left before she could say another word. Parmani went to get another flashlight, and the candles flickered as Sarah sat in her living room, thinking about Seth. It was one thing to be a workaholic and another to dash off down the peninsula, hours after a major earthquake, leaving his wife and children to fend for themselves. She wasn't happy about it at all. It seemed like irrational, obsessive behavior to her.

She and Parmani sat in the living room talking softly until almost sunrise. She thought about going upstairs to her bedroom, and putting the children in bed with her, but she felt safer downstairs, able to leave the house if there was another quake. Parmani told her a tree had fallen in the garden, and there were things all over the floor upstairs, a huge mirror had fallen and cracked, and several of the back windows had popped out and shattered on the cement outside. Most of their china and crystal lay smashed on the kitchen floor, along with groceries that had literally flown off the shelves. Parmani said several jars of juice and bottles of wine had broken, and Sarah wasn't looking forward to cleaning up the mess. Parmani had apologized for not doing it, but she'd been too worried about the children, and didn't want to leave them for the amount of time it would have taken her to deal with it. Sarah said she would do it herself. At one point she walked into the kitchen to look, after she set Oliver down on the couch, still sleeping soundly. She was horrified at the disaster area the kitchen had turned into in a matter of hours. Most of their cupboard doors had opened, and everything had fallen out. It looked like it would take days to clean up.

As the sun came up, Parmani went to make coffee, and then remembered they had neither electricity nor gas. Stepping gingerly over the debris and shards of glass, she poured some water from the hot tap into a cup, and dropped a teabag into it. It was barely lukewarm, but she brought it back to Sarah, and it was comforting to drink it. Parmani was peeling a banana for herself. Sarah had insisted she didn't want anything to eat, she was still too shaken and upset.

She had barely finished the tea when Seth came through the door, looking grim.

'That was quick,' Sarah commented.

'The roads are closed.' He looked stunned. 'I mean *all* the roads. The entrance to 101, the whole on ramp is down.' He didn't tell her about the horrifying carnage below it. There had been ambulances and police everywhere. The highway patrol had turned him back and sternly told him to go home and stay there. This was no time to be going anywhere. He tried to tell them he lived in Palo Alto, and the officer had told him he would have to stay in the city until the roads were open again. And in answer to Seth's question, he said not for several days. Maybe even a week, given the enormity of the damage to the roads. 'I tried Nineteenth Avenue to get on 280, same thing. The beach to get to Pacifica, they've got landslides there. They have it all blocked off. I didn't bother to try the bridges, because we heard on the radio they were closed. Fuck, Sarah,' he said angrily, 'we're trapped!'

'For a little while. I don't know why you can't calm down. Besides, it looks like we have a lot to clean up. No one in New York is going to expect your call. They know more about what's happening here than we do. Believe me, Seth, no one is going to miss your call.'

'You don't understand,' he muttered darkly, and then ran up the stairs and slammed their bedroom door. Sarah left the children with Parmani, who had watched the scene with interest, and then followed her husband upstairs. He was pacing around their bedroom, looking like a lion in a cage. A very angry lion, who looked like he was about to eat someone, and for lack of any other victim, he seemed as though he was going to attack her.

'I'm sorry, baby,' she said gently. 'I know you're in the middle of a deal. But you can't control natural disasters. There isn't anything we can do about it. The deal will hold for a few days.'

'No, it won't.' He spat the words angrily at her. 'Some deals don't hold. This is one of them. All I need is a fucking phone.' She would have produced one for him if she could, but she couldn't. She was just grateful that their children were safe. His obsession with continuing to do business, under the circumstances, seemed more than extreme to her. She realized at the same time that it was why he was such a huge success. Seth never stopped. He was on his cell phone night and day, making deals. Without it now, he felt utterly and totally impotent, and trapped, as though someone had severed his vocal cords and tied his hands. He was nailed to the floor in a dead city, with no possible communication with the outside world. She could see that he viewed it as a major crisis, and she wished she could convince him to calm down.

'What can I do for you, Seth?' she asked, sitting down on the bed, and patting the spot next to her. She was thinking about a massage, a bath, a tranquilizer, a back or neck rub, or holding him in her arms, or lying beside him on the bed.

'What can you do for me? Are you kidding? Is that a joke?' He was almost shouting in their beautifully decorated bedroom. The sun was up now, and the soft yellows and sky blues she had done it in looked exquisite in the early morning light. Seth was oblivious to the room, as he stared angrily at her.

'I mean it,' she said calmly. 'I'll do whatever I can.' He stared at her as though she were insane.

'Sarah, you have no idea what's going on. None. No concept.'

'Try me. We went to business school together. I'm not a moron, you know.'

'No, I am,' he said, sitting down on the bed and running a hand through his hair. He couldn't even look at her. 'I have to transfer sixty million dollars out of our fund accounts by noon today.' His voice sounded dead as he said it, and Sarah looked impressed.

'You're making an investment that size? What are you buying? Commodities? Sounds like risky stuff in quantities like that.' Admittedly, buying commodities was not only high risk but equally high profit if you did it right. She knew Seth was a genius with the investments he made.

'I'm not buying, Sarah,' he said, glancing at her, and then away again. 'I'm covering my ass. That's all I'm doing, and if I can't, I'm fucked . . . we're fucked . . . everything we own will be gone . . . I could even go to jail.' He was staring at the floor beneath his feet as he spoke.

'What are you talking about?' Sarah looked panicked. He was kidding obviously, but the look on his face said he wasn't.

'We had auditors in this week, to check on our new fund. It was an investors' audit to make sure we have as much in the fund as we claimed. We will eventually, of course, there's no question of it. I've done it before. Sully Markham has covered me for audits like that before. And eventually we make our money and put it in the account. But sometimes in the beginning, when we don't have it, Sully helps me pad things a little when the investors do an audit.' Sarah stared at him, stunned.

'A little? You call sixty million dollars' worth of padding a "little"? Jesus, Seth, what were you thinking of? You could have gotten caught, or not been able to make the money up.' And then, as she said it, she realized that that was what was happening. He was there now.

'I have to get the money, or Sully *will* get caught in New York. He has to have the money back in his accounts today. The banks are closed. I don't have a fucking cell phone to use, I can't even call Sully to tell him to cover it somehow.'

'He must be able to figure that much out. With the whole city down, he must know you can't do it.' Sarah looked pale as they talked. It had never even remotely occurred to her that Seth was dishonest. And sixty million was no small slip. It was major. It was criminal fraud on the grandest scale. She had never for a moment thought that Seth would be corrupted by greed into doing a thing like that. It

64

put everything between them in question, in fact their whole life, and more importantly, who he was.

'I was supposed to do it yesterday,' Seth said grimly. 'I promised Sully I would, by close of business. But the auditors stayed till almost six o'clock. That's why I got to the Ritz late. I knew he had till two o'clock today, and I had till eleven, so I figured I could take care of it this morning. I was worried about it, but I didn't panic. Now I'm panicked. We are utterly, totally, and completely screwed. He has an audit that starts Monday. He has to put it off. The banks here won't be open by then. And I can't even goddamn call him to warn him.' Seth looked as though he was about to cry as Sarah stared at him in shock and disbelief.

'He must have checked by now and seen you didn't make the transfer,' she said, feeling slightly dizzy. She felt as though she were on a roller-coaster ride, barely able to hang on, without a seatbelt. She couldn't even imagine what Seth felt. He was risking prison. And if so, what would happen to them?

'Yeah, so he knows I didn't make the transfer. And then what? With the goddamn earthquake shutting the whole city down, I can't get the money back to him now. He's going to have a sixty million shortfall when his auditors show up on Monday morning, and I can't do anything about it.' He and Sully Markham were both guilty of every kind of fraud and theft, crossing state lines. Sarah knew, as Seth had when he did it, that it was a federal offense, and about as bad as it could get. It didn't even bear thinking. She felt as though the room were spinning as she looked at him.

'What are you going to do, Seth?' Sarah said in barely more than a whisper. She fully understood the implications of what he'd done. What she couldn't understand was why he'd done it, or when he'd become a criminal. How could this be happening to them?

'I don't know,' he said honestly, and then looked her in the eye. He looked terrified, and so was she. 'I may go down on this one, Sarah. I've done this kind of thing before. And I've helped Sully out too. We're old friends. We just never got caught before, and I was always able to clean it up at my end. This time I'm up shit creek.'

'Oh, my God,' Sarah said softly. 'What happens if they prosecute you?'

'I don't know. This one's going to be hard to cover. I don't think Sully can postpone the audit anyway. The timing of it is at the discretion of his investors, and they don't like giving anyone time to do fancy footwork or cook the books. And we sure cooked them. We fucking fried them. I don't know if he tried to postpone his audit once he saw we had an earthquake and I didn't transfer the funds back to him. Sixty million is a little tough to slip under the rug. And it's a hole they'll notice. Worse yet, the trail leads directly to my door. Unless Sully pulls off a miracle at his end before Monday, we're totally fucked.

'If the auditors figure it out, the SEC will be after me in about five minutes. And I'm a sitting duck waiting for it to happen here, but I can't run away from it now. If it happens, it happens. We'll have to get a terrific lawyer and see if we can make a deal with the federal prosecutor, if it comes to that. Other than that, I'd have to run away to

66

Brazil, and I'm not doing that to you. So I guess we sit here, waiting for the other shoe to drop, after the dust settles from the earthquake. I tried my BlackBerry a little while ago, and it's as dead as a doornail. We just have to wait and see what happens . . . I'm sorry, Sarah,' he added. He didn't know what else to say to her, and there were tears in her eyes when she looked at him. She had never, ever suspected him of being dishonest, and now she felt as though a wrecking ball had hit her.

'How could you do something like that?' she asked, with tears rolling down her cheeks. She hadn't moved. She just sat staring at him, unable to believe what he had said. But it was obvious that it was true. Her life had instantly become a horror movie.

'I figured we'd never get caught,' he said, shrugging. It seemed incredible to him too, but for different reasons than what was upsetting Sarah. Seth didn't get it. He had no idea how betrayed Sarah felt by his confession to her.

'Even if you didn't get caught, how could you do something so dishonest? You broke every imaginable law, misrepresenting your assets to your investors. What if you'd lost all their money?'

'I figured I could cover it. I always did. And what are you complaining about? Look how fast I built my business. How do you think you got all this?' He waved his arms grandly around their bedroom, and she realized she didn't know him. She thought she did, but she didn't. It was as though the Seth she knew had vanished, and a criminal had taken his place.

'And what happens to all this if you go to prison?' She had never expected him to be this

67

successful, but they had a big lifestyle now. The house in the city, another mammoth house in Tahoe, their plane, cars, assets, jewelry. He had built a house of cards that was about to fall down around them, and she couldn't help wondering how bad it could get. Seth was looking stressed and embarrassed, as well he should.

'I guess it goes down the tubes,' he said simply. 'Even if I don't go to prison. I'm going to have to pay fines, and interest on the money I borrowed.'

'You didn't borrow it, you took it. It wasn't Sully's to give either. It belongs to *his* investors, not either of you. You made a deal with your buddy so you could lie to people. Nothing about that is okay, Seth.' She didn't want him to get caught, for his sake and theirs, but she knew that it was only justice if he did.

'Thanks for the lecture on morality,' he said bitterly. 'In any case, to answer your question, all this would probably go, pretty quickly. They'd seize all our stuff, or some of it, the houses, the plane, and most of the rest. What they don't take, we can sell.' He sounded almost matter-of-fact about it. As soon as the earthquake hit the night before, he knew his goose was cooked.

'And how are we supposed to live?'

'Borrow money from friends, I guess. I don't know, Sarah. We'll have to figure that out when it happens. Right now, today, we're okay. Nobody is going to come after me in the middle of the aftermath of an earthquake. We'll just have to see what happens next week.' But Sarah could figure out as well as he could that their whole world was about to come down around their ears. There was no way to avoid it, after the fancy footwork he had done. He had put their life at risk in the worst possible way.

'Do you think they'd take our house away?' She suddenly looked panicked as she glanced around the room. This was home to her now. She didn't need a home as elaborate as this one, but this was where they lived, the house their children had been born into. The prospect of losing everything frightened her. From one minute to the next, they could be destitute, if Seth got arrested and prosecuted. She started to feel frantic about it. She'd have to find a job, a place to live. And where would Seth be? In prison? Only hours before, all she had wanted was to know that her children were alive and safe after the earthquake, that their house hadn't fallen down around them. And suddenly, with what Seth had revealed to her, everything else had, and all they had for sure now were their kids. She didn't even know who Seth was, after what he'd told her. She'd been married to a stranger for four years. He was the father of her children. She had trusted and loved him.

She started to cry harder as she thought about it, and Seth came to put his arms around her, but she wouldn't let him. She didn't know if he was ally or foe now. Without even thinking about her and the children, he had put them all in jeopardy. She was furious at him, and heartbroken over what he'd done.

'I love you, babe,' he said softly, and she looked at him in amazement.

'How can you say that? I love you too. But look what you did to us, all of us. Not just yourself and me, but the kids too. We may get thrown out into the street. And you could wind up in prison.' And

69

almost certainly would.

'It may not be that bad,' he tried to reassure her, but she didn't believe him. She knew too much about SEC regulations herself to swallow the platitudes he was handing her. He was in extreme danger of being arrested and going to prison. And if he did, their life, as they knew it, would go with him. Their lives would never be the same again.

'What do we do now?' she asked miserably, blowing her nose on a tissue. She didn't look like the glamorous young socialite of the night before. She was like a very frightened woman. She was wearing a sweater over her evening gown, her feet were bare as she sat on their bed, crying. She looked like a teenager whose world had just come to an end. And it just had, thanks to her husband.

She took down her French twist and let her dark hair fall over her shoulders. She seemed half her age as she sat there, glaring at him, feeling betrayed as she never had before. Not for the money and lifestyle they would lose, although that mattered too. Everything had seemed so secure and that had been important to her, for their children. But more than that, he had robbed them of the happy life he had set up for them, the sense of safety she counted on. He had risked all of them, when he transferred the money Sully Markham lent him. He had shot her life out of a cannon right along with his.

'I guess all we can do is wait,' Seth said quietly, as he walked across the room and stared out the window. There were fires burning below them, and in the morning sunshine, he could see damage to houses near them. Trees were down, balconies were hanging at odd angles, chimneys had toppled

70

off roofs. People were walking around outside with a dazed air. But none of them were as stunned as Sarah, crying in their bedroom. It was only a matter of time now before life as they knew it now would end, and maybe their marriage with it.

Chapter 4

Melanie stayed on the street outside the Ritz-Carlton for a long time that night, helping people, trying to get paramedics to them. She found two little girls who were lost and helped them find their mother. There wasn't much she could do. She didn't have the nursing skills of Sister Mary Magdalen, but there was a level of comfort and reassurance that she could give to others. One of her band members followed her around for a while, and then finally went to join the others in the shelter. He knew she was a big girl and could take care of herself. No one in her entourage had stayed with her. She was still wearing the dress and platform shoes she had worn onstage, and Everett Carson's rented tuxedo jacket over it, which by then was filthy, streaked with dust and the blood of people she'd assisted. But it felt good to her to be out there. For the first time in a long time, despite the plaster dust in the air, she felt like she could breathe.

She sat on the back of the fire truck, eating a doughnut and drinking a cup of coffee, talking to the firemen about what had happened that night. And they were shocked and pleased to be having coffee with Melanie Free.

'So what's it like to be Melanie Free?' one of the younger firemen asked her. He had been born in San Francisco and grown up in the Mission. His father was a cop, as were two of his brothers, and two more were firemen like him. His sisters had all gotten married right out of high school. Melanie Free was as far from his life as anyone could get, although watching her sip coffee and eat the doughnut, she looked just like everyone else to him.

'It's fun sometimes,' she admitted. 'And sometimes it sucks. It's a lot of work and a lot of pressure, especially when we play concerts. And the press are a huge pain in the ass.' They all laughed at her comment as she reached for another doughnut. The fireman who had asked her the question was twenty-two years old and had three kids. He thought her life sounded more interesting than his, although he loved his wife and kids. 'What about you?' she asked him. 'Do you like what you do?'

'Yeah. Most of the time. Especially on a night like this. You really have the feeling you're making a difference, and doing some good. It beats having beer bottles thrown at you, or having someone take potshots at you, when you show up in the Bay View to put out a fire they started themselves. But it's not always like that. Most of the time, I like being a firefighter.'

'Firemen are cute,' Melanie commented, and then giggled. She couldn't remember the last time she'd had two doughnuts. Her mother would have killed her. Unlike her mother, Melanie was permanently on a diet, at her mother's insistence. It was one of the small prices she paid for fame.

She looked less than her nineteen years as she sat on the bottom step of the fire truck, chatting with the men.

'You're pretty cute yourself,' one of the older firefighters commented as he walked by her. He had just spent four hours getting people out of an elevator where they'd been trapped. One woman had fainted, the others had been okay. It had been a long night for everyone. Melanie waved as the two little girls she'd found walked past her with their mother on the way to the shelter. Their mother looked stunned as she realized who Melanie was. Even with her long blond hair uncombed and tangled, and dirt on her face, it was easy to recognize the star.

'Do you get tired of people recognizing you?' one of the other firemen asked her.

'Yeah, a lot. My boyfriend hates it. He punched a photographer in the face, and wound up in jail. It really gets on his nerves.'

'Sounds like it.' The firefighter smiled and went back to work. The remaining ones told her she should go to the shelter then. It was safer for her there. She had been helping hotel guests and random strangers all night, but the Office of Emergency Services wanted people in shelters. There was falling debris everywhere, pieces of windows along with signs and chunks of concrete off buildings. It really wasn't safe for her outside. Not to mention the live wires that were a constant danger.

The youngest of the firefighters offered to walk her the two blocks to the shelter, and she reluctantly accepted. It was seven in the morning, and she knew her mother would be worried sick by then, and would probably be having a fit about where she was. Melanie talked easily with the young fireman on the way to the large church auditorium where people were being sent. As it turned out, the whole building was full to the rafters, and Red Cross volunteers and church members were serving breakfast. When she saw the size of the crowd, Melanie couldn't imagine how she'd find her mother. She left the fireman at the door, thanked him for providing her an escort, and threaded her way through the crowd looking for someone she knew. It was a massive group of people talking, crying, laughing, some looking worried, and hundreds of people sitting on the floor.

She finally found her mother sitting next to Ashley and Pam, Melanie's assistant. They had been worried about Melanie for hours. Janet gave a shriek when she saw her and threw her arms around her daughter. She nearly crushed Melanie in her embrace, and then scolded her loudly for disappearing for the entire night.

'For chrissake, Mel, I thought you were dead by now, electrocuted, or hit on the head by a chunk of the building falling off the hotel.'

'No, I was just helping out,' Melanie said softly. Her voice always shrank to next to nothing when she was anywhere near her mother. And she noticed that Ashley was looking very pale. The poor thing was scared to death, and had been completely traumatized by the earthquake. She had sat huddled next to Jake all night, while he ignored her, and slept off everything he'd been drinking and smoking before the quake.

He opened an eye and glanced at Melanie when

74

he heard her mother shriek. He looked massively hung over, as he looked quizzically at Melanie. He didn't even remember her performance and wasn't sure he'd been there, although he was sure he remembered the rock-and-rolling of the quake.

'Nice jacket,' he commented as he squinted at her in the filthy tuxedo jacket. 'Where you been all night?' He looked more interested than concerned.

'Busy,' she said, but didn't lean over to kiss him. He was looking very rough. He had been lying on the floor, sound asleep, with his jacket rolled up under his head like a pillow. Most of their roadies were sleeping near them, as well as the guys in the band.

'Weren't you scared to be out there?' Ashley asked her, looking terrified, as Melanie shook her head.

'No. A lot of people needed help. Lost kids, people who needed paramedics. A lot of people got cut by falling glass. I did whatever I could.'

'You're not a nurse, for chrissake,' her mother snapped at her. 'You're a Grammy winner. Grammy winners don't run around wiping people's noses.' Janet glared at her. It wasn't the image she wanted for her daughter.

'Why not, Mom? What's wrong with helping people? There were a lot of scared people out there who needed someone to do whatever they could.'

'Let someone else do it,' her mother said as she lay down next to Jake. 'Christ, I wonder how long we're going to be stuck here. They said the airport is closed because of damage to the tower. I hope to hell they still send us home on the private plane.'

Those things mattered a lot to her. She was very big on taking full advantage of the perks they were offered. She cared a lot more about all that than Melanie did. Melanie would have been just as happy on a Greyhound bus.

'Who cares, Mom? Maybe we can rent a car and drive home. Just so we get back eventually. I don't have another gig till next week.'

'Well, I'm not going to lie around here on the floor of a church auditorium for the next week. My back is killing me. They've got to put us up somewhere decent.'

'All the hotels are closed, Mom. Their generators aren't working, they're dangerous, their refrigerators are out of commission.' Melanie knew that from the firefighters she'd talked to. 'At least we're safe here.'

'I want to go back to L.A.,' her mother complained. She told Pam to keep asking when the airport would open, and Pam promised that she would. She admired Melanie for helping people all night. She had spent the night bringing Janet blankets, cigarettes, and coffee that was being prepared on butane stoves in the mess hall. And Ashley was so panicked she'd thrown up twice. Jake was out like a light, drunk out of his mind. It had been a terrible night, but at least they were all alive.

Melanie's hairdresser and manager had both been at the front of the auditorium serving sandwiches and cookies, and handing out bottles of water. The food ran out quickly, from the church's enormous kitchen where they usually fed the homeless. After that they were handing people tins of turkey, deviled ham, and beef jerky. It

76

wasn't going to be long before there was nothing left. Melanie didn't care, she wasn't hungry anyway.

At noon, they were told that they were being taken to a shelter in the Presidio. Buses would arrive for them, and they would leave the church in shifts. They were given blankets, sleeping bags, and personal supplies like toothbrushes and toothpaste, which they carried with their own belongings, since they wouldn't be coming back to the church.

Melanie and her entourage didn't make it onto a bus till three o'clock that afternoon. She had managed to sleep for a couple of hours, and was feeling fine when she helped her mother roll up her blankets, and shook Jake awake.

'Come on, Jakey, we're going,' she said, wondering just what drugs he'd taken the night before. He'd been dead to the world all day and still looked hung over. He was a handsome guy, but as he got up and looked around, he was looking very raw.

'Jesus, I hate this movie. This looks like the set for one of those disaster epics, and I feel like a dress extra. I keep waiting for someone to paint blood on my face and put a bandage on my head.'

'You'd look great even in blood and a bandage,' Melanie reassured him, tying her own hair back in a braid.

Her mother complained all the way to the bus, and said the way they were being treated was disgusting, didn't anyone know who they were. Melanie assured her it didn't make any difference, and no one cared. They were just a bunch of people who had survived the earthquake, and no

77

different from anyone else.

'You shut your mouth, girl,' her mother scolded. 'That's no way for a star to talk.'

'I'm not a star here, Mom. No one gives a damn if I can sing. They're tired, hungry, and scared, and everyone wants to go home, just like we do. We're no different.'

'You tell her, Mellie,' one of the guys in her band said, as they boarded the bus, and then two teenage girls recognized her and screamed. She signed autographs for both of them, which seemed ridiculous to her. She felt like anything but a star, half dressed and filthy, in a man's tuxedo jacket that had seen better days and the torn net and sequin dress she'd worn onstage.

'Sing something for us,' the girls pleaded with her, and Melanie laughed at them. She told them there was no way she would sing. They were young and silly and about fourteen. They lived near the church with their families and were on the bus with them. They said part of their apartment building had fallen down, and they'd been rescued by the police, but no one was hurt, except an old lady on the top floor who broke her leg. They had a lot of tales to tell.

They arrived at the Presidio twenty minutes later, and were escorted into old military hangars where the Red Cross had set up cots for them and a mess hall. A field hospital had been organized in one of the hangars, staffed by volunteer medical personnel, National Guard paramedics, doctors and nurses, an assortment of volunteers from local churches, and Red Cross volunteers.

'Maybe they can airlift us out of here by helicopter,' Janet said as she sat down on the cot, utterly horrified by the accommodations. Jake and Ashley went off to get something to eat, and Pam offered to bring back food for Janet, since she said she was too tired and traumatized to move. She wasn't old enough to be that helpless, but she saw no reason to wait in line for hours for disgusting food. The band and the roadies were outside smoking, and after everyone else left, Melanie slipped quietly through the crowd to the desk at the front of the room. She spoke to the woman in charge in a soft voice. The woman at the desk was a National Guard reserve sergeant in camouflage fatigues and combat boots. She glanced at Melanie in surprise, and recognized her immediately.

'What are you doing here?' she asked, smiling warmly. She didn't say Melanie's name. She didn't need to. They both knew who she was.

'I played a benefit here last night,' Melanie said quietly. She smiled broadly at the woman in camouflage fatigues. 'I got stuck here like everyone else.'

'What can I do for you?' She was excited to be meeting Melanie in person.

'I wanted to ask what I can do to help.' She figured it was better than sitting on her cot, listening to her mother complain. 'Do you need volunteers?'

'I know there's a bunch of them in the mess hall, cooking and serving food. The field hospital is just down the road, and I'm not sure what they need. I can put you to work at the desk, if you want. But you may get mobbed if people recognize you.' Melanie nodded. She had thought of it herself.

'I'll try the hospital first.' It sounded better to her.

'Sounds good. Check in with me later if you don't find anything there. It's been a zoo here since the buses started coming in. We're expecting another fifty thousand people in the Presidio tonight. They're busing them in from all over the city.'

'Thanks,' Melanie said, as she went back to find her mother. Janet was lying on her cot, eating a Popsicle that Pam had brought her, with a bag of cookies in her other hand.

'Where've you been?' she asked, glancing at her daughter.

'Checking things out,' Melanie said vaguely. 'I'll be back in a while,' she told her mother. She walked away and Pam followed her. She told her assistant that she was going to the field hospital to volunteer.

'Are you sure?' Pam asked, looking worried.

'Yes, I am. I don't want to sit around here doing nothing, listening to my mom bitch. I might as well be useful.'

'I hear they're pretty well staffed with National Guard and Red Cross volunteers.'

'Maybe so. I figured at the hospital, they might need more help. There's nothing much to do here except hand out water and serve food. I'll come back in a while, or if I don't, you can find me there. The field hospital is just up the road.' Pam nodded and went back to Janet, who said she had a headache and wanted aspirin and water. They were giving that out at the mess hall. A lot of people had headaches from the dust, stress, and trauma. Pam had one herself, not only from the night, but from Janet's demands as well.

Melanie left the building quietly, unnoticed, her

80

head down, her hands in the tuxedo pockets. She was surprised to find a coin there. She hadn't noticed it before. She pulled it out as she walked along. It had a Roman numeral one on it, *I,* with the letters *AA,* and on the flip side, the Serenity Prayer. She assumed it belonged to Everett Carson, the photographer who had lent her the jacket. She put it back, wishing she had different shoes on. Walking along the cement road with pebbles on it was a challenge in the platform shoes she'd worn onstage the night before. They made her feel unsteady.

She was at the field hospital in less than five minutes, and there was a hum of activity there. They were using a generator to light the hall, and had an amazing amount of equipment that had been stored in the Presidio or sent over by hospitals nearby. It looked like a very professional operation, full of white coats, military uniforms, and Red Cross armbands. For a minute, Melanie felt way out of her league, and foolish for wanting to volunteer.

They had a desk at the entrance to check people in, and as she had in the hangar they'd been assigned to, she asked the soldier at the desk if they needed help.

'Hell, yes.' He grinned broadly at her. He had an accent straight out of the Deep South and teeth that looked like piano keys as he smiled. She was relieved to see that he didn't recognize her, and he went to ask someone else about where they needed volunteers. He was back in a minute.

'How do you feel about working with the homeless? They've been busing them in all day.' So far, many of their injuries had been among people who lived on the street.

'Works for me.' She smiled back at him.

'A lot of them got hurt sleeping in doorways. We've been sewing them up for hours. Along with everyone else.' Their homeless patients were more challenging, as they'd been in bad shape before the earthquake hit, and many of them were mentally ill and hard to manage. Melanie wasn't daunted by what he said. He didn't tell her that one of them had lost a leg when a window sliced through it, but he had been taken by ambulance somewhere else. Most of what they were dealing with at the field hospital were minor injuries, but there were a lot of them, thousands in fact.

Two Red Cross volunteers were in charge of checking people in. There were also social workers on hand to see if they could help in other ways. They were offering to help sign them up for city homeless programs, or permanent shelters if they qualified, and even if they did, some had no interest in signing up. They were at the Presidio because they had nowhere else to go, just like everyone else. And everyone at the Presidio got a bed and free food. There was an entire hall set up for showers.

'Can we give you something else to wear?' One of the volunteers in charge smiled at her. 'That must have been quite a dress. You may give someone a heart attack when the jacket opens.' She was smiling broadly, and Melanie laughed and looked down at her voluptuous chest, which was exploding through both the jacket and the remains of her gown. She had forgotten all about it.

'That would be great. If you've got any, I could use some shoes too. These are killing me, and they're hard to walk in.'

'I can see why,' the volunteer commented. 'We have a ton of flip-flops at the back of the hangar. Someone delivered them to us for all the people who walked out of their houses barefoot. We've been taking glass out of people's feet all day.' More than half the people who'd arrived had come without shoes on. Melanie was grateful at the prospect of flip-flops, and someone handed her a pair of camouflage pants and a T-shirt to go with them. The T-shirt said 'Harvey's Bail Bonds,' and the pants were too big. She found a piece of rope and tied it around her, to hold up the pants. She put the flip-flops on and threw away her shoes and dress, and the tuxedo jacket. She didn't think she'd see Everett again, and she was sorry to toss his jacket, but it was a mess anyway, covered with plaster dust and dirt, and at the last minute she remembered the AA coin and slipped it into the pocket of her new army pants. It felt like a lucky token for her now, and if she ever saw him again, she could give it back to him in lieu of the jacket.

Five minutes later, she was carrying a clipboard, signing people in, talking to men who had lived on the streets for years and reeked of booze, women who were heroin addicts and had no teeth, children who had gotten hurt and were there with their parents from the Marina and Pacific Heights. Young couples, old people, people who obviously had means, and others who were indigent. People of all races, ages, and sizes. It was a typical cross-section of the city and real life. Some were still wandering around in a state of shock and said their houses had fallen down, others who had broken or sprained ankles and legs were hobbling around.

She saw a number of people with broken shoulders and arms. Melanie didn't stop for hours, not even to eat or sit down. She had never been as happy in her life or worked as hard. It was nearly midnight before things started to slow down, and she had been there for eight hours by then, without a break, and she didn't mind at all.

'Hey, blondie!' an old man shouted at her, and she stopped to hand him his cane and smiled at him. 'What's a pretty girl like you doing here? You in the army?'

'Nope. I just borrowed the pants. What can I do for you, sir?'

'I need someone to help me to the bathroom. Can you find me a guy?'

'Sure.' She got one of the National Guard reserves and brought him to the man with the cane, and they set off toward the portable latrines set up in the rear. A moment later, she sat down for the first time all night, and gratefully accepted a bottle of water from a Red Cross volunteer handing them out.

'Thanks.' Melanie smiled gratefully. She was dying of thirst, but hadn't had time to do anything about it for hours. She hadn't eaten since noon, and wasn't even hungry. She was too tired. She was savoring the water before going back to work, when a tiny woman with red hair whizzed past her, in jeans, a sweatshirt, and pink Converse high-tops. It was warm in the field hospital, and the sweatshirt was bright pink and said, 'Jesus is coming. Look busy.' The woman wearing it had brilliant blue eyes that looked at Melanie, and then she broke into a broad smile.

'I loved your performance last night,' the

woman in the pink sweatshirt whispered.

'You did? Were you there?' Obviously she had been if she said it. Melanie was touched. It seemed a million years since that performance and the earthquake that had struck before she finished. 'Thank you. It was quite a night, wasn't it? Did you get out okay?' The redheaded woman looked unhurt, and she was carrying a tray of bandages, tape, and a pair of medical scissors. 'Are you with the Red Cross?'

'No, I'm a nurse.' She looked more like a kid at camp in her pink shirt and high-top sneakers. She was also wearing a cross around her neck, and Melanie smiled at what her sweatshirt said. Her blue eyes looked electric, and she certainly seemed busy. 'Are you Red Cross?' she inquired. She could use some help. She'd been sewing up minor cuts for hours and sending people back to other halls to sleep. They were trying to keep the hordes in the hospital hangar moving in and out at a rapid clip, and doing triage as best they could. The worst cases were being shipped out to hospitals with life support. But the field hospital was keeping the minor injuries from winding up in hospital emergency rooms, and leaving them free to deal with the seriously injured. So far the system was working.

'No, I was just here, so I thought I'd help out,' Melanie explained.

'Good girl. How are you about watching people get sewn up? Do you faint at the sight of blood?'

'Not yet,' Melanie said. She'd seen a lot of it since the night before, and so far hadn't been squeamish, although her friend Ashley was, and Jake, and her mother. But Melanie was fine.

'Good. You can come and help me then.' She led Melanie to the back of the hangar, where she had set up a small area for herself with a makeshift exam table and sterile supplies. People were in line, waiting to get sewn up, and within minutes she had Melanie wash her hands with surgical solution, and had her handing her supplies as she did careful stitches on her patients. Most of the injuries were fairly minor, with a few rare exceptions. And the little woman with the red hair never stopped. There was a lull around two A.M., when they both sat down for a bottle of water, and talked for a minute.

'I know your name,' the little elf with the red hair said with a grin. 'I forgot to tell you mine. I'm Maggie. Sister Maggie,' she added.

'Sister? You're a nun?' Melanie looked astonished. It had never occurred to her that this little vision in pink with the flame-colored hair could be a nun. There was nothing to suggest it, except maybe the cross around her neck, but anyone could have worn that. 'You sure don't look like a nun,' Melanie laughed. She had gone to Catholic school as a kid, and thought some of the nuns were cool, the young ones anyway. They all agreed that the old ones were mean, but she didn't say that to Maggie. There was nothing mean about her, she was all sunlight, smiles, and fun, and hard, hard work. Melanie thought she had a lovely way with people.

'I do too look like a nun,' Maggie insisted. 'This is what nuns look like these days.'

'Not when I was in school,' Melanie said. 'I love your sweatshirt.'

'Some kids I know gave it to me. I'm not sure

the bishop would approve, but it makes people laugh. I figured today was a good time to wear it. People need some smiles right now. It sounds like there's been a huge amount of damage to the city, and a lot of homes lost, mostly to fire. Where do you live, Melanie?' Sister Maggie asked with interest as they both finished their water and got up.

'In L.A. With my mother.'

'That's nice.' Maggie approved. 'With your success, you could be out on your own, or getting into a lot of trouble. Do you have a boyfriend?' Melanie smiled in answer and nodded.

'Yes, I do. He's here too. He's probably asleep in the hall they assigned us to. I brought a friend up for the performance, and my mom is here, some other people who work for me, and the guys in my band of course.'

'That sounds like quite a group. Is your boyfriend nice to you?' The bright blue eyes searched hers, and Melanie hesitated before she answered. Sister Maggie was interested in Melanie, she seemed like such a kind, bright girl, and there was nothing about her to suggest that she was famous. Melanie was unpretentious and unassuming to the point of being humble. Maggie loved that about her. She acted like any girl her age and not a star.

'Sometimes my boyfriend's nice to me,' Melanie answered her question. 'He has his own issues. They get in the way at times.' Maggie read between the lines and figured he probably drank too much or used drugs. What surprised her more was that Melanie looked like she didn't, and had come to work in the hospital on her own,

87

genuinely wanted to help and was truly useful, and sensible about what she did. She was totally down to earth.

'That's too bad,' Maggie commented about Jake, and then told Melanie she had worked long enough. She had been working for nearly eleven hours after almost no sleep the night before. She told her to go back to her hall and get some rest, or she'd be useless the next day. Maggie was going to sleep on a cot in an area of the hospital they'd set up for volunteers and medical personnel. They were planning to open a separate building to house them, but hadn't yet.

'Should I come back tomorrow?' Melanie asked hopefully. She had loved the time she'd spent there, and she felt genuinely useful, which made the time they had to spend waiting to go home more interesting and pass more quickly.

'Come on over, as soon as you wake up. You can have breakfast in the mess hall. I'll be here. You can come in whenever you want,' Sister Maggie said kindly.

'Thank you,' Melanie said politely, still surprised that she was a nun. 'See you tomorrow, Sister.'

'Goodnight, Melanie,' Maggie smiled warmly. 'Thank you for your help.' Melanie waved as she left, and Maggie watched her go. She was such a pretty girl, and Maggie wasn't sure why, but she had the feeling she was looking for something, that some important element was missing in her life. It was hard to believe with looks and a voice like that, and the success she had. But whatever she was looking for, Maggie hoped she'd find it.

Maggie went to check out then, and get some

sleep herself, and as Melanie walked back to the hall where she had left the others, she was smiling. She had loved working with Maggie. She still couldn't believe the lively woman was a nun. Melanie couldn't help wishing she had a mother like that, full of compassion, warmth, and wisdom, instead of the one she had, who had always pushed her, and lived vicariously through her daughter. Melanie was well aware that her mother wanted to be a star herself, and thought she was because her daughter had made it and achieved stardom. It was a heavy burden for her sometimes, being her mother's dream, instead of having her own. Melanie wasn't even sure what her dreams were. All she knew was that for a few hours, more than she ever had on stage, she felt as though she'd found her dream that night on the heels of the San Francisco earthquake.

Chapter 5

Melanie was back at the field hospital by nine o'clock the next morning. She would have been there earlier, but she had stopped to listen to the announcement being made over the PA system in the main quad. Hundreds of people had stood around to hear about conditions throughout the city. The death toll was over a thousand by then, and they said it would be at least a week, if not more, before they had electricity again. They listed the areas that had been the most severely damaged, and they said that they doubted that cell phone service would return before at least ten more days. They said emergency supplies were being flown in from all over the country. The president had come in to see the ravaged city the day before, and then had flown back to Washington, promising federal aid, and commending San Franciscans for their courage and compassion toward each other. They told the temporary residents of the Presidio that a special shelter had been set up by the ASPCA where lost pets were being brought, in the hope of bringing pets and their owners together again. The announcement also said that translators were available in both Mandarin and Spanish, and the person making the announcement thanked everyone for their cooperation in obeying the rules of the temporary camp. They said over eighty thousand people were now living in the Presidio, and two more mess halls were opening that day. They promised to keep everyone informed of further developments as they occurred, and wished everyone a pleasant day.

When Melanie found Maggie at the field hospital, the little nun was complaining that the president had toured the Presidio by helicopter but hadn't visited the field hospital. The mayor had come through briefly the day before, and the governor was due to make a tour of the Presidio that afternoon. Plenty of press had been there as well. They were becoming a model city within one that had been badly shattered by the earthquake nearly two days before. Considering how hard they had been hit, the local authorities were impressed by how well organized they all were, and what good sports San Franciscans were. There was an atmosphere of kindness and compassion that prevailed everywhere in the camp, a sense of camaraderie like that among soldiers in a war zone.

'You're up bright and early,' Sister Maggie commented, when Melanie turned up. She looked young and beautiful, and clean, although she was wearing the same clothes as the day before. She had no others, but she had gotten up at seven to line up at the shower stalls. It had felt wonderful to wash her hair and take a hot shower. And she'd had oatmeal and dry toast in the mess hall.

Fortunately the generators were keeping the food cold. The medical personnel were worried about food poisoning and dysentery if they didn't. But so far their biggest problems were injuries, not diseases, although eventually that could become a problem too. 'Did you sleep last night?' Maggie asked her. Sleeplessness was one of the key symptoms of trauma, and many of the people they were seeing said they hadn't slept in two days. A fleet of psychiatrists had volunteered to deal with trauma victims, and were set up in a separate hall. Maggie had sent many people over to see them, particularly the elderly and the very young, who were frightened and badly shaken.

She set Melanie to work doing intakes then, writing down the details, symptoms, and data about patients. There was no charge for what they were doing, no billing system, and all the administration and paperwork was being done by volunteers. Melanie was glad she was there. The night of the earthquake had been terrifying, but for the first time in her life, she felt as though she was doing something important instead of just hanging out backstage in theaters, recording studios, and singing. At least here, she was doing people some good. And Maggie was very pleased with her work.

Several other nuns and priests were also working at the Presidio, from a variety of orders and local churches. There were ministers who walked around, talking to people, and had set up offices where people could come for counseling. Clergy members of all denominations were visiting the injured and sick. Very few of them were identified by Roman collars or habits, or religious paraphernalia of any kind. They said who they were and readily talked to people as they wandered around. Some of them were even serving food in the mess hall. Maggie knew a lot of the priests and nuns. She seemed to know everyone. Melanie commented on it later that morning, when they took a break, and Maggie laughed.

'I've been around for a long time.'

'Do you like being a nun?' Melanie was curious about her. She thought she was the most interesting woman she'd ever met. In her nearly twenty years on earth, she had never met anyone with as much kindness, wisdom, depth, and compassion. She lived her beliefs and exemplified them, instead of talking them. And she had a gentleness and poise about her that seemed to touch everyone she met. One of the other workers at the field hospital said that Maggie had an amazing grace about her, and the expression made Melanie smile. She had always loved the hymn by that name and sang it often. From now on, she knew it would remind her of Maggie. It had been on the first CD Melanie ever made, and allowed her to really use her voice.

'I love being a nun,' Maggie answered. 'I always have. I've never regretted it for a minute. It suits me perfectly,' she said, looking happy. 'I love being married to God, the bride of Christ,' she added, which impressed her young friend. Melanie noticed then the thin white gold wedding band she wore, which Maggie said she had been given when she took her final vows ten years before. It had been a long wait for that ring, she said, and it symbolized the life and work she loved so much and was so proud of.

'It must be hard to be a nun,' Melanie commented with deep respect.

'It's hard to be anything in this life,' Maggie said wisely. 'What you do isn't easy either.'

'Yes, it is,' Melanie disagreed. 'It is for me. The singing is easy and what I love. That's why I do it. But concert tours are hard sometimes, because you travel a lot, and you have to work every day. We used to go on the road in a big bus, and we drove all day, and performed all night, with rehearsals as soon as we arrived. It's a lot easier now that we fly.' The good times had finally come with her enormous success.

'Does your mother always travel with you?' Maggie asked, curious about her life. She had said that her mother and several other people were with her in San Francisco. Maggie knew it was in the nature of her work to travel with an entourage, but she thought that the addition of her mother was unusual, even for a girl her age. She was nearly twenty.

'Yes, she does. She runs my life,' Melanie said with a sigh. 'My mom always wanted to be a singer

93

when she was young. She was a showgirl in Vegas, and she's pretty excited that things have gone well for me. A little too excited sometimes.' Melanie smiled. 'She's always pushed me hard to do my best.'

'That's not a bad thing,' Sister Maggie commented, 'as long as she doesn't push too hard. What do you think?'

'I think sometimes it's too much,' Melanie said honestly. 'I'd like to make my own decisions. My mom always thinks she knows best.'

'And does she?'

'I don't know. I think she makes the decisions she would have made for herself. I'm not always sure they're what I want for me. She nearly died when I won the Grammy.' Melanie smiled, and Maggie's eyes danced as she watched her.

'That must have been a big moment, the culmination of all your hard work. What an incredible honor.' She hardly knew the girl but was proud for her anyway.

'I gave it to my mother,' Melanie said softly. 'I felt like she won it. I couldn't have done it without her.' But something about the way she said it made the wise nun wonder if that kind of stardom was what Melanie wanted for herself, or just to please her mother.

'It takes a lot of wisdom and courage to know what path we want to take, and what path we're taking to please others.' The way she said it made Melanie look pensive.

'Did your family want you to be a nun? Or were they upset?' Melanie's eyes were filled with questions.

'They were delighted. In my family, that was a

94

big deal. They'd rather have their kids be priests or nuns than get married. Today, that sounds a little crazy. Twenty years ago, in Catholic families, parents always bragged about it. One of my brothers was a priest.'

'"Was"?' Melanie questioned her, and Sister Maggie smiled.

'He left after ten years and got married. I thought it would kill my mother. My father was already dead by then, or it would have killed him. In my family, once you take your vows, you don't leave religious orders. To be honest, I was kind of disappointed in him myself. He's a great guy though, and I don't think he ever regretted it. He and his wife have six children, and they're very happy. So I guess that was his real vocation, not the Church.'

'Do you wish you had children?' Melanie asked wistfully. The life Maggie led seemed sad to her, far from her family, never married, working on the streets with strangers, and living in poverty all her life. But it seemed to suit Maggie to perfection. You could see it in her eyes. She was a happy, totally fulfilled woman, who was obviously content with her life.

'All the people I meet are my children. The ones I know on the streets and see year after year, the ones I help and get off the streets. And then there are special people like you, Melanie, who happen into my life and touch my heart. I'm so glad I met you.' She gave her a hug, as they put their conversation aside and went back to work, and Melanie returned the hug with obvious affection.

'I'm so happy I met you too. I want to be like you when I grow up,' she giggled.

'A nun? Oh, I don't think your mother would like that! There are no stars in the convent! It's supposed to be a life of humility and cheerful deprivation.'

'No, I mean helping people the way you do. I wish I could do something like that.'

'You can, if you want to. You don't have to be in a religious order to do it. All you have to do is roll your sleeves up and get to work. There are people in need everywhere around us, even among fortunate people. Money and success don't always make people happy.' It was a message for Melanie, and she knew it, and more importantly for her mother.

'I never have time to do volunteer work,' Melanie complained. 'And my mother doesn't want me around people with diseases. She says if I get sick, I'll miss concert dates or tours.'

'Maybe one day you'll find time for both. Maybe when you're older.' And when her mother loosened her grip on her career, if she ever would. It sounded to Maggie as though Melanie's mother was living vicariously through her. She was living her dreams through her daughter. It was lucky for her Melanie was a star. The blue-eyed nun had a sixth sense for people, and she could sense that Melanie was her mother's hostage, and somewhere deep inside, even without knowing it, she was struggling to get free.

They got busy with Maggie's patients then. They saw an endless stream of injured people all day, most of them minor injuries that could be ministered to by a nurse and not a doctor. The others, in the triage system they were using at the field hospital, went to someone else. Melanie was a good little assistant, and Sister Maggie praised her often.

They took a lunch break together later that afternoon, and were sitting outside in the sunshine, eating turkey sandwiches that were surprisingly good. Some very decent cooks seemed to be volunteering for the cooking, and food was appearing from somewhere, donated in many cases by other cities, or even other states, being airlifted in, and often delivered by helicopter right on the Presidio grounds. Medical supplies, clothes, and bedding for the thousands of people living there now were airlifted in as well. It was like living in a war zone, and there were helicopters constantly whirring overhead, night and day. Many of the older people said it interfered with their sleep. The younger people didn't care and had gotten used to it. It was a symbol of the shocking experience they were living.

They had just finished their sandwiches, when Melanie noticed Everett walk by. Like so many others, he was still wearing the same black tux pants and white dress shirt he had had on the night the earthquake struck. He walked past them, without noticing them, with his camera around his neck, and his camera bag slung over his arm. Melanie called out to him, and he turned, and saw them with a look of surprise. He came over quickly, and sat down on the log where they were sitting.

'What are you two doing here? And together yet. How did that happen?'

'I'm working at the field hospital here,' Sister Maggie explained.

'And I'm her assistant. I volunteered when they

moved us here from the church. I'm becoming a nurse,' Melanie beamed proudly.

'And a very fine one,' Maggie added. 'What are you doing here, Everett? Taking pictures, or are you staying here too?' Maggie asked him with interest. She hadn't seen him since the morning after the quake, when he sauntered off to see what was happening in the city. She hadn't been home herself since then, if he had tried to find her, which she doubted.

'I may have to now. I've been staying at a shelter downtown, and they just had to close it. The building next to it is starting to lean badly, so they cleared us out, and suggested we come here. I thought I was going to be out of here by now, but there's no way. Nothing is leaving San Francisco, so we're all stuck here. There are worse fates,' he said to both women with a smile, 'and I've gotten some great shots.' As he said it, he pointed his camera at both of them, and took a picture of the two women smiling in the sunshine. Both looked happy and relaxed, despite the circumstances they were in. But both were being productive and enjoying what they were doing. It showed on their faces and in their eyes. 'I don't think anybody would believe this vision of Melanie Free, the world-famous superstar, sitting on a log in camouflage pants and flip-flops, working in a field hospital as a medical tech after an earthquake. This is going to be a historical shot.' And he had some great ones of Maggie from the first night. He could hardly wait to see them when he got back to L.A. And he was sure his editors would be thrilled with whatever shots he got out of the aftermath of the earthquake. And whatever they didn't use, he

98

might be able to sell elsewhere. He might even win another prize. He knew instinctively that the material he had gotten had been great. The photos he had taken seemed historically important to him. This was a unique situation that hadn't happened in a hundred years, and maybe wouldn't for another hundred. He hoped not. But in spite of the enormous tremor, the city had withstood it surprisingly well, as had the people.

'What are you two up to now?' he inquired. 'Going back to work, or taking some time off?' They had only been gone for half an hour when they saw him, and were about to go back.

'Back to work,' Maggie answered for them both. 'What about you?'

'I thought I'd sign up for a cot. And maybe then I'll come in to see you. I might get some good shots of you at work, if your patients don't object.'

'You'll have to ask them,' Maggie said primly, always respectful of her patients, no matter who they were. And then Melanie suddenly remembered his jacket.

'I'm so sorry. It was a total mess, and I didn't think I'd see you again. I threw it away.'

Everett laughed at the apologetic look on her face. 'Don't worry. It was rented. I'll tell them it was ripped off my back in the earthquake. They should give it to me without charge. I don't think they'd have wanted it back if I had returned it. Honestly, Melanie, it was no loss. Don't worry about it.' And then she remembered the coin as well, slipped her hand into her pants pocket, pulled it out, and handed it to him. It was his one-year sobriety chip, and he looked thrilled to have it back.

'Now that I do want back. It's my lucky coin!' He ran his fingers over it as though it were magic, and for him it was. He had missed going to meetings for the past two days, and having the chip back felt like a link to what had saved him more than a year before. He kissed it, and slipped it into the pocket of his pants, which were all that was left now of the rented suit. And the pants were too battered now to return too. He was going to throw them away when he got home. 'Thank you for taking good care of my chip for me.' He missed his AA meetings to help cope with the stress, but he didn't want a drink. He was exhausted. It had been a very long and trying two days, and truly tragic for some.

Maggie and Melanie walked back to the field hospital then, and Everett went to sign up for a bed for that night. There were so many buildings in the Presidio to house people that there was no risk of their running out of room. It was an old military base that had been shut down years before, but all the structures were still intact. George Lucas had built his legendary studio there in the old hospital on the Presidio grounds.

'I'll catch up with you two later,' Everett promised. 'I'll be back in a while.'

It was later that afternoon, in a brief lull, that Sarah Sloane showed up with both of her children and her Nepalese nanny. The baby had a fever and was coughing and holding one ear. She had brought her daughter with her too, because she said she didn't want to leave her at home. She didn't want to be away from them now for a minute, after the traumatic experience of Thursday night. If another quake hit, as everyone

100

feared it might, she wanted to be with them. She had left Seth alone at home, in the same state of anguished desperation he had been in since Thursday night. It was only getting worse, and he knew there was no hope of banks opening or his being able to communicate with the outside world anytime soon, to cover what he'd done. His career, and maybe his life as it had been for several years, was over. And Sarah's too. In the meantime, she was worried about their baby. This was no time for him to get sick. She had gone to the emergency room of the hospital nearest them, but they were accepting only seriously injured people for treatment. They had referred her to the field hospital in the Presidio, so she had come in Parmani's car. Melanie had spotted her at the front desk, and told Maggie who she was. They approached Sarah together, and Maggie had the baby cooing and laughing in less than a minute, although he was still pulling at his ear. Sarah told her what was wrong. And he looked a little flushed.

'Let me find you a doctor,' Maggie promised, and disappeared, and a few minutes later she beckoned to Sarah, who had been talking to Melanie about the benefit and how fabulous her performance had been, and how shocking when the earthquake hit.

Melanie and Sarah, the little girl, and the nanny all followed Maggie to where the doctor was waiting to see them. As Sarah had feared, the baby had an ear infection. His fever had come down a little in the balmy May air, and the doctor said he had the beginnings of a red throat. He gave her an antibiotic that she said Oliver had taken before, and he gave Molly a lollipop and ruffled her hair. The doctor was very sweet with both of them, although he had been working since right after the earthquake on Thursday night, with almost no sleep. Everyone had been putting in an incredible number of hours, especially Maggie, and Melanie was right up there with her.

They were just leaving the cubicle where they'd seen the doctor, when Sarah saw Everett walk in. He looked as though he were trying to find someone, and Melanie and Maggie both waved at him. He came over in the familiar black lizard cowboy boots that were his prize possession. They had survived the rigors of the earthquake unharmed.

'What is this? A reunion of the benefit?' he teased Sarah. 'That was quite a party you put on. A little dicey at the end of the evening, but up till then, I thought you did a terrific job.' He smiled at her and she thanked him, and as Maggie watched her, with her baby in her arms, she saw that Sarah looked upset. She had noticed it at first, and thought she was just worried about Oliver's fever and earache, but having been reassured, Maggie now wondered if it was something else. Her powers of observation were both accurate and acute.

Maggie suggested that the nanny hold the baby, and Molly stayed close beside her, while the nun asked Sarah to come and chat with her for a minute. They left Melanie and Everett talking animatedly, while Parmani kept track of the kids. She walked Sarah far enough away so the others wouldn't hear what they said.

'Are you all right?' Maggie asked her. 'You look

upset. Is there anything I can do to help?' She saw tears bulging in Sarah's eyes and was glad she had asked.

'No . . . I . . . really . . . I'm fine . . . well . . . actually . . . I have a problem, but there's nothing you can do.' She started to open up to her, and then knew she couldn't. It could be too dangerous for Seth if she did. She was still praying, unreasonably she knew, that no one would find out what he'd done. With sixty million dollars misdirected and illegally in his hands, it was impossible that his crime would go unnoticed, or unpunished. She felt sick every time she thought of it, and she looked it. 'It's my husband . . . I can't go into it right now.' She wiped her eyes and looked gratefully at the nun. 'Thank you for asking.'

'Well, you know where I am, for now anyway.' Maggie grabbed a pen and a piece of paper then, and wrote her cell phone number down. 'Once we get cell phone service again, you can call me at that number. Until then, I'll be here. Sometimes it helps to talk to someone, just as a friend. I don't want to intrude, so you call me if you think I can do anything to help.'

'Thank you,' Sarah said gratefully. She remembered that Maggie was one of the nuns at the benefit. And just as Melanie and Everett had, Sarah thought she didn't look anything like a nun, particularly in jeans and pink Converse high-top sneakers. She looked very cute, and surprisingly young. But she had the eyes of a woman who had seen it all. There was nothing young about her eyes. 'I'll call you,' Sarah promised, and a few minutes later they went back to the others. As they did, Sarah wiped her eyes. Everett had noticed

103

something too, but said nothing. He just complimented her again on the benefit and the money they had raised. He said it had been a class act, especially with Melanie's help. He had something pleasant to say to everyone. He was an easygoing nice guy.

'I wish I could volunteer here,' Sarah added, impressed by the efficiency of the operation they were running.

'You need to be at home with your children,' Maggie answered. 'They need you.' And she could sense that right now Sarah needed them. Whatever the problem with her husband was, it was obvious that Sarah was deeply upset.

'I don't think I'll ever leave them again,' Sarah said with a shudder. 'I was crazed until I got home on Thursday night, but they were fine.' And the bump on Parmani's head had already gone down. She was staying with them now, as she had no way to get home. Her entire neighborhood was a shambles and had been cordoned off. They had driven by to check. And the police wouldn't let her into her apartment building, as part of the roof had fallen in.

All of the city's businesses and services were still shut down. The Financial District was closed and blocked off. Without electricity throughout the city, with no open stores, gas, or telephone service, it was impossible for anyone to work.

Sarah left a few minutes later with the nanny and her children. They got into Parmani's ancient car and drove off, after thanking Maggie for her help. She had given Maggie her phone number and address, and her cell phone, and she couldn't help wondering how long they'd be there, or if they'd lose their house. She hoped they'd be there for a while, and maybe Seth could strike a deal, worst case. Sarah had said goodbye to Everett and Melanie too when she left. She doubted that she'd ever see either of them again. Both were from L.A., and they were unlikely to meet again. Sarah had really liked Melanie, and her performance had been flawless, just as Everett had said. Everyone in the room would have agreed, in spite of the horrifying finale.

Maggie sent Melanie to get supplies after Sarah left, and she and Everett stood talking. Maggie knew the main supply warehouse where they were storing things was a fair distance away, so she wouldn't be back for a while. It hadn't been a ploy, she really did need the supplies. Particularly the surgical thread. All the doctors she had ever worked with had always told her she had an impeccably neat stitch. It came from years of doing needlework in the convent. When she was younger, it had been a nice thing to do at night when the nuns congregated after dinner and sat and talked. In the years since she'd been living alone in the apartment, she rarely did needlework, if ever. But she still had a tidy little stitch.

'She seems like a nice woman,' Everett said about Sarah. 'I really thought it was an exceptionally terrific event.' He praised her, even though she had already left. And although she was far more traditional than the people Everett usually hung out with, he really liked Sarah. There was something of substance and integrity about her that shone through her conservative exterior.

'It's funny how people's paths keep crossing, isn't it? Destiny is a wonderful thing,' Everett said.

105

'I ran into you outside the Ritz, and followed you for an entire evening, even on the streets. And now here I am, I run into you in a shelter. And I met Melanie that night too and gave her my jacket. Then you and she meet here. And I find you both again, and the head of the benefit that brought us all together walks into the field hospital with her kid with an earache, and here we are again. Old home week. In a city the size of this one, it's a goddamn miracle if two people ever meet again, and we've done nothing but for the past few days. At least it's comforting to see familiar faces. I like that a lot.' He smiled at Maggie.

'So do I,' Maggie agreed. She met so many strangers in her life, now she particularly enjoyed seeing friends.

They continued to talk for a while, and eventually Melanie returned. She had the supplies with her that Maggie had wanted, and Melanie looked delighted. She was anxious to find ways to help and felt victorious that the supply officer had everything on Maggie's list, which had been long. He had given her all the medicines Maggie had asked for, he had bandages in the right sizes, both elastic and gauze, and had sent over a full box of tape.

'Sometimes I think you're more nurse than nun. You minister a lot to the wounded,' Everett commented, and she nodded, but didn't totally agree.

'I minister to the wounded of body and spirit,' Maggie said quietly. 'And you only think I'm more of a nurse, because that probably seems more normal to you. But in truth, I'm more nun than anything else. Don't let the pink shoes fool you. I do that for fun. But being a nun is serious business, and it's the most important thing in my life. I think "discretion is the better part of valor," I've always liked that quote, although I have no idea who said it, but I think they were right. It makes people uncomfortable if I run around saying I'm a nun.'

'And why is that?' Everett asked her.

'I think people are afraid of nuns,' Maggie said practically. 'That's why it's so great we no longer have to wear our habits. They always put people off.'

'I think they used to be really pretty. I was always impressed with nuns when I was younger. They were so beautiful, some of them anyway. You just don't see young nuns like that anymore. Maybe it's a good thing.'

'You could be right. People don't go in as early anymore. In my order, they took in two women in their forties last year, and I think one that was fifty and was a widow. Times have changed, but at least they know what they're doing when they go in now. In my day, a lot of people made mistakes, they went into the convent and shouldn't have. It's not an easy life,' she said honestly. 'And it's a big adjustment, whatever your life was like before. Living in community is always a challenge. I have to admit, I miss it now. But the only time I'm in my apartment is when I sleep.' It was a small studio in a terrible neighborhood. He had only glimpsed the building from outside when he was there.

A flood of new patients came in after that, with minor problems, and Melanie and Maggie had to get back to work. Everett made a date to meet them in the mess hall that night, if they could get away. Neither of them had had dinner the night before. And as it turned out, they missed dinner again. An emergency came in, and Maggie needed Melanie's help to get the woman sewn up. Melanie was learning a lot from her, and she was still thinking about it that night when she went back to the building where the rest of her entourage was camping out. They were sitting around bored out of their minds, with nothing to do. Melanie had suggested to Jake and Ashley several times that they should volunteer for something too, as they might be stuck there for at least another week, according to the bulletins in the morning. The tower at the airport had been knocked flat, and there was no way they could leave. The airport was closed, and so were the roads.

'Why are you spending all that time in the hospital?' Janet complained. 'You'll wind up catching something from someone.' Melanie shook her head and looked her mother in the eye.

'Mom, I think I want to be a nurse.' She was smiling as she said it, half teasing her mother, and half wanting to annoy her. But she was happy to help at the field hospital. She loved working with Maggie, and she was learning so many new things.

'Are you insane?' her mother said to her with a look and tone of outrage. 'A nurse? After all I've done for your career? How dare you say something like that to me? You think I've worked my ass off to make you who you are, so you can throw it all away and empty bedpans?' Her mother looked panicked as much as hurt, at the very idea that Melanie might choose another career path, when she had stardom, and the world at her feet.

'I haven't emptied a bedpan yet,' Melanie said firmly.

'Believe me, you would. Don't ever say that to me again.'

Melanie said nothing in answer. She chatted with the rest of the group, traded jokes for a while with Ashley and Jake, and then still in her T-shirt and camouflage pants, she lay on her cot and fell asleep. She was utterly exhausted. And as she fell into a deep sleep, she had a dream that she ran away and joined the army. But as soon as she did, she discovered that the drill sergeant riding her night and day was her mother. Melanie remembered the dream in the morning, and wondered if it had been a nightmare, or her real life.

Chapter 6

On Sunday, the morning announcement at the Presidio told everyone that many people had been rescued all over the city, pulled out from where they were trapped, taken out of elevators downtown and from under collapsed houses, or pinned under structures that had fallen. The building codes since the quake of 1989 had been stricter, so there was less damage than expected, but the size of this most recent earthquake had been so enormous that there had been huge destruction nonetheless, and the known death toll had risen to over four thousand. And there were still many areas being explored. Emergency Services workers were searching for survivors among the rubble, and under the fallen overpasses leading to the freeway. It was only sixty hours since the earthquake had struck on Thursday night, and there was still hope of rescuing many people who had not been freed yet.

The news was both terrifying and encouraging all at once, and people looked somber as they walked away from the grassy area where the announcements were being made every day. Most of them headed for the mess hall afterward for breakfast. They had also been told that it would probably be several weeks before they could return to their homes. The bridges, freeways, airports, and many areas of the city were still not open. And there was no way of telling when the electricity would be on again, and even less when life might return to normal.

Everett was talking quietly to Sister Maggie when Melanie walked in, after breakfast with her mother, assistant, Ashley, Jake, and several members of the band. They were all getting restless and were anxious to get back to L.A., which obviously wasn't even remotely possible for the moment. They just had to sit tight and see what happened. There was word in the camp by then that Melanie Free was there. She had been spotted in the mess hall with her friends, and her mother had been foolishly bragging about her. But so far, no one in the hospital had paid much attention to her. Even when they recognized her, they smiled and moved on. It was easy to see that she was working hard as a volunteer. Pam had signed up at the camp's check-in desk as people continued to filter in, as food ran out in the city, and people came to the Presidio for shelter.

'Hi, kid,' Everett greeted her unceremoniously, and she grinned. She had gotten a new T-shirt

110

from one of the donation tables, and a huge man's sweater with holes in it, which made her look like an orphan. She was still wearing the camouflage pants and flip-flops. Sister Maggie had changed clothes too. She had brought a few things in a bag with her, when she came to volunteer. The T-shirt she wore today said 'Jesus is my homeboy,' and Everett laughed out loud when he saw it.

'I guess this is the modern-day version of a habit?' She was wearing red high-tops with it, and still looked like a counselor in training at summer camp. Her diminutive size contributed to the impression that she was years younger than she was. She could easily have passed for thirty. She was a dozen years older, and only six years younger than Everett, although he seemed a lifetime older. He seemed old enough to be her father. It was when one spoke to Maggie that one was aware of the seasoning of age, and the benefits of wisdom.

He went off to take photographs around the Presidio that day, and said he was going to walk into the Marina and Pacific Heights to see if anything was happening there. They were urging people to stay out of the Financial District and the downtown area as buildings were taller, more dangerous, and the damage far more extensive. The police were still afraid of heavy objects or broken pieces falling off buildings. It was easier to wander into the residential neighborhoods, although many of them had been blocked off by police and Emergency Services too. Helicopters were continuing to patrol the entire city, usually flying low, so you could even see the pilots' faces. They landed from time to time at Crissy Field in the Presidio, and the pilots chatted with people

111

who approached to ask further news of what was happening in the city, or outlying regions. Many of the people staying in the shelters at the Presidio actually lived in the East Bay, on the Peninsula, and Marin, and had no way of getting home for the moment with the bridges and freeways closed. Real news was scarce among them, and rumors rampant, of death, destruction, and carnage elsewhere in the city. It was always reassuring to hear from people who knew, and the helicopter pilots were the most reliable source of all.

Melanie spent the day helping Maggie, as she had for the two days before. Injured people were still trickling in, and hospital emergency rooms around the city were still referring people to them. There was a huge airlift that afternoon, which brought them more medicines and food. The meals in the mess hall were plentiful, and there seemed to be an abundance of surprisingly decent, creative cooks. The owner and chef of one of the city's best restaurants was living in one of the hangars with his family, and he had taken charge of the main mess hall, much to everyone's delight. The meals were actually very good, although neither Melanie nor Maggie ever seemed to have time to eat. Instead of stopping for lunch, the two of them went out with most of the camp's doctors to greet the airlift and carry the supplies back inside.

Melanie was struggling to carry an enormous box, when a young man in torn jeans and a tattered sweater reached out to help just before she dropped it. It was marked fragile, and she was grateful for his help. He lifted it gently from her with a smile, and she thanked him, relieved that he

112

had helped her avoid disaster. There were vials of insulin inside it, with syringes, for the diabetics in the camp, and apparently there were many. They had all registered at the hospital as soon as they arrived. A hospital in Washington State had sent them all they needed.

'Thanks,' Melanie said, out of breath. The box was huge. 'I almost dropped it.'

'It's bigger than you are.' Her benefactor smiled. 'I've seen you around the camp,' he said pleasantly as he walked toward the hospital with her, carrying the box. 'You look familiar. Have we met before? I'm a senior at Berkeley, my major is engineering, specializing in underdeveloped countries. Do you go to Berkeley?' He knew he had seen her face before, and Melanie just smiled.

'No, I'm from L.A.,' she said vaguely, as they approached the field hospital. He was tall, blue-eyed, and as blond as she was. He looked healthy and young and wholesome. 'I was just up here for one night,' she explained as he smiled at her, bowled over by how beautiful she was, even without combed hair, makeup, or clean clothes. They all looked like they'd been shipwrecked. He was wearing someone else's sneakers, after spending the night in the city at a friend's house, and running out in boxers and bare feet just before it collapsed. Fortunately, everyone living there had survived.

'I'm from Pasadena,' he countered. 'I used to go to UCLA, but I transferred up here last year. I like it. Or at least I did till now.' He grinned. 'But we have earthquakes in L.A. too.' He helped her bring the box inside, and Sister Maggie told him where to put it. By now he was interested in staying to

113

talk to Melanie. She hadn't said anything about herself, and he couldn't help wondering where she went to college. 'My name is Tom. Tom Jenkins.'

'I'm Melanie,' she said softly, without adding a last name. Maggie smiled as she walked away. It was obvious he had no idea who Melanie was, which she thought was nice for her. For once, someone was talking to her just like any other regular human being, and not because she was a star.

'I'm working in the mess hall,' he added. 'You guys look pretty busy here.'

'We are,' Melanie said lightly as he helped her open the box.

'I guess you're going to be here for a while. We all are. I hear the tower at the airport fell over like a house of cards.'

'Yeah, I don't think we'll be leaving anytime soon.'

'We only had two weeks of classes left. I don't think we'll be going back. I don't think we'll be having graduation either. They'll have to mail us our diplomas. I was going to spend the summer here. I got a job with the city, but I guess that's pretty much out the window now too, although God knows, they're going to need engineers. But I'm going to head back to L.A. when I can.'

'Me too,' she said, as they began unloading the box. He seemed in no hurry to leave and go back to the mess hall. He was enjoying talking to her. She seemed gentle and shy, and like a really nice girl.

'Do you have medical training?' he asked with interest.

'Not till now. I'm getting it firsthand here.'

114

'She's an excellent medical tech,' Maggie vouched for her, as she came back to check out the contents of the box. Everything they'd been promised was there, and she was greatly relieved. They'd gotten an initial supply of insulin from the local hospitals and the military, but had been rapidly running out. 'She'd make a terrific nurse,' Maggie added with a smile and then carried the contents of the box to where they were stocking supplies.

'My brother is in medical school. Syracuse,' he explained. He was lingering now, and Melanie looked at him with a long, slow smile.

'I'd love to go to nursing school,' she admitted to him. 'My mother would kill me if I did. She has other plans.'

'Like what?' he was intrigued by her, and was still struck by the familiar face. In some ways, she looked like the proverbial girl next door, only better. And he had never lived next door to a girl who looked like her.

'It's complicated. She has a lot of dreams that I'm supposed to live up to for her. It's stupid mother-daughter stuff. I'm an only child, so her whole wish list is on me.' It was nice complaining to him, even though she didn't know him. He was sympathetic, and really listened to her. For once, she had the feeling that someone cared what she was thinking.

'My dad was desperate for me to be a lawyer. He put a lot of heat on me about it. He thought being an engineer was really dull, and he points out regularly that working in underdeveloped countries, I won't make any money. He has a point, but with an engineering degree, I can always switch my specialty later. I would have hated law school. He wanted a doctor and a lawyer in the family. My sister has a Ph.D. in physics, she teaches at MIT. My parents are nuts about education. But degrees don't make you a decent human being. I want to be more than just a man with an education. I want to make a difference in the world. My family is more interested in getting educated to make money.' His was obviously a family of highly educated people, and there was no way Melanie could explain to him that all her mother wanted was for her to be a star. Melanie still dreamed of going to college eventually, but with her recording schedule and concert tours, she never had time, and at this rate never would. She read a lot to make up for it, and was at least well informed on what went on in the world. The show business life had never seemed like quite enough to her. 'I'd better get back to the mess hall,' he said finally. 'I'm supposed to help make carrot soup. I'm a lousy cook, but so far no one's noticed.' He laughed easily, and said he hoped to see her around the camp again. She told him to come back if he got hurt, although she hoped he wouldn't, and with a wave as he walked away, he left. Sister Maggie wandered by and commented on their meeting with a smile.

'He's cute,' she said with a twinkle in her eye, as Melanie giggled like the teenager she was, and not a world-famous star.

'Yeah, he is. And nice. He's just graduating from Berkeley as an engineer. He's from Pasadena.' He was a far cry from Jake, with his slick looks and acting career, and frequent trips to rehab, although she had loved him for a while. But she had complained to Ashley recently that he was incredibly self-centered. She wasn't even convinced he was completely faithful. Tom looked like a totally decent, wholesome, nice guy. In fact, as she would have said to Ashley, he was really, really cute. Hot. A hunk. With brains. And a great smile.

'Maybe you'll see him sometime in L.A.,' Maggie said hopefully. She loved the notion of nice young people falling in love. She hadn't been impressed so far with Melanie's current boyfriend. He had only dropped by the hospital to see her once, said it smelled terrible, and went back to their hangar to lie around. He hadn't volunteered for any of the services that others were providing for him, and thought it was ridiculous for someone of Melanie's stature to be playing nurse. He expressed the same views as her mother, who was seriously annoyed by what Melanie was doing, and complained about it every night when Melanie got back and collapsed onto her cot.

Maggie and Melanie got busy then, and Tom was in the mess hall talking to the friend he'd been staying with the night the earthquake happened. His host on that fateful night was a senior at USF.

'I saw who you were talking to,' he said with a sly smile. 'Aren't you the clever devil, picking her up.'

'Yeah,' Tom said, blushing, 'she's cute. Nice too. She's from L.A.'

'No kidding.' His friend laughed at him, as they put vats of carrot soup on the enormous butane stove that had been supplied by the National Guard. 'Where did you think she lived? Mars?' Tom had no idea why his friend was so amused by his brief details about her.

'What's that supposed to mean? She could have been from here.'

'Hell, don't you read any of the Hollywood gossip? Of course she lives in L.A. with a career like hers. Shit, man, she just won a Grammy.'

'She did?' Tom looked stunned as he stared at him. 'Her name is Melanie . . .' And then he looked mortified as he realized what he'd done and who she was. 'Oh, for chrissake, she must think I'm a total moron . . . I didn't recognize her. Oh my God . . . I just thought she was some nice blond kid about to drop a package. Nice ass, though,' he chuckled to his friend. But better than that, she seemed like a nice person, and had been totally unassuming and down to earth. Her comments about her mother's ambitions for her should have given it away. 'She said she wished she could go to nursing school, and her mom won't let her.'

'Damn right. Not with the kind of money she makes singing. Shit, I wouldn't let her go to nursing school either if I was her mother. She must make millions from her records.' Tom looked annoyed then.

'So what? If she hates what she does. It's not all about money.'

'Yes, it is, when you're in her league,' the USF senior said practically. 'She could sock a lot of it away, and do whatever she wants later. Although I can't see her as a nurse.'

'She seems to like what she's doing, and the volunteer she's working for said she's good at it. It must be nice for her being here with no one recognizing her.' And then he looked embarrassed

118

again. 'Or am I the only person on the planet who didn't know who she is?'

'I would guess you are. I heard she was here, at the camp. But I didn't see her myself until this morning, when you were talking to her. No doubt about it, she's hot. That was a score, man.' His friend congratulated him for his good taste and judgment.

'Yeah, right. She must think I'm the dumbest guy in the camp. And probably the only one who didn't know who she was.'

'She probably thought it was cute,' his friend reassured him.

'I told her she looked familiar and asked her if we'd met before,' he said groaning. 'I thought maybe she's at Berkeley.'

'No,' his friend said with a broad grin. 'Much better than that! Are you going to go back to see her?' He hoped so. He wanted to meet her himself. Just once, so he could say he had.

'I might. If I can get over feeling stupid.'

'Get over it. She's worth it. And besides, you're not going to get another chance like this to meet a big star.'

'She doesn't act like one. She's totally real,' Tom commented. It was one of the things he had liked about her, that she seemed so down to earth. And it didn't hurt either that she was smart and nice. And obviously a hard worker.

'So stop whining about how dumb you feel. Go see her again.'

'Yeah. Maybe,' Tom said, sounding unconvinced, and then got busy stirring the soup. He wondered if she'd come to the mess hall for lunch.

119

*   *   *

Everett came back from his walk around Pacific Heights late that afternoon. He had taken shots of a woman being pulled out from under a house. She lost a leg, but was alive. It had been a very moving scene as they pulled her out, and even he had cried. It had been a very emotional few days, and in spite of his experience in war zones, he had seen a number of things at the camp that touched his heart. He was telling Maggie about it as they sat outside during her first break in hours. Melanie was inside handing out insulin and hypodermics to the people who'd come to pick them up after an announcement made over the PA system.

'You know,' he said, smiling at Maggie, 'I'm going to be sorry to go back to L.A. I like it here.'

'I always have,' she said quietly. 'I fell in love with the city when I came here from Chicago. I came out here to join a Carmelite order, and wound up in another order instead. I loved working with the poor on the streets.'

'Our very own Mother Teresa,' he teased, unaware that Maggie had been compared to the saintly nun many times. She had the same qualities of humility, energy, and bottomless compassion, all of which sprang from her faith and good nature. She seemed almost lit from within. 'I think the Carmelites would have been too tame for me. Too much praying, and not enough hands-on work. I'm better suited to my order,' she said, looking peaceful, as they both sipped water. Once again the day was warm, as it had been, unseasonably so, since before the quake. San Francisco was never

120

hot, but now it was. The late-afternoon sun felt good on their faces.

'Have you ever gotten fed up, or questioned your vocation?' he asked with interest. They were friends now, and he was fascinated by her.

'Why would I do that?' She looked stunned.

'Because most of us do that at some point, wonder what we're doing with our lives or if we chose the right path. I've done that a lot,' he admitted, and she nodded.

'You've made harder choices,' she said gently. 'Getting married at eighteen, getting divorced, leaving your son, leaving Montana, taking on a job that was almost a vocation too, not a job. It meant sacrificing any kind of personal life. And then giving up the job, and giving up drinking. Those were all big decisions that must have been hard to make. My choices have always been easier than that. I go where I'm sent, and do as I'm told. Obedience. It makes life very simple.' She sounded serene and confident as she said it.

'Is it as simple as that? You don't ever disagree with your superiors, and want to do something your own way?'

'My superior is God,' she said simply. 'In the end, I work for Him. And yes,' she said cautiously, 'sometimes I think what the mother superior wants or the bishop says is silly, or short-sighted, or too old-fashioned. Most of them think I'm fairly radical, but now they pretty much let me do what I want. They know I won't embarrass them, and I try not to be too outspoken about local politics. That gets everyone upset, especially when I'm right.' She grinned.

'You don't mind not having a life of your own?'

He couldn't imagine it. He was far too independent to live in obedience to anyone, particularly a church or the people who ran it. But that was the essence of her life.

'This *is* my life. I love it. It doesn't matter if I do it here in the Presidio, or in the Tenderloin, or with prostitutes or drug addicts. I'm just here to help them, in the service of God. Kind of like the military serving their country. I just follow orders. I don't need to make the rules myself.' Everett had always had problems with rules and authority, which at one time in his life was why he drank. It was his way of not playing by the rules, and escaping the crushing pressure he felt when others told him what to do. Maggie was a lot more easygoing about it than he was, even now that he no longer drank. Authority still rankled him at times, although he was better about tolerating it now. He was older, mellower, and being in recovery had helped.

'You make it sound so simple,' Everett said with a sigh, finishing his water, and looking at her carefully. She was a beautiful woman, yet she kept herself back somehow, careful not to engage with people in any kind of personal, womanly way. She was lovely to look at, but there was always an invisible wall between them, and she kept it there. It was more powerful than the habit she didn't wear. Whether others could see it or not, she was always completely aware that she was a nun, and wanted it that way.

'It is simple, Everett,' she said gently. 'I just get my directions from the Father, and do whatever I'm told, what seems right at the time. I'm here to serve, not to run things, or tell anyone else how to

122

live. That's not my job.'

'It's not mine either,' he said slowly, 'but I have strong opinions about most things. Don't you wish you had a home of your own, a family, a husband, kids?' She shook her head.

'I've never really thought about it. I never thought that was for me. If I were married and had children, I would only be caring for them. This way I can take care of so many more.' She seemed totally content.

'And what about you? Don't you want more than that? For yourself?'

'No.' She smiled at him honestly. 'I don't. My life is perfect as it is, and I love it. That's what they mean by a vocation. I was called to do this, and meant to. It's like being chosen for a special purpose. It's an honor. I know you see it that way, but it doesn't feel like a sacrifice to me. I didn't give anything up. I got so much more than I ever dreamed or wanted. I couldn't ask for more.'

'You're lucky,' he said sadly for a minute. It was obvious to him that she wanted nothing for herself, had no needs she allowed herself to think about, no desire to advance herself or acquire anything. She was completely happy and fulfilled giving her life to God. 'I always want things I've never had, wondering what they might be like. Sharing my life with someone, having a family and kids I could have watched grow up, instead of the one I never knew. Just someone to enjoy my life with. Past a certain age, it's not fun doing everything alone. It feels selfish and empty. If you don't share it all with someone you love, what's the point? And then what, you die alone? Somehow I never had time to do any of that. I was too busy covering war zones. Or maybe I was too scared of that kind of commitment, after getting roped into marriage as a kid. It was less scary getting shot at than staying married.' He sounded depressed as he said it, and she gently touched his arm.

'You should try to find your son,' she said softly. 'Maybe he needs you, Everett. You could be a great gift to him. And he might fill a void for you.' She could see that he was lonely, and rather than looking forward to the empty future he saw before him, she thought he should double back, at least for a while, and find his son.

'Maybe so,' he said, thinking about it, and then he changed the subject. There was something about looking up his boy that scared him. It was just too damn hard. That had all been a long time ago, and Chad probably hated him for abandoning him and losing touch. At the time Everett had been only twenty-one himself, and all that responsibility had been too much for him. So he took off, and drank for the next twenty-six years. He had sent money to support his son until he turned eighteen, but that had ended a dozen years before. 'I miss my meetings,' he said then as he sat there. 'I always feel like shit when I don't get to AA. I try to go twice a day. Sometimes more.' And he hadn't been to any in three days. There were none in the destroyed city, and he hadn't done anything about organizing an AA meeting in the camp.

'I think you should start one here,' she encouraged him. 'We could be here for another week or more. That's a long time for you to go without a meeting, and everyone else here who is missing their meeting too. With this many people in one place, I'll bet you'd get an amazing response.'

'Maybe I will,' he said, smiling at her. She always made him feel better. She was a remarkable person in every way. 'I think I love you, Maggie, in a nice way,' he said comfortably. 'I've never known anyone like you. You're like the sister I never had, and wish I did.'

'Thank you,' she said sweetly, smiling up at him, and then stood up. 'You still remind me a little of one of my brothers. The one who was a priest. I really think you should go into the priesthood,' she teased him. 'You'd have a lot to share. And think of all the lurid confessions you'd hear!'

'Not even for that!' Everett said, rolling his eyes. He left her at the hospital, then went to see one of the Red Cross volunteers in charge of the administration of the camp, and then went back to his hall to make a sign. 'Friends of Bill W.' The members of AA would know what it meant. It was a code that signified an AA meeting, using the name of its founder. In the warm weather, they could even hold the meeting outside, a little off the beaten path. There was a small peaceful grove he had discovered while walking around the camp. It was the perfect spot. The camp administrator had promised to announce it the following morning over the PA system. The earthquake had brought them all there, thousands of them, each with their own problems and lives. Now they were becoming a city within a city, all their own. Once again, Maggie had been right. He felt better already after deciding to organize an AA meeting at the camp. And then he thought of Maggie again, and the positive influence she had on him. In his eyes, she wasn't just a woman or a nun, she was magic.

125

Chapter 7

Tom went back to see Melanie at the hospital the next day, looking sheepish. He caught sight of her as she was heading back to a shed where they were using butane washing machines to do laundry. She had her arms full, and nearly tripped when she saw him, and he helped her load the machines, while apologizing for his stupidity when they met.

'I'm sorry, Melanie. I'm not usually that dumb. I didn't make the connection. I guess I didn't expect to see you here.'

She smiled at him, undisturbed by his previous lack of recognition. In fact, she preferred it. 'I played a benefit here on Thursday night.'

'I love your music, and your voice. I thought you looked familiar,' he laughed, finally relaxing. 'I thought I must have known you from Berkeley.'

'I wish you did,' she grinned as they went back outside. 'I liked that you didn't know who I was. It's a pain sometimes having everyone know and kiss my ass,' she said bluntly.

'Yeah, I'll bet it is.' They went back to the main quad and helped themselves to water bottles from a hand truck, and sat down on a log to talk. It was a pretty, natural setting, with the Golden Gate Bridge in the distance, and the bay glittering in the sunlight. 'Do you like what you do, your work, I mean?'

'Sometimes. Sometimes it's hard. My mom pushes me a lot. I know I should be grateful. She made my career happen, and my success. She always tells me that. But she wants it more than I do. I just like to sing, and I love the music. And sometimes the gigs are fun, the concert tours and stuff. But other times it's too much. And you don't get to pick and choose. You either have to do it full-on or not at all. You can't be half-baked about it.'

'Have you ever taken a break? Or time off?' She shook her head, and then laughed, aware of how juvenile she sounded. 'My mom won't let me. She says that would be professional suicide. She said you don't take breaks at my age. I wanted to go to college, but there was no way with what I was doing. I started to get hot in my junior year of high school, so I quit school, had tutors, and got my GED. I wasn't kidding, I'd love to go to nursing school. She'd never let me.' Even to her, it sounded like the tales of Poor Little Rich Girl. But Tom was sympathetic, and got a glimpse of the kind of pressure Melanie was under. It didn't sound like fun to him, whatever other people thought. She looked sad when she talked about it, as though she had missed a big piece of her youth, which she had. He was sensitive to it as he looked at her, and felt sorry for her.

'I'd love to see you perform sometime,' Tom said thoughtfully. 'I mean now that I know you.'

'I'm doing a concert in L.A. in June. I go on the road after that. First to Vegas, and then all around the country. July, August, and part of September. Maybe you can come in June.' She liked that idea, and so did he, although they had just met.

They wandered slowly back to the field hospital then, and he left her at the front door, promising to catch up with her later. He hadn't asked if she had a boyfriend, and she had forgotten to mention

Jake. He had been so unpleasant since they'd been there, and complained all the time. He wanted to go home. So did eighty thousand other people, and they seemed to be living through it. The inconveniences they were all experiencing hadn't been designed just to annoy him. She had said something about it to Ashley the night before, that Jake was such a baby. And she was getting tired of dealing with him. He was so immature and selfish. She forgot about him, and even Tom, when she went back to work with Maggie.

*   *   *

Everett's AA meeting that night at the camp was a huge success. Much to his amazement, nearly a hundred people showed up, thrilled to have a meeting. The 'Friends of Bill W.' sign had attracted the knowledgeable and initiated, and the public announcement that morning in the quad had told people where to find it. They kept it going for two hours, and an astounding number of people shared. Everett felt like a new man when he walked into the hospital at eight-thirty to tell Maggie about it. He noticed that she looked tired.

'You were right! It was fantastic!' His eyes were ablaze with light and excitement when he told her what a success the meeting had been. She was delighted for him. He hung around the hospital for an hour, while things were quiet. She had sent Melanie back to her own hall by then. And she and Everett sat and talked for a long time.

Eventually she left the hospital with him, when she signed out, and he walked her back to the building where all the religious volunteers were staying. There were nuns, priests, ministers, brothers, several rabbis, and two Buddhist priests in orange robes. They came and went as Maggie and Everett sat on the front step. She enjoyed talking to him. And he felt renewed after the meeting, and thanked her again when he got up to leave.

'Thank you, Maggie. You're a terrific friend.'

'So are you, Everett.' She smiled at him. 'I'm glad it worked out.' For a minute she had worried about what would happen if no one came. But the group had agreed to meet every day at the same time, and she had a feeling it was going to grow exponentially. Everyone was under a lot of stress. She was even feeling it herself. The priests in her building said mass every morning, and it got her day off to a good start, just as Everett's meeting had done for him. And she prayed for at least an hour at night before she went to sleep, or as long as she could stay awake. She was working long, hard, exhausting days.

'See you tomorrow,' he promised, and then left. She walked into the building where she was staying. There were battery-operated lanterns in the hall as she went up the stairs. She was thinking about him as she walked into the room she was sharing with six other nuns, all of whom had assorted volunteer jobs at the Presidio, and for the first time in years, she felt separate from them. One of them had been complaining for two days that she couldn't wear her habit. She had left it at the convent, when the building caught fire from a gas leak, and they fled, and arrived at the Presidio in bathrobes and slippers. She said she felt naked without her habit. Maggie hated wearing hers in

129

recent years, and had only worn it the night of the benefit because she didn't own a dress, just the clothes she wore while working on the streets.

For the first time in her life, she felt isolated from the other nuns. She wasn't sure why, but they seemed small-minded to her somehow, and she found herself thinking of the conversations she'd had with Everett about how much she loved being a nun. She did, but sometimes other nuns, or even priests, got on her nerves. She forgot that sometimes. Her connection was with God, and the lost souls she worked with. People in religious orders seemed irritating to her at times, particularly when they were righteous or narrow-minded about their own choices in life.

But what she was feeling worried her. He had asked if she had ever questioned her vocation, and she never had. She wasn't now. But suddenly she missed talking to him, their philosophical exchanges, the funny things he said. And as she thought of him, it worried her. She didn't want to get too attached to any man. She wondered if the other nun was right. Perhaps nuns needed habits to remind other people of who they were and to keep a distance. There was no distance between her and Everett. In the unusual circumstances they were all living, powerful friendships had been formed, unseverable bonds, and even budding romances. She was willing to be Everett's friend, but surely nothing more. She reminded herself of that as she washed her face in cold water, and then lay on her cot, praying as she always did. She didn't allow him to intrude on her prayers, but there was no question, he kept meandering into her head, and she had to make a conscious effort to shut him

130

out. It reminded her, as she hadn't been reminded in years, that she was God's bride and no one else's. She belonged to no one but Him. That was the way it always had been, always would be, and would stay forever. And as she prayed, with particular fervor, she finally managed to shut out the vision of Everett from her mind, and fill it only with Christ. She breathed a long sigh when she finished praying, closed her eyes, and fell peacefully to sleep.

*   *   *

Melanie was exhausted when she went back to her own building that night. It had been her third day of hard work at the field hospital, and although she loved the work she was doing there, on her way back to the hall where she was staying, she had to admit to herself for a minute that it would have been great to have a hot bath, and settle into her comfortable bed with the TV on and fall asleep. Instead she was sharing an enormous room with several hundred people. It was noisy, crowded, smelled bad, and her cot was hard. And she knew they'd be there for at least several more days. The city was still completely shut down, and there was no way to leave. They had to make the best of it, as she told Jake every time he complained. She was disappointed by how whiny he had been, and a lot of the time he took it out on her. And Ashley was no better. She cried a lot, said she was suffering from post-traumatic stress syndrome, and wanted to go home. Janet didn't like it there either, but at least she was making friends, and talked about her daughter constantly, in order to let everyone know how important and special she was. Melanie didn't care. She was used to it. Her mother did that everywhere they went. And the guys in her band, and roadies, had made a lot of friends. They hung out and played poker a lot. She and Pam were the only ones in the group who were working, so Melanie hardly saw the others now.

She helped herself to a cherry soda on the way in. The hall was dimly lit with the battery-operated torches that lit up the edges of the room at night. It was just dark enough to stumble over people, or fall if you weren't careful. There were people in sleeping bags in the aisles, others on cots, and all night long there seemed to be children crying. It was like being on a ship in steerage, or a refugee camp, which was in fact what it was. Melanie made her way to where her group was sleeping. They had more than a dozen cots all grouped together, with some of the roadies on the floor in sleeping bags. Jake's cot was right next to hers.

She sat down on the edge of it, and patted his bare shoulder, which was poking out of the sleeping bag. He had his back to her.

'Hi, baby,' she whispered in the semidarkness. The hall had already quieted down for the night. People went to bed early. They were upset, frightened, depressed over what they'd lost, and there was nothing to do at night, so they went to bed. He didn't move at first, so she assumed he was asleep, and was about to move to her own cot. Her mother wasn't there, and had wandered off somewhere. As Melanie was about to shift to her own cot, there was sudden movement in Jake's sleeping bag, and two heads popped out at once, looking startled and embarrassed. The first face

132

staring at her was Ashley's, the second one was Jake's.

'What are you doing here?' he asked, sounding angry and surprised.

'I sleep here, I think,' Melanie said, unable to understand what she was seeing at first, and then suddenly she realized only too well. 'That's nice,' she said to Ashley, who had been her friend almost all her life. 'Really nice. What a shit thing for the two of you to do,' she said, keeping her voice down so the others didn't hear. Ashley and Jake were sitting up by then. She could see they had no clothes on. Ashley did some minor gymnastics, and crawled out of the bag in a T-shirt and thong. Melanie recognized it as hers. 'You're a prick,' Melanie said to Jake and started to walk away. He grabbed her arm, and struggled out of the bag, wearing only his underwear.

'For chrissake, babe. We were just fooling around. It was no big deal.' People were starting to stare by then. Worse yet, they knew who she was. Her mother had seen to that.

'It looks like a big deal to me,' Melanie said as she turned around to stare at them again, and spoke to Ashley first. 'I don't mind you stealing my underwear, Ash, but I think stealing my boyfriend is a little much, don't you?'

'I'm sorry, Mel,' Ashley said, and hung her head, as tears rolled down her cheeks. 'I don't know, it's so scary here . . . I'm so freaked out . . . I had an anxiety attack today. Jake was just trying to make me feel better . . . I . . . it wasn't . . .' She was crying harder, and Melanie felt sick looking at her.

'Spare me. I wouldn't have done it to you. And maybe if both of you got off your dead asses and

133

did something useful around here, you wouldn't have to fuck each other for entertainment. You both make me sick,' Melanie said, her voice shaking as she spoke.

'Don't be such a righteous bitch!' Jake spat at her, deciding that the best defense was a great offense. It didn't fly with her.

'Fuck you!' she shot at him, as her mother arrived, looking confused by what was happening. She could see they were having a heated argument, but had no idea why. She'd been playing cards with some new friends, and a couple of really good-looking men.

'Oh fuck you, you're not as hot as you think you are!' Jake threw back at her, as Melanie walked away and her mother ran after her, looking worried.

'What happened?'

'I don't want to talk about it,' Melanie said, heading out for some fresh air.

'Melanie! Where are you going?' her mother called after her, as people on their path woke up and stared.

'Out. Don't worry. I'm not going back to L.A.' She ran out the door then, and Janet went back to find Ashley sobbing, and Jake having a tantrum of some kind. He was throwing things, and people on neighboring cots were telling him to knock it off, or they'd kick his ass. He wasn't popular in the area where they slept. He had been rude to everyone around them, and they didn't find him charming, even if he was a TV star. Janet was looking deeply concerned, and asked one of the band members to talk to him and tell him to stop.

'I hate this place!' Jake shouted, and went

134

outside, with Ashley running behind him. It had been a stupid thing to do, and she knew it. She knew how Melanie was, loyalty and honesty meant everything to her. She was afraid Melanie would never forgive her and said as much to Jake, as they sat outside wrapped in blankets, with bare feet. Ashley glanced around and didn't see Melanie anywhere. 'Oh, fuck her,' Jake added. 'When the fuck are they going to get us out of here?' He had asked one of the helicopter pilots about airlifting them out, and taking them back to L.A. He had looked at Jake like he was insane. They were flying for the government and were not for hire.

'She'll never forgive me,' Ashley whimpered.

'So what? What do you care?' He took a deep breath of the cool night air. It had just been a little fun with Ashley, they had had nothing else to do, and Melanie was so goddamn busy playing Florence Nightingale. He told himself and Ashley that if she'd stuck around, this would never have happened. It was her fault, not theirs. 'You're twice the woman she is,' he told Ashley, who lapped it up as she cuddled up to him.

'Do you really think so?' she asked, looking hopeful and a lot less guilty than she had a few minutes before.

'Sure, baby, sure,' he said, and a few minutes later they went back inside. She slept in his sleeping bag with him, since Melanie wasn't there anyway. Janet pretended not to see it, but understood fully what had happened. She had never liked Jake anyway. In her opinion, he wasn't a big enough star for her daughter, and Janet took a dim view of his history with drugs.

Melanie had gone back to the field hospital, and

135

slept on one of the empty cots they kept waiting for new patients. The nurse in charge said she could sleep there, when Melanie explained that there had been a problem in her own hall. She promised to get up if they needed the bed for a patient.

'Don't worry about it,' the nurse told her kindly. 'Get some sleep. You look beat.'

'I am,' Melanie said, and then lay awake for hours, thinking about Ashley and Jake's faces coming out of his sleeping bag. It didn't totally surprise her that Jake had done it, although she hated him for it, and thought he was a pig for cheating on her with her best friend. But it was Ashley's betrayal that hurt her most. They were both weak and selfish, users, and shameless about exploiting her. She knew it came with the territory, and she had lived through other betrayals. But she was sick of all the disappointments that came with stardom. Whatever happened to love, honesty, decency, loyalty, and real friends?

Melanie was sound asleep on the hospital cot when Maggie found her there the next morning, and covered her gently with a blanket. She had no idea what had happened, but whatever it was, she knew instinctively that nothing good had brought her there. Maggie left her to sleep as long as she could. Melanie looked like a sleeping child, as Maggie left her, and started her day. There was so much to do.

Chapter 8

The tension at Seth and Sarah's house on Divisadero on Monday morning was palpable and overwhelming. As he had since the earthquake, Seth tried all their house phones, their cell phones, their car phones, even his BlackBerry, to no avail. San Francisco was still completely cut off from the world. Helicopters were still buzzing overhead, flying low to check on people and report back to Emergency Services. They could still hear sirens throughout the city. And if they were able to, people stayed in their homes. The streets looked like a ghost town. And inside their home, there was a sense of impending doom. Sarah stayed away from Seth and kept busy with her babies. They still had their usual routines. But she and Seth hardly spoke to each other. What he had confessed to her had shocked her into silence.

She fed the children breakfast, although their food supplies were dwindling. She played with them in the garden afterward and pushed them on the swingset they had there. Molly thought it was funny that the tree had fallen down. And Oliver's cough and earache were better, from the antibiotics he'd taken. Both children were in good spirits; the same could not be said about their parents. She and Parmani made them peanut butter and jelly sandwiches for lunch, with sliced bananas, and then put them down for their naps. The house was quiet when she finally went to see Seth in his study. He look ravaged, and was staring blindly at the wall, lost in thought.

'Are you okay?' He didn't even bother to answer. He just turned to look at her with broken eyes. Everything he had built for them was about to come tumbling down. He looked devastated and gray. 'Do you want lunch?' she asked him, and he shook his head, and then looked at her with a sigh.

'You understand what's going to happen, don't you?'

'Not really,' she said softly, and sat down. 'I know what you told me, that they're going to audit Sully's books, and find the investors' money gone, and then they'll trace it to your accounts.'

'It's called theft and securities fraud. Those are federal felonies. Not to mention the lawsuits that will set off among Sully's investors, and even mine. It's going to be a hell of a mess, Sarah. Probably for a long, long time.' He had thought of nothing else since Thursday night and she since Friday morning.

'What does that mean? Define *mess*,' she said sadly, thinking that she might as well know what was coming. It was going to be happening to her too.

'Prosecution probably. A grand jury indictment. A trial. I'll probably be convicted and go to prison.' He glanced at his watch. It was four o'clock in New York, four hours past the time when he had to have the money back to Sully in time for his investors' audit. It was shit luck that their respective audits had been so close together, and even worse luck that the San Francisco earthquake had shut down all communications and the city's banks. They were dead in the water, and sitting ducks with no way to cover their tracks. 'By now, Sully has been caught red-handed, and sometime

138

this week the SEC will start an investigation of his books, and mine when this city opens up again. He's in the same boat I am. The investors will start suing in civil suits, for misappropriation of their funds, theft, and fraud.' And then as though to make matters worse, he added, 'I'm pretty sure we'll lose the house, and everything else we have.'

'And then what?' Sarah asked in a hoarse voice. She wasn't as horrified about losing their property and possessions as she was about discovering that Seth was a dishonest man. A crook and a fraud. She had known and loved him for six years, only to find out that she didn't know him. She couldn't have looked more shocked if he had turned into a werewolf in front of her eyes. 'What'll happen to me and the kids?'

'I don't know, Sarah,' he told her honestly. 'You may have to get a job.' She nodded. There were worse fates. She was more than willing to work if it would help them, but if he was convicted, what was going to happen to their life, their marriage? If he went to prison, then what, and for how long? She couldn't even get the words out to ask him, and he just sat there, shaking his head, as tears rolled slowly down his cheeks. What scared her too was that he seemed to be thinking of himself in all this, and not of them. What was going to happen to her and the children if he went to jail?

'Do you suppose as soon as the city opens up again, the police are going to show up?' She had no idea what lay ahead. In her worst nightmares, she could never have conceived of anything like this.

'I don't know. I guess they would start with an SEC investigation first. But it could get very bad

139

very quickly. As soon as the banks open, the money is going to be sitting there, and I'm screwed.' She nodded, trying to absorb it, remembering what he had said.

'You said you and Sully did this before. A lot of times?' Her eyes were bleak, and her voice was hoarse. Seth had been dishonest not just once, but maybe for several years.

'A few.' He sounded tense as he answered.

'How many is a few?' She wanted to know.

'Does it matter?' She saw a muscle in his jaw go taut. 'Three . . . maybe four. He helped me set it up. The first time I did it was right after we started, to give us a little push and get investors interested in the fund. Kind of like window dressing, to make us look good. It worked . . . so I did it again. It brought the big investors in, thinking we had that kind of money in the bank.' He had lied to them, cheated, committed outright fraud. It was inconceivable to her, and accounted now for his rapid and astonishing success. The wonder boy everyone talked about was a liar and a thief, a con man. And even more horrifying was the fact that she was married to him. He had fooled her too. She had never wanted all the extravagant luxuries he had provided. She didn't need them. They had even worried her at first. And Seth had insisted that he was making money hand over fist, and they deserved all the toys and the fabulous lifestyle he was providing for her. Houses, jewelry, fancy cars, his plane. And he had built all of it on ill-gotten means. Now he was about to get caught, and everything he had worked for would disappear, out of her life too.

'Are we in trouble with the IRS too?' she asked,

looking panicked. If so, it might implicate her as well since they filed joint returns. What would happen to their children if she went to prison? The mere thought of it terrified her.

'No, we're not,' he reassured her. 'Our tax returns are clean as a whistle. I wouldn't do that to you.'

'Why not?' she said, with tears bulging in her eyes, and then spilling slowly down her cheeks. She was overwhelmed. The earthquake that had just hit the city was peanuts compared to what was about to happen to them. 'You've done everything else. You put yourself at risk, and you're going to take all of us down with you.' She couldn't even imagine what she was going to tell her parents. They were going to be horrified, and deeply ashamed once this hit the press. There would be no way to keep it quiet. She could easily see the story being a major item on the news, even more so if he was convicted and went to prison. The newspapers were going to have a field day with it. The higher he had climbed, the harder he would hit when he fell. It was easily predictable, she realized as she stood up and walked around the room. 'We need a lawyer, Seth, a really good one.'

'I'll take care of it,' he said, watching her stand staring out the window. The neighbor's window boxes had fallen, and were still lying all over the sidewalk, with dirt and flowers everywhere. They had gone to the shelter in the Presidio when their chimney fell through their roof, and no one had cleaned up any of the mess. There was going to be a lot of cleaning up to do in the city. But it would be nothing compared to the mess that Seth was going to have to deal with. 'I'm sorry, Sarah,' he

141

whispered.

'So am I,' she said, turning to look at him. 'I don't know if it means anything to you, but I love you, Seth. I did from the minute we met. I still do, even after this. I just don't know where we go from here. Or even if we do.' She didn't say it to him, but she didn't know if she could ever forgive him for being so dishonest and having so little integrity. It had been a horrifying revelation about the man she loved. If he was in fact so different than she had believed him to be, who in fact did she love? He looked like a stranger to her now, and in fact, he was.

'I love you too,' he said miserably. 'I'm so sorry. I never thought it would come to this. I didn't think we'd get caught.' He said it as though he had stolen an apple from a cart, or failed to return a book to a library. She was beginning to wonder if he fully realized how major this was.

'That's not the point. It's not just about your getting caught. It's about who you were and what you were thinking when you set it up. The risk you took. The lie you were living. The people you were willing to hurt and lie to, not just your investors, but me and the kids. They're going to be damaged by this too. If you go to prison, they'll have to live with that for the rest of their lives, knowing what you did. How are they going to look up to you when they grow up? What does this tell them about you?'

'It tells them that I'm human and I made a mistake,' he said sorrowfully. 'If they love me, they'll forgive me, and so will you.'

'Maybe it's not as simple as that. I don't know how you come back from something like this, any of us. How do you forget that someone you completely trusted turned out to be a liar and a fake, a thief . . . a fraud . . . how do I ever trust you again?' He said nothing, and sat staring at her. He hadn't come near her in three days. He couldn't. She had put a wall between them ten feet high. Even in their bed at night, each of them had huddled toward their respective sides, with a vast expanse of empty space between them. He didn't touch her, and she couldn't bring herself to reach out to him. She was too wounded and in too much pain, too disillusioned and disappointed. He wanted her to forgive him, and understand, and be supportive of him, but she had no idea if she ever would, or could. It was just too huge.

She was almost grateful that the city was cut off. She needed the time to absorb it before the roof fell in on them. But then again, if the earthquake hadn't hit the city, none of this would have happened. He would have sent the money back to Sully, so he could cook his own books. And then, at some point, they would have done it again, and maybe gotten caught later. Sooner or later it would have had to happen. No one was that clever, or got away with a crime of this magnitude forever. It was so simple it was pathetic, and so dishonest that it boggled the mind.

'Are you going to leave me, Sarah?' That would have been the icing on the cake for him. He wanted her to stand by him, and she didn't look as though she would. Sarah had extremely rigid ideas about honesty and integrity. She set extremely high standards for herself and everyone else. He had violated them all. He had even put their family at risk, which he suspected would be the final straw for her. Family was sacred to her. She lived by the values she believed in. She was a woman of honor, and she expected and believed the same of him.

'I don't know,' she said honestly. 'I have no idea what I'm going to do. I'm having trouble getting my mind around the whole concept. What you did is so enormous, I'm not sure I even get it yet.' Nothing that had happened in the earthquake had shocked her as much as this. She looked as though the world had collapsed in on her and their kids.

'I hope you don't leave,' he said, sounding sad and vulnerable. 'I want you to stay.' He needed her. He didn't think he could face this alone. But he realized he might have to, and at some level, recognized that it was his own fault.

'I want to stay,' she said, crying again. She had never felt as devastated in her life, except when they thought their baby was going to die. Thank God, Molly had been saved. But she couldn't imagine now that anything would be able to save Seth. Even if he had a brilliant lawyer and they negotiated like crazy, she couldn't imagine him being acquitted, not with the proof they would have from the bank. 'I just don't know if I can,' she added. 'Let's see what happens when we're in communication with the world again. I imagine that the shit will hit the fan pretty fast.' He nodded. They both knew that this time of being cut off from the world was a reprieve for both of them. There was no way that they could act, or react. They just had to sit there and wait. It added immeasurably to the stress of the days after the earthquake, but she was grateful for the time it gave her to think. It did more for her than for Seth, who prowled the house like a caged lion,

144

thinking about what was going to happen to him, and worrying about it constantly. He was desperate to talk to Sully, to find out what had happened to him in New York. Seth checked his BlackBerry constantly, as though it would suddenly come alive. It was still as dead as everything else, and possibly their marriage.

As they had for the three nights before that, they stayed well away from each other in bed that night. Seth wanted to make love to her, just for the comfort it would give him, the reassurance that she still loved him, but he didn't go near her, and didn't blame her for how she felt. He lay awake on his side of the bed, long after she fell asleep. Halfway through the night, Oliver woke up, crying and pulling on his ears again. He was teething, and Sarah wasn't sure if his ears were hurting or his teeth. She held him in her arms for a long time, rocking him in the big comfortable rocking chair in his room, until he finally went back to sleep again. She didn't put him back in his crib, she just sat there, holding him, looking at the moon, and listening to the helicopters patrolling the city through the night. It sounded like a war zone, as she listened, and as she sat there, she realized that it was. She knew this was going to be a terrible time for them. There was no way to avoid it, change it, turn the clock back to before it happened. Just as the city had been shaken to its roots by the earthquake, their life had come down around their ears, or was about to. It had fallen from the sky, hit the pavement, and been smashed to bits.

She spent the rest of the night in the rocking chair, holding Ollie, and never went back to bed.

She couldn't bring herself to go back and lie next to Seth, and maybe never could again. She moved out of their bedroom into the guest room the next day.

Chapter 9

On Friday, the eighth day after the earthquake, the shelter residents at the Presidio were told that the freeways and airport would reopen the next day. A temporary tower had been set up. It would be months before the old one was rebuilt. The opening of Highways 280 and 101 meant that people could move freely to the south, but the Golden Gate Bridge wouldn't open for a few more days, making direct movement toward the north still impossible. They were told that the Bay Bridge would be closed for many months, until it was repaired. That would mean that commuters from the East Bay would have to travel to the city via the Richmond and Golden Gate Bridges, or the Dumbarton or San Mateo Bridges to the south. Commuting would be a nightmare, and traffic would be extremely slow. And for now, only those who lived on the peninsula would be able to go home on Saturday.

Several neighborhoods were being opened again, and people would be able to check the condition of their homes. Others had to face police barricades and yellow tape, if conditions were too dangerous to enter. The Financial District was still a disaster and off limits to everyone, which meant that many businesses could not reopen. And electricity would become available to only a small portion of the city over the weekend. There were rumors that electricity would not be fully restored for perhaps as long as two months, or one if they were lucky. The city was on all fours, but it was beginning to crawl. After being completely flattened for the past eight days, it was showing signs of life, but it would be months before San Francisco would stand fully upright again. There had been much talk in the shelters about people saying they would move away. They had lived with the threat of a major earthquake for years, and now that it had come, it had hit too hard. Some were ready to quit, others were determined to stay. Old people said they wouldn't live long enough to see another one like it, so it didn't matter to them. Young people were anxious to rebuild and start again. And many in between said they had had it with the city. They had lost too much and were too frightened. There was a constant cacophony of worried voices in the sleeping halls, the mess hall, and on the walkways where people strolled, and even along the beaches bordering Crissy Field. On a sunny day, it was easier to forget what had happened to them. But late at night, when they all felt the aftershocks that had begun to hit them a day later, everyone looked panicked. It had been a traumatic time for everyone in the city, and it wasn't over yet.

After they heard the news that the airport was going to open the next day, Melanie and Tom sat on the beach, talking, looking out at the bay. They had come to sit here every day. She had told him what had happened with Jake and Ashley, and she had been sleeping at the hospital ever since. She was anxious to get home and get away from them, but she had enjoyed getting to know Tom better.

'What are you going to do now?' she asked him quietly. Sitting with him always felt comfortable and peaceful. He had an easy way about him, of confidence and decency.

It was nice being with someone who wasn't directly involved in her business, or any aspect of show business. She was tired of actors, singers, musicians, and all the crazy people she dealt with every day. She had gone out with several of them, and it always ended as it had with Jake, or sometimes worse. They were narcissists, drug addicts, lunatics, or just generally badly behaved people who wanted to take advantage of her in some way. From what she had seen, they had no conscience, no morality, and they did whatever felt good to them at the time. She wanted something better than that in her life. Even at nineteen, she was far more stable than they were. She didn't do drugs and never had, had never cheated on anyone, didn't lie, wasn't obsessed with herself, and was a decent, moral, honest person. She wanted the same from someone else. She and Tom had talked a lot about her career in the past few days and where she wanted to go with it. She didn't want to abandon it, but wanted to take charge of it herself. It was unlikely her mother would ever let that happen. Melanie had said to Tom that she was tired of being run, controlled, used, and pushed around by everyone else. He was impressed by how logical, rational, and sane she was.

'I've got to go back to Berkeley and move out of my apartment,' Tom said, in answer to her question. 'It sounds like it may be a while before I

148

can do that. At least the Golden Gate and Richmond Bridges have to reopen, so I can get over to the East Bay. Then I'll go back to Pasadena after that. I was going to stick around for the summer. I have a job here in the fall, but everything could change now, depending on how soon businesses can reopen. I may look for something else down there.' Like her, he was practical, had a level head, and kept a clear view of his goals. He was twenty-two years old, wanted to work for a few years, and then go to business school, maybe at UCLA. 'What about you? What have you got on your agenda for the next few weeks?' They hadn't talked about it in any detail before. He knew she was leaving on tour in July, after a concert in Las Vegas. She had told him how much she hated it there, but it was an important venue for her, and the tour was going to be huge. After that, she was planning to be back in L.A. in September after the tour. But he had no idea what she had planned through June. It was still only May.

'I have a recording session next week for a new CD. We're doing some of the material I'll be using on the tour. It's a good warm-up for me. Other than that, I'm pretty free till my L.A. concert in June right before I leave. Do you think you'll be back in Pasadena by then?' She gave him the date, and looked hopeful. He smiled, listening to her. Getting to know her had been wonderful, seeing her again would be like a dream. He couldn't help thinking that she would forget him as soon as she got back to L.A. 'I'd love you to come to the L.A. concert as my guest. It gets pretty crazy when I'm working, but it might be fun for you. You can bring a couple of friends if you want.'

'My sister would go nuts,' he said, smiling at her. 'She'll be home in June too.'

'Why don't you bring her,' Melanie said, and then her voice dropped down to a whisper. 'I hope you call me when you get back.'

'Will you take my call?' he asked, looking worried. Once out of the Presidio and back to her real life, she was a major star. What could she possibly want with him? He was just a fledgling engineer and no one on her radar screen. But she seemed to like being with him, as much as he enjoyed being with her.

'Of course I will,' she reassured him. 'I hope you call me.' She jotted down her cell phone number for him. Cell phones were not operating in the San Francisco area yet, and wouldn't be for a while. Computer and telephone service hadn't been restored either. There was some talk that they would be up and running in another week.

They walked back to the hospital again then, and he teased her as they wandered in. 'I guess you won't be going to nursing school for a while, if you're going on tour.'

'Yeah, right. Not in this lifetime.' She had introduced Tom to her mother the day before, and Janet hadn't been impressed. As far as she was concerned, he was just a kid, and his engineering degree meant nothing to her. She wanted Melanie to go out with producers, directors, lead singers, and well-known actors, anyone who would catch the eye of the press or in some way help her career. Whatever his other failings, Jake had been in those leagues, as a lure for the press. Tom never would be. And his boring, wholesome, well-educated Pasadena family was of no interest to Janet whatsoever. She wasn't worried about it, she figured Melanie would forget him as soon as they left San Francisco, and she wouldn't see him again. She had no idea about their plans to meet up again in L.A.

Melanie worked with Maggie all day and well into the evening. They had a pizza together that Tom brought them that night from the mess hall. The food had actually remained surprisingly good, thanks to a continual supply of fresh meats, fruits, and vegetables that were flown in by helicopter, and the creative skills of the chefs. Everett joined them after his final AA meeting, and said he had turned it over to a new secretary, a woman whose house in the Marina had been destroyed, and she was planning to stay at the shelter in the Presidio for several months. The meeting had grown remarkably just in the past few days, and had been a source of immense support to him. He thanked Maggie again for encouraging him to do it. She assured him gracefully that he would have done it anyway. And they continued to sit and talk, after the young people left for a last stroll on their final night together. This was a time they would all long remember, some of them in poignant ways.

'I hate to go back to L.A. tomorrow,' Everett confessed, after Tom and Melanie had left. They had promised to come back and say goodnight. The L.A. contingent were leaving early the next morning, and Melanie wouldn't be back to work again. 'Are you going to be okay here?' He looked worried about her. She was full of fire and brimming with energy, but there was also something vulnerable about her that he had come

151

to love.

'Of course I will. Don't be silly. I've been in much worse places than this. My own neighborhood, for instance.' She laughed, and he smiled at her.

'So have I. But it was nice being here with you, Maggie.'

'Sister Maggie to you,' she reminded him, and then chuckled. There was something between them that worried her at times. He had started treating her like a woman, not just a nun. He was protective of her, and she reminded him that nuns weren't ordinary women, they were under God's protection. 'My Maker is my husband,' she said, quoting the Bible. 'He takes good care of me. I'll be fine here. You make sure you'll be fine in L.A. too.' She was still hoping he would go to Montana to find his son one of these days, although she knew he wasn't ready to do it. But they had spoken of it a couple of times, and she encouraged him to think about it.

'I'm going to be busy editing all the shots I took here. My editor is going to go crazy.' He smiled at her, anxious to see the shots he had taken of her the night of the earthquake and since. 'I'll send you copies of the ones I took of you.'

'I'd like that.' She smiled. It had been a remarkable time for all of them, tragic for some, and life-altering in good ways for others. She had said as much to Melanie that afternoon. She was hoping that at some point Melanie would get involved in volunteer work. She was so good at that kind of thing and had comforted so many people with so much gentleness and grace. 'She'd make a great nun,' Maggie commented to Everett, and he guffawed.

'Stop recruiting. Now that's one girl who's never going to enlist. Her mother would kill her.' Everett had met Janet once, with Melanie, and hated her on sight. He thought she was loud, overbearing, pushy, pretentious, and rude. She treated Melanie like a five-year-old, while exploiting her daughter's success to the hilt.

'I suggested that she look up some kind of Catholic mission in L.A. She could do some wonderful work with the homeless. She told me she'd love to stop everything she's doing one day, and go away for six months, to work with poor people in a foreign country. Stranger things have happened. It might do her a lot of good. That's a crazy world she works in. She might need a break from it someday.'

'She might, but I don't think that's going to happen, with a mother like hers. Not while she's selling platinum records and winning Grammys. It may be a while before she can do something like that. If she ever does.'

'You never know,' Maggie said. She had given Melanie the name of a priest in L.A. who did wonderful work with people on the streets, and went to Mexico for several months every year, to help there.

'And what about you?' Everett asked her. 'What are you going to do now? Go back to the Tenderloin as soon as you can?' He hated her neighborhood. It was so dangerous for her, whether she acknowledged it or not.

'I think I'll stay here for a while. The other nuns are going to stay too, and a few of the priests. A lot of people living here now have nowhere else to go.

153

They're going to keep the shelters running at the Presidio for at least six months. I'll work at the field hospital, but I'll go home to check on things from time to time. There's probably more for me to do here. I can use my nursing skills.' And she had used them well.

'When am I going to see you again, Maggie?' He looked worried about it. He had loved seeing her every day, and he could already feel her slipping out of his life, possibly for good.

'I don't know,' she admitted, looking sad for a minute herself, and then she smiled, remembering something she had meant to tell him for days. 'You know, Everett, you remind me of a movie I saw when I was a kid. It was already an old movie then, with Robert Mitchum and Deborah Kerr. A nun and a marine get stranded on a desert island. They almost fall in love, but not quite. Or at least they're sensible enough not to let it happen, and they become friends. He behaves very badly at first and shocks her. He drinks a lot, and I think she hides his booze. She reforms him somewhat, and he takes very good care of her, and she of him. They were hiding from the Japanese while they were on the island. It was during World War II. And in the end, they get rescued. He goes back to the Marines and she to the convent. It was called *Heaven Knows, Mr. Allison,* and it was a very sweet film. I loved it. Deborah Kerr made a great nun.'

'So do you,' he said sadly. 'I'm going to miss you, Maggie. It's been so wonderful talking to you every day.'

'You can call me when we get cell phone service back, though I don't think that will happen for a while. I'll be praying for you, Everett,' she said, looking him in the eye.

'Maybe I'll pray for you too,' Everett said. 'What about that movie, the part where they almost fall in love but become friends. Did that happen to us?'

She was silent for a long moment, thinking about it, before she answered. 'I think we're both more sensible than that, and more realistic. Nuns don't fall in love.'

'What if they do?' he persisted, wanting a better answer than that.

'They don't. They can't. They're already married to God.'

'Don't give me that. Some nuns leave the convent. They even get married. Your brother left the priesthood. Maggie . . .'

She stopped him in his tracks before he could say more, or something they'd both regret. She couldn't be his friend if he didn't respect her very firm boundaries and crossed the line. 'Everett, don't. I'm your friend. I think you're mine. Let's be grateful for that.'

'And if I want more?'

'You don't.' She smiled at him with her electric blue eyes. 'You just want what you can't have. Or you think you do. There's a whole world of people out there for you.'

'But no one like you. I've never known anyone like you.'

She laughed at him then. 'That may be a very good thing. You'll be grateful for that one day.'

'I'm grateful to have met you,' he said seriously.

'So am I. You're a wonderful man, and I'm proud to know you. I'll bet you win another Pulitzer for the photographs you took.' He had finally admitted it to her, somewhat sheepishly, in one of their long talks about his life and work. 'Or some kind of prize! I can't wait to see what gets published.' She was gently steering him onto safer ground, and he knew it. She was not going to open any other door to him, or even let him try.

It was ten o'clock when Melanie and Tom came back to say goodbye. They looked happy and young and a little giddy with the newness of their budding romance. Everett envied them. Life was just starting for them both. He felt as though his was nearly over, the best part anyway, although AA and his recovery had changed his forever, and improved it immeasurably. He was just bored with his job, and missed his old war zones. San Francisco and the earthquake had put a little spark in his life again, and he was hoping the pictures would be great. But he also knew that he was going back to a job that offered little challenge and used few of his skills and too little of his expertise. His drinking, before he conquered it, had put him in that position.

Melanie kissed Maggie goodnight, and she and Tom left. Everett would be leaving with Melanie and her entourage the next day. They were going to be among the first people to leave San Francisco, and a bus was coming for them at eight. The Red Cross had arranged it. There were others leaving later for assorted destinations. They had already been warned that they might have to get to the airport by side streets and back roads as there were a lot of detours on the freeway, and it could take them as long as two hours to get there, if not more.

Everett said goodnight to Maggie regretfully

156

then. He gave her a hug before he did, and slipped something into her hand. She didn't look at it until he'd walked away, and then she opened her hand and saw his one-year AA chip in her palm. He called it his lucky coin. She smiled as she looked at it, with tears brimming in her eyes, and slipped it in her pocket.

Tom walked Melanie back to her hangar. She was sleeping there for her last night. It was the first time she was going back there since the incident with Jake and Ashley. She had seen them in the quad, but avoided them otherwise. Ashley had come to the hospital to talk to her several times, and Melanie had pretended to be busy, or slipped out the back door and asked Maggie to deal with her. She didn't want to hear the lies, excuses, or stories. As far as Melanie was concerned, they deserved each other. She was much happier spending time with Tom now. He was a very special person, with a depth and kindness that matched her own.

'I'll call you as soon as we have phone service, Melanie,' Tom promised. He was thrilled to know that she would be delighted to take his calls. He felt like he had won the lottery, and still couldn't believe his good fortune. He didn't care who she was professionally, he thought she was the nicest girl he had ever known. And she was equally impressed with him, for the same reasons.

'I'll miss you,' she said softly.

'So will I. Good luck with the recording session.'

She shrugged. 'They're easy, and fun sometimes. If they go well. We'll have to do a lot of rehearsing after we get back. I already feel rusty.'

'That's hard to imagine. I wouldn't worry about

157

it.'

'I'll be thinking about you,' she assured him, and then laughed. 'I never thought I'd be homesick for a refugee camp in San Francisco.' He laughed with her, and then without warning, he reached down gently, took her in his arms, and kissed her. She was breathless when she smiled up at him. She hadn't expected it, but she had loved it. He had never kissed her before, during their walks, or quiet time together. They had been friends until that moment, and hopefully still would be, even if they added more.

'Take good care of yourself, Melanie,' he said softly. 'Sleep tight. I'll see you in the morning.' In the mess hall, they were packing lunches for all those who would be traveling the next morning. There was no way of knowing how long they'd have to wait at the airport, or if there would be food there. It didn't seem likely, so the mess hall was providing enough food to take with them and tide them over.

Melanie floated into the hangar with a wistful smile on her face, and found her group in the same place they'd been camped out before. She noticed that Ashley was sleeping on a separate cot from Jake that night, and she no longer cared. Her mother was sound asleep, fully dressed, and snoring. It was going to be their last night in the shelter. The next day it would all feel like a dream, when they got back to the comforts of their life in L.A. But Melanie knew she would remember this week forever.

Melanie saw that Ashley was awake, and ignored her. Jake had his back to her and didn't move when she came in, which was a relief. She

158

wasn't anxious to see him, or to travel with him the next day. But they had no other choice. They were all flying on the same plane with about fifty other people from the camp.

Melanie slipped under the blanket on her cot, and then heard Ashley whisper to her. 'Mel . . . Mel . . . I'm sorry.'

'It's okay, Ash . . . don't worry about it,' Melanie said, thinking of Tom. She turned her back to her childhood friend who had betrayed her, and five minutes later, she was asleep, with a clear conscience. Ashley lay awake and tossed and turned all night, knowing she had lost her best friend forever. And she already knew Jake wasn't worth it.

Chapter 10

Tom and Sister Maggie came to see the others off the next morning. They were using two school buses to transport them. And they all knew it would be a long ride to the airport. The food for the travelers had been prepared and put on the buses for them. Tom and a number of other workers from the mess hall had finished putting it together at six o'clock that morning. Everything was ready.

Much to everyone's surprise, there were tearful goodbyes as they left. They had all expected to be thrilled to leave, but instead they suddenly found it hard to part from new friends. There were promises to call and write, or even visit. The people in the Presidio had shared so much grief, fear, and trauma. It was a bond they would share forever.

Tom was talking quietly to Melanie as Jake, Ashley, and the others got on the bus, while Janet told her to hurry up. She didn't even bother to say goodbye to Tom. She waved at two women who had come to see her off. Others wished they were going home too, although many had lost their homes and had nowhere to go. The L.A. contingent were lucky to be leaving the area and going back to normalcy again. It would be a long time before anything in San Francisco was normal.

'Take care, Melanie,' Tom whispered to her, as he held on to her gently and then kissed her again. She had no idea if Jake was watching, but after what he had done, she no longer cared. It was over between them, and should have been long before. She was sure he'd be using drugs again as soon as they got back to L.A. At least he'd been forced to stay off them in the camp, or maybe he'd found some after all. She no longer gave a damn about that either. 'I'll call you as soon as I get to Pasadena.'

'Take care of yourself,' she whispered, kissed him lightly on the lips, and hopped onto the bus with the others. Jake shot her an evil look as she walked past him. And Everett was right behind her in line before they boarded. He was saying goodbye to Maggie, and she showed him that she had his chip in her pocket.

'Hang on to that, Maggie,' he told her. 'It will bring you luck.'

'I've always been lucky,' she said, smiling at him. 'I was lucky when I met you,' she added.

'Not as much as I was. Stay safe and be careful.

160

I'll be in touch,' he promised, kissed her on the cheek, looked into those bottomless blue eyes for a last time, and climbed aboard.

Everett opened the window next to him, and waved at Maggie as they drove away. She and Tom stood and looked after the bus for a long time, and then went back to their respective jobs. Maggie was quiet and sad as she walked into the hospital, wondering if she would ever see Everett again, and knowing that if not, it was the will of God. She felt she had no right to ask for more right now. She had shared a remarkable week with him even if they never met again. She felt his AA chip in her pocket, touched it briefly, and went back to work, throwing herself into it with vigor, so she didn't let herself think of him. She knew she couldn't allow herself to do that. He was going back to his own life, and she to hers.

*　　　*　　　*

The ride to the airport turned out to be even longer than everyone had predicted. There were still obstacles in the road, parts of it had been torn up, and looked severely mangled. Overpasses had fallen, they saw buildings that had come down, and the drivers of the two buses took a long and circuitous road to the airport. It was nearly noon when they got there, and they saw damage to several terminals when they arrived. The tower that had been standing only nine days before had completely disappeared. There were only a handful of travelers, and only a few planes had come in, but theirs was waiting. It was scheduled to leave at one o'clock. They looked like a ragtag group as they checked in. Credit cards had been lost, and only a few people still had money on them. For those who needed it, the Red Cross had paid for their trip. Pam had Melanie's credit cards on her, and paid for all of their tickets. She had left a large group of friends behind her in the Presidio after working hard for a week. And as Pam paid for their seats, Janet insisted that she and Melanie be in first class.

'We don't need to do that, Mom,' Melanie said quietly. 'I'd rather sit with the others.'

'After what we've just been through? They should be giving us the plane.' Janet had apparently forgotten that the others had been through the same ordeal too. Everett was standing near them, paying for his ticket with the magazine's credit card, which he still had, and glanced at Melanie. She smiled and rolled her eyes, just as Ashley walked over with Jake. She still looked mortified whenever she was around her old friend. Jake looked totally fed up.

'Christ, I can't wait to get back to L.A.,' Jake said, almost snarling, as Everett looked at him with a grin.

'The rest of us are dying to stay here,' Everett quipped, as Melanie laughed, although in his case it was true, and hers too. They both had left people they cared about at the camp.

The airline personnel who were assisting them were exceptionally nice. They were well aware of what these people had been through, and they were all treated like VIPs, not just Melanie and her entourage. The band and roadies were flying home with them. Theoretically, they were still on the benefit's tickets, but those had been lost at the

162

hotel. Pam was going to sort it out with them later. For now, all any of them wanted was to get home. They had had no way of reassuring their families they were okay since the earthquake, except through the Red Cross, which had been very helpful. Now the airline took over for them.

They took their seats on the plane, and as soon as they took off, the pilot made an announcement, welcoming them, and saying that he hoped the past nine days hadn't been too traumatic for them. As soon as he said it, several passengers burst into tears. Everett had taken a few last photos of Melanie and her group. It was a far cry from the way they'd all looked when they arrived. Melanie was wearing yet another pair of combat pants, held up with a rope, with a T-shirt that must have belonged to a man ten times her size. Janet was still wearing some of her own clothes that she had worn backstage at the benefit. Her polyester pants had served her well, although she, like everyone else, had finally helped herself to some sweatshirts from the donation tables. The one she was wearing was several sizes too tight. It wasn't a great look with the polyester pants and high heels, which she had refused to exchange for the flip-flops everyone else was wearing by then. Pam was wearing a full set of army clothes that had been given to her by the National Guard. And the roadies and band looked like convicts in overalls. As Everett said, it made one hell of a great picture. It was one he knew that *Scoop* would run, possibly on the cover, in sharp contrast to the ones he had taken of her performing at the benefit in the slinky sequin and net dress and platform shoes. As Melanie said, her feet looked like a farmer's, her fancy L.A. pedicure had entirely disappeared in the dirt and gravel of the camp as she ran around in rubber flip-flops. Everett still had his beloved black lizard cowboy boots.

They served champagne, cocktail nuts, and pretzels on the flight, and less than an hour later they landed at LAX, among war whoops and screams, wolf whistles and tears. It had been a shocking nine days for them all. Better for some than for others, but even in the best of conditions they had all been through the mill. And the stories they told were legion, of escape and survival, injury and fear. One man had his leg in a cast and was on crutches, provided by the field hospital, and several people had broken their arms and were in casts too. Melanie recognized among them several people whom Maggie had stitched up. On some days, she had the feeling they'd sewn up half the camp. Just thinking about it made her miss Maggie. She was planning to call her on her cell phone, when she could.

The plane taxied up to the terminal, and there was a wall of press waiting when they emerged. They were the first survivors of the San Francisco earthquake to return to L.A. There were TV cameras there too, and they pounced on Melanie the moment she came through the gate, looking a little dazed. Her mother had told her to comb her hair, just in case, but she hadn't bothered. She truly didn't care. She was happy to be home, although she hadn't thought about it much when she was in the camp. She was too busy there.

The photographers recognized Jake too, and took a few pictures of him, but he walked right by Melanie without saying a word, and headed toward

164

the street. He said to someone standing nearby that if he never saw her again, it would be too soon. Fortunately, none of the members of the press taking pictures of her heard him.

'Melanie! . . . Melanie!! . . . Over here . . . here . . . How was it? . . . Were you scared? . . . Did you get hurt? . . . Come on, give us a smile . . . You look great!' Everett couldn't help thinking to himself wryly, at nineteen who didn't? They never even saw Ashley in the crowd. She stepped back and waited with Janet and Pam as she had a thousand times before. The roadies and band took off on their own, after saying goodbye to Melanie and her mother. The guys in the band told her they would see her at rehearsal the following week, and Pam said she'd call them to set it up. Melanie's next recording session was in less than a week.

It took them half an hour to press through the crowd of photographers and reporters. Everett helped run interference for them, and accompanied them to several taxis at the curb. For the first time in several years, there was no waiting limousine. But all Melanie wanted now was to get away from the press hounding her. Everett slammed the door to her cab, waved, and watched them pull away. He couldn't help thinking it had been one hell of a week. Within minutes of Melanie's departure, the rest of the press disappeared. Melanie had taken the first cab with Pam, and Ashley was in the second one with Janet. Jake had long since left on his own. And the roadies and musicians had fended for themselves.

Everett took a long look around him, relieved to be back in spite of himself. L.A. looked as though nothing had ever happened. It was hard to believe

165

that life was normal here. It seemed impossible to fathom that the world had nearly ended in San Francisco, and here it was all business as usual. It was a weird feeling to see it. Everett got in a cab then, and gave the driver the address of his favorite AA meeting. He wanted to go there before he even went home. And the meeting was terrific. In his share, he told them all about the earthquake, the meeting he had organized in the Presidio, and then before he could stop himself, he blurted out that he had fallen in love with a nun. Since cross-talk wasn't allowed at twelve-step meetings, no one made any comment. It was only afterward, when he got up and people came over to ask him about the earthquake, that one of the men he knew there made a comment.

'Talk about unavailable, man. How's that going to work?'

'It's not,' Everett said quietly.

'Will she leave the convent for you?'

'No, she won't. She loves being a nun.'

'So what happens to you then?'

Everett thought about it for a minute before he answered. 'I go on with my life. I keep coming to meetings. And I love her forever.'

'Does that work for you?' his fellow AA member asked with a look of concern.

'It'll have to,' Everett said. And with that, he walked quietly out of the meeting, hailed a cab, and went home.

Chapter 11

Melanie planned to spend a quiet weekend lying by the pool, and enjoying her house in the Hollywood Hills as she never had before. It was the perfect antidote to nine days of stress and trauma. And she knew she had been far less traumatized than many others. Compared to people who had been injured, lost loved ones or their homes, she had fared very well, and even felt useful during her time working at the field hospital at the camp. And she had met Tom.

Predictably, and much to her relief, Jake didn't call her once they got back. Ashley did several times, and spoke to her mother, but Melanie didn't take the calls. She told her mother she was done.

'Don't you think you're being a little hard on her?' her mother said on Saturday afternoon, while Melanie got her nails done at the side of the pool. It was a gorgeous day. Pam had booked a massage for her later that afternoon. But Melanie felt guilty now, being so lazy, and wished she were back at the field hospital with Maggie, and seeing Tom. She was hoping to see him soon. It was something to look forward to now that she was back in her familiar world in L.A. She missed them both.

'She slept with my boyfriend, Mom,' she reminded Janet about Ashley.

'Don't you think that was more his fault than hers?' Janet liked Ashley, and had promised her she would talk to Melanie when they got home, and everything would be fine. As far as Melanie was concerned, it was not so fine, in fact not at all.

'He didn't rape her. She's a consenting adult. If she cared anything about me, or our friendship, she shouldn't have done it. She didn't care. And now neither do I.'

'Don't be childish. You two have been friends since you were three.'

'That's my point,' Melanie said coldly. 'I think that was worth a little loyalty. I guess she didn't think so. She can have him. But I'm out. Over and out. That was a shitty thing to do. I guess friendship doesn't mean as much to her as it does to me. That's a good thing to know.' Melanie wasn't budging an inch.

'I told her I would talk to you and everything would be okay. You don't want to make me look stupid, do you? Or like a liar?' Her mother's wheedling and interference only made Melanie's position more firm. Integrity and loyalty were a big deal to her. Particularly given the life she led, where everyone wanted to use her, every chance they got. It went with the territory of her success and stardom. She expected it from outsiders, or even from Jake, who had turned out to be scum. But she didn't expect it, nor would she accept it, from her best friend. She was angry at her mother for even trying to convince her otherwise.

'I told you, Mom, I'm done. That's the way it's going to stay. I'll be polite to her when I see her, but that's all she's going to get out of me.'

'That's going to be very hard on her,' Janet said sympathetically, but she was wasting her breath. Melanie didn't like the fact that her mother was championing Ashley's cause.

'She should have thought of that before she

168

crawled into Jake's sleeping bag. And I assume she did that all week.' Janet didn't comment for a minute and then tried again.

'I think you should give it some thought.'

'I did. Let's talk about something else.'

Janet looked distressed and walked away. She had promised Ashley she'd call her, and now she didn't know what to say. She hated to tell her that Melanie said she'd never speak to her again, but that was essentially the case. As far as Melanie was concerned, their friendship was dead. Sixteen years of friendship down the tubes. And her mother knew that once Melanie felt betrayed and said it was over, that was it. She had seen her do it before, about other things. A boyfriend who had cheated on her before Jake, and a manager she'd trusted who had stolen money from her. Melanie could only be pushed so far and had healthy boundaries. Janet called Ashley that afternoon and told her to give Melanie a little time to cool off, she was still very hurt. Ashley said she understood and burst into tears. Janet promised to call her again soon. Ashley was like a second daughter to her, but she hadn't been like a sister to her best friend when she slept with Jake. And Ashley knew her well enough to realize that Melanie wasn't going to forgive her.

When the manicurist finished doing her nails, Melanie jumped in the pool. She did laps for a while, and then her trainer came at six. Pam had set that up for her too, and then had gone home. After the trainer left, Janet ordered Chinese takeout, and Melanie ate two soft-boiled eggs. She said she wasn't hungry and needed to lose a little weight. The food had been too good at the camp, and too fattening. It was time to get serious again before her concert in a few weeks. She thought of Tom and his sister coming to it, and smiled. She still hadn't told her mother about them yet. She figured there was time before he showed up. He was going to be in San Francisco for a while. There was no way of telling how soon he would come to L.A. And then, as though her mother had read her mind, she asked Melanie about him as she sat in the kitchen eating her soft-boiled eggs. Her mother was gorging on Chinese food, saying she had been starving for the past nine days, which was hardly the case. Every time Melanie had seen her, she'd been eating doughnuts, a Popsicle, or a bag of chips. She looked like she'd gained five pounds in the last week, if not ten.

'You're not getting all wound up over that boy you met at the camp, are you? The one with the engineering degree from Berkeley.' She was surprised that her mother remembered. She had been so dismissive of him that Melanie found it hard to believe that her mother remembered his education. But she certainly seemed to be well aware of who he was, right down to his degree.

'Don't worry about it, Mom,' Melanie said noncommittally. She thought it was none of her mother's business. She was turning twenty in two weeks. As far as she was concerned, she was old enough to pick her own men. She had learned a lot from the mistakes she'd made, getting together with Jake. Tom was a different kind of human being, and she loved being part of his life, which was so much more wholesome and healthy than Jake's.

'What does that mean?' her mother asked her,

looking worried.

'It means he's a nice guy, I'm a big girl, and yes, maybe I'll see him again. I hope so. If he calls.'

'He'll call. He looked crazy about you, and you're Melanie Free after all.'

'What difference does that make?' Melanie asked, feeling upset.

'It makes a big difference,' Janet reminded her, 'to everyone on the planet, except you. Don't you think you're carrying humility a little too far? Look, no man can separate out who you are as a person, and who you are as a star. It's not in their DNA. I'm sure this guy is as impressed by you as everyone else. Who wants to go out with a nothing, if you can be with a star? You'd be a real feather in his cap.'

'I don't think he's into feathers, or caps. He's into serious stuff, he's an engineer, and a good man.'

'How boring,' her mother said, with a look of disgust.

'It's not boring. He's smart,' Melanie persisted. 'I like smart guys.' She wasn't apologizing for it. It was a fact.

'Then it's a good thing you got rid of Jake. He drove me nuts for the past nine days. All he did was whine.'

'I thought you liked him.' Melanie looked surprised.

'I thought so too,' Janet said. 'I was sick to death of him by the time we left. Some people are not the right ones to go through a crisis with. He's one of them. All he talks about is himself.'

'Apparently, Ashley is one of these people too, that you wouldn't want to go through a crisis with.

171

Especially if she sleeps with your guy. She can have him now. He's a totally narcissistic pain in the ass.'

'You could be right. Just don't throw Ashley away in the deal.' Melanie didn't comment. She already had.

Melanie went to her room early then. It was all done in pink and white satin, by her mother's design, with a pink and white fox throw on the bed. It looked like the bedroom of a Las Vegas showgirl, which was precisely what her mother was at heart, to this day. She had told the decorator exactly what she wanted in Melanie's room, right down to a pink fur teddy bear. All of Melanie's requests for stark simplicity had been ignored. This was what her mother said she had to have. But at least it was comfortable, Melanie acknowledged to herself, as she lay down on the bed. It felt heavenly to be so pampered again. She felt a little guilty for it, particularly when she thought of the people in San Francisco in the shelter, and the fact that they would be there for months, for the most part, while she was at home on her satin-and-fur-covered bed. Somehow, it felt wrong, even if in a way it felt right. But not right enough. If nothing else, it wasn't her style, it was her mother's. That was becoming clearer to Melanie every day.

Melanie lay on her bed and watched TV until late that night. She watched an old movie, the news, and finally MTV. In spite of herself and the interesting experience she'd had, it felt great to be home.

*   *   *

172

On Saturday afternoon, as Melanie and her group winged their way to L.A., Seth Sloane was sitting in his living room, staring into space. It had been nine days since the earthquake, and they were still isolated and cut off. Seth was no longer sure if it was a blessing or a curse. He could get no news from New York. Nothing. Zero. Zip.

As a result, it was an agonizingly stressful weekend. In desperation, he finally tried to take his mind off his troubles and play with his kids. Sarah hadn't spoken to him in days. He hardly saw her, and at night as soon as she put the children to bed, she disappeared into the guest room. He hadn't commented on it to her, he didn't dare.

On Monday morning, eleven days after the earthquake, Seth was sitting at the kitchen table, drinking a cup of coffee, when the BlackBerry he had set on the table next to him suddenly came to life. It was the first chance he'd had to communicate with the outside world, and he grabbed it. He text-messaged Sully immediately and asked him what had happened. The answer came back two minutes later.

Sully's answer was succinct. 'The SEC is all over me. You're next. They know. They got the records from the bank. Good luck.' Shit, Seth whispered under his breath, and text-messaged him again.

'Did they arrest you?' he inquired of Sully.

'Not yet. Grand jury next week. They got us, bro. We're fucked.' It was precisely the confirmation he had been fearing for over a week. But even knowing what would probably happen, Seth felt his stomach sink when he read the words. 'We're fucked' was an understatement, particularly if they had the records from Sully's bank. Seth's

173

was still closed, but wouldn't be for much longer.

It opened the following day, and Seth's lawyer had told him to do nothing. Seth had literally walked to his house to talk to him, since he couldn't reach him by phone. Anything Seth did now could incriminate him further, especially since Sully was under investigation. And having lost part of his house in the earthquake, Seth's lawyer couldn't meet with him till Friday. As it turned out, the FBI beat him to it. On Friday morning, two weeks after the earthquake, two special agents from the FBI showed up at the house. Sarah let them in. They asked to see Seth. She showed them into the living room and went to get Seth. He'd been sitting in his office upstairs, where he had been holed up in terror for two weeks. It was starting to unravel, and there was no telling where it would go.

The FBI special agents spent two hours with Seth, questioning him about Sully in New York. He refused to answer any questions about himself without a lawyer present and said as little as possible about Sully. They had threatened to arrest him on the spot for obstruction of justice if he refused to respond to any questions about his friend. Seth looked gray when they left. But at least he hadn't been arrested. He was sure that would come soon.

'What did they say?' Sarah asked him nervously after they left.

'They wanted to know about Sully. I didn't say much, as little as I could.'

'What did they say about you?' Sarah asked, looking anxious.

'I told them I wouldn't discuss it without my

174

lawyer present, and they said they'd come back. You can be damn sure they will.'

'What do we do now?' Seth was relieved to hear her say 'we.' He wasn't sure if it was just out of habit, or showed her state of mind. He didn't dare ask. She hadn't spoken to him all week. And he didn't want to lose that again now.

'Henry Jacobs is coming here this afternoon.' They finally had their phones back. It had taken two weeks. But he was terrified to talk to anyone. He had had one cryptic phone call with Sully, and that was all. If the FBI were investigating him, he knew they might be tapping his phones, and he didn't want to make things any worse than they already were.

When he came, the lawyer stayed with Seth in his office for nearly four hours. They covered the waterfront. Seth told him everything, and when it was over, his attorney wasn't encouraging. He said as soon as they got his records from the bank, he would probably be called before the grand jury and indicted. And arrested shortly thereafter. He was almost sure that he would have to stand trial. He didn't know what else would happen, but the preliminary visit from the FBI agents was not a good sign.

It was a nightmarish weekend for Seth and Sarah. The Financial District was still closed, without electricity or water, so Seth still couldn't go downtown. He just sat at home, waiting for the other shoe to drop. It did on Monday morning. The head of the local FBI bureau called Seth on his BlackBerry. He said their main offices were closed, and he asked for Seth and his attorney to meet with them at Seth's home the following

175

afternoon. He reminded him not to leave town, and informed him that he was under investigation, and that the FBI had been notified by the SEC. He told Seth that Sully was appearing in front of the grand jury in New York that week, which Seth already knew.

He found Sarah in the kitchen feeding Ollie. The baby had applesauce all over his face, and Sarah had been talking to him and Molly, with *Sesame Street* on in the background. They had gotten their electricity back over the weekend, which much of the city still hadn't. But it was coming back on here and there. They were among the lucky few, probably because of the neighborhood they were in. The mayor lived a few blocks away, which never hurt. The electricity was being turned on by grid. They were in the first grid, which was fortunate for them. And a few stores were open again, mostly supermarkets, food chains, and banks.

Sarah looked terrified when Seth told her about the FBI meeting scheduled for the next day. The only good news for her was that as his wife, she could refuse to testify against him. But she didn't know anything about it anyway. He had never said anything to her about his illegal transactions at the hedge fund. It had come as a complete shock to her.

'What are you going to do?' she asked in a choked voice.

'Meet them with Henry tomorrow. I have no choice. If I refuse, it looks worse, and they can get a court order to force me. Henry is coming over this afternoon to prepare me.' He had called his lawyer the minute he hung up the call from the

FBI and insisted he come over immediately.

Henry Jacobs arrived looking somber and official that afternoon. Sarah opened the door for him, and led him to the upstairs den where Seth was waiting, doodling nervously at his desk, and staring bleakly out the window from time to time. He had been lost in thought all day, and after his brief conversation with Sarah earlier, Seth had closed the door to the room. She knocked softly and let Henry in.

Seth stood up to greet him, waved him to a chair, and sighed as he sat down. 'Thanks for coming, Henry. I hope you have a magic wand in your briefcase. It's going to take a magician to get me out of this mess.' He ran a hand through his hair as the somber-looking lawyer sat down across from him.

'That's possible,' Henry said noncommittally.

Henry was in his early fifties and had handled similar cases before. Seth had consulted him several times, in reverse actually, wanting detailed information about how he could cover his shady dealings before they occurred. It had never dawned on his attorney that that was what he had in mind. It had all seemed very theoretical, and Henry had assumed that the questions had been to assure that Seth didn't do anything wrong. He had admired Seth for being so diligent and so cautious, and only now did he realize what was going on. He passed no judgment on it, but there was no question, Seth was in a serious bind, with potentially catastrophic results.

'I take it you've done this before,' Henry commented as they went over it again. Seth's dealings sounded too practiced, too thorough, and too detailed for this to have been the first time. Seth nodded. Henry was astute, and good at what he did. 'How often?'

'Four times.'

'Has anyone else been involved?'

'No. Only the same friend in New York. We've been friends since high school. I trust him totally. I guess that's not the point now.' Seth smiled grimly, and then threw a pencil across his desk. 'If the fucking earthquake hadn't happened, we'd have been fine this time too. Who would have thought? We were running a little tight on time, but it was just rotten luck that his investors' auditors were coming in so quickly after mine. It would have worked if the earthquake hadn't shut everything down.' The money had sat there frozen in the banks, which had allowed their scheme to be discovered.

For two full weeks, Seth's hands had been tied, with Sully's investors' money in his accounts. The point he was missing was not the misfortune of the earthquake to keep them from covering up their crime, but the fact that they had transferred the funds at all. It didn't get much more illegal than that, other than emptying the accounts and absconding with the money. They had lied to two sets of investors, created an illusion of enormous funds in their accounts, and been discovered. Henry wasn't shocked—defending people like Seth was his business—but nor was he sympathetic about the problem the earthquake had caused. Seth could see it in his eyes. 'What are we looking at here?' Seth asked bluntly. There was terror stamped all over his face and leaping from his eyes, like a rat in a cage.

He knew he wouldn't like the answer, but Seth wanted to know. He was running scared. The grand jury was meeting in New York that week to indict Sully, by special request of the federal prosecutor. Seth knew he wouldn't be far behind, given what he'd heard from the FBI.

'Realistically, the evidence is fairly solidly against you, Seth,' Henry said quietly. There was no way to dress it up for him. 'They have hard evidence against you, in your accounts at the bank.' Henry had told him not to touch the money the moment he'd called. He couldn't have anyway, there was nowhere to go with it. Sully's ac-counts were already frozen in New York. And he couldn't just take out sixty million dollars in cash and hide it in a suitcase under his bed. For now at least, the money was just sitting there. 'The FBI is acting for the SEC in an investigative capacity here. As soon as they report their findings after they talk to you, I think it's safe to assume they'll have a grand jury hearing here. They may not even ask you to be present, if the evidence is strong enough against you. If the grand jury moves for an indictment, they'll bring charges against you pretty quickly, probably arrest you, and move toward prosecution. After that, it's up to me. But there's only so much we can do. It may not even make sense to push this to trial. If the evidence is rock solid, you may do better making a deal with them, and trying to plea-bargain. If you plead guilty, we may be able to give them enough information to nail down their case against your friend in New York. If that appeals to the SEC, and they need us, you may do less time. But I don't want to mislead you. If what you say is true, and they can prove it, I think you'll go to prison, Seth. It's going to be tough, worse than tough, to get you out of this. You left a neon-lit trail behind you. We're not talking breadcrumbs here. This is big money. A sixty-million-dollar fraud is no small thing to the government. They're not going to back down on this.' He thought of something else then. 'Are your taxes in order?' That would be a whole other can of worms, and Sarah had asked Seth the same question. If he had committed tax fraud too, he was going to be away for a very, very long time.

'Totally,' Seth said, looking offended. 'I never cheat on my taxes.'

Only his investors, and Sully's. Honor among thieves, Henry thought. 'That's good news,' Henry said drily. Seth interrupted him quickly. 'What am I looking at here, Henry? How much time could I do, worst case, if everything goes wrong?'

'Worst case?' Henry said, musing, taking all the elements into consideration, or as much as he knew for now. 'It's hard to say. The law and the SEC take a dim view of defrauding investors . . . I don't know. Without any kind of modification or plea-bargaining, twenty-five years, maybe thirty. But that's not going to happen, Seth,' he reassured him. 'We can balance out some of this with other factors. Worst case, maybe five to ten. If we're lucky, two to five. I think that would be best case in this instance. I hope we could get them down to something like that.'

'In a federal penitentiary? You don't suppose they'd agree to some kind of electronic incarceration at home? I could live with that a lot more easily than going to prison,' he said, sounding frightened. 'I have a wife and kids.'

Henry didn't tell him that he should have thought of that before, but it crossed his mind. Seth was thirty-seven years old, and out of sheer greed and lack of integrity, he had destroyed their lives as well as his own. This was not going to be pretty, and he didn't want to give Seth the false impression that he could save him from paying society back for what he'd done. The feds who would be involved in this didn't kid around. They hated guys like Seth who were consumed with greed and their own egos, and thought they were above the law. The governing laws on hedge funds, and institutions like them, were made to protect investors from men like him. The laws on hedge funds still had some loopholes in them, but not big enough for an offense like this. And Henry's job was to protect Seth, for better or worse. In this case, possibly worse. There was no denying it was a tough case, at best.

'I don't think keeping you at home with a bracelet is realistic,' Henry said candidly. He wasn't going to lie to him. He didn't want to frighten him unduly, but he had to tell him honestly what his chances were, as best he could assess them. 'Maybe I can get you early parole. But not in the beginning. Seth, I think you have to face the fact that you're going to have to do some time. Hopefully, not too long. But given the amount that you and Sully passed around, this is going to be a big ticket, unless we can come up with something that appeals to them to make a deal. And even then, you won't get off scot free.' It was roughly what Seth had said to Sarah the morning after the earthquake. The minute it hit and their phones went down, he knew then that he was screwed.

181

And so did she. Henry was just spelling it out for him more clearly. They went over the details again then, and Seth was truthful with him. He had to be. He needed his help, and Henry promised to be at the FBI meeting with him the following afternoon. The grand jury would be meeting in New York about Sully at exactly the same time. It was six o'clock when Henry left, and Seth came out of his office, looking drained.

He went downstairs to find Sarah in the kitchen, feeding their children. Parmani was doing laundry downstairs. Sarah looked worried as Seth walked in.

'What did he say?' Like Seth, she was hoping for a miracle. It was going to take one to save him. Seth sat down heavily in a kitchen chair, and looked miserably at his children, and then back at her. Molly was trying to show him something, and he ignored her. He had too much on his mind.

'About what I thought.' He decided to tell her the worst case first. 'He said I could get up to thirty years in prison. If I'm lucky, and they want to make a deal with me, maybe two to five. I'd have to sell Sully out to do that, and I don't really want to.' He sighed then, and showed her yet another side of who he was. 'But I may have to. My ass is on the line.'

'So is his.' She had never liked Sully. She thought he was sleazy, and he had always been condescending to her. She'd been right. He was a bad guy. But so was Seth. And he was willing to sell out his friend, which somehow made it seem even worse. 'What if he sells you out first?' Seth hadn't thought of that. Sully was further into the process than he was. It was entirely possible that at that very moment Sully was singing to the SEC and FBI. He wouldn't put it past him. And Seth was willing to do it himself. He had already made up his mind, after everything his attorney had said. He had no intention of doing thirty years, and was willing to do everything possible now to save his hide. Even if it meant burying his friend. Sarah could see it on his face, and it made her feel sick, not that he would sell out Sully, who deserved it in her opinion, but that nothing was sacred to him, neither his investors, nor his partner in crime, nor even his wife and kids. It told her where she stood and who he was.

'What about you? Where are you in all this?' Seth asked her, looking worried, after Parmani took the children upstairs for a bath. The conversation had been over Molly's head anyway, and Ollie was a baby.

'I don't know,' Sarah said thoughtfully. Henry had told him that it would be important for her to attend the hearings and the trial. Whatever look of respectability they could give him was crucial to them now.

'I'm going to need you through the trial,' he said honestly, 'and even more after that. I could be gone for a long time.' Tears filled her eyes as he said it, and she got up to put the baby's dishes in the sink. She hadn't wanted her children to see her cry, or even him. But Seth followed her to where she stood. 'Don't leave me now, Sarrie. I love you. You're my wife. You can't bail on me now.' He was begging her.

'Why didn't you think of that before?' she said in a whisper as tears rolled down her cheeks, as she stood in the beautiful kitchen, in the house she loved so much. Her problem with their current state was that this wasn't about saving their house or their lifestyle, but about being married to a man who was so corrupt and so dishonest that he had destroyed their life and their future, and said he needed her now. What about what she needed from him? And their children? What if he was gone for thirty years? What would happen to all of them? What life would she and the children have?

'I was building something for us,' Seth explained to her weakly, standing near her at the sink. 'I was doing it for you, Sarah, for them.' He waved vaguely toward their children upstairs. 'I guess I tried to do it too quickly, and it all blew up in my face.' He hung his head and looked ashamed. But she could see that he was manipulating her now, and just as he was willing to betray his friend, this was more of the same. It was only about him. The rest of them could burn.

'You tried to do it dishonestly. That's different,' Sarah reminded him. 'This wasn't about building something for us. This was about you, being a big shot and a big winner, whatever it took, at everyone else's expense, even the kids'. If you go to prison for thirty years, they'll never even know you. They'll see you once in a while for visits. For chrissake, you might as well be dead,' she said, finally angry, instead of just heartbroken and afraid.

'Thanks a lot,' Seth said, with something ugly coming to light in his eyes. 'Don't count on it. I'm going to spend every penny I have paying for the best attorneys I can get, and appeal it forever if I have to.' But they both knew that sooner or later the price of his crimes would have to be paid. This last time would lead the way to all the other times he and Sully had done the same thing. They were going down, together, and hard, and Sarah didn't want him taking her and their children with him, whatever it took. 'Whatever happened to "for better or worse"?'

'I don't think that was meant to include securities fraud and thirty years in prison,' Sarah said, her voice shaking.

'It was meant to include standing by your husband when he's up to his neck in shit. I tried to build a life for us, Sarah. A good one. A big life. I didn't hear you complaining about the "better" when I bought this house and let you fill it with art and antiques, and bought you a shitload of jewelry, expensive clothes, a house in Tahoe, and a plane. I didn't hear you telling me it was too much.' She couldn't believe what he was saying to her now. Just listening to him made her feel sicker.

'I told you it was too expensive and I was worried,' she reminded him. 'You did it all so fast.' But now they both knew how. He had done it with ill-begotten gains, conning investors into believing he had more than he did so they would give him more money for risky investments. And for all she knew, he had skimmed some of it off the top. Thinking about it now, she realized he probably had. He had stopped at nothing to rise to the top, and now he was going to take a fatal fall to the bottom. Maybe even fatal for her, after he destroyed their life.

'I didn't see you giving any of it back, or trying to stop me,' he reproached her, and she looked him in the eye.

'Could I have stopped you? I don't think so,

185

Seth. I think you were driven to do what you did by your own greed and ambition, whatever it took. You crossed all the lines here, and now we all have to pay the price.'

'I'm going to be the one sitting in prison, Sarah, not you.'

'What do you expect when you do shit like this? You're not a hero, Seth, you're a con. That's all you are.' She was crying again, and he stormed out of the room and slammed the door. He didn't want to hear that from her. He wanted to know that she was going to stick by him whatever happened. It was a lot to ask, but he felt he deserved it.

It was a long, agonizing night for both of them. He stayed locked in his office till four A.M., and she stayed in the guest room. He finally lay down on their bed at five o'clock that morning, and slept till noon. He got up in time to dress for the meeting with his attorney and the FBI. Sarah had already taken the children to the park. She still didn't have a car after losing both of theirs in the earthquake, but Parmani had her ancient Honda, which they were using to do errands. Sarah had been too upset to even rent a car, and Seth wasn't going anywhere so he hadn't rented one either. He was locked up in their house, too terrified about his future to move or go out.

They were on the way back from the park when Sarah had an idea, and asked Parmani if she could borrow her car to do an errand. She told her to take the children home for their naps. The sweet-natured Nepalese woman said that Sarah was welcome to it. She knew that something was wrong, and feared that something bad was happening to them, but she had no idea what, and

186

would never have asked. She thought maybe Seth was having an affair, or they had a problem in their marriage. It would have been inconceivable to her that Seth was about to be indicted and might go to prison, or even that they could lose their house. As far as she knew, they were young, rich, and solid, which was exactly what Sarah had thought two and a half weeks before. Now she knew they were anything but. Young maybe, but rich and solid had gone out the door with an earthquake of their own. She realized now that he would have gotten caught sooner or later. You couldn't do what he had done, and not have it come out at some point. It had been inevitable, she just hadn't known.

When Parmani lent her the car, Sarah drove straight down the hill north on Divisadero. She turned left on Marina Boulevard, and drove into the Presidio past Crissy Field. She had tried to call Maggie on her cell phone, but it was turned off. She didn't even know if Maggie was still at the field hospital there, but she needed to talk to someone, and couldn't think of who else. There was no way she could tell her parents about the disaster Seth had caused. Her mother would have been hysterical, her father furious at Seth. And if things got as bad as they feared they would, her parents would read about it soon enough. She knew she'd have to tell them before it made the news, but not yet. Right now she just needed a sane, sensible person to talk to, to pour out her heart and share her woes. She knew instinctively that Sister Maggie was the right one.

Sarah got out of the small battered Honda outside the field hospital, and walked inside. She was about to ask if Sister Mary Magdalen was still working there, when she saw her hurrying toward the back of the room, carrying a stack of surgical linens and towels that was almost taller than she was. Sarah walked back toward her, and as soon as she saw her, Maggie looked up in surprise.

'How nice to see you, Sarah. What brings you here? Are you sick?' Emergency rooms in all of the city's hospitals were fully operative again, although the field hospital in the Presidio was still in use. But it wasn't quite as busy as it had been even a few days before.

'No . . . I'm okay . . . I . . . I'm sorry . . . do you have time to talk?' Maggie saw the look in her eyes and immediately set the clean linens down on an empty bed.

'Let's go. Why don't we go sit on the beach for a few minutes? It'll do us both good. I've been here since six o'clock this morning.'

'Thank you,' Sarah said quietly, and followed her outside. They walked down the road to the path to the beach, making casual conversation. Maggie asked her how Ollie's ears were, and Sarah told her they were fine. And then finally, they reached the beach, and both sat down on the sand. They were both wearing jeans, and the bay looked shimmering and flat. It was another lovely day. It was the prettiest May Sarah could remember, although to her right now, the world seemed very dark. Particularly hers and Seth's.

'What's happening?' Maggie asked gently, watching the younger woman's face. She looked deeply troubled, and there was bottomless agony in her eyes. Maggie suspected a problem in her marriage. Sarah had hinted at something before when she brought the baby in with his earache. But

188

whatever it was, Maggie could see it had gotten considerably worse. She looked distraught.

'I don't even know where to start.' Maggie waited, while Sarah found the words. Before she did, tears filled her eyes and started running down her cheeks. She made no move to brush them away, as the gentle nun sat beside her and silently prayed. She prayed for the burdens Sarah was carrying to be lifted from her heart. 'It's Seth . . . ,' she finally started, and Maggie wasn't surprised. 'Something terrible has happened . . . no . . . he did something terrible . . . something very wrong . . . and he got caught.' Maggie couldn't even begin to imagine what it was, and wondered if he'd had an affair that Sarah had just learned about, or perhaps suspected before.

'Did he tell you about it himself?' Maggie asked gently.

'Yes, he did. The night of the earthquake, when we got home, and the next morning.' She searched Maggie's eyes before she told her the whole story, but she knew she could trust her. Maggie kept everyone's secrets to herself, and shared them only with God, when she prayed. 'He did something illegal . . . he transferred funds he shouldn't have to his hedge fund. He was going to move them out again, but with the earthquake, all the banks were closed, so the money was sitting there. He knew it would be discovered before the banks opened again.' Maggie was silent but taken aback. This was obviously a much bigger problem than she had thought.

'And was it discovered?'

'Yes.' Sarah nodded miserably. 'It was. In New York. On the Monday after the earthquake. It was

189

reported to the SEC. And they contacted the FBI here. There's an investigation, and there will probably be a grand jury indictment and a trial.' She cut to the chase. 'If he's convicted, he could go to prison for thirty years. Maybe less, but that would be worst case. And now he's talking about selling out the friend who helped him do it. He's already under investigation in New York.' She began crying harder then, and reached out and took the nun's hand in her own. 'Maggie . . . I don't even know who he is. He's not the man I thought he was. He's a con man and a fraud. How could he do this to us?'

'Did you suspect any of it?' Maggie looked worried for her. This was indeed an awful story.

'Never. Nothing. I thought he was completely honest, and just incredibly smart and successful. I thought we spent too much money, and he kept saying we had it to spend. Now I don't even know if it was really our money or not. God only knows what else he did. Or what's going to happen now. We'll probably lose our house . . . but even worse, I've already lost him. He's already a condemned man. He'll never be able to get out of this. And he wants me to stand by him and stay with him. He says that's what I signed on for, "for better or worse" . . . and what's going to happen to me and the kids if he goes to prison?' Maggie knew that she was young, and whatever happened, she could start her life again. But there was no question, this was a terrible way for things to end with Seth, if they did. It sounded terrifying even to her, with the little she knew.

'Do you want to stand by him, Sarah?'

'I don't know. I don't know what I want or what

190

I think. I love him, but now I'm not even sure who I love, or who I've been married to for four years, or knew for two years before that. He really is a fraud. And what if I can't forgive him for what he's done?'

'That's another story,' Maggie said wisely. 'You can forgive him, but decide not to stay with him. You have a right to decide who and what and how much hardship you want in your life. Forgiveness is an entirely other story, and I'm sure in time you will. It's probably too soon for you to make any major decisions. You need to sit with it for a while and see how you feel. You may decide to stay with him in the end, and stand by him, or maybe not. You don't have to make that decision right now.'

'He says I do,' Sarah said, looking grief-stricken and confused.

'That's not for him to say. It's up to you. He's asking an awful lot of you, after what he did. Have the authorities come to see him yet?'

'The FBI is with him right now. I don't know what will happen next.'

'You have to wait and see.'

'I'm not sure what I owe him, or what I owe my kids and myself. I don't want to go down the tubes with him, or be married to a man who's in prison for twenty or thirty years, or even five. I don't know if I could do it. I could end up hating him for this.'

'I hope not, Sarah, whatever you decide. You don't need to hate him, that would only poison you. He has a right to your compassion and your forgiveness, but not to ruin your life or your children's.'

'Do I owe this to him, as his wife?' Sarah's eyes

were infinite pits of pain, confusion, and guilt, and Maggie felt deeply sorry for her, for them both in fact. They were in an awful mess, and whatever he'd done, she suspected that Seth was in no better shape than his wife, and she was right.

'You owe him your understanding, pity, and compassion, not your life, Sarah. You can't give him that, whatever you do. But the decision to stand by him or not is entirely yours, whatever he says. If it's better for you, and your children, you have a right to walk away. The only thing you owe him now is forgiveness. The rest is up to you. And forgiveness brings with it a state of amazing grace. That alone will bless you both in the end.' Maggie was trying to give her practical advice, colored by her own powerful beliefs, which were entirely based on mercy, forgiveness, and love. The very spirit of the risen Christ.

'I've never been in a situation like this,' Maggie admitted honestly. 'I don't want to give you bad advice. I just want to tell you what I think. What you do is up to you. But it may be too soon for you to decide. If you love him, that's already a lot. But how that love manifests in the end, and how you express it, will be your choice. It may be more loving for you and your children in the end to let him go. He has to pay the price for his own mistakes, and it sounds like they were big ones. You don't. But to some degree, you will anyway. This won't be easy for you either, whatever you decide to do.'

'It already isn't. Seth says we'll probably lose the house. They could seize it. Or he may have to sell it to pay his lawyers.'

'Where would you go?' Maggie asked with a

look of concern. It was obvious that Sarah felt lost, which was why she had come to see her. 'Do you have family here?' Sarah shook her head.

'My parents moved to Bermuda. I can't stay with them, that's too far away. I don't want to take the kids away from Seth. And I don't want to say anything to my parents yet. I guess if we lose the house, I could get a little apartment, and I'd have to get a job. I haven't worked since we got married, because I wanted to stay home with the kids, and it's been great. But I don't think I'll have much choice. I can find a job if I have to. I have an MBA. That's how Seth and I met, at Stanford Business School.' Maggie smiled at her, and thought that her husband had certainly misused his advanced degree in business. But at least Sarah had the education to get a good job and support herself and her children if need be. That wasn't the point. The big question mark was their marriage, and Seth's future if he was prosecuted, which sounded like a sure thing. As did an eventual conviction, if what Sarah said was true, and it seemed that way.

'I think you need to give this some time, if you're willing to, and see how it shakes out. There's no question that Seth has made a shattering mistake here. Only you know if you can forgive him, and want to stay with him. Pray about it, Sarah,' she urged her. 'The answers will come as things unfold. It will come clear to you, maybe sooner than you think.' Or sooner even than she wanted. Maggie reminded herself that often when she prayed for clarity in a situation, the answers were blunter and more obvious than she wanted, particularly if she didn't like them. But she didn't

193

say that to Sarah.

'He says he'll need me at the trial,' Sarah said grimly. 'I'll be there for him. I feel like I owe him that. But it's going to be so awful. He's going to look like a total criminal in the press,' which in fact he was, they both knew. 'This is so humiliating.'

'Don't let pride make this decision for you, Sarah,' Maggie warned her. 'Make it with love. If you do, it will bless everyone. That's really what you want here. The right answer, the right decision, the right future for you and your children, whether or not that includes Seth. He'll always have his children, he's their father, wherever he winds up in all this. The question is if he'll have you. And most important, if you want him.'

'I don't know. I don't know who "him" is. I feel like I was in love with an illusion for the last six years. I have no idea who he really is. He's the last man on the planet I would have expected to commit fraud.'

'You never know,' Maggie said as they looked out at the bay. 'People do strange things. Even people we think we know and love. I'm going to pray for you,' she reassured her. 'And you pray too, if you can. Give it to God. Let Him try to help you figure it out.' Sarah nodded, and turned to her with a small smile.

'Thank you. I knew it would help if I talked to you. I don't know what I'm doing yet, but I feel better. I was freaking out when I came to see you.'

'Come and see me anytime, or call me. I'll be here for a while.' There was still a lot for her to do for all the people who had been displaced in the earthquake and would be living in the Presidio for

194

many months. It was a fertile field of activity for her, and fit well with her mission as a nun. She brought love, peace, and comfort to all she touched. 'Be merciful' were her final words of advice to Sarah. 'Mercy is an important thing in life. That doesn't mean you have to stay with him, or give up your own life for him. But you do have to be merciful and kind to him and yourself, once you make your decision, whatever it is in the end. Love doesn't mean you have to stay with him, it only means you have to be compassionate. That's where the grace comes in. You'll know it when you're there.'

'Thank you,' Sarah said as she hugged her, as they stood outside the field hospital again. 'I'll stay in touch.'

'I'll be praying for you,' Maggie reassured her, and waved with a loving smile as Sarah drove away. The time they had spent together had been just what Sarah needed.

She drove back down Marina Boulevard in Parmani's car, and south up the hill on Divisadero. She pulled up just as the two FBI agents left, and she was grateful not to have been there. She waited until they drove away, and then went in. Henry was summing things up with Seth. She waited until he had left too, and then walked into Seth's office.

'Where were you?' he asked, looking utterly exhausted.

'I needed to get some air. How was it?'

'Pretty bad,' he said solemnly. 'They didn't pull any punches. They're asking for an indictment next week. This is going to be tough, Sarah. It would have been nice if you'd stuck around today.' His eyes were full of reproach. She had never seen him this needy. She remembered what Maggie had said, and tried to feel compassion for him. Whatever he had done to her indirectly, he was in a hell of a mess, and she felt sorry for him, more so than she had before she went to see Maggie that day.

'Did the FBI want to see me?' she asked, looking worried.

'No. You have nothing to do with this. I told them you knew nothing about it. You don't work for me. And they can't force you to testify against me anyway, you're my wife.' Sarah looked reassured by what he said. 'I just wanted you here for me.'

'I'm here, Seth.' For now at least. It was the best she could do.

'Thank you,' he said quietly, and then she left the room, and went upstairs to see her children. He didn't say anything more to her, and as soon as she walked out, he put his face in his hands and dissolved in tears.

Chapter 12

For the next ten days, Seth's life continued to unravel. His case was presented to the grand jury by the federal prosecutor, and they granted the indictment. Two days later federal agents came to arrest him. He was informed of his rights, taken to the federal courthouse, photographed, formally charged, and booked. He spent the night in jail, until bail was set by a judge the next morning.

The funds he had fraudulently deposited in the bank were returned to New York, by a court order, to cover Sully's investors. So Sully's investors had suffered no loss, but Seth's had been shown books that looked sixty million dollars fatter than they really were. And they had invested in his hedge fund accordingly, as a result of Seth's fraudulent representations to them. The nature and severity of Seth's crime caused the judge to set his bail at ten million dollars. He had to pay one million to the bail bondsman to be released on bail. That wiped out all the cash they had on hand. He was assessed as not being a flight risk, and he was eligible for bail because there had been no loss of life or physical violence involved. What he had done had been far subtler than that. They had no choice except to put their house up as bail. It was worth about fifteen million, and the night he got out of jail, he told Sarah they had to sell the house. The bail bondsman could keep ten million of it as collateral, and the other five he needed to pay his attorneys. Henry had already told him that their fee would probably be in the vicinity of three million dollars through trial. It was a complicated case. He told Sarah they had to sell the house in Tahoe too. They needed to sell as much as they could. The only good news was that they owned the house on Divisadero free and clear. There was a mortgage on Tahoe that was going to eat into their profit, but they could use the difference for his defense and related expenses.

'I'll sell my jewelry too,' she said, looking wooden. She didn't care about the jewelry, but was crushed to lose their home.

'We can rent an apartment.' He had already

given up his plane. It wasn't fully paid for yet, and he had taken a loss. His hedge fund was closed. There would be no income coming in, but a lot of money going out to defend him. His sixty-million-dollar caper was liable to cost them everything they had. In addition to whatever prison sentence they gave him, if he was convicted, there would be staggering fines. And then lawsuits from his investors would wipe him out. They were becoming paupers overnight.

'I'll get my own apartment,' Sarah said quietly. She had made the decision the night before, when he was in jail. And Maggie had been right. She didn't know what else she was going to do, but it had become clear to Sarah that she didn't want to live with him right now. They might get back together later, but for now, she wanted to get an apartment for her and the children, and she was going to get a job.

'You're moving out?' Seth looked stunned. 'How will that look to the FBI?' It was all he cared about right now.

'We're both moving out, as it so happens. And it'll look like you made a hell of a mistake, I'm shaken up, and we're taking a break.' All of which was true. She wasn't filing for divorce, she just wanted space. She couldn't stand being part of the process of the unraveling of their lives, because he had chosen to be a con instead of an honest man. She had been praying a lot since seeing Maggie, and she felt comfortable about what she was doing. Sad, but it felt right, just as Maggie had said it would, she knew. One step at a time.

Sarah called the real estate brokers the next day, and put the house on the market. She called the bail bondsman to tell him what they were doing, so he didn't think there was something sneaky going on. He had the deed to the house anyway. He explained to her that he had a right to approve the sale, hang on to his ten million dollars, and anything over and above that was theirs. He thanked her for the call, and didn't say it, but he felt sorry for her. He thought her husband was a jerk. Even when he'd met with him in jail, Seth was pompous and full of himself. The bail bondsman had seen others like him before. They were always run by their egos, and wound up screwing over their families and wives. He wished her good luck with the sale.

After that, she spent her days calling people she knew in the city and Silicon Valley, looking for a job. She wrote up a résumé, which gave the details of her MBA program at Stanford, and her work on Wall Street in an investment banking firm. She was willing to take anything—trader, analyst. She was willing to get a stockbroker's license, or work in a bank. She had the credentials and the brains, all she needed was the job. And meanwhile, out of both curiosity and real interest, potential buyers were crawling all over their house.

Seth got himself a penthouse in what was referred to as the Heartbreak Hotel on Broadway. It was a modern apartment building, full of small, expensive furnished apartments, heavily populated by men who had just broken up with their wives. Sarah got a small cozy flat in a Victorian on Clay Street. It had two bedrooms, one for her, and one for the children. It had parking space for one car, and a tiny garden. Rents had plummeted since the earthquake, and she got it at a good price, and it

199

would be hers on the first of June.

She went to see Maggie in the Presidio to tell her what she was doing. Maggie was sorry for her, but impressed that she was moving forward and making cautious, wise decisions. Seth went out and bought a new Porsche to replace the Ferrari he'd lost, on some sort of deal with no money down, which infuriated his lawyer. He told him this was a time to be humble and not showy. He had hurt a lot of people with the deals he'd made, and the judge was not going to be favorably impressed by his flamboyance. Sarah bought a used Volvo station wagon to replace her crushed Mercedes. Her jewelry had gone to Los Angeles to sell. She still had said nothing to her parents, who wouldn't have been able to help her anyway, but would at least have been supportive. And so far, by some miracle, Seth's indictment hadn't appeared in the press, nor had Sully's, but she knew it wouldn't be long. And then the shit would hit the fan, even more than it already had.

*   *   *

Everett spent days after the earthquake editing pictures. He had turned in the most relevant ones to *Scoop* magazine, and they had printed a whole section on the San Francisco earthquake. And predictably, they had put one of Melanie in camouflage pants on the cover. They had printed only one of Maggie, and identified her as a nun volunteering in a field hospital in San Francisco after the quake.

He sold other photographs to *USA Today,* the AP, one to *The New York Times,* and several to

Time and *Newsweek*. *Scoop* had allowed him to do that, as they had far more than they could use, and they didn't want to overdo it on the earthquake. They liked the celebrity aspect a lot better, and had run six pages on Melanie, and only three on the rest. Everett had written the article himself, with high praise for residents and the city. He had a copy of the magazine he wanted to send to Maggie. But more than that, he had dozens of absolutely spectacular photographs of her. She looked luminous in shots of her ministering to injured people. There was one of her holding a crying child, and comforting an old man with a gash on his head in the dim light . . . several of her laughing with her bright blue eyes when she'd just been talking to him . . . and one he had shot of her as they drove away on the bus when the look in her eyes was so sad and bereft, it almost made him cry. He had clipped up photographs of her all over his apartment. She watched him as he ate breakfast in the morning, sat at his desk at night, or lay on the couch and stared at her for hours. He wanted to make copies of them for her, and he finally did. He wasn't sure where to send them. He had called her several times on her cell phone, and she never answered. She had returned his call twice, and then had missed him. They had been playing phone tag, and both of them were busy, but as a result, he hadn't spoken to her since he left. He was missing her terribly, and he wanted her to see how beautiful the photographs of her were, and show her some of the others.

He was home alone on a Saturday night, when he finally decided to go up to San Francisco and see her. He had no assignments for the next few days. And on Sunday morning, he got up at the crack of dawn, took a cab to LAX, and hopped a plane to San Francisco. He hadn't warned her, and hoped he'd find her at the Presidio, if nothing had changed in the weeks since he'd left.

The plane landed at ten A.M. in San Francisco. He hailed a cab at the curb, and gave the driver the address. He had the box of photographs under his arm to show to her. It was nearly eleven when they reached the Presidio and he noticed the helicopters still patrolling overhead. He stood staring up at the field hospital, hoping she was inside. He was well aware that what he'd just done was a little crazy. But he had to see her. He had missed her ever since he left.

The volunteer at the front desk told him that Maggie was off today. It was Sunday, and the woman who knew her well said she had probably gone to church. He thanked her and decided to check the building where the religious volunteers and assorted chaplains were living. There were two nuns and a priest standing on the front step when he asked for Maggie, and one of the nuns said she'd go inside and check. Everett's heart sank as he stood and waited, and it seemed to take forever. And then suddenly she was standing there, in a terrycloth bathrobe, with her bright blue eyes, and soaking-wet red hair. She said she'd been in the shower. She broke into a smile the minute she saw him, and he nearly cried he was so relieved to see her. For a minute, he'd been afraid he wouldn't find her, but there she was. He swept her up in a warm hug, and nearly dropped the box of photographs. He stepped back to look at her as he beamed.

'What are you doing here?' she asked him, as the other nuns and the priest walked away. Deep friendships had formed for all of them during the initial days after the earthquake, so they saw nothing unusual about the visit or the obvious delight with which they greeted each other. One of the nuns remembered him from when he'd been at the camp, before he went back to L.A., and Maggie said she'd catch up with them later. They'd already been to church, and were heading to the mess hall for lunch. It was beginning to feel like an eternal summer camp for adults. Everett had been impressed on his way in by some of the improvements he already saw in the city after just a couple of weeks. But the refugee camp in the Presidio was still going strong.

'Are you here to do a story?' Maggie asked him, and then they both spoke at once, in their excitement to see each other. 'I'm sorry I keep missing your calls. I turn my phone off when I'm at work.'

'I know . . . I'm sorry . . . I'm so glad to see you,' he said, and hugged her again. 'I just came up to see you. I had so many photographs to show you, and I didn't know where to send them, so I decided to bring them up myself. I brought you a full set of everything I got.'

'Let me put some clothes on,' she said, running a hand through her short, wet hair, smiling broadly.

She was back five minutes later, in jeans, her pink Converse, and a T-shirt from Barnum & Bailey's Circus, with a tiger on it. He laughed at the incongruous shirt, which she had picked up on the donation table. She was definitely a most unusual nun. And she was dying to see his photographs. They walked a few feet away to a bench, and sat down to look at them. Her hands were shaking when she opened the box, and when she saw them, she was moved to tears several times, and just as often laughter, as they both remembered the moments and faces, the heart-rending times. There were photographs of the woman he'd watched taken out from under her house, after they had to cut her leg off to free her, others of children, and a huge number of Melanie, but far more of Maggie. At least half his photographs were of her, and she exclaimed as she looked at each one . . . oh, I remember that! . . . oh my God, remember him? . . . oh that poor kid . . . that sweet little old lady. There were photographs of the destruction of the city, the night of the benefit when it had all started. It was an exquisite chronicle of a frightening but deeply moving time in both their lives. 'Oh Everett, they're so beautiful,' she said, looking at him with her bright blue eyes. 'Thank you for bringing them to show me. I've thought of you so often, and hoped everything was fine.' His messages had been reassuring, but she had missed talking to him, almost as much as he missed talking to her.

'I missed you, Maggie,' he said honestly, after they finished looking at the pictures. 'I have no one to talk to when you're not around, not really.' He hadn't realized how empty his life was until he met her and then left.

'I missed you too,' she confessed. 'Have you been going to meetings? The one you started here is still going strong.'

'I've been going to two a day. Do you want to go

out to lunch?' A few of the fast food places on Lombard Street had opened. He suggested they pick up something to eat and walk to the Marina Green. It was a gorgeous day. And from there, they could look at the bay and watch the boats. They could do that on the Presidio beach too, but he thought it would do her good to get out, walk, get some air, and leave the Presidio for a change. She had been cooped up in the hospital all week.

'I'd love that.' They couldn't go far without a car, but Lombard was within easy walking distance. She went back for a sweater, left the photographs that were his gift to her in her room, and a few minutes later they left.

They walked along in comfortable silence for a while, and then chatted about what they'd been doing. She told him about what was happening in the reconstruction of the city, and her work in the hospital. He told her about the assignments he'd been on. He had brought her a copy of the earthquake edition of *Scoop* too, with all the photographs of Melanie, and they talked about what a nice girl she was. At the first fast food place they saw, they bought sandwiches and then headed toward the bay. And finally they sat down on the vast expanse of grass at the Marina Green. Maggie didn't say anything to him about Sarah's problems, because that had been told to her in confidence. She'd heard from Sarah several times by then, and things were not going well. She knew Seth had been arrested, and was out on bail. And she said they were selling the house. It was a terrible time for Sarah, who didn't deserve any of what had happened to her.

'What are you going to do when you leave the

Presidio?' Everett asked Maggie as they ate their sandwiches, and then lay on the grass facing each other, like two kids in the summer. She didn't look anything like a nun in her circus T-shirt and pink high-tops, as she lay on the grass talking to him. Sometimes he forgot she was.

'I don't think I'll be leaving for a while, maybe not for months. It's going to take a long time to get all these people housing again.' So much of the city had been destroyed. It could take as long as a year to rebuild, or more. 'After that, I guess I'll go back to the Tenderloin, and do the same old stuff.' As she said it, she suddenly realized how repetitious her life was. She had been working on the streets with the homeless for years. But it had always felt right to her. Now suddenly she wanted more, and she was enjoying hospital nursing again.

'You don't want more than that, Maggie? Your own life someday?'

'This is my life,' she said gently, smiling at him. 'This is what I do.'

'I know. Me too. I take photographs for a living, for magazines and newspapers. It's been strange since I went back, though. Something shook me up when I was here. I just feel like there's something missing in my life.' And then as he looked at her as they lay there, he spoke softly. 'Maybe it's you.' She didn't know what to say in answer. She just looked at him for a long moment and then lowered her eyes.

'Be careful, Everett,' she said in a whisper. 'I don't think we should go there.' She had thought of it too.

'Why not?' he said stubbornly. 'What if you change your mind one day and don't want to be a

206

nun anymore?'

'What if I don't? I love being a nun. That's all I've ever been since I left nursing school. It was all I wanted as a kid. This is my dream, Everett. How can I give that up?'

'What if you trade it for something else? You could do the same kind of work if you left the convent. You could be a social worker, or nurse practitioner with the homeless.' He had thought about it from every angle.

'I do all that, and I'm a nun. You know how I feel about it.' He was scaring her, and she wanted him to stop before they said too much and she felt she couldn't see him again. She didn't want that to happen, and if he went too far, it could. She had to live by her vows. She was still a nun, whether he liked it or not.

'I guess I'll just have to keep coming up to visit you then, to bug you from time to time. Is that okay with you?' He tried to back off and smiled at her in the bright sunshine.

'I'd like that, as long as we don't do anything foolish,' she reminded him, relieved that he didn't press her further.

'And what would that be? Define *foolish* for me.' He was pushing her and she knew it, but she was a big girl and could take care of herself.

'It would be foolish if you or I forgot that I'm a nun. But we won't do that,' she said firmly. 'Isn't that right, Mr. Allison?' she said, referring to the old Deborah Kerr-Robert Mitchum movie with a chuckle.

'Yeah, yeah, I know,' Everett said, rolling his eyes. 'In the end, I go back to the Marines, and you stay a nun, just like in the movie. Don't you know any movies where the nun leaves the convent?'

'I don't go to see those,' she said primly. 'I go to the ones where the nun keeps her vows.'

'I hate those,' he said, teasing her. 'They're so boring.'

'No, they're not. They're very noble.'

'I wish you weren't so noble, Maggie,' he said gently, 'and so true to your vows.' He didn't dare say more, and she didn't answer. He was pushing. And she changed the subject.

They lay in the sun until the late afternoon, and could see building and reconstruction starting in the areas behind them. They walked back to the Presidio, as the air got cool, and she invited him to eat something in the mess hall before he left. She told him that Tom had gone back to Berkeley to close up his apartment. But many of the same faces were still there from before Everett left.

They both had soup, and he walked her back to her building after they ate, and she thanked him for the visit.

'I'll come up and see you again,' he promised. He had taken a few pictures of her that day, as she lay in the sun talking to him. Her eyes had been the same color as the sky.

'Take care of yourself,' she told him, as she had before. 'I'll be praying for you.' He nodded and kissed her cheek. It was as soft as velvet. She had an ageless quality to her, and looked amazingly young, in her silly circus shirt.

She watched as he walked away, and saw him leave through the main gate. He had the familiar gait she had come to recognize, in his black lizard cowboy boots. He waved once, then turned toward

Lombard to find a cab to take him back to the airport, and she went upstairs to her room to look at his photographs again. They were beautiful. He had an extraordinary talent. But more than that, there was something about his soul that drew her to him. She didn't want it to be so, but she was powerfully attracted to him, not just as a friend, but as a man. That had never happened to her, in all of her adult life, since she had entered the convent. He touched something in her that she had no idea had ever been in her, and maybe until Everett, it wasn't. But it troubled her deeply.

She closed the box of photographs and set it on the bed beside her. And then she lay down and closed her eyes. She didn't want this to be happening to her. She couldn't let herself fall in love with him. It was impossible. And she told herself it was not going to happen.

She lay there praying for a long time, before the other nuns came back to the room she shared with them. She had never prayed as fervently in her life, and all she kept saying to herself over and over again was 'Please, God, don't let me love him.' All she could do was hope that God would hear her. She knew she could not let this happen, and she kept reminding herself that she belonged to God.

Chapter 13

Tom got to Pasadena and his family a week after Melanie left San Francisco, and he called her as soon as he arrived. He had packed up his apartment in two days, put everything in his van, which had been miraculously unharmed, and drove south. He could hardly wait to see Melanie again.

He spent his first evening at home with his parents and sister, who'd been worried sick about him during the earthquake. They wanted to hear all about it, and he had a very pleasant evening with them. He told his sister he was taking her to a concert soon, and then headed to Hollywood immediately after breakfast the next day. He mentioned as he left that he probably wouldn't be back until late that night. At least he hoped not. Melanie had invited him over to spend the day with her, and he was planning to take her out to dinner afterward. After having such easy access to her at the Presidio, he had missed her terribly once she was gone, and he wanted to spend all the time with her that he could now, particularly knowing she was leaving on tour in July. He had to get busy himself. It was obvious the job in San Francisco wasn't going to work out. In the aftermath of the earthquake, there would be long delays, and he had decided to look for a job in L.A.

Melanie was waiting for him when he arrived. She saw him drive up, and buzzed him in through the gate. He pulled up in his van, and she ran out to greet him with a huge smile. Pam noticed him when she glanced outside, and she smiled too when she saw them kissing. And then they disappeared into the house, as Melanie showed him around. They had a gym, a pool table in a playroom downstairs, and a wide-screen TV with comfortable chairs to watch movies, and a huge pool. Melanie had told him to bring a bathing suit. But the only thing he was interested in seeing was her. He put his arms around her and kissed

210

her gently on the lips, and time stood still for both of them.

'I missed you so much,' he said, smiling happily. 'Camp was awful after you left. I kept hanging around and bugging Maggie. She said she really missed you too.'

'I have to call her. I miss her too . . . and I missed you,' Melanie whispered, and then they giggled as the cleaning service people came clattering down the stairs. She took him upstairs then to see her room. It looked almost like a child's room to him with the pink and white decor her mother had arranged. There were photographs of her with actors, actresses, and other singers, most of them very well known. There was a photograph of her receiving the Grammy, which her mother had framed for her. There were photographs of her favorite rappers and stars. He followed her back out, and down the back stairs to the kitchen, where they both helped themselves to sodas and then went outside to sit by the pool.

'How did the recording session go?' He was fascinated by what she did, without being unduly impressed by her stardom. He had gotten to know her as a normal person, and he liked it that way. He was relieved to see that she hadn't changed, and was the same adorable girl he'd met and fallen in love with in San Francisco. If anything, they were even more in love. She was wearing shorts, a tank top, and sandals instead of the flip-flops she'd worn in camp, but her appearance was the same. She was no more done up or starlike than she had been when he first met her. She was totally herself, as she sat next to him on a deck chair, and then at the edge of the pool dangling her feet. He still had

211

a hard time believing that she was the world-famous star he knew she was. It meant nothing to him. And Melanie could sense that about him, just as she had in San Francisco. He was entirely genuine, and oblivious to her fame.

They were sitting at the pool, talking quietly. She was telling him about her recording session, when her mother drove into the driveway, and then stopped at the pool to see what her daughter was doing and with whom. She looked anything but pleased to see Tom. And her greeting wasn't warm.

'What are you doing here?' she asked bluntly as Melanie looked embarrassed, and he stood up to shake her mother's hand. Janet looked unimpressed.

'I just got back to Pasadena yesterday,' he explained. 'I thought I'd come and say hi.' Janet nodded and shot a look at Melanie. She hoped he wouldn't stay long. There was nothing about him that appealed to Janet as a suitable escort for her daughter. It didn't matter to Janet that he was well educated, came from a nice family, and would presumably have a decent job once he got situated in L.A., that he was a kind, compassionate person, and loved her daughter. A nice boy from Pasadena was of no interest to her, and she made it clear without spelling it out that she didn't approve of his being there to visit her. Two minutes after she'd arrived, Janet walked into the house and slammed the door. 'I don't think she was too pleased to see me,' he said, looking embarrassed, and Melanie apologized for her mother, as she often did.

'She'd like it better if you were some half-baked

movie star on drugs, as long as you're in the tabloids at least twice a week, and preferably stay out of jail. Unless it gets you really good press.' She laughed at her description of her mother, which he suspected was painfully accurate.

'I've never been in jail or the tabloids,' he said apologetically. 'She must think I'm a real dud.'

'I don't,' Melanie said, as she sat close to him and looked into his eyes. Melanie liked everything about him so far, especially the fact that he wasn't part of any of the Hollywood nonsense. She had come to hate the problems she'd had with Jake. His drinking, going to rehab, winding up in the tabloids with him, and the time he'd punched someone out in a bar. Paparazzi had appeared on the scene in an instant, and he'd been taken away by the police while flashes from the photographers went off in her face. And even more than that, she hated what he had done with Ashley. She hadn't spoken to him since they got back, and didn't plan to again. In contrast, Tom was honorable, decent, wholesome, well behaved, and cared about her. 'Want to go for a swim?' He nodded. He didn't care what he did, as long as it was with her. He was a regular, healthy twenty-two-year-old boy. In fact, nicer, smarter, and better-looking than most. He was someone with a future, Melanie could tell. Not the kind of future her mother wanted for her, but the kind Melanie wanted to be part of when she grew up, and even now. He was down to earth, and real, just as she was. There was nothing fake about him. He was as far from the Hollywood scene as you could get.

She showed him to the cabana at the end of the pool, and the room where he could change. He came out a minute later, wearing a Hawaiian-style bathing suit. He had gone surfing there at Easter with friends, in Kauai. Melanie went into the cabana after him, and came out in a pink bikini that showed off her dazzling figure. She had been working with her trainer again since she got back. It was part of her daily drill. As were two hours every day in the gym. She had been going to rehearsal every day too, getting ready for the concert in June. It was going to be at the Hollywood Bowl, and it was already sold out. It would have been anyway, but after the story about her in *Scoop,* about surviving the San Francisco earthquake, tickets had sold even faster than before. They were being sold by scalpers now for five thousand dollars a ticket. She had two, with backstage passes, reserved for him and his sister.

They swam together and kissed in the pool, and then drifted around on a large inflatable raft as they lay side by side in the sun. She had put tons of sunscreen on. She wasn't allowed to get a tan—it looked too dark in the lights on stage. Her mother preferred her pale. But it was nice lying on the raft with Tom. They lay in silence for a while just holding hands. It was all very innocent and friendly. She felt incredibly comfortable with him, just as she had when she spent time with him in the camp.

'The concert's going to be really cool,' she said when they talked about it. She told him about the special effects and the songs she was going to sing. He knew them all, and he told her again that his sister would go nuts. He said he hadn't told her yet whose concert it was, or that they'd be going backstage to visit her after the show.

214

When they got tired of lying in the sun, they went inside and made lunch. Janet was sitting in the kitchen, smoking, talking on the phone, and glancing at a gossip magazine. She was disappointed not to see Melanie in it. So as not to disturb her, they took their sandwiches outside, and sat at a table under an umbrella near the pool. Afterward they lay in a hammock together, and she told Tom in a whisper that she'd been trying to figure out how she could do volunteer work, like what she'd done at the Presidio. She wanted to do more with her life than just go to rehearsals and sing.

'Do you have any ideas?' he asked her in the same whisper.

'Nothing my mom would let me do.' They were co-conspirators as they talked in hushed tones, and then he kissed her again. The more he saw her, the crazier he was about her. He could hardly believe his luck, not because of who she was, but because she was such a sweet, unassuming girl, and fun to be with. 'Sister Maggie told me about a priest who runs a Catholic mission. He goes to Mexico for a few months every year. I'd love to call him, but I don't think I could ever do that. I've got my tour, and my agent is lining up engagements till the end of the year. We'll be starting on next year soon.' She sounded disappointed as she said it. She was tired of traveling so much, and she wanted time to spend with him.

'Will you be away a lot?' He looked worried about it too. They had just found each other, and he wanted time to be with her. It was going to get complicated for him, too, once he found a job. They'd both be busy.

'I'm gone about four months a year. Sometimes five. Otherwise I just fly in and out, like I did for the benefit in San Francisco. I'm only gone a couple of nights for gigs like that.'

'I was thinking that maybe I could fly up to see you in Vegas, and maybe I could hit some of the hot spots on your tour. Where are you going?' He was trying to figure out ways for them to see each other. He didn't want to wait till early September when she got back. It seemed centuries away to both of them. They had gotten so close to each other during the aftermath of the earthquake in San Francisco that their feelings for each other had hit 'fast forward' in a way they wouldn't have otherwise. She was going to be gone for ten weeks, which was a standard tour, although it seemed an eternity now, to both of them. And her agent wanted her to tour Japan next year. Her CDs flew off the shelves in Japan. She had just the look and sound they loved.

She laughed when he asked her where she was going on tour, and started reeling off cities. She was going to be traveling all across the States. But at least they would be traveling by chartered plane. It had been agonizing during the years they did it on a bus. Sometimes they had traveled all night. In fact, most of the time. Her life and tours were a lot more civilized now. When she told him the dates, he said he hoped to be able to visit her once or twice on tour. It depended on how fast he found a job, but it sounded great to her.

They dove back into the pool then and swam laps until they were too winded to do it anymore. He was in fantastic shape and was an excellent swimmer. He said he had been on the swimming team at UCB, and had played soccer for a while till he hurt his knee. He showed her the small scar of a minor surgery. He talked about his college years, and childhood before that, and of his career plans. He wanted to go to graduate school eventually, but was planning to work for several years first. He had it all mapped out. Tom knew where he was going, more than most young men his age.

They discovered that they both loved skiing, tennis, water sports, and a variety of other athletic pursuits, most of which she had no time for. She explained to him that she had to stay in shape, but actual sports were never on her agenda. She was too busy, and her mother didn't want her to get hurt, and be unable to go on tour. She made a fortune doing tours, although she didn't spell that out to Tom. She didn't have to. The money she pulled in now was outrageous, as he could only guess. She was far too discreet to say it, although Janet hinted often at how much money her daughter made. It still embarrassed Melanie, and her agent had warned Janet to be discreet, or it would put Melanie at risk. They had enough security headaches as it was, keeping her safe from her fans. It was something every major star in Hollywood had to think about these days—no one was exempt. Janet always minimized the dangers when talking to her daughter, so as not to frighten her, but often used a bodyguard herself. She pointed out that fans were dangerous sometimes. What she often forgot was that the fans were Melanie's, not hers.

'Do you ever get threatening letters?' he asked, as they lay drying off by the pool. He'd never thought about what it involved to protect someone

217

in her position. Life had been so much simpler for her in the Presidio, but not for long. And he had had no idea that some of the men in her entourage were bodyguards who traveled with her.

'Sometimes,' she said vaguely. 'I have. The only people who threaten me are nuts. I don't think they'd ever do anything about it. Some of them have written to me for several years.'

'To threaten you?' He looked horrified.

'Yes,' she laughed. It came with the territory, and she was used to it. She even got scary, passionate fan letters from men in maximum security prisons. She never responded. That was how stalkers happened, when they got out. She was extremely cautious about not wandering around public places on her own, and when she took them with her, her guards took good care of her. Whenever possible, she preferred not to use them when she was running around L.A. doing errands or visiting friends, and she said she preferred to drive herself.

'Does all of that ever scare you?' Tom asked, with ever-increasing concern. He wanted to protect her but wasn't quite sure how.

'Not usually. Once in a while, depending on what the police say about the stalker. I've had my share, but no worse than anyone else here. It used to scare me when I was younger, but it really doesn't anymore. The only stalkers I worry about now are press. They can eat you alive. You'll see,' she warned him, but he couldn't see how it would ever involve him. He was still naïve about a life like hers and all it entailed. There were definitely some downsides, but lying in the sun with her and talking, everything seemed so simple, and she was just like any other girl.

They went for a drive in the late afternoon. He took her out for ice cream, and she showed him where she'd gone to school before she dropped out. She told him she still wanted to go to college, but for now it was only a dream for her, and not a possibility. She was away too much, so she read everything she could get her hands on. They stopped at a bookstore together and found they liked to read the same things, and had loved many of the same books.

They drove back to her house then, and later, he took her out for dinner at a little Mexican restaurant she liked, and afterward they went back to her place and watched a movie in the playroom downstairs on the gigantic plasma screen. It was almost like being in a theater. When Janet came home, she seemed surprised he was still there. Tom looked mildly uncomfortable, sensing her displeasure. She made no effort to hide it. It was eleven o'clock when he left. Melanie walked him out to his van in the driveway, and they stood kissing through his window. He said he'd had a wonderful day, and so had she. It had been a very respectable and thoroughly enjoyable first date. He said he'd call her the next day, and instead called her as soon as he left the driveway. Her cell phone rang in her pocket just as she was walking back into the house, thinking of him.

'I miss you already,' he said as she giggled.

'Me too. It was so much fun today. I hope you weren't bored just hanging around here.' It was hard for her to get out sometimes. People recognized her everywhere. It had been fine when they went out for ice cream, but people in the bookstore had stared at her, and three people had asked her for autographs while they paid. She hated that whenever she went out on dates. It always felt like an intrusion and bothered the man she was with. Tom had been amused.

'I had a great time,' he reassured her. 'I'll call you tomorrow. Maybe we can do something this weekend.'

'I love going to Disneyland,' she confessed. 'It makes me feel like a kid again. But it's too crowded this time of year. It's better in winter.'

'You are a kid,' he said, smiling. 'A really terrific kid. Goodnight, Melanie.'

' 'Night, Tom,' she said, and hung up with a happy smile. Her mother came out of her room then and saw her, as Melanie headed toward hers.

'What was that all about today?' Janet asked, still looking disgruntled. 'He was here all day. Don't start something with him, Mel. He doesn't live in your world.' It was precisely what Melanie liked about him. 'He's just using you for who you are.'

'No, he's not, Mom,' Melanie said hotly, outraged on his behalf. Tom wasn't that kind of guy. 'He's a decent, normal person. He doesn't care who I am.'

'That's what you think,' Janet said cynically. 'And if you go out with him, you'll never be in the press again, and that's not good for your career.'

'I'm tired of hearing about my career, Mom,' Melanie said, looking sad. It was all her mother talked about. Melanie had dreams about her sometimes, brandishing a whip. 'There's more to life than that.'

'Not if you want to be a big star.'

'I am a big star, Mom. I still need to have a life. And Tom is a really nice guy. He's a hell of a lot nicer than the Hollywood types I've gone out with.'

'You just haven't met the right one,' she said firmly, unmoved by Melanie's sentiments about Tom.

'Are there any?' Melanie shot back. 'None of them seem right to me.'

'And he does?' Janet inquired, looking worried. 'You don't even know him. He was just another face in that frigging awful refugee camp.' Janet still had dreams about it, and none of them were pleasant. They had all been traumatized to some degree, particularly when the quake hit. She had never been so happy to be sleeping in her own bed again in her entire life.

Melanie didn't say to her that she didn't think the camp was awful. The only really awful thing, as far as Melanie was concerned, was her supposed boyfriend sleeping with her alleged best friend. Now both had been disposed of, without regret on Melanie's part. Only her mother's. She still talked to Ashley at least once a day, promising to patch things up with Melanie, who had no idea they were talking regularly.

Melanie had no intention of allowing Ashley back into her life. Nor Jake. The arrival of Tom in her world seemed to be her reward for losing them. She said goodnight to her mother, and walked slowly down the hall to her own room, thinking of Tom. It had been a truly flawless first date.

Chapter 14

Tom came to see Melanie several more times. They went to dinners, movies, and relaxed at her pool, despite her mother's obvious disapproval. Janet barely spoke to Tom, although he was extremely polite to her. He brought his sister over once to meet Melanie. The three of them barbecued at the pool, and had a great time. His sister was extremely impressed by Melanie, how simple she was, open and kind and understanding. There was nothing in her behavior to suggest she was a star. She really did act like the girl next door. She was thrilled when Melanie invited them to her Hollywood Bowl concert in June.

They hadn't slept with each other. They had both agreed to take things slowly, see what happened, and get to know each other first. She was still feeling bruised by Jake, and Tom didn't rush her. He kept saying they had time. They always had fun together. He brought over all his favorite movies and CDs, and shortly after she'd met his sister Nancy, he took Melanie to Pasadena to dinner. Melanie thought his parents were adorable. They were genuine, nice, friendly people. They had intelligent conversations, were well educated, liked each other, and were very respectful of her, and sensitive about her being who she was. They didn't make a fuss, they welcomed her in as they would have any of their children's friends—unlike Janet, who still acted like Tom was an intruder, or worse. Janet made every effort to be unpleasant to him, but he told

222

Melanie he didn't mind. He realized that she thought he was a threat, and not the kind of man Melanie should go out with, particularly if her mother wanted tabloids and mainstream press for her, which she did. Melanie apologized to him constantly for her mother, and started spending more time in Pasadena, when she wasn't in rehearsal.

He came to rehearsal with her twice, and was incredibly impressed by how professional she was. Her career was no accident of fate. She was brilliant at all the technical details, did her own arrangements, wrote some of her songs, and worked unbelievably hard. Both rehearsals Tom went to, for the Hollywood Bowl concert, lasted until two A.M., until Melanie felt they had it right. The technicians he talked to, as he wandered around, said she always did that. Sometimes she worked till four or five A.M., and then wanted them back at nine the next morning. She drove them hard, but she was even harder on herself. And Tom thought she had the voice of an angel.

The day of the concert, she had told him he could come early, and he and Nancy could stay in her dressing room with her until it started. He took her at her word, and when they got there, Janet was with Melanie, hovering, and giving orders and directions. She was drinking champagne and getting her own makeup done. Sometimes photographers wanted her to pose too. She ignored Tom and Nancy for as long as she could, and then stormed off to find Melanie's hairdresser, who was smoking outside with some of the men in the band. They knew Tom by name now, and thought he was a nice guy.

223

They left her half an hour before the concert started. Melanie had to finish her makeup and put on her costume. Tom thought she was amazingly calm, considering she was about to perform in front of eighty thousand people. This was what she did best. She was introducing four new songs to try them out before her tour. She was leaving soon. Tom had promised to visit whenever he could, although he was starting a job in July that he was excited about. It was with Bechtel, and they had promised some travel abroad. He said it would keep him busy while Melanie was gone, and it was much better than the job he'd had lined up in San Francisco before the earthquake. This one had just fallen into his lap, through some connections of his father's. And it had some major career opportunities for him. In fact, if they were pleased with his performance, they would consider paying for business school.

'Good luck, Mel,' Tom whispered as he left her dressing room. 'You'll be fantastic.' She had given them seats in the front row. When he left, she slithered into a skin-tight red satin dress, checked her makeup and hair, and put on mile-high silver platform sandals. She had six costume changes to do, with a single intermission. She was going to be working hard.

'I'm going to sing one of the new songs for you,' she whispered, and he kissed her. 'You'll know which one. I just wrote it. I hope you like it.'

'I love you,' he said, as her eyes grew wide. It was the first time he had said it to her, even more amazing since they hadn't made love yet. It seemed almost irrelevant at this point, they were still getting to know each other and having a

224

wonderful time.

'I love you too,' she answered, and then he slipped out of Melanie's dressing room as her mother stormed in, reminding her that she had less than twenty minutes, and to stop dicking around and get ready. There were four photographers right behind her, waiting to take Melanie's photograph.

Her mother helped her zip up her dress, and Melanie thanked her. And then Pam let the photographers in. Janet posed with her in two of the shots. Melanie was dwarfed beside her. Janet was a big woman, and a major presence wherever she was.

And then suddenly, they came to get Melanie. The concert was about to begin. She ran backstage, hopping nimbly over the wires and equipment, said a quick hello to her band, stood just out of sight, and closed her eyes. She took three long, slow breaths, and then she heard her cue, and drifted slowly into view through smoke. As the smoke cleared, there she was. She looked out into the audience with the sexiest smile Tom had ever seen and purred hello. This was nothing like rehearsal, or the girl he'd brought home to dinner in Pasadena. As Melanie worked her audience and sang her heart out till the rafters nearly shook, she was every inch and fiber of her being a star. The lights were too bright for her to see Tom or his sister in the audience. But in her heart, she felt him out there, and was singing for him that night.

'Wow!' Nancy said, touching her brother's arm, and he turned to her with a smile. 'She's *amazing!*'

'She sure is,' he said proudly. He couldn't tear

his eyes off her until intermission, and then rushed back to her dressing room to see her and tell her how great she was. He was thrilled to be there with her, and loved her performance. He couldn't say enough great things about her and to her. Melanie realized that this was so different from dating someone in show business. Tom was never jealous of her. They kissed quickly and then he went back to his seat. She had to change clothes again, and this was a tough costume change. Pam and her mother helped her into the skin-tight dress. It was even tighter than the ones she'd worn before, and she looked fabulous when she stepped onstage again for the second act.

They did seven encores that night. She always did them to please her fans. And they had loved the new song she had written to Tom. It was called 'When I Found You,' and was all about their first days together in San Francisco. It talked about the bridge, the beach, and the earthquake in her heart. He listened to it raptly, and his sister had tears in her eyes as she listened.

'Is that you?' she whispered. He nodded, and she shook her head in amazement. Whatever their relationship was going to be over time, it had clearly gotten started like a rocket shooting into space, and it was showing no signs of slowing down.

They joined Melanie afterward in her dressing room when it was over. This time there were dozens of people congratulating her, photographers, her assistant, her mother, friends, groupies who had somehow wormed their way in. Tom and Nancy were crushed in the crowd, and afterward they went to Spago for dinner, although

226

they arrived late because it took a while to get there. Wolfgang Puck had prepared their meal himself.

After dinner, Tom and Nancy went back to Pasadena, and he kissed Melanie before he left. He promised to come and see her in the morning, then they all dispersed. It had been a long night. There was a mile-long white stretch limousine waiting for her outside. It was anything but discreet, but this was her public persona, the one he had never seen before. It was the private Melanie that he loved, but he had to admit that this one was fun too.

He called her on her cell phone right after she got home, and told her again how fabulous she had been. She had made a diehard fan out of him, especially with the song she'd written just for them. It sounded like another Grammy winner to him.

'I'll be over first thing in the morning,' he promised. They were trying to spend as much time together as they could, before she left for Vegas in a week.

'We can read the reviews together when you get here. I hate that part. They always find something to bitch about.'

'I don't see how they can this time.'

'They will,' she said, sounding like the pro she was. 'Jealousy sucks.' Often bad reviews were more about that than a bad performance, but the criticism hurt anyway, even if she was used to it. It always hurt. Sometimes her mother or Pam hid reviews from her if they were really rude, which happened sometimes too.

When Tom arrived the next day, there were

newspapers spread out all over their kitchen table.

'So far so good,' Melanie whispered to Tom, as her mother handed them to her one by one. She looked pleased.

'They like the new songs,' her mother commented, glancing at Tom with a frosty smile. Even she had to admit the one to him was good.

All in all, the reviews were great. The concert had been a huge hit, which would bode well for her concert tour, and even the show in Vegas, which was smaller and was already sold out, just as the one at the Hollywood Bowl had been.

'So what are you two kids doing today?' Janet asked, glancing at both of them, looking pleased, as though she had played the concert herself. It was the first time she had willingly included Tom in anything she said. They had turned a corner, although Melanie didn't know why. Maybe she was just in a good mood, or had finally figured out that Tom didn't want to interfere with Melanie's career. He was happy to watch the goings-on, and support whatever she did.

'I just want to relax,' Melanie said. She had to be in the recording studio again the next day. And they were starting rehearsals for the show in Vegas the day after. 'What are you doing, Mom?'

'I'm going to go shopping on Rodeo,' she beamed. Nothing made her happier than Melanie performing at a huge concert and getting great reviews the next day.

She left them alone without dark looks or slamming doors this time, much to Tom's surprise.

'I think your initiation may finally be over,' Melanie said with a sigh. 'For now anyway. She must have decided you're not a threat.'

'I'm not, Mel. I love what you do. It was incredible watching you last night. I couldn't believe I was sitting there, and when you sang that song, I damn near died.'

'I'm glad you liked it.' She leaned over and kissed him. She looked tired, but pleased. She had just turned twenty, and looked prettier than ever to him. 'I wish I could take a break sometime, from all this. It gets old after a while,' she confessed. She had said it to him before, in the past few weeks. The time she'd spent working in the field hospital after the earthquake had been such a welcome relief.

'Maybe one of these days,' he tried to encourage her, but she just shook her head.

'My mom and my agent will never let that happen. The smell of success is too sweet to them. They're going to milk this till I die.' She sounded sad as she said it, and Tom put his arms around her and kissed her. The look in her eyes had touched him to the core, just as her song had. She was a remarkable woman, and he knew he was one lucky guy. Fate had dealt him an incredible hand. The San Francisco earthquake, and meeting her as a result, had been the best day of his life.

*   *   *

While Janet was reading Melanie's reviews in Hollywood that morning, Sarah and Seth Sloane were reading their own. It had finally hit the San Francisco papers, and neither of them could figure out what had taken so long. He had been arrested weeks before, and somehow no one had picked up on it. But it had finally exploded like Fourth of

July fireworks, and it had even been reported by the AP. Sarah had a feeling that the reporters covering Sully's earlier arrest and impending trial had tipped off the San Francisco press that he had had a crime partner out west. Until then, Seth's story had slipped right through the cracks, but it was front-page news now. Every lurid detail was printed in the *Chronicle,* with a photograph of Seth and Sarah at the recent Smallest Angels benefit. What they wrote about him was grim. They had the full indictment, all available details, the name of his hedge fund, and the circumstances leading up to his arrest. It said their house was on the market, mentioned that he had a house in Tahoe and a plane. And they made it sound as though everything he owned had been purchased with ill-gotten gains. He sounded like the biggest crook and fraud in town. It was profoundly humiliating for him, and excruciating for her as well. She had no doubt that her parents would even read about it in Bermuda, once the AP put it over the wires. She realized she had to call them now. With luck, she could still explain it herself. It was simpler for Seth. His parents had been much older when he was born and both were deceased. Her parents were very much alive and would be shocked, particularly since they loved Seth, and had right from the beginning.

'It's not a pretty story, is it?' Seth said, glancing at her. They had both lost a lot of weight. He looked gaunt, and she looked drained.

'There's not much they can do with it to dress it up,' she said honestly.

These were the last days of their living together. They had agreed to stay in the house on

Divisadero, for the kids' sake, until it sold, before they moved into their own apartments. They were expecting several offers that week. It wouldn't be long. Sarah knew it would make her sad to see the house go. But she was far more upset about her marriage and her husband than about the house they had owned only for a few years. The house in Tahoe was on the market, with everything in it, even kitchenware, TVs, and linens. It was easier to sell that way to someone who wanted a ski house and didn't want to bother decorating it or filling it. The house in the city would be sold empty. They were putting their antiques up for auction at Christie's, along with their modern paintings. Her jewelry was beginning to sell in L.A.

Sarah was still looking for a job, but hadn't found anything yet. She was keeping Parmani for the children, because she knew that when she found work, she'd need someone to take care of them. She hated the idea of leaving her children in day care, even though she knew that others did. What she really wished was that she could do what she had done until now, stay home with them, as she had for the past three years. But that was over. With Seth spending every penny they had on lawyers for his defense, and possibly fines, she had to work, not just to help contribute, but maybe at some point to support her children and herself, with no help from Seth. If everything they had and owned was going to be swallowed up by court orders, lawsuits, and his defense fund, and he went to prison, who was going to help them? She had to rely on herself.

After Seth's astonishing and utterly appalling betrayal, she trusted no one now but herself. She could no longer rely on him. And she knew she'd never trust him again. He read it easily in her eyes whenever their glance met. He had no idea how to make reparations to her, or if he ever could. He doubted it, given everything she'd said. She hadn't forgiven him, and he had come to doubt she ever would. And he wasn't sure he blamed her. He was feeling deeply guilty about the effect on her. Their life was destroyed.

He was shocked when he read the article in the paper. It made mincemeat of him and Sully and made them sound like common criminals. Nothing kind or compassionate was said. They were two bad guys who had set up fraudulent hedge funds, misrepresented the financial backing, and had cheated people out of money. What else could they say? Those were the allegations, and as Seth had admitted to Sarah and his own attorney, the accusations made against them were all true.

They hardly spoke to each other again all weekend. Sarah didn't insult or berate him. There was no point. She didn't say anything. She was too hurt. He had destroyed every shred of faith and confidence she'd ever had in him, and thrown her trust out the window by proving himself unworthy of it. He had put their children's future lives at risk, and heavily impacted hers. He had made her worst nightmares come true, for better or worse.

'Don't look at me like that, Sarah,' he finally said to her over the paper. There was an even bigger, uglier article in the Sunday edition of *The New York Times,* which included Seth too. As important as Seth and Sarah had become in their community, their disgrace was now commensurate. Although she had done nothing herself, and knew nothing of his illegal activities before the earthquake, she felt tarred by the same brush. Their phone had been ringing off the hook for days, and she left it on the machine. There was nothing she wanted to say to anyone, or hear from them. Sympathy would have cut through her like a knife, and she didn't want to hear the thinly veiled chortles of the jealous. She was sure there would be plenty of those. The only people she had spoken to that day were her parents. They were devastated and shocked, and couldn't understand what had happened to Seth any better than she could. In the end, it was all about lack of integrity and intense greed.

'Can't you at least try to put a good face on it?' Seth said reproachfully. 'You sure know how to make things worse.'

'I think you took care of that pretty efficiently, Seth.' After she cleared the table of their breakfast dishes, he found her crying at the sink.

'Sarah, don't . . .' His eyes held a poisonous mixture of anger and panic.

'What do you want from me?' She turned to look at him in agony. 'Seth, I'm scared . . . what's going to happen to us? I love you. I don't want you to go to prison. I want none of this to have happened . . . I want you to take it back and undo it . . . you can't . . . I don't care about the money. I don't want to lose you . . . I love you . . . and you threw our whole life out the window. Now what am I supposed to do?' He couldn't stand the pain in her eyes, and instead of putting his arms around her, which was all she wanted, he turned around and walked away. He was in so much pain and terror himself that he had nothing to give her. He

233

loved her too, but he was much too frightened for himself now to be of any help to her and the kids. He felt as though he was drowning alone. And so was she.

Sarah couldn't think of anything as devastating ever happening in her life, except when their premature baby nearly died, but she was saved by the neonatal unit. There was no way to save Seth. His crime had been too big and too shocking. Even the FBI agents had seemed somewhat disgusted by him, especially when they saw the kids. Sarah had never lost anyone in traumatic circumstances. Her grandparents had either died before she was born, or of old age without catastrophic illness. The people she had loved in her life had stood staunchly by her. Her childhood had been a happy one, her parents were solid citizens. Her boyfriends had been nice to her. Seth had always been wonderful to her. And her children were adorable and healthy. This was the worst thing by far that had ever happened to her. She had never even lost a friend to a car accident or cancer. She had passed unscathed through all thirty-five years of her life, and now a nuclear bomb had been dropped on her. And the person who had dropped it was the man she loved, her husband. She was so stunned by it that, most of the time now, she just didn't know what to say, especially to him. She didn't know where to start making it better, nor did he. The truth was that there was no way they could. His lawyers would have to do their best, with the appalling set of circumstances he'd given them to work with. And in the end, Seth would have to take his medicine, no matter how bitter it was. And so would she, even though she had done nothing to deserve it. That was the 'better or worse' part. She was going down in flames with him.

Sarah called Maggie on her cell phone on Sunday night, and they spoke for a few minutes. Maggie had seen the articles in the papers in the lounge at the Presidio, and her heart had gone out to Sarah, and even Seth. They were paying a high price for his sins. And she felt sorry for the kids. She told Sarah to pray, and she would do the same.

'Maybe they'll be lenient with him,' Maggie said hopefully.

'According to Seth's attorney, that would be two to five years. At the other end of the spectrum, it could be thirty.' She had told her all that before.

'Don't go there yet. Just have faith and keep swimming. Sometimes that's the best you can do.' Sarah hung up then, walked quietly past her husband's study, and went upstairs to bathe her children. Seth had been playing with them, and she took over from him. They did everything in turns now, and were rarely in one room at the same time. Even being near each other had become painful. Sarah couldn't help wondering if she would feel better or worse when she moved out. Maybe a lot of both.

*   *   *

Everett called Maggie that night to discuss what he'd read about Seth in the L.A. papers. The story was all over the country by then. He had been shocked by the news, particularly since he thought Seth and Sarah looked like the perfect young couple. It reminded him yet again, as he had

235

known for years, that you could never tell what evil lurked in people's hearts. Like everyone else who read of it, he felt sorry for Sarah and their children, and not at all for Seth. He was getting what he deserved, if the allegations were true, and they sounded so perfectly nailed down that he suspected they were.

'What a miserable situation for her. I saw a little of her at the benefit. She seems like a nice woman. But then again, he looked okay too. Who knew.' He had seen her briefly at the field hospital too, but hadn't talked to her for long. She looked upset then, and now he knew why. 'If you see her somewhere, tell her I'm sorry,' he said sincerely, and Maggie didn't acknowledge whether or not she would. She was faithful to Sarah and the relationship they had, and kept all her secrets, even that they saw each other.

Otherwise, Everett said he was doing fine, and so was Maggie. She was happy to hear from him, but as always, she was troubled when she hung up. Just hearing his voice touched her heart. She prayed about it after they talked, and she went for a long walk on the beach at dusk. She was beginning to wonder if she should stop taking or returning his calls. But she told herself she had the strength to deal with it. He was only a man, after all. And she was the bride of God. What man could compete with that?

Chapter 15

Melanie's concert in Las Vegas was a huge success. Tom flew in to see it, and she sang the song to him again. The show they did in Vegas had more special effects, and made a bigger impression, although the audience and the venue were significantly smaller than the concert he'd gone to before. They went wild for Melanie in Las Vegas. She sat at the edge of the stage when she did the encores, and Tom could reach out and touch her from his front row seat. Fans were pressed all around her, while security tried to hold them back. The finale was an explosion of lights while Melanie rode a platform to the sky, singing her heart out. It was the most impressive show Tom had ever seen, although he was upset to discover that she'd sprained her ankle getting off the platform, and she had two more shows to do the next day.

When the time came, she went on anyway, in platform silver sandals and with an ankle the size of a melon. He took her to the emergency room after her second show. He and Melanie left without saying anything to her mother. They gave her a cortisone shot so she could go on again the next day. The last three days in Vegas were smaller shows. The opening concert had been the big one, and she was on crutches at the end of the weekend when he left.

'Take care of yourself, Melanie. You work too hard.' He looked worried. They'd had a nice weekend together, but she had been busy with rehearsals or doing a show most of the time. They managed to get to one of the casinos the first night. And Melanie's suite was fabulous. He stayed in her suite in the second bedroom, and they were very circumspect for the first two nights. And on the last night they had finally given in to nature's urges and all the strong emotions they felt for each other. They had waited long enough, and it felt right. She felt even closer to him now as he left. 'You're going to wreck your ankle, if you don't slow down.'

'I'll get another cortisone shot tomorrow.' She was used to injuries onstage, they had happened before. She always went on no matter what happened to her. She had never canceled a show. She was a pro.

'Mellie, I want you to take care of yourself,' Tom said, genuinely concerned about her. 'You can't just take cortisone like that. You're not on a football team.' He could see her ankle was painful and still swollen in spite of the shot the day before. All it had done was allow her to abuse herself and perform again, in high heels. 'Get some rest tonight.' He knew she was leaving for Phoenix in the morning, to do another show.

'Thank you,' she said, smiling up at him. 'Nobody ever worries about me the way you do. They just expect me to go onstage and perform, dead or alive. I knew that platform was wonky when I stepped on. The rope broke as I got off. That's how I fell.' They both knew that if it had broken earlier, she would have fallen a long way down, and might even have been killed. 'I guess you've seen the flip side of show business now.' She stood close to him as they waited for his plane.

238

She had taken him to the airport in the long white stretch limousine the hotel gave her for the duration of her stay. The perks in Vegas were fabulous. It wasn't going to be as comfortable when they hit the road. She had ten weeks ahead of her and wouldn't be back in L.A. till early September. Tom had promised to fly out and meet her over a few weekends. They were both looking forward to it.

'Make sure you see the doctor again before you leave.' They called his flight then, and he had to go. He pulled her into his arms and kissed her, careful of the crutches she was resting on, and she was breathless when he let go. 'I love you, Mellie,' he said softly. 'Don't forget that while you're on the road.'

'I won't. I love you too.' They had been dating now for over a month. It wasn't long, and things had started to move quickly since they came to Vegas. But they had been through so much together in San Francisco that their romance had taken off at a rapid rate. He was the nicest man she'd ever known. 'See you soon.'

'You bet!' He kissed her one last time, and was the last to board the plane. She hobbled back through the terminal then on her crutches, and crawled into the limousine at the curb. Her ankle was killing her, more than she had wanted to admit to Tom.

When she got back to her suite at the Paris, she put an ice pack on it, which hardly helped, and took some Motrin to bring the swelling down. Her mother found her lying on the couch in the living room at midnight, and Melanie admitted to her that the ankle really hurt.

'You've got to go on in Phoenix tomorrow,' her mother warned her. 'They're sold out too. We'll get you another shot in the morning. You can't miss that show, Mel.'

'Maybe I can do it sitting down,' Melanie said as she touched it and winced.

'Your dress will look like shit if you do,' her mother commented. Melanie had never missed a single performance, and she didn't want her to start now. Rumors about that kind of thing spread like wildfire, and could destroy the reputation of a star. But her mother could see that she was really hurt. Melanie was always a good sport about injuries, and she never complained, but this one seemed more serious.

Tom called her before she went to sleep that night, and she lied and told him the ankle was better, so he wouldn't worry. He said he already missed her. She had a picture of him next to her bed when she fell asleep.

Her ankle was more swollen in the morning, and Pam took her to the hospital. The head ER doctor recognized her immediately and escorted her into a stall. He said he didn't like the look of it and wanted another X-ray. When she had hurt it, the medics who saw her the first time had said that it was just a bad sprain. The head of the emergency room wasn't convinced. And he was right. When he checked the X-ray, he showed her a hairline crack. He said she had to wear a hard cast for the next four weeks, and try to stay off it as much as she could.

'Yeah. Right,' she laughed, and then groaned. It hurt every time she moved. The performance was going to be agony that night, if she could even do

240

it. 'I'm playing to a packed house in Phoenix at eight o'clock,' she explained. 'And I still have to get there. They didn't pay to watch me hobble onstage in a cast,' she said, as she almost cried moving it.

'What about a boot?' the ER doctor suggested. He treated a lot of performers, some of whom had fallen offstage or worse. 'You can take it off when you go on. But don't even think of wearing platforms or high heels.' He knew the breed well, and she looked guilty the minute he said it.

'My costumes will look like shit with combat boots,' she said.

'You'll look worse in a wheelchair if it gets any more swollen. The boot ought to do it. Just wear flats when you perform. And you gotta use the crutches,' he informed her. She had no other choice. The ankle was excruciatingly painful, and she couldn't put any weight on it at all.

'Okay, I'll try the boot,' she conceded. It went up to her knee, was made of a shiny black plastic material, and had Velcro straps to hold her leg in. And as soon as she stood on it, it gave her considerable relief. She hobbled out of the emergency room in the boot, with the crutches, while Pam paid the bill.

'Looks cute,' Janet said jauntily, as she helped Melanie into the limousine. They had just enough time to pick up their bags, meet the others, and head to the airport for their flight to Phoenix. Melanie knew it would be crazy from now on. Their concert tour had begun, and she'd be all over the States for the next ten weeks.

She put her leg up on a pillow in their chartered plane. The band played liar's dice and poker, and Janet joined them. She glanced over at her daughter a couple of times and tried to make her more comfortable. In the end, Melanie took a couple of pain pills and went to sleep. Pam woke her up when they got to Phoenix and one of the guys from the band carried her down the stairs. She was looking sleepy and a little pale.

'You okay?' Janet asked her as they got into another limousine, a white one again. They would have hotel suites and limousines waiting for them in every city where they went.

'I'm fine, Mom,' Melanie reassured her, and when they got to their hotel rooms, Pam ordered lunch for all of them, while Melanie called Tom. 'We're here,' she said, trying to sound livelier than she was. She was still groggy from the pain pills, but the boot helped when she walked. She could hardly move without the crutches.

'How's your ankle?' he asked, sounding concerned.

'I've still got it. They put me in some kind of a removable cast thing in Vegas before we left. I look like a cross between Darth Vader and Frankenstein. But it actually helps. I can take it off when I'm onstage.'

'Is that smart?' Tom asked, sounding like the voice of reason.

'I'll be fine.' She had no other choice. She did what the doctor had suggested and wore flats that night. They had taken the rising platform out of the show because she was afraid of falling and getting hurt again. She always said she felt like the Flying Wallendas when she used it, and said she should have a net. She had fallen off it twice before, but this was the first time she had actually gotten injured. It hurt, but it could have been worse.

She hobbled onto the stage with her crutches that night and laid them down. They had given her a tall chair to sit on, and she joked about it with the crowd. She said she'd done it having sex, which they thought was funny. And the audience forgot about it as soon as she started her show. She sat down on stage for most of the performance that night, but no one seemed to mind. She had worn hot pants, fish-net stockings, and a red-sequined bra. And even in flat shoes, she looked hot. She kept the encores short that night. She was dying to get back to her room and take another pill. She went right to sleep after she did, even before she called Tom to tell him how the show went. He had told her he was going to L.A. for dinner with his sister, and didn't call her either. But normally, they talked to each other all the time on their cell phones.

They spent two days in Phoenix, and from there they flew to Dallas and Fort Worth. They did two shows in each city, one in Austin, and another at the Astrodome in Houston. She was religiously wearing the boot while she was offstage, and her foot was better. They finally got two days off in Oklahoma City, which was sheer heaven. They were flying all over the country, and she was working hard. Performing with an injury was just one of the challenges she had to face while doing concerts. One of the roadies had broken an arm, and their sound man slipped a disk, carrying heavy equipment. But whatever happened, they all knew the show had to go on. It wasn't an easy life when they were on the road. The hours were exhausting, the performances were tough, and their hotel rooms were dreary. Whenever possible, they got suites. They got stretch limousines at every airport, but there was nowhere to go in them, except between the concert hall and hotel. In a lot of cities, they played in stadiums. It was all part of life as they made their way from city to city. After a while, all the places they went looked the same and they forgot where they were.

'God, I could use a break from this,' Melanie said to her mother one particularly hot night in Kansas City. It had been a good show, but she'd turned her bad ankle hopping off the stage, and it hurt more than ever. 'I'm tired, Mom,' she admitted, and her mother gave her a nervous look.

'If you want to keep selling platinum, you have to go on the road,' her mother said practically. She knew a lot about the business, and Melanie knew she was right.

'I know, Mom.' Melanie didn't argue with her, but she looked worn out when she got back to the hotel. She couldn't wait to have a hot bath and go to bed. She had meant what she said. She was dying for some time off. They were all getting a weekend off when they got to Chicago. Tom was planning to fly in to meet her. Melanie could hardly wait.

'She looks tired,' Pam commented to Janet. 'It can't be fun to perform on that ankle.' They had gotten stools put on stage for her in every city, but it was obvious the ankle wasn't healing and Melanie was in a lot of pain. When she wasn't performing, she hobbled around on her crutches with her black boot. It gave her some relief, but not enough. And the ankle was still just as swollen. It hadn't improved at all. It would have been

244

infinitely worse without their own plane. At least she could lie down on every flight. Flying commercial with all their equipment would have been nearly impossible, and would have driven them all insane. Checking luggage and equipment in would have required their spending hours boarding the flight. This way they just loaded up and took off.

When Tom met her in Chicago, he was surprised at how tired and pale she looked, and she was absolutely exhausted.

He was waiting for her at the hotel when they got in from the air-port, and he spun her around in his arms, even with the heavy boot, and then set her down gently on a chair. She was beaming from ear to ear. He had checked in to their suite half an hour before she arrived. It was a decent hotel, and they had a giant suite. But Melanie was sick of room service, signing autographs, and performing night after night no matter how much pain she was in. Tom was shocked at how swollen and painful her ankle still was.

They were playing a concert on Tuesday. And it was only Saturday night. Tom was leaving on Monday morning, to get to work in L.A. He had started the job after she left, and said he loved it. The travel they were promising him sounded terrific. It was with an urban planner, and although most of their jobs were for profit, they had several going that were in developing countries where they offered their services for free to governments, which was right up Tom's alley. She was proud and impressed by his humanitarian side, and she was happy he had found a job he liked. Tom had been worried about finding employment when he came back to Pasadena. He didn't even mind the commute to L.A. After the earthquake in San Francisco, he was happy to be back. And finding this job had been the perfect opportunity for him.

Tom took her out to dinner that night, and she ate an enormous greasy hamburger, with fried onion rings. And after that they went back to the hotel and talked about a lot of things. She told him about all the cities they had been to and various incidents along the way. Sometimes being on the road was like kids going to camp, or young soldiers being shipped out.

There was a constant sense of temporary living, breaking camp, and moving on. It was fun at times, and the atmosphere between them was great, but it was exhausting anyway. To break the monotony of traveling so much, the band and roadies had water balloon fights and threw some out the windows of the hotel, designed to hit pedestrians on the street below. The manager caught on to them eventually, came upstairs, and gave them a sound scolding. They were like children with nothing better to do. The roadies and guys in the band got into a fair amount of mischief when they had time off, mostly going to topless bars and strip joints, hanging out in bars, and getting drunk. Tom enjoyed talking to them and thought they were a lot of fun. But what interested him most was being with Melanie. He was beginning to miss her more and more when they were apart. And Melanie had told Pam conspiratorially that she was falling more and more in love with Tom. He was the nicest boyfriend she'd ever had, and she said she felt really lucky to have him in her life. Pam reminded her that she was one of the hottest stars in the

246

world at the moment, and he was lucky too. Besides, she was a nice person. Pam had known Melanie since she was sixteen, and thought she was one of the kindest people she'd ever met, unlike her mother, who could be really tough. Pam thought Tom and Melanie were a very good match. They were similar in disposition, easygoing and friendly, they were both intelligent, and he didn't appear to be jealous of her stardom or her work, which was incredibly rare. Pam knew that there weren't many people on the planet like them, and thanks to Melanie, she thoroughly enjoyed her work.

Tom and Melanie had a fantastic time in Chicago. They went to movies, museums, and restaurants, went shopping, and spent a lot of time in bed. When she went out, she used the crutches and wore the cumbersome black boot. Tom wanted her to. It was a terrific weekend, and Melanie was grateful that he was able to fly around to meet her as much as he did. He was using all his free air miles. The anticipation of seeing him, and the cities they discovered together made the tour far more tolerable for her. They were headed for the East Coast next, all the way up to Vermont and Maine. They were playing concerts in Providence and Martha's Vineyard. Tom said he would try to come back for Miami and New York.

The weekend whizzed by them, and she hated to see him leave again. The air was hot and muggy when she walked out to the curb with him while he hailed a cab. The boot had helped her, and the break from working, and she was in less pain by the time Tom left. She parked the boot near her bed at night, and she felt like she was taking off a wooden leg. Tom teased her about it, and she threw it at him once. It nearly knocked him down.

'Hey you, go easy. Behave yourself!' he scolded her, and then hid it under the bed. They were like kids sometimes and always had a lot of fun. They each enhanced the other's life, and seemed to fall more and more in love. For Tom and Melanie it was a summer of discovery and joy.

*　　　*　　　*

In San Francisco, Seth and Sarah had accepted the first offer on their house. It was a good one. The people were moving to town from New York, and wanted it in a hurry. They paid just over the asking price, and wanted a rapid closing. Sarah hated to see the house go, and felt bereft about it, but she and Seth were both relieved that it had sold. It went into escrow immediately, and Sarah shipped the things they were selling to Christie's. She sent the master bedroom furniture, a few things from the living room, and the children's clothes and some of their furniture to her new flat on Clay Street. They would be sharing a room now, instead of each having their own, so they didn't need as much. All the files and papers in Seth's office went to the Heartbreak Hotel on Broadway. They divided up the kitchen things. She sent a couch and two club chairs to Seth. And the rest went into storage. The art was sent to auction in New York. She was saddened to see how fast their home came apart, not unlike their lives. In a matter of days, the house was empty, and looked ransacked and unloved. Watching it happen reminded her of their marriage coming apart. It was amazing how little it

248

took to undo it. It depressed her as she walked around the house for a last time on their final day. She found Seth standing in his office, looking as depressed as she felt. She had just come down from the children's rooms, to make sure everything was on the truck. Parmani had taken the children to her house for the night, so Sarah could get everything set up on Clay Street.

'I hate to leave,' Sarah said, looking at him. He nodded, and then looked into her eyes with deep regret.

'I'm sorry, Sarah . . . I never thought this would happen to us.' She noticed that for once he said 'to us,' instead of just 'to me.'

'Maybe it'll all work out.' She didn't know what else to say, and neither did he. She went and put her arms around him then, to give him comfort. He stood there for a long moment with his arms at his sides, and then he put his arms around her too. 'Come and see the kids whenever you want,' she said generously. She hadn't been to see a lawyer for a divorce. There was time for that, and she had to be at the trial with him anyway. Henry Jacobs said her presence would be an unspoken but crucial positive factor in her husband's defense. They had hired two more attorneys to defend him. They and Henry would work as a team. Seth needed all the help he could get. Things were not looking good for him.

'Are you going to be okay?' Seth asked her with a look of deep concern. For the first time in a long time, his narcissism actually included someone else on the screen, other than himself. Sarah thought it was a first, and it meant a lot to her. They had had such a tough time ever since Seth's arrest.

'I'll be all right,' Sarah said to him as they stood in the dining room for the last time.

'Call me if you need me, any hour, any time,' Seth said, looking mournful, and then they both went outside. It was the end of their life together, the disappearance of their home. He had put an end to life as they had known it. And as she looked back at the brick house she loved, Sarah just stood there and cried. She was crying for their marriage and lost dreams, not the house. It nearly ripped Seth's heart out to see how upset she was. 'I'll come by and take the kids out tomorrow,' he said hoarsely. Sarah turned away and nodded, slipped into her car, and drove toward Clay. It was the beginning of her new life, and in her rearview mirror, she saw Seth get into his new silver Porsche that wasn't even paid for yet, and drive away. Her heart sank as she watched him. It was as though the man she had loved and married, and had two children with, had just died.

Chapter 16

Sarah's new flat on Clay Street was in a small Victorian house that had recently been renovated and painted. It was a duplex, and was neither elegant nor pretty, but Sarah knew it would look better to her when she unpacked their things. The first room she unpacked was the children's. She wanted them to feel at home the next day when they returned. She put out their favorite possessions and treasures lovingly and slowly, afraid that something might have broken in the boxes, but nothing had. So far, everything looked okay. She spent hours unpacking books, and two hours organizing linens and beds. They had gotten rid of so many things, that their lives suddenly seemed very spare. It was still hard to believe that, thanks to Seth's incredible perfidy, everything in their lives had changed. The articles that had continued to appear in the local and national press had been humiliating beyond belief. But humiliation or not, what she needed most was a job. She had called some contacts, but needed to make an all-out effort in the next few days.

And then, while she was going through some papers for the benefit, she had an idea. It was far below her skill level, but at this point, she was going to be grateful for any job she could get. She called the head of the neonatal unit on Wednesday afternoon, while both her children were taking a nap. She had cut Parmani's hours down as much as she could, and once she found a job, she was planning to increase them again. The sweet Nepalese woman was gentle and understanding. Her heart went out to Sarah and the children, and she wanted to do everything she could to help. By then, she had read all the articles too.

The head of the neonatal ICU gave Sarah the name she wanted, and promised to put in a good word for her. In order to give him time to do that, she waited until the next morning, until she got a message from him that the call had been made. The woman's name was Karen Johnson. She was the head of development at the hospital, in charge of fund-raising on a major scale, and whatever investments the hospital made. It wasn't Wall Street, but Sarah thought it could be an interesting job, if they had a spot in the department for her. When Sarah called her, Karen gave her an appointment for Friday afternoon. She was very warm and welcoming, and thanked Sarah for the enormous contribution she'd made with the benefit for the neonatal unit. They had made well over two million dollars. It was less than she'd hoped, but still a slight improvement over the year before.

Parmani came in on Friday afternoon and took the children to the park while Sarah went to her appointment at the hospital. She was nervous about it. It was the first time in ten years that she had gone to a job interview. The last one she'd had had been on Wall Street, before she went to business school, where she met Seth. She redid her résumé, and included the benefits she had organized for the hospital. But she knew it would be hard to get a job, as she hadn't worked since she completed business school. Since then, she had married Seth and taken care of her children. So she was out of the business loop.

Karen Johnson was a tall, spare, gracious woman with a Louisiana accent, who was kind and interested during the interview. Sarah was candid about the reverses she'd had, Seth's indictment, the fact that they were currently separated, and that she needed employment for obvious reasons. But more important, she had the abilities they needed.

She was more than capable of handling their investment portfolio, and then suddenly she panicked, worrying that they might think she might be as dishonest as her husband. Karen saw the look of anxiety and humiliation come over her face, and correctly guessed the reason for it. She was quick to reassure her, and offered her sympathy for the problems they were having.

'It's been very difficult,' Sarah said honestly. 'It came as a terrible shock . . . I had no idea what was going on, until the day after the earthquake.' She didn't want to go into the details of the case with her, but they'd been all over the newspapers anyway. It was no secret that Seth was going to trial for fraud, and was currently out on bail. Everyone in the country knew what he'd done, if they read the papers or listened to the news.

Karen explained to her then that she had an assistant in the department who had recently moved to L.A. There was in fact a job opening in the development department, but she was quick to say that hospitals weren't known for the salaries they paid. She mentioned a figure to Sarah, which sounded wonderful to her. It was modest, but it was something she could count on. And the hours were from nine to three. She could be home when her children woke up from their naps, and still have the afternoons and evenings with them, and weekends of course. At Karen's request, Sarah left three copies of her résumé with her. Karen said they would get in touch with her the following week, and thanked Sarah warmly for her interest in the position.

Sarah was excited when she left the building. She liked Karen, and the scope of the job. The hospital meant a lot to her, and the kind of investment portfolio that Karen had described was right up her alley. And she liked the prospect of fund-raising too. All she could do was hope now that she would get the job. Even the location worked well for her. The hospital was within walking distance of her new home. And the hours would give her time to spend with her children. The only drawback was the salary, which wasn't terrific, but it would have to do. And on her way home, Sarah had an idea.

She drove down to the Presidio and looked up Sister Maggie at the field hospital. She told her about the interview she'd just had at the hospital. Maggie was thrilled for her.

'That's fantastic, Sarah!' She admired her courage in the face of everything she was going through. Sarah had just told her that they had sold their house, she and Seth had separated, and she had moved into the flat on Clay Street with her children. It had only been a few days since they last talked. Things were moving fast.

'I just hope I get the job. We can really use the money.' Two months before she would never have had to say those words. They would have been inconceivable to either her or Seth. How quickly everything had changed. 'I love that hospital. They saved Molly's life. That's why I do the benefit for them.' Maggie remembered Sarah's speech right before the earthquake, and Melanie's performance.

'How are you and Seth?' Maggie asked her, as they walked into the mess hall for a cup of tea. Things were a little slower at the Presidio these days. A number of the residents had been able to go home, to areas of the city that had electricity and water again.

'Not so good,' Sarah said honestly. 'We hardly spoke to each other before we gave up the house. He's living in an apartment on Broadway, and ever since we moved to our new flat, Molly keeps asking me where Daddy is.'

'What do you tell her?' Maggie asked gently, as they sat down with their cups of tea. She liked talking to Sarah. She was a good woman, and Maggie was enjoying her friendship although they didn't know each other very well. But Sarah had bared her soul to her and trusted Maggie completely.

'I tell her the truth, as best I can. That Daddy isn't living with us right now. That seems to work for her. He's coming to take them out this weekend. Molly's going to spend the night with him. Oliver is too little.' She sighed then. 'I promised Seth I'd be at the trial with him.'

'When is it?'

'It's set for March.' It was still a long time away, nine months. Long enough for her to have the third baby she had been hoping to start with Seth, and that now they would never have. She couldn't imagine putting their marriage back together. Not now anyway. She felt too betrayed.

'That must be stressful for you both,' Maggie commented, looking sympathetic. She was always so kind. 'How are you doing with forgiveness, by the way? I know that's not a small endeavor, particularly in a case like this.'

'That's true,' Sarah said quietly. 'To be honest, I don't think I'm doing so well with that. I'm so angry sometimes, and so hurt. How could he do it? We had such a wonderful life. I love him, but I just don't understand how he could do something like that, and be so dishonest. He has no integrity whatsoever.'

'Something must have gone very wrong. It was

255

certainly a shocking error of judgment. And it sounds like he may pay a terrible price for it. Maybe that's punishment enough. And losing you and the children must be the final blow.' Sarah nodded. The problem for her was that she was paying the price too. She had lost her husband, and her children their father. But worst of all, she had lost all respect for him, and doubted she could ever trust him again. Seth knew it, and had barely dared to look her in the eye before he left. The look on her face had said it all.

'I don't mean to be hard on him. It's just such a terrible thing. He blew our whole life apart.' Maggie nodded, thinking about it. It was definitely hard to understand. Greed probably. And the need to be even more than he was. It was like some terrible character flaw in him that had surfaced, and turned into a tidal wave that had taken everyone with it. But Sarah looked better than Maggie had hoped. She almost said something to her then about her own problems, but she wouldn't even have known where to start. The big blue eyes looked into Sarah's, and the younger woman saw something deeply worried there. 'Are you okay?' Sarah asked her, and then Maggie nodded.

'More or less. I have my challenges too sometimes.' She smiled. 'Even nuns have nutty thoughts and do crazy things. I forget sometimes that we have the same human frailties as everyone else. Just when I think I have things all figured out, and think I have a direct channel to God, He turns the sound off, and I can't figure out what I'm doing or where I am. It reminds me of my own failings and humanity and keeps me humble,' she said cryptically, and then laughed. 'I'm sorry. I don't know what I'm talking about.' She had been so confused lately, so tormented, but she didn't want to burden Sarah with her problems. She had enough of her own. And there was nothing to do about what was troubling Maggie. She knew it. She just had to put it out of her mind. She had promised God and herself that she would.

They walked back to the field hospital then. Sarah said goodbye to Maggie, and promised to come back and see her soon.

'Let me know if you get the job!' she called out as Sarah walked away. Sarah wondered if she'd get it. She was qualified certainly, but her luck hadn't been running strong of late. Maybe this time it would. She needed the job. No one had responded to the résumés she had sent out in case the hospital job didn't pan out, although she hoped it would.

Sarah drove back to the house on Clay Street then, and was happy to see that Parmani and the children were home from the park, as she walked into the flat. Molly squealed in delight and ran to her, and Oliver crawled across the floor with a big grin for his mom. She tossed him up in the air, and sat down on the couch with him on her lap, as Molly cuddled up next to her, and Sarah realized again that whatever else had happened, the greatest blessing in her life was them. And as she started to get dinner ready, she thought about how nice it had been to see Maggie that afternoon. She wondered what the problem was that she'd been referring to. Whatever it was, she hoped it was nothing major. She was such a kind woman, and such a remarkable soul that Sarah couldn't

257

imagine a problem she couldn't solve. She certainly helped Sarah with hers. Sometimes all it took was a willing ear and a good heart, although Sister Maggie offered far more than that. She tossed in wisdom, love, and humor too.

*　　*　　*

Melanie's ankle was still bothering her when she came back to L.A. at the beginning of September. It had been hurting for the whole two months she'd been on tour. She had gone to see a doctor in New Orleans, and another one with Tom when he visited her in New York. Both orthopedists had told her it would just take time. At her age, most things were easy to repair, but hopping on and off stages and running around the country for two months doing one- or two-night stands was hard even on her. She finally went to see her own doctor when she got back to L.A., and he said it wasn't healing as well as it should have. He told her she was working too hard. That was nothing new. She had described the tour to him, and what she did when she was on it. He had been horrified. She was still wearing the big black boot, because the ankle hadn't healed, and the boot gave her some relief and protection from further damage. The only time her ankle didn't hurt was when she wore it. Onstage, even in normal street shoes now, even flats, the ankle always killed her.

Tom was worried when she called him on her way home. 'What did he say?'

'That I need a vacation, or maybe I should retire,' Melanie teased. She loved how attentive Tom was. Jake had been such a jerk. Tom wanted to know everything about her, even what her doctor had said when he ran another X-ray. 'Actually,' she answered him, he says there's still a hairline crack, and if I don't take it easy, I could wind up with surgery and pins in my foot. I think I'll pick "take it easy." I don't have a lot to do right now.' Tom laughed.

'Since when do you not have a lot to do?' She had taken care of everything on her desk when she got home the day before. Melanie was always busy. And Tom worried about her.

Her mother asked her the same questions about the ankle when she got home. Melanie shared with her that the doctor said it wasn't a big deal. Unless she went on tour again, then it might be.

'It's starting to look like a big deal,' her mother said casually. 'Every time I look at you, the foot is swollen. Did you tell the doctor that? You can't even wear high heels.'

Melanie looked sheepish. 'I forgot.'

'So much for being grown up at twenty,' Janet added. Melanie didn't have to be completely grown up. In some ways, she was just a kid. It was part of her charm. And she had a flock of people around her to take care of her. In other ways, Melanie was far older and had matured from years of hard work and discipline in her career. She was both woman of the world, and enchanting child. Her mother would have preferred to convince her she was still a baby. It gave her all the power, but in spite of Janet's efforts, Melanie was growing up, and becoming a woman in her own right.

Melanie tried to take care of the ankle. She went to physical therapy, did the exercises they gave her, and soaked it at night. It was better, but she was afraid to wear platform shoes or high heels, and when she stood for a long time in rehearsal, it hurt. It was like a constant reminder now of the price she paid for the work she did, and that it wasn't as easy as it looked. The money, fame, and razzle-dazzle of her business didn't come easily. She had performed with a nasty injury all summer, getting on stage with it at night, traveling constantly, and having to make it look as though everything was fabulous, or at least fine, even when it wasn't. She thought about it all one night as she lay awake in bed, with her ankle hurting, and in the morning she made a call. She'd had the name and number in her wallet since she left the Presidio in May. She made an appointment for the following afternoon, went to meet him by herself, and told no one.

The man she went to see was a small rotund man with a bald head and the kindest eyes she'd ever seen, except Maggie's. They talked for a long, long time. And when Melanie drove back to the house in Hollywood, she was crying. They were tears of love, joy, and relief. She needed to find some answers now, and all of his suggestions had been good. And the questions he had asked her about her life had plunged her into ever deeper thought. She had made only one decision that day. She didn't know if she could do it, but she had promised him and herself she would try.

'Something wrong, Mel?' Tom asked her when he came to pick her up for dinner that night. They went to a sushi restaurant that they both loved. It was quiet, pretty, and the food was good. It had a serene Japanese look to it, and as Melanie looked across the table at him, she smiled.

'No, something right, I think.' She told him about the meeting she'd had that day with Father Callaghan. She said Maggie had given her his name when she said she wanted to do volunteer work. He ran two orphanages in L.A., and a mission in Mexico, and was only in L.A. part of the time. She'd been lucky to call him when she did. He was leaving the next day.

She told Tom about the work he did, mostly with abandoned children, young girls he rescued from brothels, boys who'd been selling drugs since they were seven or eight. He housed them, fed them, loved them, and turned their lives around. There was a shelter for battered women, and he was helping to build a hospital for people with AIDS. He worked with similar people in Los Angeles, but his real love was what he did in Mexico. He had been doing it for more than thirty years. Melanie had asked him what she could do to help him. She had wanted to volunteer in L.A., and thought he might ask her to write a check to help with the missions in Mexico too. Instead, he smiled at her, and invited her to come and visit there, and told her he thought it might do her a lot of good. It might give her answers she was seeking and had talked to him about, in her own life. She had everything in the world to be thankful for, she told him, success, fame, money, good friends, adoring fans, a mother who did everything for her, whether she wanted her to or not, and a boyfriend who was wonderful to her, a really good person whom she loved.

'So why am I so unhappy?' she had asked the priest, with tears running down her cheeks in rivers. 'I hate what I do sometimes. I feel like everyone owns me, except me, and I have to do everything they want, for them . . . and this stupid ankle has been killing me for three months. I worked on it all summer, and now I can't get it better. My mom is mad at me because I can't wear heels on stage and she says it looks like shit.' It was all jumbled in her head as it came tumbling out like building blocks from a child's dump truck. Her thoughts were scattered all over the place. She could identify them, almost, but she couldn't make sense out of them, or make anything useful out of her concerns. He handed her a couple of tissues, and she blew her nose.

'What do *you* want, Melanie?' Father Callaghan asked her gently. 'Never mind what everyone else wants. Your mom, your agent, your boyfriend. What does Melanie want?'

Before she could stop them, the words blurted out, 'I want to be a nurse when I grow up.'

'I wanted to be a fireman, and I wound up being a priest instead. Sometimes we take other paths than the ones we expected to take.' He told her he had studied to be an architect, before going into the priesthood, which he found useful in the buildings they were putting up in the Mexican villages where he now worked. He didn't tell her he had a Ph.D. in clinical psychology that was even more useful to him, even in his dealings with her. He was a Franciscan, which worked well in his chosen line of work, but he had toyed with the idea of being a Jesuit. He loved the intellectual side of his Jesuit brothers, and enjoyed heated debates with them whenever the opportunity arose. 'You have a wonderful career, Melanie. You've been blessed. You have a tremendous talent, and I get

262

the feeling you enjoy your work, some of the time anyway, when you're not performing on a broken ankle, and no one is exploiting you.' In her own way, she was no different than the girls he rescued from brothels in Mexico. Too many people had been using her. They just paid her better for it, and the costumes were more expensive. But he could sense that everyone, including her mother, was pumping her to do their bidding, until the well ran dry. It had started to run dry for Melanie on her last concert tour, and all she wanted now was to run away and hide. She wanted to help others, and get in touch with what she'd experienced in the Presidio after the earthquake. It had been a time of epiphany and transformation for her, and then she had to go back to real life.

'What if you could do both? Do the work you love to do, when it's not overwhelming, maybe even on your terms. Maybe you need to take some of that control away from others. You can take some time to think about that. And take some time out of your life to help others, people who really need you, like the earthquake survivors you helped with Sister Maggie. Maybe the balance in your life would make more sense then. You have a lot to give people, Melanie. And you'd be amazed at what they'll give you back.' Right now, no one was giving her anything, except Tom. She was being bled dry.

'You mean like work with you here in L.A., or in your mission in Mexico?' She couldn't imagine being able to find the time. Her mother always had plans for her, interviews, rehearsals, recording sessions, concerts, benefits, special appearances. Her life and time were never her own.

'Possibly. If that's what you want. Don't do it to please me. You make a lot of people happy as it is, with your music. I want you to think about what would make you happy. It's your turn, Melanie. All you have to do is get in line, step up to the booth, and get your ticket. It's waiting for you. No one can take that away from you. You don't have to get on the rides everyone else wants you on. Get your ticket, pick your ride, and have a little fun here for a change. Life is a lot more fun than you're allowing it to be. And no one should take that ticket away from you. It's not their turn, Melanie. It's yours.' He was smiling at her, and as she listened to him, she knew.

'I want to go to Mexico with you,' she said in a whisper. She knew she had no major engagements for the next three weeks. She had a few interviews lined up, a photo shoot for a fashion magazine. She was recording in September and October, and was scheduled to do a benefit sometime after that. But none of them were things that couldn't be changed or canceled. All of a sudden, she knew she had to get away, and it might do her ankle good to stop working for a while, instead of trying to hobble around in high heels to make her mother happy. Suddenly, it was all too much. And he was offering her a way out. She wanted to take that right he was talking about. She had never done what she wanted in her whole life. She did what her mother told her, and what everyone expected her to do. She had always been the perfect little girl, and now she was sick of it. She was twenty years old and wanted to do something that meant a lot to her for a change. She had a feeling this was it. 'Could I stay at one of the missions for a while?'

Melanie asked him, and he nodded.

'You can live in our home for teenage girls. Most of them have been prostitutes and drug addicts. You wouldn't know it to look at them, they look like angels now. But your being there might do them a world of good. And you too.'

'How do I get hold of you when you're down there?' she asked, feeling breathless. Her mother was going to kill her if she did this. Although who knew, she'd probably try to turn it into a golden press opportunity. She always did.

'My cell phone works, and I'll give you some numbers,' he said, jotting them down. 'If it doesn't work for you to come down now, it might be easier for you in a few months, like next spring. This is pretty short notice in a life like yours. I'll be there till after Christmas, so come whenever you want, and stay as long as you feel like it. Whenever you show up, Melanie, we'll have a bed for you.'

'I'm coming,' she said with a look of determination, realizing that things had to change. She couldn't keep her mother happy forever. She needed to make her own decisions too. She was tired of living her mom's dreams, or being her dream. She needed her own. And this was a good place to start.

She was deeply pensive when she left the meeting. Father Callaghan hugged her, and then made the sign of the cross on her forehead with his thumb. 'Take care of yourself, Melanie. I hope we see you down there. If not, I'll catch up with you when I get back. Stay in touch.'

'I will,' she promised, and she thought about it all the way home. She knew what she wanted to do, she just didn't know how to pull it off, even for

265

a few days. But she wanted to go for longer than that. Maybe even a few months.

She told Tom all about it over their sushi dinner. He looked impressed and stunned, and then just as quickly, worried.

'You're not going to join a convent, are you?' She saw panic in his eyes and, as she shook her head and laughed, relief.

'No, I'm not. I'm not a good enough person to do that. Besides, I'd miss you too much.' She reached out across the table and took his hand in hers. 'I'd just like to do this for a while, help some people, clear my head, get out from under the pressure of all my obligations. I don't know if they'd let me, and my mom will have a fit. I just feel like I need to get away, and figure out what's important to me, other than my work and you. Father Callaghan says I don't need to give up my career to help other people, he says I give people hope and joy with my music. But I just want to do something more real for a while, like in the Presidio.'

'I think it's a great idea,' Tom seconded it. Ever since she'd gotten back from her tour, Melanie looked drained, and he knew her ankle was still hurting her a lot. It was no wonder after running around on it for three months, and dancing around on stage, taking pills at night, and cortisone shots like football players trying to fool their bodies into thinking they weren't injured and could play. Tom had learned a lot about the pressures she lived with, and the heavy dues she paid for her fame. It looked like too much to him, and he thought her going to Mexico for a while sounded like just what she needed, for her soul as well as her body. What

266

her mother would say about it was another thing. He was coming to know Janet well, and how she controlled everything in Melanie's life. She tolerated him now, and even liked him at times, but Janet always kept her daughter on a very, very short leash. She wanted Melanie to be a puppet, while she pulled all the strings. Anything that interfered with that had to be disposed of immediately. Tom was careful not to cross her, or to challenge her overwhelming influence on Melanie's life. He didn't think it could last forever. But he also knew that if Melanie challenged her mother's control now, Janet would go insane. She wanted to give up that power to no one, least of all to Melanie herself. And Melanie knew it too.

'I think I'll set it up first, and talk to her about it after I do. So she can't stop me. I have to see if my agent can get me out of some stuff, and my manager, without letting her know. She wants me to do everything, as long as it gets national press, major publicity, and I'm on the cover of whatever it is. She means well, she just doesn't understand that sometimes it's too much. I can't complain, she really made my career happen. She's had all this in her head since I was a little kid. I just don't want all of it as much as she does. I want to pick and choose, not get buried by all the shit she makes me do. And there's a lot of it!' She grinned at Tom. He knew Melanie was telling the truth. He had seen it at close range since May. Just keeping track of what she did exhausted him. And he had as much energy as she did. But he hadn't broken his ankle performing in Vegas. That had taken a toll too. It all had. Melanie had been looking exhausted, and now suddenly she had come alive again after her meeting with the priest.

'Would you come down and visit me in Mexico?' she asked Tom hopefully, and he smiled as he nodded.

'Of course I will. I'm so proud of you, Mellie. I think you'd love it, if you can pull it off.' They both knew her mother would be a fear-some opponent, and deeply threatened by any sign of independence from her daughter. This was going to be tough on Melanie. It was going to be the first time she had made a major decision on her own. And this was a big one, particularly since it had nothing to do with her career. That would frighten Janet even more. She didn't want Melanie distracted from her goals or, more important, her mother's goals. Melanie was not supposed to have her own dreams, only her mother's. That was changing. And change was going to scare her mother. Big time.

They talked about it on the way home. Janet was out when they got there, and they discreetly went to Melanie's bedroom and locked the door. They made love, cuddled up in bed afterward, and watched movies on TV. Her mother didn't mind his spending the night occasionally, although she didn't want anyone moving in, for herself or her daughter. As long as whatever guy in question didn't get too cocky, or have too much influence over Melanie, Janet was willing to tolerate his existence. Tom was smart enough to be discreet, and never face off with her.

In the end, he decided to go home around two in the morning, so he could get to work early the next day. Melanie was asleep when he left, but before she drifted off, he told her he'd be going.

She smiled sleepily and kissed him. She woke up early the next day, and started making calls to further advance her project. She swore her agent and manager to secrecy, and both said they'd see what they could do to get her out of the commitments she had, most or all of them made by her mother. They both warned her that her mother would hear about it fairly soon, one way or the other. Melanie said she was going to talk to her about it, but only after she canceled her commitments, so there was nothing Janet could do. Her manager told her that her stay in Mexico would be a great press opportunity for her, if she was willing to exploit the trip a little.

'No!' Melanie said firmly. 'That's the whole point. I need to get away from all that bullshit. I need some time to figure out who I am and what I want to do.'

'Oh Jesus, not one of those trips. You're not thinking about retiring, are you?' her agent asked. Janet would kill them all if that happened. She was a decent woman at heart, she just wanted her daughter's career to be the biggest thing since the birth of Jesus. She loved Melanie, but she was living vicariously through her. Her agent had thought it was a good thing that Melanie was trying to cut the umbilical cord a little. It had to happen sooner or later, and it was healthy for her. He had seen it coming. The problem was that Janet didn't, and she was guarding that umbilical cord with her life. No one was going to touch it. And only Melanie had that right. 'How long are you thinking?'

'Maybe till Christmas. I know we have the concert in Madison Square Garden on New Year's

269

Eve. I don't want to cancel that.'

'That's a good thing,' he said, sounding relieved. 'I probably would have had to slit my wrists on that one. Till then, it's all pretty minor stuff. I'll get on it,' he promised.

Two days later, both her agent and her manager had done what they had said they'd do. Melanie was free and clear until two weeks after Thanksgiving. Some of it had been rescheduled, and other things just had to be canceled, to be addressed at some distant, later date, if ever. None of it was a big deal. This had been the perfect time to do it. All she'd be missing were the press opportunities that came up at parties and benefits she'd be invited to. And there was no way to predict those. Janet liked her to do them all. And Melanie always did. Until now.

As expected, Janet wandered into Melanie's room two days after all of her engagements had been canceled. No one had said anything to her yet, and Melanie had told Tom she was going to tell her mother that night. She was planning to leave the following Monday and had already made her reservations. She wanted to spend the weekend with Tom before she left. He was a hundred percent behind her. And he was planning to come down to visit her when he could. He was excited about what she was doing and wanted to volunteer some time too. He had a strong urge to help his fellow man, as she did, and wanted to balance a serious career with the humanitarian traditions that he firmly believed in.

Three months wasn't a long time to be apart, but he said he would miss her. What they had was solid and good, and could withstand the distraction

270

of their respective obligations. Their relationship was going full speed ahead, and was turning into a great thing for both of them. They were kind, compassionate, intelligent, and supportive. They couldn't believe their good luck in having found each other. In many ways, they were so much alike and inspired each other in constructive ways. Together, their world had grown. Tom was even thinking of taking a week or two off himself, and volunteering at one of the Mexican missions with her, if they gave him the time off work. He loved working with kids, and in high school had been a Big Brother to a boy in Watts, and another in East L.A., and was still in touch with both. This was just his kind of thing. As a kid, he had dreamed of joining the Peace Corps, and had later chosen a career path instead. But now he envied what she'd be doing in Mexico, and wished he could spend three months there himself.

'That's weird,' Janet muttered to her, glancing at a stack of papers in her hand. 'I just got a fax that says your interview with *Teen Vogue* was canceled. How did they manage to screw that up?' She shook her head and glanced at her daughter, looking annoyed. 'And I got an e-mail this morning from the colon cancer benefit, saying they hope you can do it for them next year. That was in two weeks. It sounds like they dumped you for someone else. They said Sharon Osbourne is going to do it. Maybe they thought you were too young. Anyway, you'd better get out there and shake your booty, girl. You know what all that means? It means they're starting to forget you, and you were only on the road for just over two months. Time to show your face and get some press.' She smiled at

271

Melanie, lying on her bed and watching TV. Melanie had been thinking about what she had to pack for her trip to Mexico. Not much. And she had half a dozen books on her bed, about Mexico, which miraculously escaped her mother's notice. She glanced up at her mother, and wondered if this was the time to tell her. It wasn't going to be easy, she knew, whenever she did. The proverbial shit was going to hit the fan.

'Uh . . . actually, Mom,' Melanie spoke up just as her mother was about to leave the room, 'I canceled those two things . . . and some others . . . I'm kind of tired . . . I thought I'd go away for a few weeks.' She had been debating about telling her mother up front how long she was going to be away, or letting her know as time went on. She had not yet figured that out. But she had to tell her something, since she was about to leave. Janet stopped in her tracks and turned to frown as Melanie lay on her pink satin bed.

'What's that all about, Mel? What do you mean, you're "going away for a few weeks"?' She looked at her as though Melanie had said she had just grown horns or wings.

'Well, you know . . . my ankle . . . it's really been bothering me . . . I just thought . . . you know . . . it might be good to get away.'

'You canceled commitments without asking me?' Melanie could see that the fan was speeding up. The shit was near.

'I was going to talk to you about it, Mom, but I didn't want to bother you. The doctor said I should stay off my feet.'

'Is this Tom's idea?' Her mother was now glaring at her, trying to figure out where the evil influence had come from that had led Melanie to cancel two engagements without consulting her first. She smelled heavy interference.

'No, Mom, it isn't. It's just something I want to do. I'm tired after the tour. I didn't want to do that benefit, and I can do *Teen Vogue* anytime I want. They ask us all the time.'

'That's not the point, Melanie,' her mother said as she approached the bed with fury in her eyes. 'You don't cancel commitments. You talk to me, and I do. And you can't just disappear off the face of the earth because you're tired. You have to keep your face out there.'

'My face is on a million CD covers, Mom. No one's going to forget me if I'm gone for a few weeks, or don't do a colon cancer benefit. I just need some time to myself.'

'What the hell is that all about? This has to be Tom's doing. I see that kid lurking around. He probably wants you all to himself. He's jealous of you. He doesn't understand, and neither do you, what it takes to make a major career and keep you right up there on top. You can't lie around, fucking around and watching TV, or with your nose in a bunch of books. You need to be out there, Mel. And I don't know where you think you're going for a few weeks, but you can cancel that plan right now. When I think you need to get away, I'll tell you. You're fine. Now get off your dead ass and stop feeling sorry for yourself with that ankle. It's just a small crack, for chrissake. And that was almost four months ago. Get up and get moving, Mel. I'll call *Teen Vogue* and set the interview up again. I'll leave the benefit alone, because I don't want to piss off Sharon. But don't you *ever* cancel

273

any of your commitments again! Do you hear me?' She was trembling with rage, and Melanie with terror. She felt sick listening to her mother. It was all there. Janet thought she owned her. Whatever her intentions, good or bad, Melanie knew that her mother's constant control would ruin her life, if she continued to allow it.

'I hear you, Mom,' she said quietly, 'and I'm sorry you feel that way. But this is something I need to do for myself.' She bit the bullet then and jumped into the deep end. 'I'm going to Mexico till after Thanksgiving. I'm leaving Monday.' She almost winced as she said it, but managed not to. This was the worst it had ever been, although they'd had some major run-ins, whenever Melanie tried to make her own decisions or exercise some independence.

'You're *WHAT?* Are you insane? You have a million bookings from now till then. You're not going anywhere, Melanie, unless I tell you to. Don't you dare tell me what you're going to do. Let's not forget who put you on top here.' Her voice had, with her mother's help, but it was a cruel thing to say, and Melanie felt it like a blow. This was the first time she had stood up to her mother in just this way. And it was anything but pretty. Melanie wanted to crawl under her covers and cry, but she didn't. She held her ground. She knew she had to. And what she was doing wasn't wrong. She refused to let her mother make her feel guilty for wanting some time off.

'I canceled the other bookings, Mom,' she said honestly.

'Who did that?'

'I did.' She didn't want to get her agent and

274

manager in trouble, so she took the blame. She had told them to do it, which was what mattered. 'I need this time away, Mom. I'm sorry if it upsets you, but it's important to me.'

'Who's going with you?' She was still looking for the culprit, the person who had stolen her power from her. But in fact, only time had. Melanie had finally grown up and wanted at least some control of her own life. It had been a long time coming. And maybe Tom's love had helped her.

'No one. I'm going alone, Mom. I'm going to work in a Catholic mission that takes care of children. It's something I want to do. I promise I'll come back and work my ass off when I get home. Just let me do this without going crazy.'

'I'm not going crazy. *You* are,' Janet shouted at her. Melanie hadn't raised her voice once, out of respect for her mother. 'We can turn it into a press opportunity if you want to do it for a few days,' she said hopefully, 'but you can't go running off to Mexico for three months. For chrissake, Melanie, what were you thinking?' And then she thought of something else. 'Is that little nun in San Francisco behind this? She looked like a sneaky little piece of work to me. Watch out for that type, Melanie. She'll have you joining a convent next. And you can tell her that if that's what she has in mind, it'll be over my dead body!' Melanie smiled at the mention of Maggie, however rude.

'No, I went to see a priest here.' She didn't tell her the connection was through Maggie. 'He runs this great mission in Mexico. I just want to go there, have some peace, and then I can come back and work as hard as you want. I promise.'

'You make it sound like I'm abusing you,' her

275

mother said, bursting into tears as she sat down on her daughter's bed and Melanie put her arms around her.

'I love you, Mom. I appreciate everything you've done for my career. I just want something more than that in my life now.'

'It's the earthquake,' Janet said, shaking as she sobbed. 'You have post-traumatic stress. God, that would make such a good story in *People,* wouldn't it?' Melanie laughed as she looked at her. Her mother was a caricature of herself. Her heart was in the right place, but all she thought about was publicity for Melanie, and how to make her career even bigger than it was, which would have been hard to do. She had already done everything she had set out to accomplish, but her mother still couldn't let go, and have her own life. That was the essence of the problem. She wanted to live Melanie's life, not her own.

'You should go away somewhere too, Mom. A spa or something. Or London with some of your friends, or Paris. You can't think about me all the time. It's not healthy. For either of us.'

'I love you,' Janet wailed. 'You don't know what I gave up for you . . . I could have had a career, I gave it to you . . . all I've ever done is what I thought was best for you.' It was a two-hour speech, which Melanie had heard too often and tried to head off at the pass this time.

'I know, Mom. I love you too. Just let me do this. I'll be good after that, I promise. But you have to let me figure things out for myself, and make my own decisions. I'm not a kid anymore. I'm twenty.'

'You're a baby,' Janet said angrily, mortally

276

threatened.

'I'm a grown-up,' Melanie said firmly.

Janet spent the next few days alternately crying, complaining, and accusing. She bounced between grief and rage. She could feel the early signs of power slipping from her, and she was totally panicked. She even tried to get Tom to talk Melanie out of her plan, and he diplomatically said he thought it might do her good and thought it was noble of her, which only enraged Janet further. It was a nightmarish few days around their house, and Melanie could hardly wait to leave on Monday. After spending the weekend with him at her own house, she spent the last night at Tom's apartment, just to get away from her mother, and only went back to her own home at three A.M., to sleep before she left for the airport the following morning at ten. Tom had taken the morning off to drive her. She didn't want to leave in a white stretch limousine and attract attention, which her mother would have insisted on, if she'd had her way. She probably would have called the press and leaked the story, and might still anyway.

The scene with her mother as she left was out of a bad soap opera, with her mother clutching her and crying, saying she would probably be dead when Melanie got back, since she had been having chest pains ever since Melanie told her she was leaving. Melanie told her she'd be fine, promised to call her often, left all the pertinent phone numbers, and ran out the door to Tom's car, with a backpack and a duffel bag. It was all she was taking with her. She looked like she was escaping from prison as she slid into the car beside him.

'Go!' she shouted at him. 'Go! Go! Go! Before

she runs out and throws herself on the hood of the car.' He took off, and they were both laughing as they reached the first stoplight. It felt like a getaway car to both of them, and it was. Melanie almost felt high at the prospect of leaving and what she'd be doing when she got to Mexico.

Tom kissed her when he left her at the airport, and she promised to call him when she arrived. He was planning to come down in two or three weeks. But in the meantime, Melanie knew she would have lots of new adventures. Her three-month sabbatical in Mexico was just what the doctor ordered.

She was sitting on the plane, just before the doors closed, when she decided to call her mother. She was getting to do what she wanted, and she knew it was hard for Janet. Melanie knew it felt like a huge loss to her. Losing her control over Melanie to any degree was frightening for her, and Melanie felt sorry for her.

Janet answered at the house, and sounded depressed. She brightened noticeably when she heard her daughter's voice.

'Did you change your mind?' she asked, sounding hopeful, and Melanie smiled.

'No. I'm on the plane. I just wanted to give you a kiss. I'll call you from Mexico, when I can.' They made the announcement then to turn off all cell phones, and she told her mother she had to get off. Her mother sounded tearful for a moment.

'I still don't understand why you're doing this.' It felt like punishment to her, and rejection. It was much more than that to Melanie. It was a chance to do some good in the world.

'I just need to, Mom. I'll be back soon. Take

care. I love you, Mom,' Melanie said as a flight attendant reminded her to turn off her phone. 'I gotta go.'

'I love you, Mel,' her mother said hastily, as with a last kiss, Melanie turned off her phone. She was glad she had called. This trip had nothing to do with hurting her mother. It was something she needed to do for herself. She needed to discover who she was, and if she could exist on her own.

Chapter 17

Maggie heard from Melanie after she got to Mexico. She loved it and said the place was beautiful, the children were wonderful, and Father Callaghan was fantastic. She said she had never been happier in her life and wanted to thank Maggie for the suggestion that she call him.

Maggie had heard from Sarah too. She got the job at the hospital, and was happy and busy. She still had a lot to face, adjusting to her new life, but she seemed to be doing well, and keeping busy helped her. Maggie knew, as Sarah did herself, that she had some tough times ahead, particularly when Seth went to trial. And after that, she had to make some major decisions. She had promised Seth and his lawyers that she would stand by him at the trial. But Sarah was trying to make up her mind about whether or not to divorce him. The key for her was whether or not she could forgive him. She didn't have the answer to that question yet, and had talked about it to Maggie a lot. Maggie told her to keep praying and the answer

279

would come. But so far nothing had. All Sarah could think of was the terrible thing Seth had done when he betrayed everyone and himself and broke the law. It seemed an almost unforgivable sin to Sarah.

Maggie was still at the field hospital in the Presidio herself. They had been there for four months, and the office of Emergency Services was thinking of closing the camp the following month, in October. There were still people living in the residence halls and hangars, and some of the old brick barracks, but not nearly as many as before. Most people had gone home by then, or made other arrangements. And Maggie was planning to move back to her apartment in the Tenderloin later in the month. She realized that she was going to miss the companionship of all the people she lived with and had met there. In a strange way, it had been a good time for her. And the studio apartment in the Tenderloin was going to seem very lonely. She told herself it would give her more time for prayer, but nonetheless she would miss the camp. She had made some wonderful new friends.

Everett called her at the end of September, a few days before she was moving back home. He said he was coming to San Francisco to do a story on Sean Penn, and said he wanted to take Maggie to dinner. She hesitated, and then started to say she couldn't, desperately groping for some excuse, but couldn't find one that sounded plausible, so feeling stupid for it afterward, she accepted his invitation. She prayed about it that night, asking not to be confused, and to be only grateful for his friendship, and want nothing more.

But the moment she saw him, Maggie felt her heart pound. He walked toward her down the walk outside the hospital where she was waiting, and his long thin legs and cowboy boots made him look more like a cowboy than ever. He beamed as soon as he saw her, and in spite of herself, a smile lit up her face. They were so happy to see each other. He put his arms around her in a big bear hug, and then stepped back to look at her, drinking her in.

'You look terrific, Maggie,' he said happily. He had come straight from the airport. He wasn't doing the interview until the next day. Tonight was just for them.

He took her to a small French restaurant on Union Street for dinner. The city was back in order now. Debris had been cleared, and there was construction everywhere. Almost five months after the earthquake, nearly every neighborhood was habitable again, except the very worst ones, some of which had been without salvation and had had to be torn down.

'I'm moving back to my own apartment next week,' Maggie said sadly. 'I'm actually going to miss living with the other sisters here. Maybe I would have been happier living in a convent than on my own,' she commented as they started dinner. She had ordered fish, and Everett was digging into a huge steak as they chatted. And as always between them, the conversation was lively and intelligent and flowed. They talked about a myriad of subjects, and then finally Everett mentioned Seth Sloane's upcoming trial. Just hearing or reading about it always made Maggie sad, especially for Sarah. It was such a senseless waste of a good man and four lives. He had been so foolish, and had hurt so many. 'Do you think you'll cover the trial?' she asked with interest.

'I'd like to. I don't know how interested *Scoop* will be in that, although it's a hell of a story. Have you seen Sarah again? How's she doing?'

'She's okay,' Maggie said, not divulging any secrets. 'We talk occasionally. She's working at the hospital now, in fund-raising and development. This isn't going to be easy for her either. He sure took a lot of people down with him.'

'That kind of guy always does,' Everett said without a lot of sympathy. It was Sarah he felt sorry for, and Seth's kids, who would never really know him now, if he spent the next twenty or thirty years in prison. Thinking about it reminded him of his son again. For some reason, he always thought of Chad when he was with Maggie, as though they were somehow invisibly connected. 'Is Sarah divorcing him?'

'I don't know,' Maggie said vaguely. Sarah didn't know yet either, but Maggie didn't think she should be discussing that with Everett, and the conversation moved on to other topics.

They sat at the table in the French restaurant for a long time. It was cozy and comfortable and the waiter left them alone while they talked.

'I heard a rumor that Melanie is in Mexico,' Everett commented, and Maggie smiled. 'Did you have anything to do with that?' He smelled her hand in it, and she laughed.

'Only indirectly. There's a wonderful priest who runs a mission down there. I thought they'd be a good match. I think she's staying until almost Christmas, although she's not telling anyone officially where she is. She just wants to spend a

282

few months as a regular person. She's a very sweet girl.'

'I bet her mother went nuts over it when she left. Working at a mission in Mexico is not exactly on her usual star track, or in her mother's plans for her. Don't tell me she's down there too!' He chuck-led at the vision, and Maggie shook her head, laughing.

'No, she's not. I think that was the whole point. Melanie needs to try her wings a little. It will do her a world of good to get away from her mother. And it will do her mother good too. It's hard to cut those ties sometimes. Some people have more trouble with it than others.'

'And then there are guys like me who have no ties at all.' He said it regretfully, and she watched him.

'Have you done anything about finding your boy yet?' She nudged him gently, but didn't push too hard. She never did. She always found a light touch more effective, and it was in his case too.

'No, but I will one of these days. I guess it's time, or something like that. I'll do it when I'm ready.'

He paid the check then, and they walked down Union Street. There were no left-over signs of the earthquake here. The city looked clean and beautiful. It had been a beautiful September, with lots of warm weather, and now there was the faint chill of autumn in the air. Maggie tucked her hand into his arm comfortably, as they strolled along, and continued talking about a variety of subjects. They hadn't intended to walk all the way back to the Presidio, but in the end they did. It gave them a little more time together, and was all on level

283

ground, which was rare in San Francisco.

He walked her to the building where she lived, and it was after eleven, late enough so no one was outside. They had taken their time with dinner, and always seemed to fit together like two halves of one whole, each one complementing the other, in their thinking and opinions.

'Thanks for a nice time,' she said, feeling foolish for having tried to avoid him. The last time she had seen Everett had confused her. She had felt such a powerful pull toward him, but now all she felt was warmth and deep affection. It was perfect, and he was looking down at her with all the love and admiration he felt for her.

'It was good to see you, Maggie. Thanks for having dinner with me. I'll call you when I leave tomorrow. I'll stop by if I can, but I think the interview may run long, so I'll be rushing to catch the last plane. If not, I'll come by for a cup of coffee.' She nodded, looking up at him. Everything about him was so perfect. His face. His eyes, the deep soul and ancient suffering that peeked through them, along with the light of resurrection and healing. Everett had been to hell and back, but it had made him who he was. As she looked at him, she saw him gently lean his face toward her. She was going to kiss his cheek, and then before she knew what had happened, she felt his lips on hers, and they were kissing each other. She hadn't kissed a man since nursing school, and even then, it hadn't been often. And now suddenly she felt her whole being, heart and soul, pulled toward him, and his spirit mingling with hers. It was the sudden blending of two beings becoming one through a single kiss. She felt dizzy when they finally stopped. He hadn't just kissed her, she had kissed him as well, and she stared at him afterward with a look of terror. The unimaginable had happened. And she had prayed so hard for it not to.

'Oh my God . . . Everett! . . . no! . . .' She took a step back, and he grabbed her arm and pulled her gently toward him, and with her head bowed in grief, he held her.

'Maggie, don't . . . I didn't mean to do that . . . I don't know what happened . . . it was like a force too powerful to resist pulled us together. I know that wasn't supposed to happen, and I just want you to know I didn't plan it . . . but I have to be honest with you. It's how I feel, and have since the moment I met you. I love you, Maggie . . . I don't know if that makes a difference to you or not . . . but I do . . . I'll do anything you want me to do. I don't want to hurt you. I love you too much for that.' She looked up at him without a sound, and saw love in his eyes, pure, raw, and honest. His eyes mirrored what was in hers.

'We can't see each other again,' she said, looking heartbroken. 'I don't know what happened.' And then she gave him the gift of the same honesty he had given her. He had a right to know it. 'I love you too,' she whispered. 'I can't do this . . . Everett, don't call me again.' It broke her heart to say it, and he nodded. He would have given her both his arms and legs. She already owned his heart.

'I'm sorry.'

'So am I,' she said sadly, and turned away from him then and walked silently into the building.

He stood watching the door as it closed, and felt

his heart go with it. He dug his hands into his pockets, turned, and walked back to his hotel on Nob Hill.

In her bed, in the dark, Maggie looked as though her world had come to an end. She was too devastated and stunned for once to even pray. All she could do was lie there, thinking of the moment when they'd kissed.

Chapter 18

Melanie's time in Mexico had been everything she hoped it would be. The children that she worked with were loving, lovable, and so grateful for the smallest things people did for them. Melanie had worked with eleven- to fifteen-year-old girls, all of whom had been prostitutes, many of them previously addicted to drugs, and she knew that three of them had AIDS.

It was a time of growth and deep meaning for her. Tom came down to see her twice, for long weekends, and was impressed by what she was doing. She told him she was anxious to work when she got back, she missed singing and even performing, but there were some things she wanted to change. Above all, she wanted to start making her own decisions. They both agreed it was time, although she knew her mother would have a hard time with it. But she had to have her own life now too. Melanie said Janet seemed to be keeping busy without her. She had gone to New York to see friends, and even to London, and had spent Thanksgiving with friends in L.A. Melanie had stayed in Mexico for Thanksgiving, and she wanted to go back and volunteer there again next year. The trip had been a success in every way.

She stayed a week longer than planned and landed at LAX the week before Christmas. The airport was decorated, and she knew Rodeo Drive would be by then too. Tom picked her up, and she looked tanned and happy. In three months, she had slipped from child to woman. Her time in Mexico had been a rite of passage. Her mother hadn't come to the airport but had a surprise party waiting for her at home, with all the people who were important to Melanie. She threw her arms around her mother's neck and they both cried, happy to see each other. She could tell that her mother had forgiven her for flying away, and had somehow found it in herself to understand and accept what had happened, although during the party, she told Melanie about all the things she'd booked for her. Melanie started to object, and then they both laughed, knowing what had happened. Old habits died hard.

'Okay, Mom. I'll give you a pass this time. Just this once. Next time, ask me.'

'I promise,' her mother said, looking slightly sheepish. It was going to be a major adjustment, for both of them. Melanie had to take on the responsibility of her own life now. And her mother had to hand it over. No small feat for either of them, but they were trying. The time away from each other had helped to make the transition.

Tom spent Christmas Day with them, and gave Melanie a promise ring. It was a narrow band of diamonds that his sister had helped pick out for her. Melanie loved it, and he slipped it on her right hand.

'I love you, Mel,' he said softly, as Janet came out in a red-and-green-sequined Christmas apron, with a tray of eggnog. And several friends had dropped by. She was in good spirits, and seemed busier than ever. Since she got back, Melanie had spent the week rehearsing for her concert at Madison Square Garden on New Year's Eve. It was a hell of a reentry, and hardly a gentle beginning. Tom was coming to New York with her two days before the concert. And her ankle was completely healed. She'd been wearing sandals for three months.

'I love you too,' she whispered to Tom. He was wearing the Cartier watch she had given him. He loved it. But most of all he loved her. It had been an amazing year for them both, from the San Francisco earthquake to Christmas.

*　　*　　*

Sarah dropped the children off with Seth on Christmas Day. He had offered to come by, but she didn't want him to. It made her uncomfortable when he came to her house. She still hadn't decided what to do. She had talked to Maggie about it several times. And Maggie had reminded her that forgiveness was a state of grace, but no matter what she did, Sarah couldn't seem to reach it. She still believed in 'for better or worse,' but she no longer knew what she felt for him. She couldn't process what had happened. She was numb.

She had celebrated Christmas with the children the night before, on Christmas Eve, and that morning they had dug through their stockings, and opened the gifts from Santa Claus. Oliver just loved ripping off the wrappings, and Molly loved everything Santa had given her. They had checked, and Santa had drunk most of the milk and eaten all the cookies. Rudolph had gnawed on all the carrots, and two were missing.

It pained Sarah to share their familiar traditions with the children without Seth, but he said he understood. He was seeing a psychiatrist and taking medication for anxiety attacks he was having. And Sarah felt terrible about that too. She felt as though she should have been there with him, at his side, and bringing him comfort. But he was a stranger to her now, even if one she had loved and still did. It was an odd and painful feeling.

He smiled when he saw her standing outside his door with the children and asked her to come in, but she said she couldn't. She said she was meeting friends, and she was actually having tea at the St. Francis with Maggie. She had invited her there, as it wasn't far from where Maggie lived, although it was a whole universe away in spirit.

'How are you doing?' Seth asked her, as Oliver toddled in. He was walking now. And Molly dashed in to see what was under his tree. He had gotten her a pink tricycle, a doll as big as she was, and a stack of other presents. His finances were in the same shape as Sarah's, but Seth had always spent more money than she did. She was trying to be careful now, with her salary, and the money he gave her for the kids. Her parents were helping her too and had invited her to Bermuda for the holidays, but she didn't want to go. She had wanted to stay here, and keep the children near him. For all they knew, it might be his last Christmas out of prison for a long time, and she didn't want to deprive him of his children, or them of him.

'I'm okay,' she answered Seth, and smiled in the Christmas spirit, but there was so much wreckage between them. It showed in his eyes and hers too, so much disappointment and sorrow, and the force of his betrayal, which had hit her like a bomb. She still couldn't understand what had happened, or why. She realized now that once again there was a piece of him she just never knew, one that had more in common with people like Sully, and nothing in common with her. That was the scary part. There had always been a stranger living in the house with her. It was too late to meet him now, and she didn't want to. That stranger had destroyed her life. But she was rebuilding it quietly on her own. Two men had asked her out recently, and she had turned both down. As far as Sarah was concerned, she was still married, until they decided otherwise, which they hadn't yet. She was putting that decision off until after the trial, unless it came to her in a blinding flash before that. She was still wearing her wedding band, and Seth was too. For now, at least, they were still husband and wife, even if living apart.

He handed her a Christmas present before she left, and she had one for him too. She had bought him a cashmere jacket and some sweaters, and he got her a beautiful little mink jacket. It was exactly what she liked, and it was gorgeous in a lush dark brown. She put it on when she opened it, and kissed him.

'Thank you, Seth. You shouldn't.'

'Yes, I should,' he said sadly. 'You deserve a lot more than that.' In the old days, he would have given her some huge piece of jewelry from Tiffany or Cartier, but this was not the year for that, and it never would be again. All her jewelry was gone. It had finally been sold at auction the month before, and the money frozen with the rest of their assets, as his legal bills mounted sky high. He felt terrible about it.

She left him with their children then. They were spending the night with him. He had bought a portable crib for Ollie, and Molly was going to sleep in his bed with him, since he only had one bedroom in the small apartment.

Sarah kissed him when she left, and had a heavy heart as she drove away. The burdens they shared now were almost too much to bear. But they had no other choice.

*   *   *

Everett went to an AA meeting on Christmas morning. He had volunteered to be the guest speaker, and share his story. It was a big meeting he liked to go to. There were a lot of young people, some rough-looking types, a handful of affluent Hollywood folk, and even a few homeless people who wandered in. He loved the mix, because it was so real. Some of the meetings he'd been to in Hollywood and Beverly Hills were a little too manicured and polished for him. He preferred his meetings rougher and more down to earth. This one always was.

He shared during the regular part of the meeting too. He said his name and that he was an alcoholic, and fifty people in the room said 'Hi, Everett!' at once. Even after nearly two years, it gave him a warm feeling and made him feel at home. His shares were never practiced or rehearsed. He just said whatever came to mind, or was bothering him at the time. He mentioned Maggie this time, that he loved her and she was a nun. He said she was in love with him too, was remaining faithful to her vows, and had asked him not to call her again, so he hadn't. He had felt the loss sorely for the past three months, but respected her wishes. And then, as he left the meeting and got into his car to go home, he thought about what he'd said. That he loved her as he had never loved any other woman before, nun or not. That was worth something, and he suddenly wondered if he had done the right thing, or if he should have fought for her. It had never occurred to him before. He was on the way home, when he made a sharp turn and headed for the airport. Traffic was light on Christmas Day. It was eleven o'clock in the morning, and he knew he could catch a one o'clock flight to San Francisco, and be in the city by three. Nothing could have stopped him then.

He paid for his ticket, got on the flight, and sat staring out the window at the clouds and the countryside and highways below. He had no one else to spend Christmas with, and if she refused to see him, he hadn't lost much. Just some time, and a round-trip ticket from L.A. It was worth a shot. He had missed her unbearably in the last three months, her wise views, her thoughtful comments, her delicate ventures into advice, the sound of her voice, and the brilliant blue of her eyes. He could hardly wait to see her now. She was the best

Christmas gift of all, and the only one he had. He had nothing for her either, except his love.

The flight landed ten minutes early, just before two o'clock, and the cab he hailed got him into the city at twenty to three. He went to her address in the Tenderloin, feeling like a schoolboy visiting his girlfriend, and started to worry about what would happen if she wouldn't let him in. She had an intercom and might tell him to go away, but he had to try anyway. He couldn't just let her slip out of his life. Love was too rare and important to throw away. And he had never before loved anyone like her. He thought she was a saint. Others said it about her too.

He paid the cabdriver when they got to her building, and he walked nervously to her front steps. They were badly battered and chipped. And two drunks were sitting on the stoop, sharing a bottle. Half a dozen hookers were wandering up and down the street, looking for 'dates.' It was business as usual here, Christmas Day or not.

He rang her bell, and no one answered. He thought of calling her cell phone, but didn't want to warn her. He sat down on the top step in his jeans and heavy sweater. It was chilly, but the sun was out and it was a pretty day. However long it took, he was going to wait. He knew she'd turn up eventually. She was probably serving Christmas lunch or dinner to the poor in a dining room somewhere.

The two drunks on the step below him were still passing the bottle to each other, and then one of them looked up and offered it to him. It was bourbon, the cheapest brand they could buy, in the smallest size. They were filthy dirty, smelled bad,

293

and both of them smiled toothlessly up at him.

'Drink?' one of them offered, slurring. The other one was drunker and looked half asleep.

'Have you guys ever thought of going to AA?' Everett asked amiably, declining the bottle, as the one who'd offered it looked at him in disgust and turned away. He nudged his buddy, gestured toward Everett, and without a word the two of them got up and walked away to another stoop, where they sat down and continued drinking while Everett watched. 'There but for the grace of God go I,' he whispered to himself, still waiting for Maggie. It seemed like the perfect way to spend Christmas Day, waiting for the woman he loved.

*   *   *

Maggie and Sarah had a nice time having tea at the St. Francis Hotel. They were serving a proper English high tea, with scones, pastries, and an assortment of tea sandwiches. And they chatted easily as they both sipped Earl Grey. Maggie thought Sarah looked sad, but didn't press her about it. And Maggie had been feeling down herself. She missed talking to Everett, their laughter and conversations, but after what had happened between them the last time, she knew she couldn't see or talk to him again. She didn't have the strength to resist him if she saw him. She had gone to confession about it, and strengthened her resolve since. But she missed him anyway. He had become a treasured friend.

Sarah talked about seeing Seth, how much she missed him, and the easy days of their old life. She had never, ever dreamed that it would all come to

294

an end. It was the farthest thing from her mind.

She said she liked her job and the people she was meeting. But she was still keeping very much to herself socially. She was still too embarrassed to go out or see friends. She knew the city was still buzzing with gossip about them, and it was going to be worse around the time of the trial in March. There had been long discussions about whether to try to get continuances to delay the proceedings, or press for a speedy trial. Seth had decided he wanted to get it over with. And he seemed to get more stressed about it every day. She was deeply worried about it too.

The conversation meandered pleasantly as they talked about things in the city, Sarah taking Molly to *The Nutcracker,* Maggie serving at an ecumenical Christmas midnight mass the night before at Grace Cathedral. It was just a warm and cozy meeting between two friends. Their friendship had been a gift to each of them that year, an unexpected blessing as a result of the earthquake in May.

They left the St. Francis at five o'clock. Sarah dropped Maggie off at the corner of her block and headed uptown. She was thinking about going to a movie on her own, and invited Maggie, but she said she was tired and wanted to go home. And the film Sarah wanted to see sounded too depressing to her. Maggie waved as Sarah drove away, and then walked slowly up her block. She smiled at two of the hookers, both of whom lived in her building. One was a pretty Mexican girl, the other was a transvestite from Kansas who was always very nice to Maggie, and respectful of the fact that she was a nun.

Maggie was just about to walk up the steps, when she looked up and saw him. She stopped, no longer moving, and he smiled down at her. He had been sitting there for two hours, and he was getting cold. He didn't care if he froze to death sitting there, he wasn't going to move until she came home. And suddenly there she was.

She stood looking at him, unable to believe what she was seeing, and slowly he came down the stairs to where she stood.

'Hi Maggie,' he said gently. 'Merry Christmas.'

'What are you doing here?' she asked, staring at him. She had no idea what else to say.

'I was at a meeting this morning . . . and I shared about you . . . so I flew up to say Merry Christmas to you myself.' She nodded. It was conceivable to her. She could imagine him doing it just that way. No one had ever done anything like that for her before. She wanted to reach out and touch him to see if he was real, but she didn't dare.

'Thank you,' she said softly, her heart racing. 'Do you want to go somewhere for a cup of coffee? My place is a mess.' And she didn't think it was proper to take him upstairs. The most important piece of furniture she had in the studio's only room was her bed. And it was unmade.

He laughed in answer to her question. 'I'd love that. I've been freezing my ass off on your steps, literally, since three o'clock.' He brushed off the seat of his jeans then, as they walked to a coffee shop across the street. It was a dismal-looking place, but convenient, well lit, and the food was actually halfway decent. Maggie stopped there for dinner sometimes on the way home. The meat loaf was fairly good, and the scrambled eggs. And they were always nice to her because she was a nun.

Neither of them said another word until they sat down, and ordered coffee. Everett ordered a turkey sandwich, but Maggie had just eaten her fill at the lovely Christmas tea she'd shared with Sarah at the St. Francis.

He was the first to speak. 'So how've you been?'

'Okay.' She felt tongue-tied for the first time in her life, and then relaxed a little, and almost looked like herself. 'This is the nicest thing anyone has ever done for me. Flying up here to wish me a Merry Christmas. Thank you, Everett,' she said solemnly.

'I've missed you. A lot. That's why I'm here today. It suddenly seemed stupid that we can't talk to each other anymore. I guess I should apologize for what happened last time, except that I'm not sorry we did it. It was the best thing that's ever happened to me.' He was always honest with her.

'Me too.' The words fell out of her mouth without her permission, but it was how she felt. 'I still don't know how that happened.' She looked remorseful and penitent.

'Don't you? I do. I think we love each other. Or at least I do. And I get the feeling you do too. At least I hope you do.' He didn't want her to suffer for her feelings for him, but he couldn't help hoping that they were in love with each other, and it wasn't just happening to him. 'I don't know what we'd ever do about it, if anything. That's another story. But I wanted you to know how I feel.'

'I love you too,' she said sadly. It was the single greatest sin she had ever committed against the Church, and the greatest challenge to her vows, but it was true. She thought he had a right to

297

know.

'Well, that's good news,' he said, taking a bite out of his sandwich. After he had swallowed it, he smiled at her, relieved by what she'd said.

'No, it's not,' she corrected him. 'I can't give up my vows. This is my life.' But now, in some way, he was too. 'I don't know what to do.'

'How about if we just enjoy it for right now, and think about it? Maybe there is some right way for you to move on into a different life. Kind of like an honorable discharge maybe.' She smiled at what he'd said.

'They don't give you those when you leave the order. I know people do it, my brother did, but I could never imagine doing that myself.'

'Then maybe you won't,' he said fairly. 'Maybe we just stay like this. But at least we know we love each other. I didn't come up here to ask you to run away with me, although I'd love it if you did. Why don't you think about it, without torturing yourself? Give it some time, and see how you feel.' She loved how reasonable and sensible he was.

'I'm scared,' she said honestly.

'Me too,' he said, and took her hand in his own. 'This is scary stuff. I'm not sure I've ever been in love with anyone in my life. I was too drunk to give a damn about anyone for about thirty years, including myself. Now I wake up, and there you are.' She loved what he had said.

'I've never been in love,' she said quietly, 'till you. I never in a million years thought this would happen to me.'

'Maybe God figured it was time.'

'Or He's checking my vocation. I'll feel like an orphan if I leave the Church.'

'I may have to adopt you then. That's a possibility. Can you adopt nuns?' She laughed at what he said. 'I'm so happy to see you, Maggie.'

She started to relax then, and they talked the way they always did. She told him about what she'd been doing, he told her about stories he'd covered. They talked about Seth's impending trial. He said he had talked to his editor at length, and might cover it for *Scoop*. He said if so, he'd be in San Francisco for many weeks, starting in March, when the trial was scheduled to begin. She liked the idea of his being there, and the fact that he wasn't rushing her. By the time they left the coffee shop, they were comfortable with each other again. He held her hand as they crossed the street. It was nearly eight o'clock by then and time for him to catch a plane back to L.A.

She didn't invite him up, but they stood there for a long minute. 'This is the best Christmas gift I've ever had.' She smiled at him.

'Me too.' He kissed her gently on the forehead. He didn't want to frighten her, and people in the neighborhood knew she was a nun. He didn't want to compromise her reputation by kissing her. And she wasn't ready for it anyway. She needed to think. 'I'll call you, and see how things are going.' And then he caught his breath, and felt like a kid when he spoke. 'Will you think about things, Maggie? I know this is a big decision for you. They don't come bigger than this. But I love you, and I'm here for you, and if you were ever crazy enough to do it, I would be honored to marry you. Just so you know what I'm offering is respectable.'

'I wouldn't expect anything less of you, Everett,' she said primly, and then beamed. 'I've never been proposed to before either, come to think of it.' She felt giddy as she looked at him, stood on tiptoe, and kissed his cheek.

'Can a recovering alcoholic and a nun be happy together? Stay tuned.' He was laughing as he said it, and suddenly out of the blue, he realized that she was still young enough to have babies, maybe even a few of them, if they got started soon. He liked that idea, but didn't mention it to her. She had enough on her mind as it was.

'Thank you, Everett,' she said, as she unlocked the front door, and he whistled to a passing cab that stopped in front of them. 'I'll think about it. I promise.'

'Take as long as you want. I'm in no hurry. There's no pressure on you.'

'Let's see what God has to say about all this,' she said, smiling at him.

'Okay. You ask Him. Meanwhile, I'll start lighting candles.' He had loved doing that as a kid.

She waved as she disappeared into the building, and he ran down the steps to the waiting cab. He looked up at the building as they drove away, thinking that this was possibly the best day of his life. He had love, and better yet, he had hope. And best of all, he had Maggie . . . almost. And for dead-ass sure, she had him.

Chapter 19

The day after Christmas, filled with the energy of seeing Maggie, Everett sat down at his computer, got on the Internet, and started playing. He knew there were sites that did particular searches. He typed in some information, and a questionnaire appeared on his screen. He carefully answered all the questions, although he didn't have much information. Name, birthdate, place of birth, parents' names, last known address. That was all he had to go on. No current address, Social Security number, or any other type of information. He kept it limited to Montana. If nothing turned up there, he could search other states. He sat quietly at his computer waiting to see what would come back. There was hardly a pause before a name and address were on his screen. It had all been so simple and so quick. After twenty-seven years, there he was. Charles Lewis Carson. Chad. With an address in Butte, Montana. It had taken twenty-seven years to look for him, but now he was ready. There was a phone number and e-mail address too.

He thought about e-mailing and decided not to. He jotted all the information down on a piece of paper, sat thinking about it for a while, walked around his apartment, and then took a deep breath, called the airline, and made a reservation. There was a flight out at four o'clock that afternoon. Everett decided to be on it. He could call him when he got there, or maybe just drive by and see what the house looked like. Chad was thirty years old, and Everett hadn't even seen a photograph in all these years. He and his ex-wife had completely lost contact, after he stopped sending her support checks when Chad turned eighteen, and the only contact between them before that, as Chad grew up, were the checks he sent her every month, and her signature on the back when she endorsed them. They had stopped exchanging letters when Chad was four, and he hadn't had a single photograph since, nor asked for one.

Everett knew nothing about him now, married, single, whether or not he went to college, what he did for a living. He had another thought then and typed in the same questions for Susan, but didn't find her. She might have moved to another state, or gotten remarried. There were a number of reasons why she might not turn up on the screen. All he really wanted to do was see Chad. He wasn't even sure if he wanted to meet him. Everett wanted to take a look and decide once he was there. This had been a hard decision for him, and he knew that both Maggie and his recovery had a lot to do with it. Before both of those factors entered his life, he wouldn't have had the courage to do this. He had to face his own failures in this case, his inability to relate or engage, to even try to be a father. He had been eighteen when Chad was born, a baby himself. Now Chad was older than he had been when his son was born. Everett was twenty-one the last time he saw him, and went off to become a photographer floating around the world, like a soldier of fortune. But no matter how he dressed it up or tried to romanticize it, for all intents and purposes and from Chad's perspective, Everett had abandoned him and disappeared. Everett was ashamed of having done it, and it was entirely possible that Chad hated him. He certainly had a right to. Everett was finally willing to face him now after all these years. Maggie had given him the push he needed.

He was quiet and pensive on the way to the

airport, bought a cup of coffee at Starbucks and took it on the plane with him, and then sat staring out the window while he drank it. This was different than the trip he'd taken the day before, when he went to San Francisco to see Maggie. Even if she was angry, or was avoiding him, they had some kind of relationship, all or most of which had been pleasant. He and Chad had nothing, except Everett's total failure to be a father. There was nothing to draw from or build on. There had been no communication and no bridge between them for twenty-seven years. Other than DNA, they were total strangers.

The plane landed in Butte and Everett asked a cabdriver to drive him past the address he had taken off the Internet. It was a small, clean, cheaply built house in a residential district of the city. It wasn't a fancy neighborhood, but it wasn't a slum either. It looked ordinary, mundane, and pleasant. The patch of grass outside was small but neatly tended.

After they'd seen it, Everett asked the driver to take him to the nearest motel. It was a Ramada Inn, and had nothing distinctive about it. He asked for the smallest, cheapest room, bought a soda from a vending machine, and went back to his room. He sat there for a long time, staring at the phone, wanting to dial the number, but too afraid to, and finally he got up the guts to do it. He was feeling like he wanted to go to a meeting. He knew he could do that eventually, but first he wanted to call Chad. He could always share about it later, and probably would.

The phone was answered on the second ring. It was a woman, and for a minute Everett wondered if he had the wrong number. If he did, it could get complicated. Charles Carson wasn't an unusual name, and there could have been many in the phone book.

'Is Mr. Carson in?' Everett asked in a polite, pleasant voice. Everett could feel his voice shake, but the woman didn't know him well enough to hear it.

'I'm sorry, he's out. He should be back in half an hour.' She readily gave out the information. 'Should I give him a message?'

'I . . . no . . . uh . . . I'll call back,' Everett said, and hung up before she could ask him any questions. Everett wondered who the girl was. Wife? Sister? Girlfriend?

He lay on the bed then, turned on the TV, and dozed off. It was eight o'clock when he woke up, and stared at the phone again. He rolled over on the bed and dialed the number. A man answered this time in a strong, clear voice.

'Is Charles Carson in, please?' Everett asked the voice on the other end, and waited breathlessly. He had a feeling this was it, and the prospect of it made him feel dizzy. This was much harder than he had expected. And once he identified himself, then what? Chad might not want to see him. Why would he?

'This is Chad Carson,' the voice corrected. 'Who is this?' He sounded mildly suspicious. The use of his full name told him that the caller was a stranger.

'I . . . uh . . . mmmm . . . I know this sounds crazy, and I don't know where to start.' He blurted it out then. 'My name is Everett Carson. I'm your father.' There was dead silence at the other end of the phone, as the man who'd answered tried to figure out what had just hit him. Everett could easily imagine the kind of things Chad might say to him, 'get lost' being by far the nicest of them. 'I'm not sure what to say to you, Chad. I guess I'm sorry is the first thing, although it doesn't cover twenty-seven years. I'm not sure anything could. And if you don't want to talk to me, that's okay. You don't owe me a thing, not even conversation.' The silence continued as Everett wondered if he should continue talking, or hang up discreetly. He decided to wait through a few more seconds of silence, before he gave up completely. It had taken him twenty-seven years to reach out to his son and initiate a reunion. Chad had no idea what was going on and was shocked into silence.

'Where are you?' was all he said, as Everett wondered what he was thinking. This was all pretty scary.

'I'm in Butte.' Everett still said it like a native, although he had lived in other places. He still had the faint accent of Montana.

'You are?' Chad sounded astonished again. 'What are you doing here?'

'I have a son here,' Everett said simply. 'I haven't seen him in a long time. I don't know if you want to see me, Chad. And I wouldn't blame you if you don't. I've been thinking about doing this for a long time. But I'll do whatever you want. I came to see you, but it's up to you if you want to. If not, I understand. You don't owe me anything. I'm the one who owes you an apology for the last twenty-seven years.' There was silence at the other end, while the son he didn't know digested what he said. 'I came to make amends.'

'Are you in AA?' Chad asked cautiously, recognizing the familiar words.

'Yes, I am. Twenty months. It's the best thing I ever did. That's why I'm here.'

'Me too,' Chad said with some hesitation. And then he had an idea. 'Do you want to go to a meeting?'

'Yes, I do.' Everett took a deep breath.

'There's one at nine o'clock,' Chad offered. 'Where are you staying?'

'The Ramada Inn.'

'I'll pick you up. I drive a black Ford pick-up. I'll honk twice. I'll be there in ten minutes.' In spite of everything, he wanted to see his dad, as much as his father wanted to see him.

Everett threw some cold water on his face, combed his hair, and looked in the mirror. What he saw was a forty-eight-year-old man who'd seen a lot of rough road in his day, and had abandoned his three-year-old son at twenty-one. It was something he wasn't proud of. There were a lot of things that still haunted him, and that was one. He hadn't hurt many people in his life, but the one he had hurt most was his son. There was no way he could make it up to him, or give him back his years without a father, but at least he was here now.

He was standing outside the hotel in jeans and a heavy jacket when Chad pulled up. Everett saw that he was a tall, handsome boy, with blond hair and blue eyes, a powerful build, and the gait of Montana as he got out of his truck and approached. He walked to where Everett stood, looked at him long and hard, and held out his hand to shake his father's. The two men looked into each other's eyes, and Everett had to fight

306

back tears. He didn't want to embarrass this man who was a total stranger to him but looked like a good man, the kind of son any father would have been proud to know and love. They shook hands, and Chad nodded acknowledgment. He was normally a man of few words.

'Thanks for coming to pick me up,' Everett said as he got into his truck, and saw photographs of two little boys and a girl. 'Are those your kids?' Everett looked at them in surprise. It had never even occurred to him that Chad would have children of his own. Chad smiled and nodded.

'And another one on the way. They're nice kids.'

'How old are they?'

'Jimmy is seven, Billy's five, and Amanda is three. I thought we'd done it, but then we got a surprise six months ago. Another girl.'

'That's quite a family.' Everett smiled and then laughed. 'Holy shit, I've had my son back for five minutes, and I'm already a grandfather, times four. Serves me right, I guess. You got started early,' Everett commented, and this time Chad smiled.

'So did you.'

'A little earlier than planned.' He hesitated for a moment then, afraid to ask, but decided to anyway. 'How's your mom?'

'She's okay. She got married again, but she never had any other kids. She's still here.' Everett nodded. He was leery of seeing her again. Their brief adolescent marriage had left a bitter taste in his mouth and probably hers too. They had shared a miserable three years, which finally drove him away. They were the worst possible match he could have imagined, a nightmare right from the beginning. She had threatened to shoot him once with her father's rifle. A month later, Everett walked out. He figured if he didn't, he'd kill her or himself. It had been three years of constant battles. He had started drinking heavily then, and kept at it for twenty-six years.

'What do you do?' Everett asked Chad with interest. He was a strikingly handsome young man, far more so than he himself had been at Chad's age. Chad had a chiseled face and was a rugged man. He was even taller than Everett and had a far more powerful build, as though he worked in the outdoors, or should.

'I'm the assistant foreman at the TBar7 Ranch. It's twenty miles out of town. It's all horses and cattle.' He looked like the perfect cowboy.

'Did you go to college?'

'Junior college. Two years. At night. Mom wanted me to go to law school.' He smiled. 'That's not my thing. College was okay, but I'm a hell of a lot happier on a horse than at a desk, although I have to put in a fair amount of desk time now too. I don't like it much. Debbie, my wife, teaches school. Fourth grade. She's a hell of a rider. She's in the rodeo in the summer.' They were the perfect cowboy and wife, and Everett didn't know why, but he sensed that they had a good marriage. He looked like the kind of guy who would. 'Did you get married again?' Chad looked at him with curiosity.

'No. I was healed,' he said, and they both laughed. 'I've been roaming around the world for all these years, until twenty months ago, when I put myself in rehab and dried up, long overdue. I was too busy and too drunk for all this time for any decent woman to want me. I'm a journalist,' he added, and Chad smiled.

'I know. Mom shows me your pictures sometimes. She always did. You do some pretty cool stuff, mostly wars. You must have been to some interesting places.'

'Yeah, I have.' He realized that he sounded more Montana himself now, talking to the boy. Short sentences, clipped words, and fewer of them. Everything here was spare, just like the rugged terrain. There was an incredible natural beauty to it, and he thought it was interesting that his son had stayed close to home, unlike his father, who had gone as far as he could from his roots. He had no family here now, the little he had were all dead. He had never come back again, except finally, for his son.

They reached the little church then, where the meeting was, and as he followed Chad down the stairs to the basement, he realized how lucky he was to have found him, and that Chad had been willing to see him at all. It could easily have been otherwise. He gave silent thanks to Maggie as he walked into the room. It was only due to her gentle, persistent persuasion that he had come, and he was thrilled now that he had. She had asked him about his son the night they met.

Everett was surprised to see that there were thirty people in the room, mostly men and a few women. He and Chad sat down next to each other on folding chairs. The meeting had just started and followed the familiar format. Everett spoke up when they asked newcomers or visitors to identify themselves. He said that his name was Everett, he was an alcoholic, and had been in recovery for twenty months. Everyone in the room said 'Hi,

Everett!' and they went on.

He shared that night, and so did Chad. Everett spoke first, and found himself talking about his early drinking, his unhappy shotgun marriage, leaving Montana, and abandoning his son. He said it was the single event in his life he most regretted, that he was there to make amends and clean up the wreckage of the past, if possible, and that he was grateful to be there. Chad sat and looked at his feet while his father spoke. He was wearing well-worn cowboy boots, not unlike his father's. Everett was wearing his favorite pair of black lizard. Chad's were the boots of a working cowboy, splattered with mud, dark brown, and well worn. All the men in the room were wearing cowboy boots and even some of the women. And the men held Stetsons on their laps.

Chad shared that he had been in recovery for eight years, since he got married, which was interesting information for his father. He said he'd had a fight again that day with the foreman, and would have loved to quit his job but couldn't afford to, and that the baby in the spring would put additional pressure on him. He said that sometimes he got scared of all the responsibilities he had. And then he said that he loved his kids anyway, and his wife, and things would probably work out. But he admitted that the new baby locked him even more into his job, and he was resentful about it at times. And then he glanced at his father, and said that it was weird meeting a father he had never known, but he was glad he had come back, even if long overdue.

The two men mingled with the crowd afterward, after the whole group held hands and said the

Serenity Prayer. And once the official format of the meeting was over, everyone welcomed Everett, and spoke to Chad. They all knew each other. There were no strangers at the meeting, except Everett. The women had brought coffee and cookies, and one of them was the secretary of the meeting. Everett had liked the shares and said he had thought it was a good meeting. Chad introduced his father to his sponsor, a grizzled-looking old cowboy with a beard and laughing eyes, and his two sponsees, who were about his own age. Chad said he had been a sponsor in AA for almost seven years.

'You've got some time in recovery,' Everett commented when they left. 'Thanks for letting me come with you tonight. I needed a meeting.'

'How often do you go?' Chad inquired. He had liked his father's share. It was open and honest and seemed sincere.

'When I'm in L.A., twice a day. Once, when I'm on the road. What about you?'

'Three times a week.'

'That's a heavy load you're carrying with four kids.' He had a lot of respect for him. Somehow he had assumed that Chad had lived in suspended animation for all these years, a child forever, and instead he was a man with a wife and family of his own. In some ways, Everett recognized, he had made more of his life than his father. 'What's with the foreman?'

'He's a jerk,' Chad said, looking suddenly young and annoyed. 'He rides my ass all the time. He's very old-fashioned, and he runs the ranch the same way he did forty years ago. He's going to retire next year.'

'Think you'll get the job?' Everett asked with fatherly concern, and Chad laughed and turned to look at him as they drove up to the hotel.

'You've been back an hour, and now you're worrying about my job? Thanks, Dad. Yeah, I damn well better get the job or I'll be pissed. I've been working there for ten years, and it's a good job.' Everett beamed when he called him Dad. It was a good feeling, and an honor he knew he didn't deserve. 'How long are you going to be here?'

'That's up to you,' Everett said honestly. 'What do you think?'

'Why don't you come to dinner tomorrow? It won't be fancy. I have to do the cooking. Debbie's been pretty sick. She always is when she's pregnant, right until the last day.'

'She must be a good sport to have done it so often. And so are you. That's no easy deal supporting all those kids.'

'They're worth it. Wait till you meet them. Actually'—Chad squinted, looking at him—'Billy looks like you.' Chad actually didn't, he looked like his mother, Everett had noticed, and her brothers, who had looked a lot like her. They had been big solid Swedish stock who had come to Montana two generations before from the Midwest, and Sweden before that. 'I'll pick you up tomorrow at five-thirty when I get back from work. You can get to know the kids while I cook. And you'll have to forgive Debbie. She feels like shit.' Everett nodded and thanked him. Chad was being incredibly welcoming, so much more than Everett felt he deserved. But he was grateful that after all these years Chad was so willing to open up his life

312

to him. Everett had been a piece missing from his life for too long.

Both men waved at each other as Chad drove away, and Everett hurried back to his room. It was freezing outside, and there was ice on the ground. He sat down on his bed with a smile and called Maggie. She answered on the first ring.

'Thanks for coming up yesterday,' Maggie said warmly. 'It was nice,' she continued softly.

'Yes, it was. I've got something to tell you. It may come as a surprise.' She got nervous listening to him, wondering if he was going to put more pressure on her than he had the day before. 'I'm a grandfather.'

'What?' She laughed. She thought he was kidding. 'Since yesterday? That was quick.'

'Apparently not so quick. They're seven, five, and three. Two boys and a girl. And another one on the way.' He was beaming as he said it. He suddenly liked the idea that he had a family, even if grandchildren made him feel ancient. But what the hell.

'Wait a minute. I'm confused. Did I miss something? Where are you anyway?'

'I'm in Butte,' he said proudly, and all thanks to her. It was yet another gift she had given him, one of many.

'Montana?'

'Yes, ma'am. I flew in today. He's a terrific kid. Not a kid, a man. He's the assistant foreman at a ranch here, and he has three kids and another one on the way. I haven't met them yet, but I'm going to dinner at their place tomorrow. He even cooks.'

'Oh, Everett,' she said, sounding as excited as he was. 'I'm so pleased. How's it going with Chad? Is he okay about things . . . about you . . .'

'He's a noble man. I don't know what his childhood was like, or how he feels about that. But he seems pleased to see me. Maybe we were both ready. He's in AA too, and has been for eight years. We went to a meeting here tonight. He's a really solid guy. He's a lot more grown-up than I was at his age, or maybe even now.'

'You're doing fine. I'm so glad you did that. I always hoped you would.'

'I never would have done it without you. Thank you, Maggie.' With her gentle, persistent urging, she had given him back his son, and a whole new family.

'Yes, you would have. I'm so glad you called and told me. How long are you staying?'

'A couple of days. I can't stay too long. I have to be in New York on New Year's Eve, to cover a concert Melanie is doing there. But I'm having a great time here. I wish you could come to New York with me. I know you'd enjoy seeing one of her concerts. She does an incredible job onstage.'

'Maybe I'll get to one, one of these days. I'd like to.'

'She's doing a concert in L.A. in May. I'll invite you down.' And with any luck at all, she might have made some kind of decision by then about leaving the convent. It was all he wished now, but he didn't mention it. It was a huge decision, and he knew she needed time to think. He had promised not to pressure her. He had just called to tell her about Chad and the kids, and to thank her for getting him there, in her usual quiet way.

'Have fun with the children tomorrow, Everett. Call and tell me how it went.'

'I promise. Goodnight, Maggie . . . and thank you . . .'

'Don't thank me, Everett.' She smiled. 'Thank God.'

He did as he fell asleep that night.

*   *   *

The next day Everett went shopping for some toys to bring to the children. He bought a bottle of cologne for Debbie, and a big chocolate cake for dessert. He was carrying all of it in shopping bags when Chad picked him up, and helped him put it in the back of the truck. He told his father they were having barbecued chicken wings that night and mac and cheese. He and the kids were designing the menus these days.

The two men were happy to see each other, and Chad drove him to the small, neat house Everett had seen when he looked around to see where his son lived. It was warm and cozy inside, although there were toys in the living room, children lying on all the furniture, the television was on, and a pretty blond girl looking pale was reclining on the couch.

'You must be Debbie.' He spoke to her first, and she got up and shook his hand.

'I am. Chad was really happy to see you last night. We've talked about you a lot over the years.' She made it sound as though the comments in the past had been pleasant, although realistically he couldn't imagine that that would have been the case. Any mention of him would have had to be angry, or sad, for Chad anyway.

Everett turned to the children then, amazed by

315

how sweet they were. They were as beautiful as their parents, and didn't seem to fight with each other. His granddaughter looked like an angel, and the two boys were sturdy little cowboys and big for their age. They looked like a poster family for the state of Montana. And while Chad cooked dinner and Debbie lay on the couch again, visibly pregnant, Everett played with the kids. They loved the toys he gave them. Then he showed the boys card tricks, sat Amanda on his lap, and when dinner was ready, he helped Chad dish it up for the kids. Debbie couldn't sit at the table, the sight and smell of the food made her feel too sick, but she joined in the conversation from the couch. Everett had a ball, and hated to leave when it was time for Chad to take him back to the motel. Everett thanked him profusely for a great evening.

When they pulled up in front of the motel, Chad turned to ask him a question. 'I don't know how you feel about it . . . do you want to see Mom? It's okay if you don't. I just thought I'd ask.'

'Does she know I'm here?' Everett asked, looking nervous.

'I told her this morning.'

'Does she want to see me?' Everett couldn't imagine that she did after all these years. Her memories couldn't be any better than his, and possibly worse.

'She wasn't sure. I think she's curious. Maybe it would be good for you both, for some kind of closure. She said she always thought she'd see you again and you'd come back. I think she was angry for a long time that you never did. But she got over all that a long time ago. She doesn't talk about you much. She said she could see you tomorrow morning. She's coming into town to see the dentist. She lives thirty miles out of town, past the ranch.'

'Maybe it would be a good idea,' Everett said, thinking. 'It might help us both bury old ghosts.' He didn't think about her much either, but now that he'd seen Chad, it didn't seem so uncomfortable to see her, for a few minutes anyway, or whatever they could tolerate. 'Why don't you ask her what she thinks? I'll be at the motel all day. I've got nothing much to do.' He had invited Chad and his family out to dinner the following day. Chad said they all loved Chinese and there was a good one in town. And then he was leaving the next day, for one night in L.A., and then off to New York for Melanie's concert.

'I'll tell her to come by if she wants.'

'Whatever works for her,' Everett said, trying to sound casual, but still feeling somewhat strained at the idea of seeing Susan again. After she left, he could go to a meeting, just as he had that day, in the afternoon before he saw Chad and the kids. He was religious about his meetings, wherever he was. There were plenty to choose from in L.A., though fewer here.

Chad said he'd relay the message and pick his father up for dinner the following night. And Everett reported on the evening to Maggie. He told her what a good time he'd had, how beautiful the children were, and well behaved. And for some reason, he didn't tell her about possibly seeing his ex-wife the next day. He hadn't quite absorbed it yet himself, and he was apprehensive about it. Maggie was even more thrilled for him than she'd been the day before.

317

Susan showed up at the motel at ten o'clock the next morning, just as Everett was finishing a Danish and coffee. She knocked on the door of his room, and when he opened it, they stood staring at each other for a long moment. There were two chairs in the room, and he invited her in. She looked both different and the same. She was a tall woman, and she had gotten heavy, but her face was the same. Her eyes explored his and looked him over. Seeing her was like examining a piece of his own history, a place and person he remembered, but no longer felt anything for. He couldn't remember loving her, and wondered if he had. They had both been so young, confused, and angry at the situation they were in. They sat in the room's two chairs, looking at each other, struggling for words. He had the same feeling he had then, of having absolutely nothing in common with her, a fact that, in his youthful lust and enthusiasm, he had failed to notice when they started dating, and she got pregnant. And then he remembered how trapped he had felt, how desperate, how bleak the future had looked to him when her father had insisted they get married, and Everett had agreed to what felt like a life sentence. The years had stretched ahead like a long lonely road, whenever he thought about it, and had filled him with despair then. He felt breathless again just remembering it, and recalled perfectly all the reasons why he had run away and began drinking heavily before that. An eternity with her had felt like suicide to him. He was sure she was a good person, but she had never been the right one for him. He had to fight to bring his mind back to the present, and for a fraction of a second he wanted a

318

drink, and then remembered where he was, and that he was free. She couldn't trap him anymore. Circumstances had trapped him more than she had. They were both victims of their own destinies, and he hadn't wanted to share his with her. He had never been able to adjust to the idea of being with her forever, even for the sake of their son.

'Chad's a great kid,' he complimented her, and she nodded, with a small wintry smile. She didn't look like a happy person, nor miserable either. She was very bland. 'And so are his children. You must be very proud of him. You did a great job with him, Susan. No thanks to me. I'm sorry about all those years.' It was his chance to make amends to her too, no matter how unhappy their time together had been. He realized even more acutely now what a lousy husband and father he had been then. He was just a kid himself.

'It's okay,' she said vaguely, while he thought that she looked older than her years. Her life in Montana hadn't been easy, nor was his on his travels. But it was more interesting than hers. She was so different than Maggie, who was so full of life. There was something about Susan that made him feel dead inside, even now. It was hard for him to even remember when she was pretty and young. 'He was always a good boy. I thought he should have stayed in college, but he'd rather be outdoors on a horse than doing anything else.' She shrugged. 'I guess he's happy where he is.' As Everett looked at her, he saw love in her eyes. She loved their son. He was grateful for that.

'He seems to be.' It was a father-mother discussion that seemed odd between them. It was probably the first and last they'd ever have. He hoped she was happy, although she didn't look like a cheerful, extroverted person. Her face was solemn and devoid of emotion. But this meeting wasn't easy for her either. She looked content as she looked at Everett, as though their meeting put something to rest for her too. They were so totally different, they would have been miserable if they'd stayed together. And as their visit ended, they both knew things had happened as they should.

She only stayed a short time, and he apologized to her again. And then she left for the dentist, and he went for a walk, and then to his AA meeting. He shared about seeing her and how it had reminded him of how desperate he had felt and how unhappy and trapped he felt when he was married to her. He felt as though he had finally closed the door on the past and double-locked it. She was all the reminder he needed of why he had left. A lifetime with her would have killed him, but he was grateful now to have Chad and his grandchildren. So in the end, she had shared something good with him. It had all happened for a reason, and now he could see what that was. He couldn't have known then that thirty years later it would all make sense, and Chad and his children would become the only family he had. She had actually brought something good into his life, and he was grateful to her for that.

Dinner at the Chinese restaurant that night was a huge amount of fun. He and Chad talked constantly, the children chattered and giggled and slopped Chinese food all over the place. Debbie came and tried to be a good sport about the food smells. She only had to go outside for air once. And when Chad dropped his father off at the

320

motel afterward, he gave him a big hug, as did all the children and Debbie. And then Chad said, 'Thanks for seeing Mom. I think it meant a lot to her. She never really felt like she said goodbye to you. She always thought you'd come back.' He could see why he never had, but he didn't say that to his son. Susan was his mother, after all, and she had been the one who'd been around to take care of him and love him. She might have been boring to Everett, but she had done a great job with their son, and he respected her for that.

'I think it did us both good to meet again,' Everett said honestly, and to remind him of the realities of the past.

'She said you had a nice time.' By her definition, not his. But it served its purpose, and he could see it was important to Chad, which made it all the more worthwhile.

He promised to come back and see them again, and to stay in touch. He left them his cell phone number and told them he moved around a lot when he was on assignments.

They all waved when they drove off. The visit had been a huge success, and he called Maggie again that night and told her all about it. He was genuinely sad to leave Butte the next day. His mission had been accomplished. He had found his son. He was a wonderful man, with a sweet wife and a great family. And even his ex-wife wasn't a monster, she just wasn't the woman he would have wanted or could have lived with. The trip to Montana had brought Everett a cornucopia of gifts. And the one who had made it possible for him was Maggie. She was the source of so many good things in his life.

Everett watched Montana drift away below him as the plane took off. As they circled before heading west, they passed over where he knew the ranch was, where Chad worked. He looked down with a quiet smile, knowing that he had a son, and grandchildren, and he would never lose them again. Now that he had faced his demons, and his own failings, he could return to see Chad and his family again and again. He looked forward to doing it, and maybe even bringing Maggie. He wanted to see the new baby in the spring. The visit he had dreaded for so long was the piece of him that had been missing for years, maybe all his life. And now, he had found it. The two greatest gifts in his life were Maggie and Chad.

Chapter 20

Everett covered Melanie's concert in New York on New Year's Eve. Madison Square Garden was packed with her fans, and she was in great form. Her ankle was healthy, her soul was peaceful, and he could see that she was happy and strong. He stood backstage with Tom for a few minutes, and took a picture of him with Melanie. Janet was there as usual, ordering everyone around, but she seemed a little more tempered about it, and less obnoxious. All seemed to be well in their world.

He called Maggie on New Year's Eve, at midnight for her. She was at home, watching TV. It was after the concert, and he had stayed up to call her. She said she was thinking about him, and she sounded troubled.

'Are you okay?' he asked, worried. He was always afraid that she might close the door on him, if it seemed the right thing to do, to her. He knew how powerful her loyalties were to her vows, and he represented a huge challenge and even threat to her, and all that she believed.

'I have a lot on my mind,' she admitted. She had decisions to make, a whole life to evaluate, her future and his to decide. 'I pray about it constantly these days.'

'Don't pray too hard. Maybe if you just let it flow for a while, the answers will come.'

'I hope so,' she said with a sigh. 'Happy New Year, Everett. I hope it's a great year for you.'

'I love you, Maggie,' he said, suddenly feeling lonely. He missed her, and had no idea how things would work out. He reminded himself, one day at a time, and said as much to her.

'I love you too, Everett. Thank you for calling me. Say hello to Melanie for me, if you see her again. Tell her I miss her.'

'I will. Goodnight, Maggie. Happy New Year . . . I hope it's a great one for us, if that's possible.'

'It's in God's hands.' She was leaving it up to Him. It was all she could do, and she would listen to whatever answer came to her in prayer.

As he turned off the light in his hotel room, his thoughts were full of Maggie, and so was his heart. He had promised her he wouldn't pressure her, even if sometimes he was scared. He said the Serenity Prayer to himself that night before he went to sleep. All he could do now was wait and hope that everything would turn out all right, for both of them. He was thinking about her as he fell asleep, wondering what lay ahead.

He didn't see Maggie again for the next two and a half months, although he spoke to her often. She said she needed time to think, and space. But in mid-March, he arrived in San Francisco, sent by *Scoop* magazine, to cover Seth's trial. Maggie knew he was coming in, and how busy he would be. She had dinner with him the night before it started. It was the first time he had seen her in nearly three months, and she looked great. He told her Debbie, Chad's wife, had had a baby girl they named Jade the night before. She was genuinely thrilled for him.

They had a quiet easy dinner, and he took her home. He left her on her front steps, and they talked about Sarah and Seth. Maggie said she was worried about her. It was going to be such a hard time for them both. She and Everett had both expected him to plea-bargain with the federal prosecutor at the last minute, and avoid the trial, but apparently he hadn't. So he was going to have to go through a jury trial. It was hard to believe the outcome would be good for him. Maggie said she prayed for the right outcome all the time.

Neither of them made any mention of their own situation, or the decision that Maggie was trying to make. Everett assumed that when she had come to some conclusion, she would tell him. And so far she hadn't, obviously. Mostly, they talked about the trial.

*   *   *

Sarah was at her Clay Street apartment that night, and she called Seth before she went to sleep.

'I just want you to know that I love you, and I want this to come out okay for you. I don't want you to think I'm mad. I'm not. I'm just scared, for both of us.'

'So am I,' he admitted. His doctor was giving him tranquilizers, and beta-blockers for the trial. He didn't see how he'd get through it, but he knew he had to, and he was grateful for her call. 'Thanks, Sarah.'

'I'll see you in the morning. Goodnight, Seth.'

'I love you, Sarah,' he said sadly.

'I know,' she said, sounding equally sad, and hung up. She had not yet achieved the state of grace or forgiveness that she and Maggie had talked about. But she felt sorry for him. She was expressing compassion toward him, which was all she could do right now. More was just too much to ask.

*   *   *

When Everett got up the next day, he put his camera in his shoulder bag. He couldn't take it out in court, but he could take pictures of all the activity outside, and of the people who came and went. He got a shot of Sarah as she solemnly walked into the courthouse next to her husband. She was wearing a dark gray suit and looked pale. Seth looked considerably worse, which was hardly surprising. Sarah didn't see Everett. But later that morning Everett saw Maggie arrive. She took a seat in the courtroom to watch the proceedings from a discreet seat in the back. She wanted to be there for Sarah, if it helped her at all.

Afterward she came out and chatted with Everett for a few minutes. He was busy, and Maggie had to meet with a social worker to get a homeless man she knew into a shelter. She and Everett both had busy lives, and enjoyed what they did. She had dinner with him again that night, after he finished work at the trial. They were working on jury selection, and they both thought the trial could take a long time. The judge was warning jurors it could last a month, with detailed financial material to examine, and extensive reading to do on the matter at hand. Everett told her that night that Seth had looked grim all afternoon, and he and Sarah had hardly spoken to each other, but she was there, staunchly at his side.

It took two weeks for jury selection, which seemed agonizingly slow to Seth and Sarah, but finally they were set. They had twelve jurors and two alternates. Eight women and six men. And then finally the trial began. The prosecutor and defense attorney made their opening arguments. The prosecutor's description of Seth's immoral and illegal behavior made Sarah wince as she listened. Seth sat stone-faced, while the jury watched. He had the benefit of tranquilizers. She didn't. She couldn't imagine the defense team overcoming those arguments, as day after day, the prosecution presented evidence, witnesses, experts, all of it condemning Seth.

By the third week of the trial, Seth looked exhausted, and Sarah felt like she could hardly crawl when she went home to her children at night. She had taken time off from work to be with him, and Karen Johnson at the hospital told her not to worry about it. She was desperately sorry for Sarah, as was Maggie. She called Sarah every night to see how she was. Sarah was holding up despite the incredible pressure of the trial.

Everett dined with Maggie often during the agonizing weeks of the trial. It was April when he finally mentioned their situation again. Maggie said she didn't want to talk about it, she was still praying, so they discussed the trial instead, which was always depressing, but obsessed them both. It was all they talked about when they saw each other. The prosecution was burying Seth daily, and Everett said he had been suicidal to go to trial. The defense was doing their best, but the federal prosecutor's case was so damning that there was little they could do to balance the avalanche of evidence against him. As the weeks wore on, whenever she came to court to support her, Maggie could see Sarah getting thinner and paler by the hour. There was no way out but through it, but it was truly a trial by fire for them and their marriage. Seth's credibility and reputation were being utterly destroyed. It was upsetting for everyone who cared about them, particularly for Sarah's sake, to see where this was going. It became clearer to everyone that Seth should have plea-bargained for a lesser charge or sentence, rather than go to trial. It didn't seem possible that he could be acquitted given the accusations against him, and the testimony and evidence to support it. Sarah was innocent in all this, she had been duped just as his investors had been, but in the end, she was paying just as high a price, perhaps more. Maggie was devastated for her.

Sarah's parents came out for the first week of the trial, but her father had a heart condition. Her mother didn't want him wearing himself out, or sitting through the stress of the proceedings, so they went home as the case was still building against Seth, and they still had weeks ahead of them before it would be over.

The defense put an enormous amount of energy into defending Seth. Henry Jacobs was masterful in his demeanor, and solid in his talent as a lawyer. The problem was that Seth had given them little to work with, and their case was mostly smoke and mirrors, and it showed. The defense was about to rest the next day, as Everett and Maggie had dinner in the coffee shop across the street from her apartment, where they met often at the end of their days. Everett was writing daily items about the trial for *Scoop*. And Maggie was pursuing her normal activities, while spending any spare time she had at the trial. It gave her a chance to stay abreast of the proceedings, catch a few minutes with Everett during recesses and breaks, and to hug Sarah whenever possible to buoy her spirits as the nightmare went on.

'What's going to happen to her when he goes?' Everett asked Maggie. He was worried about Sarah too. She was beginning to look so broken and frail, but she hadn't missed a day beside her husband. And outwardly, she was always gracious and poised. She tried to exude a confidence and faith in him that Maggie knew only too well she didn't feel. She talked to her on the phone sometimes late at night. And more often than not, Sarah just sat at the other end and sobbed, completely distraught from the unrelenting stress.

'I don't think there's a hope in hell that he'll get off.' After what he had heard in the past weeks, there was no doubt in Everett's mind. And he couldn't imagine the jury seeing it differently than he did.

'I don't know. She'll have to manage somehow. She has no choice. Her parents are there for her, but they live far away. They can only help her so much. She's pretty much on her own. I don't think they have a lot of close friends, and most of them have abandoned them in this mess. I think Sarah is too proud and too embarrassed by all this to reach out for help. She's very strong, but if he goes to prison, she'll be alone. I don't know that the marriage will survive it if he goes. That's a decision she'll have to make.'

'I give her credit for hanging in this long. I think I'd have dumped the bastard the day he got indicted. He deserves it. He took her life down with him. No one has the right to do that to another human being, out of sheer greed and dishonesty. If you ask me, the guy's a shit.'

'She loves him,' Maggie said simply, 'and she's trying to be fair.'

'She's been more than fair. This guy totally screwed up her life, and sacrificed her and their kids' future for his own benefit, and she's still sitting there, hanging in. It's a lot more than he deserves. Do you think she'll stick by him, Maggie, if he takes a fall?' He had never seen loyalty like Sarah's before, and knew he wouldn't have been capable of it himself. He admired her immensely, and felt desperately sorry for her. He was sure the whole courtroom did.

'I don't know,' Maggie said honestly. 'I don't

think Sarah knows either. She wants to do the right thing. But she's thirty-six years old. She has a right to a better life than this, if he goes to prison. If they divorce, she could start over again. If they don't, she's going to spend a lot of years visiting him in prison, and waiting for him, while life passes her by. I don't want to advise her, I can't. But I have mixed feelings about it myself. I told her that. Whatever happens, she needs to forgive, but that doesn't mean she has to give up her life for him forever, because he made a mistake.'

'This is a lot to forgive,' he said somberly, and Maggie nodded in agreement.

'Yes, it is. I'm not sure I could do it. Probably not,' she said honestly. 'I'd like to think I'd be a bigger person than that, but I'm not sure I am. But only Sarah can decide what she wants. And I'm not sure she knows. She doesn't have a lot of options. She could even stay with him and never forgive him or forgive him and let him go. Grace expresses itself in strange ways sometimes. I just hope she finds the right answer for her.'

'I know what mine would be,' Everett said grimly. 'Kill the bastard. But I guess that wouldn't help Sarah either. I don't envy her sitting there day after day, hearing what a dishonest sonofabitch he is. And she still walks out of court next to him every day and kisses him goodbye before she goes home to their kids.' While they waited for dessert, Everett decided to broach a much more delicate subject with her again. On the day after Christmas Maggie had agreed to think about them. It had been almost four months, and like Sarah, she had made no decision either, and avoided discussing it with him. The suspense was starting to kill him. He

330

knew she loved him, but didn't want to leave the convent either. This was an agonizing decision for her too. And like Sarah, she was seeking answers and a state of grace, which would allow her to finally discover the right thing to do. In Sarah's case, all solutions were onerous, and in some ways, in Maggie's too. Either she had to leave the convent for Everett, to share a life with him, or she had to give up that hope and remain faithful to her vows for the rest of her years. In either case, she lost something she loved and wanted, and in either case, she won something in return. But she had to trade one for the other, she couldn't have both. Everett searched her eyes as he gently tried to open the subject again. He had promised not to pressure her and to give her all the time she needed, but there were times when he just wanted to reach out to her and hold her, and beg her to run away with him. He knew that she wouldn't. If she came toward him and chose a life with him, it would be precise, well thought out, not precipitous, and above all, it would be honest and clean.

'So what are you thinking about us these days?' he inquired cautiously, as she stared into her coffee cup and then at him. He saw the agony in her eyes when she did, and was suddenly terrified she had made a decision that was not in favor of him.

'I don't know, Everett,' she said with a sigh. 'I love you. I know that. I just don't know what my path is meant to be now, which direction to go. I want to be sure I choose the right one, for both of us.' She had been giving it her every attention and thought for the past four months, and even before, ever since their first kiss.

'You know what my vote is,' he said with a small nervous smile. 'I figure God will love you whatever you do, and so will I. But I sure would love to have a life with you, Maggie.' And even kids, though he never pressed her on that either. One major decision was enough for the time being. If appropriate, they could discuss other things later. Right now she had to tackle a far bigger decision. 'Maybe you should talk to your brother. He went through it. How did he feel?'

'He never had as strong a vocation. And the minute he met his wife, he was out the door. I don't think he was ever as torn by it. He said that if God put her on his path, it was meant to be. I wish I were as sure. Maybe this is some extreme form of temptation to try me, or perhaps this is destiny knocking at the door.' He could see how tormented she still was, and couldn't help wondering if she'd ever really make a decision, or finally just give up.

'You can still work with the poor on the streets, just as you do now. You could be a nurse practitioner, or a social worker, or both. You can do whatever you want to, Maggie. You don't have to give that up.' He had said that to her before. The problem for her was not so much her work as her vows. They both knew that was the issue for her. What he didn't know was that she had been talking to the provincial of the order for three months now, her mother superior, her confessor, and a psychologist who specialized in the problems that arose in religious communities. She was doing everything possible to make the decision wisely, not just wrestling with it alone. He would have

332

been encouraged to know it, but she didn't want to give him false hope, if she didn't come through for him in the end.

'Can you give me a little more time?' she asked, looking pained. She had set herself a deadline of June to make up her mind, but she didn't tell him that either, for the same reasons.

'Of course I can,' he said reasonably, and walked her back to her building across the street. He had been up to see her apartment by then and was horrified by how small, spare, and depressing it was. She insisted she didn't mind and said it was much nicer and larger than any nun's cell in any convent. She took the vow of poverty seriously, just as she did the others she'd taken. He didn't say it, but he couldn't have lived in her apartment for a day. And the only decoration was a simple crucifix on one wall. Other than that, the apartment was bare, except for her bed, a chest of drawers, and a single broken chair she'd found on the street.

He went to a meeting after he dropped her off, and then went back to his hotel room to write his report on the trial for the day. *Scoop* liked what he was sending them. His editorials were well written, and he had gotten some terrific photographs outside the courthouse.

The defense took nearly a full day to rest its case. Seth sat frowning, looking anxious, while Sarah closed her eyes several times, listening with total concentration, as Maggie sat in the back of the courtroom and prayed. Henry Jacobs and his team of defense attorneys had made a good case, and defended Seth as best they could. Under the circumstances, they had done a fine job. But the circumstances were not good.

The judge instructed the jury the next day, thanked the witnesses for their testimony, the attorneys for their excellent work, on behalf of the defendant and the government, and then the jury retired to do their job. Other than that, court was adjourned, pending the jury's decision. Sarah and Seth were left to hang around with their attorneys and wait. They all knew it could take days. Everett walked Maggie out then. She had stopped for a minute to talk to Sarah, who insisted she was all right but didn't look it, and then Maggie walked out to the street with Everett, talked to him for a few minutes, and left for an appointment. She was meeting with the provincial again, but didn't mention it to Everett. She just kissed him on the cheek and left. And he went back inside to wait with the others, while the jury deliberated.

Sarah sat beside Seth in two chairs at the back of the courtroom. They had gotten some air for a few minutes, but nothing really helped. Sarah felt like she was waiting for yet another bomb to hit them. They both knew it was coming. The only question was how hard it would hit, and how much destruction it would do when it did.

'I'm sorry, Sarah,' Seth said softly. 'I'm so sorry I put you through this. I never thought anything like this could happen.' It would have been nice if he had thought of it before instead of after, but Sarah didn't say it. 'Do you hate me?' He searched her eyes, and she shook her head, crying as she did constantly now. Every emotion she'd ever had was brought up to the surface. She felt as though she had no emotional resources left. She had used them all to stand by him.

'I don't hate you. I love you. I just wish this hadn't happened.'

'So do I. I wish I had copped a plea instead of putting you through all this bullshit. I just thought maybe we could win it.' She feared he had been as delusional about that as he had been when committing the crime with Sully. In the end, both men had given each other up during investigation. So much so that their respective information about each other had only served to confirm their respective guilt, rather than saving either of them from the consequences of their actions, or diminishing their punishment. The federal prosecutors in California and New York had made no deal with either of them. They had given Seth the opportunity to plea-bargain early on, and then rescinded it later. Henry had warned him that going to trial could possibly make his sentence worse, but a gambler at heart, more than anyone had realized, Seth had decided to take the chance, and now he feared the result, as they waited for the jury to make the decision. Once they did, the judge would sentence him a month later.

'We'll just have to wait and see what they decide,' Sarah said quietly. Their fate was in the jury's hands.

'What about you?' Seth said anxiously. He didn't want her to desert him now. He needed her too badly, whatever it cost her. 'Have you made any decisions about us?' She shook her head and didn't answer. They had too much on their plates just then to add divorce to the mess they were dealing with. She wanted to wait for the jury's decision, and Seth didn't press her. He was too afraid of what would happen if he did. He could see that Sarah was at the breaking point already, and had been for a while. The trial had taken a toll on her, but she had been staunch and faithful to the end, just as she had promised. She was a woman of her word, which was more than anyone could have said for him. Everett referred to him as a scumbag to Maggie. And others had said worse, although not to Sarah's face. She was the hero in the story, and the victim, and in Everett's eyes, the saint.

They waited six days for the jury to finish their deliberations. The evidence was complicated, and the wait agonizing for Sarah and Seth. Night after night, they went home to their separate apartments. Seth had asked if she would come home with him one night, he was too terrified to be alone, but Molly was sick, and in truth, she didn't want to spend the night with Seth. It would have been too hard for her. She was trying to protect herself a little, although she felt sad to say no to him. She knew how badly he was hurting, but so was she. He went back to his apartment and got drunk instead. He called her at two in the morning, incoherent, telling her he loved her. And he was visibly hung over the next day. The jury finally came back into the courtroom, late that afternoon. And everyone started scurrying, as court was reconvened.

The judge was solemn as he asked them if they had reached a verdict in the matter of *United States v. Seth Sloane,* and the foreman stood, looking equally solemn and serious. He owned a pizzeria, had attended a year of college, and was a Catholic with six children. He was extremely respectful of his duties, and had worn a suit and tie to court every day.

'We have, your honor,' the foreman said. There were five felony charges against Seth. The judge reeled each of them off, and in each case the foreman answered the question of how the jury had found Seth. The entire courtroom held its breath as he responded. They had found him guilty of each charge.

There was a momentary silence as spectactors in the courtroom absorbed it, and then an explosion of talk and sounds, as the judge rapped his gavel soundly, called them all to order, thanked the jury, and dismissed them. The trial had taken five weeks, and their deliberations had added a sixth. And as Sarah understood what had happened, she turned to look at Seth. He was sitting in his chair and crying. He looked up at her in desperation. The only hope they had for appeal, according to Henry Jacobs, was in the case of new evidence or some irregularity during the proceedings of the trial. He had already told Seth that, barring some unforeseen later development, he had no grounds for appeal. It was over. He had been found guilty. And in a month it would be up to the judge to sentence him. But he was going to jail. Sarah looked as devastated as he did. She knew it was coming, she had done everything to prepare herself for it, and she wasn't surprised. She was just heartbroken for him, for herself, and for their children, who would grow up with a father they scarcely knew in prison.

'I'm sorry,' she whispered to him, and then their attorneys helped get them out of the courtroom.

Everett sprang into action then, to get the photographs he knew he had to get for *Scoop*. He

337

hated to intrude on Sarah, at such a time of distress for her. But he had no choice but to rush at them outside the courtroom, in the press of photographers and news cameras. It was his job. Seth was almost snarling as he pushed his way through the crowd, and Sarah looked as though she might faint as she followed him to their waiting car. They had a driver and town car waiting for them outside the courthouse. They were gone in minutes, as the crowd milled around.

Everett saw Maggie on the courthouse steps. She hadn't been able to get near Sarah to say anything to her. He waved at her, and she saw him and came down the steps to meet him. She was grave-faced and looked worried, although the verdict was no surprise. And the sentencing was liable to be worse. There was no telling how long the judge would send him away for, but it was likely to be a very long time. Particularly since he hadn't pled guilty, and had pushed for a jury trial, which wasted taxpayers' money, in the hope of having a fleet of highly paid lawyers do their fancy footwork to get him off. It hadn't worked, but made an inclination toward leniency less likely for him. He had pushed it to the max, and there was a good chance the judge would push back. He had a certain amount of discretion in the range of sentencing for Seth's crimes. Maggie feared the worst for him, and for Sarah now.

'I'm so sorry for her,' Maggie said to Everett as they walked to his rented car parked in the garage. It was all at *Scoop*'s expense. His job was over in San Francisco. He would fly up for the day of the sentencing, and maybe get a couple of shots of Seth being escorted into a federal prison. In thirty days, it would be all over for Seth. He was out on bail till then. And once the money was returned by the bail bonds-man, it was going straight into a fund for his defense for the civil suits that had been filed against him by the investors he had defrauded. His conviction was all the evidence they needed to justify their suits, and even win them. After that, there would be nothing left for Sarah and the children. Sarah was well aware of that, as were Everett and Maggie. She had gotten screwed, just as his investors had. They could sue him, the government could penalize him, and all Sarah could do was pick up the pieces of her and her children's lives. It seemed so desperately unfair to Maggie, but some things were in life. She hated to see things like that happen to good people, and she looked profoundly depressed as she got into Everett's car.

'I know, Maggie,' he said gently. 'I don't like it either. But there was no way he should have gotten off.' It was an ugly story with a sad ending. Not the happy ending Sarah had hoped to live with Seth, or that anyone who knew her would have wanted for her.

'I just hate this for Sarah.'

'So do I,' Everett said as he started the car. The Tenderloin wasn't far from the courthouse, and he stopped in front of her building a few minutes later.

'Are you flying back tonight?' Maggie asked him sadly.

'I guess so. They're going to want me in the office tomorrow morning. I need to check the pictures and coordinate the story. Do you want to have something to eat before I go?' He hated to leave her, but he had been in San Francisco for well over a month, and *Scoop* would want him back.

'I don't think I could eat,' she said honestly. And then she turned to him with a wistful smile. 'I'll miss you, Everett.' She had gotten so used to having him there, and seeing him every day, at the courthouse and afterward. They had had dinner almost every night. His leaving was going to leave a terrible void in her life. She also realized that it would give her a chance to see how she felt about him. She had important decisions to make, not unlike Sarah. Sarah didn't have anything to look forward to if she stayed with Seth, except his release from prison a long time from now. His sentence hadn't even started, or been determined yet. And her sentence would be just as long as his. It seemed like cruel and unusual punishment for her to Maggie. In her own case, there were blessings whatever she decided, although there were losses too. In each case, there was a loss and a gain woven into each other. It was impossible to separate them, which was what made the decision so difficult for Maggie.

'I'm going to miss you too, Maggie,' Everett said as he smiled at her. 'I'll see you when I come up for the sentencing, or I can come for a day sometime, if you want me to. It's up to you. All you have to do is call me.'

'Thank you,' Maggie said quietly, as she looked at him, and he leaned over and kissed her. She felt her heart go out to him as he did. She clung to him for a minute, wondering how she could ever give that up, but knowing she might have to. She left the car without saying another word to him. He

340

knew she loved him, just as she knew he loved her. There was nothing more for them to say to each other for now.

Chapter 21

Sarah walked into the Broadway apartment with Seth to make sure he would be all right. He looked alternately dazed and angry and as though he was going to cry again. He didn't want to go to her place and see the children. He knew they would pick up on his sense of devastation and despair, even though they knew nothing about the trial. It was obvious that something terrible had happened to both their parents. In fact, it had happened months before, the first time he had defrauded his investors, thinking he would never get caught. He knew it wouldn't be long before Sully went to prison in New York. And now he was facing the same thing.

Seth took two tranquilizers as soon as he walked in, and poured himself half a glass of scotch. He took a long swig, and looked at Sarah. He couldn't stand seeing the anguish in her eyes.

'I'm sorry, baby,' he said between swallows of scotch. He didn't put his arms around her, or comfort her. He was thinking of himself. Apparently, he always had.

'So am I, Seth. Are you going to be okay here tonight? Do you want me to stay?' She didn't want to, but she would have for him, particularly the way he was drinking and taking pills. He was liable to kill himself without even trying. He needed someone there with him after the impact of the verdict, and if it had to be her, she was willing to do it for him. He was her husband and the father of her children, after all, although he seemed to have very little understanding of what this was doing to her. He was the one going to prison, as far as he was concerned, not his wife. But she was already in prison now, thanks to him, and had been since their life had imploded the night of the earthquake in May, eleven months before.

'I'll be fine. I'm going to get fucking drunk. Maybe I'll stay drunk for the next month, until that asshole sends me to the slammer for a hundred years, thirty days from now.' It wasn't the judge's fault, it was Seth's. Sarah was clear on the concept, but he wasn't. 'Why don't you go back to your place, Sarah? I'll be okay.' He didn't sound convincing, and she was worried. It was all about him, it always was. But he was right in the sense that he was going to prison and she wasn't. He had a right to be upset, even if he'd done it to himself. She could still walk away from what had happened. He couldn't. And a month from now, his life as he had known it until then would be over. Hers already was. He didn't bring up divorce that night with her. He couldn't have handled hearing it from her, nor could she have said the words to him. She hadn't formed the decision or the words in her mind yet.

The subject came up finally a week later, when he dropped the children off, after a visit. He had only taken them out for a few hours. He couldn't handle more than that right now. He was too stressed, and he was looking very rough. She was looking frighteningly thin. Her clothes were hanging off her now, and her features had gotten sharp. Karen Johnson at the hospital kept saying she should have a check-up. But Sarah knew that there was no mystery to what was happening to her. Their life had fallen apart, and her husband was going to prison for a long time. They had lost everything, and would soon lose what was left. She had no one to rely on now except herself. It was as simple as that.

When Seth dropped the children off, he looked at her, with a question in his eyes. 'Should we be talking about what we're going to do about our marriage? I think I'd like to know before I go to jail. And if we're going to stay together, maybe we should spend these last few weeks living together. It may be a long time before we can do that again.' He knew she wanted another baby, but she couldn't think about that now. She had given up the idea as soon as his criminal activities had surfaced. The last thing she wanted now was to get pregnant, although she wanted another baby, but not with him, and not now. That told her a lot. And what he was suggesting to her, about their moving in together for the next three weeks, upset her too. She couldn't see herself living with him again, making love with him, getting even more attached to him than she already was, and then having him leave her to go to prison. She couldn't do it. It had to be faced, and he was right, maybe now instead of later.

'I can't do that, Seth,' she said in an agonized voice, after the children went upstairs with Parmani for a bath. She didn't want them to hear what she was saying to their father. She didn't want them to remember that one day. They would have to know what had happened when they were old enough, but surely not now, and not later in an ugly way. 'I just can't . . . I can't come back. I want to more than anything. I wish we could turn back the clock, but I don't think we can. I still love you, and I probably always will, but I don't think I could ever trust you again.' It was painful, but brutally honest. He stood rooted to the spot, looking at her, wanting her words to be different. He needed her, particularly when he'd go away.

'I understand.' He nodded, and then thought of something. 'Would it have been different if I'd been acquitted?' Silently, she shook her head. She couldn't come back to him. She had suspected it for months, and had finally faced it herself in the last days of the trial, before the verdict. She just didn't have the heart to tell him, or even admit it to herself. But now she had no other choice. It had to be said, so they each knew where they stood. 'I guess under those circumstances, it was nice of you to stand by me at the trial.' His lawyers had asked her to, for appearance's sake, but she would have done it anyway, out of love for him. 'I'll call and start proceedings for divorce,' he said, looking devastated, and she nodded, with tears heavy in her eyes. It was one of the worst moments of her life, matched only by when their preemie baby nearly died, and the morning after the earthquake, when he had told her what he'd done. Their house of cards had been falling ever since, and it was flat on the ground now.

'I'm sorry, Seth.' He nodded, said not a word, turned, and left her apartment. It was done.

Sarah called Maggie and told her a few days later, and the little nun told her how sorry she was.

'I know how hard that decision was for you,' she said in a voice filled with compassion. 'Have you forgiven him, Sarah?'

There was a long pause as Sarah searched her heart and was honest with her. 'No, I haven't.'

'I hope you will someday. It doesn't mean you have to take him back.'

'I know.' She understood that now.

'It would free you both. You don't want to carry this forever, like a cement block on your heart.'

'I will anyway,' Sarah said sadly.

*　　　*　　　*

The sentencing was an anticlimax after the verdict at the trial. Seth had given up his apartment and was staying at the Ritz-Carlton for the last few nights. He had explained what was happening to his children, that he was going away for a while. Molly had cried, but he had promised she could visit, which seemed to reassure her. She was only four, and she didn't really understand. How could she? The concept was hard for all the grown-ups involved too. He had made arrangements with the bail bondsman to return the money to the bank, where it would be held in escrow for future lawsuits against him from investors, and a small portion was going to Sarah to help support herself and the children, but it wouldn't last long. Eventually, she'd have to rely only on her job, or her parents to do what they could for her, and it wouldn't be much. They were retired and lived on a fixed income. She might even have to live with them for a while, if she ran out of cash, and couldn't live on her salary. Seth was sorry, but he couldn't do better than that for her. He sold his new Porsche and somewhat grandly gave her the money. Every little bit helped, and he put his belongings in storage and said he'd figure out what to do with them later. Sarah had promised to do whatever his lawyers couldn't do for him. And the week of his sentencing, he had started proceedings for their divorce. It would be final in six months. Sarah cried when she got the notification, but she couldn't imagine staying married to him now. She didn't feel as though there was a choice.

The judge had investigated Seth's financial situation, and imposed a two-million-dollar fine on him, which would wipe him out, after the sale of everything he still had left. And a fifteen-year prison sentence, three years for each of the five charges he was convicted of. It was stiff, but it wasn't thirty. A muscle in Seth's jaw tightened as he listened, but he had been prepared for the bad news this time. The last time, waiting for the verdict, he had hope that a miracle would happen to let him off. He wasn't waiting for a miracle at the sentencing. And he realized, as he heard his sentence, that Sarah was right to want a divorce. If he served his full sentence, he would be out when he was fifty-three years old, and Sarah fifty-one. They were thirty-eight and thirty-six respectively now. It was a long time to wait for anyone. He might get out in twelve, if he was lucky. But even then, it was a long time. She'd be forty-eight years old, a very long time not to have her husband at her side. And Molly was going to be nineteen years old when he got out, Oliver seventeen. That really brought the point home to him that Sarah was right.

He was led out of the courtroom in handcuffs, as Sarah burst into a sob. He would be transferred to a federal prison in the next few days. His lawyers had asked for a minimum security facility, which was un-der consideration, and Sarah had promised to visit as soon as he got there, in spite of the divorce. She had no intention of shutting him out, she just couldn't be his wife anymore.

He turned to look at her once as he was led away, and just before they put the cuffs on him, he tossed her his wedding band. He had forgotten to take it off that morning, and leave it with the gold watch he had put in his suitcase and asked to have delivered to her house. He had told her to give the clothes away and save the watch for Ollie. The whole thing was ghastly, and she stood there holding his wedding ring, and sobbed. Everett led her out of the courtroom with Maggie, they took her home, and put her to bed.

Chapter 22

Maggie flew to L.A. on the Memorial Day weekend, after Seth's sentencing, for Melanie's next concert. She tried to get Sarah to come with her, but she wouldn't. She was taking the children to visit Seth in his new home in prison. It was the first time they were going to see him since he'd left, and she realized it would be a shock and adjustment for them all.

Everett had asked Maggie several times how she thought Sarah was doing, and she said technically all right. She was functioning, going to work, taking care of her children, but she was understandably terribly depressed. It was going to take time, maybe even a lot of time, for her to recover from what had happened. Hiroshima had happened to her life, and her marriage. The divorce was proceeding as planned.

Everett picked Maggie up at the airport, and took her to the small hotel where she was staying. She had an appointment with Father Callaghan that afternoon and said she hadn't seen him in ages. The concert wasn't until the next day. Everett dropped her off and left her to do a story he'd been assigned to. His coverage of the trial had been so impressive that he'd just had an offer to work for *Time,* and the AP wanted him back again. He'd been in recovery for two years now, and he felt solid as a rock. He had given Maggie his two-year chip to keep with the first one he'd given her, for luck. She cherished both and kept them on her at all times.

They had dinner with Melanie, Tom, and Janet that night. Melanie and Tom said that they had just celebrated their first-year anniversary, and Janet seemed more relaxed than Maggie had expected. She had met a man and was having fun with him. He was in the music business, and they had a lot in common. And she seemed to have adjusted to Melanie making her own decisions, although Everett would never have thought it possible. Melanie was turning twenty-one, and had come into her own in the past year.

She was going on a short concert tour that summer, four weeks instead of nine or ten, only to major cities. Tom had taken two weeks off to go with her. And Melanie had signed up with Father

Callaghan to go back to Mexico in September, although she planned to stay only a month this time. She didn't want to be away from Tom for too long. The young couple beamed and looked happy, and Everett snapped a bunch of pictures at dinner, including one of Melanie and her mother, and another of Melanie with Maggie. She credited Maggie with changing her life and helping her to grow up and be who she wanted, although she said it out of earshot of her mother. The anniversary of the San Francisco earthquake had come and gone earlier in May. It was an event they all remembered with terror and fondness. Good things had come of it for all of them, but the trauma they had experienced had not been forgotten either. Maggie commented that the Smallest Angels Ball had taken place again this year, but Sarah didn't run it or attend. She had been too involved with Seth's legal proceedings, and Maggie hoped Sarah would do it again the following year. They all agreed that it had been a beautiful event until the earthquake hit.

Everett and Maggie stayed later than usual at the dinner at Melanie's house. It was relaxed and fun, and Everett and Tom played pool afterward. Tom told Everett that he and Melanie were thinking of moving in together. It was a little awkward with her still living with her mother, and even though Janet had mellowed a little, she was certainly no angel. She drank way too much that night, and despite the fact that she had a boyfriend now, Everett sensed that she would have made a pass at him if Maggie hadn't been there. He could see easily why Tom and Melanie wanted their own place. It was time for Janet to grow up too and go

349

into the world on her own, without hiding behind Melanie's skirts and fame. It was a growing time for them all.

Everett and Maggie chatted easily on the way back to her hotel, and as always he loved being with her. They talked about the young couple, and were happy for them. And by the time they got to Maggie's motel, she was yawning and half asleep. He kissed her gently and walked her to her door with his arm around her.

'How was your meeting with Father Callaghan, by the way?' He had forgotten to ask her, and he liked to keep abreast of all her doings every day. 'I hope you're not going to Mexico too,' he teased her, and she shook her head, yawning again.

'No. I'm going to work for him here,' she said sleepily, and cuddled up against Everett before she went in.

'Here? In L.A.?' He was confused. 'Do you mean San Francisco?'

'No, I mean here. He needs someone to run the mission here while he's in Mexico, for four to six months every year. I can figure out what I'm doing after that, or he might keep me on, if I do a good job.'

'Wait a minute.' Everett stared at her. 'Explain this to me. You're taking a job in L.A. for four to six months? What did the diocese say, or have you told them yet?' He knew they were fairly liberal about letting her work in the field wherever she chose.

'Hmmm . . . I did . . . ,' she said, putting her arms around his waist. Everett still looked confused.

'And they're willing to let you come and work

350

down here?' He was smiling. He loved the idea, and he could see that she did too. 'That's amazing. I didn't think they were that cool, to let you wander off to another city like that.'

'They don't have any say in it anymore,' she said quietly, as he looked into her eyes.

'What are you saying, Maggie?'

She took a deep breath and held him tightly. It had been the hard-est thing she'd ever done. She hadn't talked to anyone outside the Church about it, not even him. It had been a choice she had to make herself, without pressure from him. 'I was released from my vows two days ago. I didn't want to say anything until I was here.'

'Maggie! . . . Maggie? . . . You're not a nun anymore?' He stared at her in disbelief, and she shook her head sadly, fighting back tears.

'No, I'm not. I don't know what I am anymore. I'm having an identity crisis. I called Father Callaghan about the job, so I can come down here and work, if you want me. Other than that, I don't know what I'd do.' She laughed through her tears then. 'And I'm the oldest virgin on the planet.'

'Oh Maggie, I love you . . . oh my God, you're *free!*' She nodded, and he kissed her. They didn't have to feel guilty anymore. They would be able to explore everything they felt for each other. They could marry and have kids. She could be his wife if they wanted, or not if they preferred. Now all the choices were theirs. 'Thank you, Maggie,' he said profoundly. 'Thank you with all my heart. I didn't think you'd be able to do it, and I didn't want to push you, but I've been worrying myself sick over it for months.'

'I know. Me too. I wanted to do it right. It was a

hard thing to do.'

'I know,' he said, and kissed her again. He still didn't want to rush her. He knew it would be a tremendous adjustment for her to no longer be a nun. She had been in religious orders for twenty-one years, almost half her life. But he couldn't help thinking of the future. The best part was that their future was now. 'When can you move down?'

'Whenever you want. The lease on my apartment is month by month.'

'Tomorrow,' he said, looking ecstatic. He couldn't wait to get home and call his sponsor. His sponsor had been suggesting he look into CODA, a twelve-step group for codependent people, since he thought Everett was hooked on her unavailability. How much more unavailable did it get than a nun? And now the nun was his! 'I'll help you move next week, if you want.' She laughed.

'I probably don't have two suitcases of stuff, and besides where would I live?' She hadn't made any arrangements yet, it was all so fresh. She had been out of religious orders for two days, and only got a job that afternoon. She hadn't had time to think about an apartment yet.

'Would you be willing to live with me?' he asked cautiously, still standing outside her hotel room. It was turning into the best night of his life, and surely hers. But she shook her head in answer to his question. There were some things she was not willing to do.

'Not unless we're married,' she said quietly. She didn't want to pressure him. But she didn't want to live with a man out of wedlock. It went against the grain of everything she believed, and was way too modern for her. She had only been out in the world, officially, for two days, and she was by no means ready to agree to live in sin with him, no matter how happy she was.

'That can be arranged,' he said, grinning. 'I was just waiting for you to get free. Wow, Maggie, will you marry me?' He had wanted to do it more elegantly, but just couldn't wait. They had already waited so long for her to make a decision and get free.

She nodded, beaming, and said the word he had waited to hear for so long. 'Yes.' He spun her around in his arms, kissed her, and set her down. They talked for a few more minutes, and then she walked into her room smiling, and he left, promising to call her first thing in the morning, or maybe even when he got home. Their whole life was beginning. He had never thought she'd do it. It was even more amazing to think that an earthquake had brought them together. She was such a brave woman. He knew he'd be grateful forever that Maggie would be his.

*   *   *

The concert the next day was fantastic. Melanie did an incredible job. Maggie had never before seen her in a major concert, only at the benefit, which was a much smaller venue. Everett had told her about Melanie's concerts, and she had all of her CDs. Melanie had sent them to her after the earthquake, but she still wasn't prepared for the incredible experience of seeing her onstage and hearing her sing in such a big space. She was bowled over by it, and it was a particularly good performance. Maggie sat in the front row with

Tom, while Everett did his job for *Scoop*. He had decided to take the job at *Time* magazine, but he still had to give *Scoop* notice. Suddenly, everything was changing in his life, and remarkably it was all good.

Maggie and Everett had dinner with Tom and Melanie after the performance, and Everett urged Maggie to share their big news. Maggie looked shy about it at first, and then she told them that she and Everett were getting married. They hadn't set a date yet, but had been making plans all afternoon. Maggie couldn't see herself having a big wedding, or even a small one. She had suggested they be married quietly by Father Callaghan, as soon as she moved to L.A. As an ex-nun, it didn't feel right to her to make a big fuss of it. She was too old for a big white dress, she said, and the day she had taken final vows felt like a first wedding to her. The important thing was that they were getting married, and how and when they did it seemed a lot less important to her. It was the ultimate symbol of her bond to Everett, and a sacred union. All she needed there, she said, was her husband, the God she had served all her life, and a priest.

Tom and Melanie were thrilled for them, although Melanie looked completely stunned.

'You're not a nun anymore?' Her eyes were wide, and for a moment she thought they were kidding, and then realized they weren't. 'Wow! What happened?' She had never even suspected that there was something between them, but now she could see it. She could also see how happy they were, how proud Everett was, and how peaceful Maggie looked. She had achieved what she always talked about, with the challenging decision, a state of grace where what they were doing felt right to her, and infinitely blessed. It was a new chapter in her life. The old one was slowly closing. She looked at Everett, while Tom poured champagne for himself, Melanie, and Maggie. Everett smiled at her with a smile that lit Maggie's world, as nothing and no one else could have.

'Here's to the San Francisco earthquake!' Tom said, holding his glass aloft to toast the happy couple. It had brought him to Melanie, and apparently had done the same for others. Some had won. Some had lost. Some had lost their lives. Others had moved away. Their lives had been shaken up, infinitely blessed, and forever changed.

Chapter 23

It took Maggie two weeks to wrap up her life in San Francisco. By then, Everett had given notice at *Scoop,* and was starting at the L.A. bureau of *Time* in late June. He was planning to take two weeks off between the two jobs to spend with Maggie. Father Callaghan had agreed to marry them the day after she arrived, and Maggie had called her family to tell them. Her ex-priest brother had been particularly pleased for her and wished her well.

She bought a simple white silk suit for the occasion, with ivory satin high heels. It was a far cry from her old habit, and the beginning of a new life for both of them.

Everett was planning to take her to La Jolla for their honeymoon, to a little hotel he knew well, and they could take long walks on the beach. She would start work for Father Callaghan in July, and had six weeks to train with him before he left for Mexico in mid-August. He was leaving earlier than usual this year, since he knew his L.A. mission would be in good hands. Maggie could hardly wait to begin. Everything in her life was so exciting now. A wedding, a move, a new job, a whole new life. It had come as a shock to her to realize that she had to use her own name now. Mary Magdalen was the name she had taken when she entered the convent. She had been Mary Margaret for her entire life before that. Everett said he would forever call her Maggie. It was how he thought of her, how he had come to know her, and who she was to him now. They both agreed that it suited her, and she had also decided to keep the name. The new name she was acquiring was Carson. Mrs. Everett Carson. She rolled it around on her tongue as she packed her bags and looked around the studio for the last time. It had served her well during her years in the Tenderloin. Those days were over now. She had packed the crucifix in her single bag. The rest she had given away.

She handed her keys to the landlord, wished him well, and said goodbye to the familiar people lingering in the hallways. The transvestite she had grown fond of waved as she got into the cab. Two of the prostitutes who knew her had seen her carrying her suitcase, and waved too as she drove by. She hadn't told anyone she was leaving, or why, but it was as though they knew she wouldn't be back. She said a prayer for them as she left.

Her flight to L.A. was on time, and Everett met her at the airport. For a moment, he had his heart in his mouth. What if she changed her mind? And then he saw Maggie, a tiny woman in blue jeans, with bright red hair, wearing pink high-top sneakers and a white T-shirt that said 'I love Jesus' coming toward him with an irresistible smile. This was the woman he had waited a lifetime for. He had been lucky enough to find her, and she looked as though she felt just as lucky as she tucked herself into his arm. He took her suitcase from her, and they walked away. Tomorrow was their wedding day.

*   *   *

The prison Seth had been sent to was a minimum security facility in northern California, and conditions there had been reported to be good. It had a forestry camp attached to it, and the inmates there served as rangers, overseeing the safety of the area, and fighting forest fires when they occurred. Seth was hoping to make it to the forestry camp soon.

In the meantime, he had been given a single cell, after his attorneys had pulled some strings. He was comfortable, and wasn't in any great danger. The other inmates were there for white-collar crimes. In fact, most of them had committed crimes similar to his, on a much smaller scale. If anything, he was considered a hero among the men. There were conjugal visits for those of them who were married, they were allowed to have packages, and the *Wall Street Journal* was widely read by most of the inmates. It was called the country club of federal prisons, but a prison was nonetheless what it was. He missed his freedom, his wife, and his children. He wasn't sorry for what he'd done, but he was desperately sorry he had gotten caught.

Sarah had come to see him with the children in the first institution he'd been in, in Dublin, southeast of Oakland, while he was being processed. It had been uncomfortable, frightening, and a shock for all of them. Visiting him in prison now was more like visiting a hospital or a bad hotel in the forest. There was a small town attached to it where Sarah and the children could stay. Sarah could have had conjugal visits with him, as their divorce wasn't final yet, but as far as she was concerned the marriage was over, and he regretted that too, as much as the sorrow he'd caused her. He had seen it so clearly in her eyes the last time she visited him with their children, two months before. This was the first time he was seeing them that summer. It wasn't an easy place to get to, and they had been away. Sarah and the children had been in Bermuda with her parents since June.

He was nervous as he waited for them on a hot August morning. He pressed his khaki pants and shirt, and shined his regulation brown leather shoes. Among all the other things he missed, he missed his custom-made British shoes.

When visiting time came, he wandered down to the grassy area at the front of the camp. Inmates' children played there, while husbands and wives talked, kissed, and held hands. And then, as he watched the road intently, he saw them drive up. Sarah parked the car, and took a picnic basket out of the back. Visitors were allowed to bring food. Oliver was walking along beside her, holding on to her skirt with a cautious look, and Molly bounced along with a doll under her arm. For a moment, he felt tears sting his eyes, and then Sarah saw him. She waved, walked through the checkpoint, where they searched the basket she'd brought, and then all three of them were allowed inside. She was smiling at him as they approached him. He could see that she had put on a little weight, and looked less gaunt than she had before the summer, after the trial. Molly rushed into his arms, and Oliver hung back for a minute and then approached him with a little bit of caution. And then Seth met Sarah's eyes. She kissed him lightly on the cheek and set down the basket, as their children ran around them.

'You look good, Sarah.'

'So do you, Seth,' she said, feeling awkward at first. It had been a while and so much had changed. He e-mailed her from time to time, and she answered him, telling him about the kids. He would have liked to say more to her, but no longer dared. She had set boundaries he had no choice but to respect. He didn't tell her that he missed her, although he did. And she didn't tell him how hard it still was for her without him. There was no longer room for that in what they shared. The anger had gone out of it for her, and all that was left was sadness, but there was also a kind of peace, as she started to move on with her life. There was nothing left to reproach him about, or regret. It had happened. It was done. It was over. And for the rest of their lives they would share children, decisions about them, and memories of another time.

She served lunch for all of them on one of the picnic tables. Seth carried chairs over, and both children took turns sitting on his lap. She had brought delicious sandwiches from a local deli, fruit, and the cheesecake she knew Seth liked. She had even thought to bring him his favorite chocolates and a cigar.

'Thank you, Sarah. The lunch was delicious.' He sat back, smoking the cigar, as the children ran off. She could see that he was doing well, and had adjusted to the turn of fate that had landed him there. He seemed to accept it now, particularly after Henry Jacobs had confirmed that there were no grounds for an appeal. The trial had been run correctly, and the proceedings had been clean. Seth didn't seem bitter, and neither did she. 'Thanks for bringing the kids.'

'Molly starts school in two weeks. And I have to get back to work.' He didn't know what to say to her. He wanted to tell her he was sorry he had lost their house, that her jewelry was gone, that everything they'd built and shared had disappeared, but he couldn't find the words. Instead, they sat there together, watching their children. She filled the awkward silences with news of her family, and he told her about prison routine. It wasn't impersonal so much as different. There were things they couldn't say anymore, and never would again. He knew she loved him, the lunch she'd brought had told him that, the loving way she'd prepared it in the picnic basket, the way she had brought their children to him. And she knew he still loved her. One day even that would be different, but for now it was the left-over glue of a bond they had shared that would crumble and alter over time, but for now much of it was still there. Until something or someone else replaced it, until the memories got too old or the time too long. He was the father of her children, the man she had married and loved. That would never change.

She and the children stayed until the end of visiting time. A whistle blew to warn them that the end of their time together was coming. It told them to pack up their things, and throw their leftovers away. She put the remains of their lunch and the red-checked napkins in the picnic basket. She had brought things from home to make it as festive as she could.

She rounded up the children and told them they were going. Oliver made a sad face when she told him to say goodbye to Daddy, and Molly threw her arms around his waist.

'I don't want to leave Daddy,' she said, looking unhappy. 'I want to stay!' This was what he had condemned them to, but he knew that even that would alter over the years. Eventually, they'd be used to seeing him here and nowhere else.

'We'll come and visit him again soon,' Sarah said, waiting for Molly to let go of her father, and eventually she did. Seth walked them as close to the checkpoint as he was allowed to go, as other inmates did the same.

'Thanks again, Sarah,' he said in the familiar voice of seven years of history between them. 'Take care of yourself.'

'I will. You too.' She started to say something to him then, and hesitated, as the children moved away. 'I love you, Seth. I hope you know that. I'm not angry at you anymore. I'm just sad for you, and for us. But I'm okay.' She wanted him to know that, that he didn't need to worry about her or feel guilty. He could regret whatever he wanted to, but over the summer she had realized that she was going to be all right. This was the hand fate had dealt her, and it was the one she was going to play, without looking back, or hating him, or even wishing things were different. She knew now that they could never be. Even if she hadn't understood what was happening, it had been happening anyway. It had only been a matter of time before it came out in the light of day. She fully understood that now. He had never been the man she thought he was.

'Thanks, Sarah . . . for not hating me for what I did.' He didn't try to explain it to her. He had already tried, and knew she would never understand. Everything that had gone through his mind at the time was completely foreign to who she was.

'It's okay, Seth. It happened. We're lucky to have the kids.' She was still sorry not to have another baby, but maybe she would one day. Her destiny was in hands other than hers. It was what Maggie said when she called to tell her she had gotten married. And as Sarah thought of her, she turned to Seth and smiled. She hadn't realized it before, but without even trying to, she had forgiven him. A million-pound weight had lifted from her heart and shoulders. Without even willing it away, it was gone.

He watched as they went through the exit gate, and walked into the parking lot again. The children waved, and Sarah turned back once to smile and gave him a long look. He waved as they drove away, and walked slowly back to his cell, thinking of them. They were the family he had

362

sacrificed, and ultimately thrown away.

As Sarah drove around a bend in the road, and the prison vanished behind her, she looked at her children, smiled to herself, and realized it had happened. She didn't know how or when, but she had gotten there somehow. It was what Maggie had referred to so often and Sarah could never find. She had found it, it had found her, and she felt so light she could fly. She had forgiven Seth, and achieved the state of grace that at first she couldn't even imagine. It was a moment of pure perfection frozen in time forever . . . amazing grace!